T0365315

LETTERS
FROM A CAPTIVE HEART

Also by Russell Lunsford

Poetry

Sweetheart and My Love

Children's History and Adventure

Benjamin Nathan Tuggle-Adventurer:
Daniel Boone and the Settlement of Boonesborough, Kentucky
Benjamin Nathan Tuggle-Adventurer
General George Washington and the American Revolution

Daniel Boone's Kentucky:
The Boone Trace and Settlement of Kentucky

Enjoy the adventure of reading!

LETTERS FROM A CAPTIVE HEART

America's Heartbreak
in the POW Camps of North Korea

A Novel

Russell Lunsford

Letters From A Captive Heart
America's Heartbreak in the POW Camps of North Korea

iUniverse books may be ordered through booksellers or by contacting:

iUniverse
1663 Liberty Drive
Bloomington, IN 47403
www.iuniverse.com
844-349-9409

Because of the dynamic nature of the Internet, any web addresses or links contained in this book may have changed since publication and may no longer be valid. The views expressed in this work are solely those of the author and do not necessarily reflect the views of the publisher, and the publisher hereby disclaims any responsibility for them.

Any people depicted in stock imagery provided by Getty Images are models, and such images are being used for illustrative purposes only. Certain stock imagery © Getty Images.

ISBN: 978-0-5954-6092-2 (sc)
ISBN: 978-0-5956-9920-9 (hc)
ISBN: 978-0-5959-0392-4 (e)

Cover art and layout by Levi Clark
Cover typography by Heather Clark

Print information available on the last page.

iUniverse rev. date: 10/16/2024

For all the warriors of the Korean War

Who fought and brought the scars of battle home
Who gave their last full measure on the battlefield
Who are still Missing In Action, but not forgotten
Who died in a North Korean Prisoner of War camp
Who are Ex-POWs and still surviving day to day

and

For those who wait at home with broken hearts

C H A P T E R 1

▼

"What da ya think, Sarge? Think they're done? I'll bet they're done. Isn't it too dark to fight? I'm out of ammo, Sarge. Can I go down and draw more ammo?"

Squatting, Sergeant Jennings looked down the hill in front of the foxhole. Visibility was only seventy-five yards. A veteran of campaigns in the Pacific during World War II, he could smell a big fight coming and the odor was pungent around the hill. Looking down at the outline of the private's helmet and shoulders, he shook his head. Darkness made it difficult to see, but there was no mistaking the strong Brooklyn accent, and the rapid-fire questions.

"Here's another bandoleer and a couple of grenades, Jawaski. Get loaded up, fix your bayonet and get ready, company's coming!"

Jawaski stood, took the bandoleer and eased back down disappearing from view. The sergeant rose and made his way to the next fighting position along the perimeter. Jawaski's small frame fit easily into the foxhole. He took the ammo out of the bandoleer pouches laying them on the dirt rim at the top of the foxhole. It was routine and he did it with little effort in complete darkness at the bottom of the hole. Sitting on the cut-out seat he thought out loud, "Was that four or five rounds I have left?"

For three consecutive days they had taken the hill, only to lose it again in the darkness. The North Korean assaults began with night flares, blowing bugles, whistles, and shouting. Waves of soldiers would run up the flare-illuminated hill, mindlessly struggling over their fallen comrades. Jawaski was a city boy, and true to that upbringing, he had never fired a weapon until he enlisted in the army. He had never held one until the unit armorer at Camp Chaffee replaced the wooden

1

stick he had carried for two weeks with a M1 Garand. Brooklyn had been home his whole life. Arkansas was as far removed from New York as one could get, and he'd spent six weeks there learning to soldier. He saw very little else, other than the areas at Chaffee he trained in and what he saw through the window of the train. If anyone asked him if he had been to Arkansas he would probably say, "I'm not sure. You been? Maybe we could go visit someday. Would you like that? I would," and on and on.

Tonight, lots of ammo was a good thing, even when you had to carry it up and down hills. Why the North Koreans wanted the hill puzzled Jawaski. Why the Americans didn't give it to them was a greater mystery. He didn't question that out loud, but just about everything else was fair game. Everybody poked fun at him because he asked so many questions, but if Jawaski had learned one thing at Chaffee, it was you did what you were told, when you were told, no questions, no hesitation. His combat experience in Korea had answered about all of his questions. You did what you were told 'cause you'd die if you didn't, or worse, you could cause buddies to die.

A loud whisper came from his left, *"Leo!"*

In a foxhole five yards away was Private Cody Inman, a product of Cheyenne, Wyoming. He was a part-time rodeo cowboy, ranch hand, cowpuncher and broncobuster. Cody had filled Leo's head with stories of riding the range, rattlesnakes and star lit nights. Leo couldn't get enough and at times, Cody redirected the discussion a bit to talk about the big city. Leo dreamed of riding a horse across endless ranges, and Cody dreamed of riding a subway beneath the largest city in the world. They were exact opposites, but best of friends. They had vowed when their tour in Korea came to an end, they would visit each other, the city boy and the cowboy.

"Hey! City Boy!"

"Yo!"

"Bet a can of peaches against that short pack of Chesterfield's in your Cs that they're done for the night. What da ya say?"

"Peaches? You got a bet cowboy."

High overhead they heard a muffled, *pop!"* and an illumination flare lit up the hillside like an evening in Manhattan. They looked back at one another and Cody smiled as he tossed a small green can of ration peaches over to Leo. The bugling and whistling began as Leo caught the can and stuck it in his pocket.

They smiled at each other in the yellowish illuminated light, turned and began firing down the hill into the first wave of charging North Koreans.

Pop, pop, pling! The clip ejected from the breach of the Garand.

"Diddly damn, I'm the King of Siam. It was two!" said Jawaski. He stooped down, grabbed a full clip off the foxhole shelf, inserted it into the breach of the weapon and grabbed a grenade from the shelf. Pulling the ring pin out with his teeth he tossed it out high over the front edge of his hole and waited. In a few seconds, there was a loud, *bang!* He counted to three and was up knocking down the screaming North Koreans as they came up the hill at him.

On it went. Reload and kill. Reload and kill. As he loaded his last clip, he unconsciously snapped his bayonet on the end of his rifle. He tossed the last grenade down the hill, waited, *bang,* one, two, three and stood just in time to see that the North Koreans had broken through the American lines to his left. The parachute flares were drifting low, but their illumination still lit the night enough to see clearly the battlefield around him. To his left he saw Inman climb out of his foxhole, weaponless, his hands in the air. He was out of ammo and surrendering as two North Koreans approached him, both with fixed bayonets, yelling wildly in Korean. Inman was shaking his arms in the air and yelling back trying to be heard above the noise and confusion of the battle. Frustrated, he brought his arms down and moved them out to the side, in a sign of confusion. As he did, one of the soldiers took a quick step forward and jammed his bayonet into his stomach.

Jawaski gasped and held his breath as he watched Inman grab the end of the bayonet at the rifle barrel. He struggled trying to pull the blade from his abdomen, as blood gushed from his stomach. The second North Korean thrust his bayonet through the American's ribcage, gave it a quick sideward motion, slicing the left lung and liver and just as quickly, withdrew the long blade. Inman fell to his knees and rolled over on his back, still clinging to the bayonet stuck in his belly. Angry and yelling, the first soldier kicked Inman in the side, and centered his left boot on the dying man's belly trying to pull his bayonet free.

The fading flare gave the scene an eerie black and white effect, like an old movie. It seemed surreal, almost dream like. As Jawaski watched the soldier struggling to remove his bayonet, his horror became intense anger. He leaped out of his foxhole screaming and charging the two North Koreans, firing the Garand from his hip as he ran. The one soldier franticly twisted his rifle in an attempt to pull the bayonet free, while the other turned, raising his rifle to fire. The last three metal-jacketed .30-06 rounds to leave the Garand hit the North Korean center mass and knocked him to the ground.

A sudden surge of energy helped the other soldier to free his bayonet, but as he swung the barrel around to fire, Jawaski was eyeball to eyeball with him. All of their training and combat experience was focused as the two faced each other in that mortal moment, one fueled by fear, the other by intense rage.

Parrying the North Korean's rifle and bayonet to the side, Jawaski brought the stock of his Garand swiftly up to the soldier's chin. The butt stroke glanced off the jawbone spinning the Korean around. Using the spinning momentum, the North Korean spun completely around attempting to bring the bayonet down on the side of Jawaski's neck and shoulder. The American went to one knee, dropped the butt of the rifle against the ground and thrust the bayonet forward, up into the upper abdomen and chest cavity of the North Korean. The force of the thrust and the Korean's spinning movement took the blade through both lungs and heart, before it exited on its own accord. Dead on his feet, the Korean's knees buckled and he folded face first to the ground.

Standing with the two dead Koreans at his feet, Jawaski extended his arms and rifle over his head and screamed at the top of his lungs. The release of anger and anguish went unnoticed on the battlefield, as other life and death struggles were shaping and concluding. Drained of emotion, he dropped to his knees in the bloodstained dirt, and stared down at his friend's lifeless body. The cowboy's eyes were open and staring. The smile that Jawaski had seen earlier was replaced with a more grotesque expression. Inman's mouth was open, his tongue protruding as if he died in mid-scream. It was the face of torment and intense pain. Jawaski rose to his feet and slowly moved away, leaving his friend behind.

Walking through the carnage, the battle intensified around him. Bullets zipped about, one tearing into his jacket sleeve and grazing the meat of his left arm, others kicking up the dirt at his feet. The rifleman's creed is "It only takes one to kill you." It might be a bullet. It might be an artillery round. It was neither for Jawaski, because it wasn't his time. In more cases than not a soldier's luck would run out, but not this time, not for Jawaski. He walked dazed through the battle as if he was on a Sunday stroll in Central Park.

Several shots fired from the right hit the dirt in front of him. Stopping, he stared at the dirt kicking up, and squatted to rub the ground where the bullets had ricocheted. He tried to process what he had seen, but nothing clicked upstairs. Mild shock kept its grip as he rested on the back of his boots, balancing himself with the butt of the Garand firmly on the ground. Resting there, his thoughts slowly caught up with the moment. Throbbing pain was suddenly stinging his left arm. He reached for the pain and felt the warm flow of blood.

"Damn! I'm hit! Damn it! Damn it! Damn it!" he repeated out loud.

The physical pain was followed by the mental recognition that he was out of ammo and would have to surrender. Since he had witnessed firsthand the enemy's attitude toward prisoners, he sprang to his feet and ran.

Fully conscious now, he saw how completely Bravo Company had been overrun and routed. During the previous two nights of fighting when it became evident they would lose the hill, there was an orderly retreat. Tonight, the ammo ran out early because the North Koreans had doubled their efforts in charging the hill. Someone should have seen it coming. No one had.

Jawaski's pace picked up until he was running as hard as he could without tumbling headfirst down the hill. As he neared the company area, he realized there wasn't a safe place to hide. The enemy was everywhere, thousands of them surrounding the hill and beyond. The deeper into the American lines, the more North Koreans there seemed to be. It was a nightmare, a horrible, devilish nightmare.

Cowboy and Indian tactics were taking place on the battlefield with close, intimate combat everywhere. Some Americans were fighting, most were screaming in panic and pain as they died at the end of a North Korean bayonet. The further he ran, the more he realized he was on his own. There was no one coming to save him, no trucks to haul him back to the rear. There were just thousands of North Koreans killing every American in sight. The chilling realization made him turn to his left away from the company area and into the night.

He ran blindly around a small hill and up a long valley, tripping over rocks and bushes. If he circled the hill and walked west for say, twenty city blocks and then south another two, he would head in the direction of brigade headquarters. It was like walking from one neighborhood to the next back home in Brooklyn. The sound of killing was beginning to dim and eventually faded out as he rounded the back of the hill.

In just a few minutes he had put considerable distance between himself and the fighting. His eyes had gained their night vision, and he maneuvered around bushes and rocks, making his way up the valley.

Above, the sky was bright with stars. He looked up and in that careless moment a rock shifted under his weight and he crashed to the ground, sending rocks sliding down the slope. Ten feet ahead he saw a shadow move behind a bush. Taking the Garand, he pulled back the bolt and let it slide forward, as if chambering a round, the bayonet still fixed to the end of the barrel. The empty gun was useless except for close, hand-to-hand fighting, but to anyone seeking to harm him it sounded as if a round was loaded and ready to fire. It would also signal to a fellow American the distinctive charge of an M1 Garand.

"Walk forward," whispered a voice. Jawaski felt elated and took two quick steps toward the voice in the bush.

"I'm American."

"*Shsss!* Take it slow . . . no quick movement . . . no noise."

Jawaski stepped carefully toward the bush, and the shadow stepped out, took his arm and pulled him to the ground. Whispering the two men continued their conversation.

"Thank God I found the American lines. They overran us before we could bug out, bayoneting everyone who surrendered. I ran out of ammo and ran for it. Can you radio back to brigade and get help?"

"There is no American line, Jawaski. It's Dan Welch. The gooks are everywhere. They came in mass and overran our lines. It looks like it's every man for himself. You and me, we're both out of ammo. If we work together, we'll get back to brigade. We're a good twenty miles from there. We've got to bug out and bug out quick, or daylight will expose us."

The two men moved quickly up the trail together. After five hours of walking and running, Welch turned up a ravine and sat down behind a large rock. Jawaski followed.

"How'd you get out? You're out of ammo too? How'd you know I wasn't one of them?"

"They hunt in packs and don't stumble around. They don't sound like they're from Brooklyn, either."

There were several moments of silence, and Jawaski said, "They murdered my best friend, Cody Inman. He was up for the big R home next week, and now he's gone."

"Inman bought the farm? I'm sorry. They killed a lot of our guys tonight, Jawaski."

"You don't understand. He raised his hands to surrender. Two Korean soldiers bayoneted him. They murdered him. He just wanted to give up. He never stood a chance."

Reaching in his pocket, Jawaski pulled out the peaches and began to softly cry. After a few moments, he regained control and wiped the tears from his dirt stained face.

"They had no right to kill him like that. We don't murder them. It's not right."

"I wish I could tell you something to make it okay, but I can't. We lost a lot of real estate tonight. I've lost all my friends since we got here. I won't take on new ones. There's just too damn much dying going on around here. We're slaughtering North Koreans like rats running around a dump, and they keep coming. They have family just like us," Welch whispered. "Too much damn dying."

The two men sat quietly for ten more minutes until the tall American stood up. Without saying a word, he picked up his empty M1 Carbine and headed out, followed quickly by the smaller Jawaski.

Walking noiselessly, Welch came to a sudden stop, dropping to his belly on the rocky ground. Jawaski followed. Within seconds, some hundred feet below several soldiers passed them making their way down the valley. Their movement was fast and silent. In seconds, they were gone.

"Are they friendlies?" asked Jawaski in a whisper.

"We couldn't take a chance. We were lucky. They were North Koreans. Smell that? North Koreans soldiers don't smell like us. They don't stink, just different. I couldn't tell until they passed down wind where I picked up their scent. We need to move. They may pick up ours." Walking quickly, the two men moved up the valley.

"We crest the hill and we should be safe. Another fifteen miles and we'll be back home briefing the brigade brass. It's a ways, but we can do it." Turning to face Jawaski as he walked, he said, "Just over yonder and we'll rest all we want."

As they climbed the hill, Welch could see the slight hue of the morning sun beginning to show on the horizon to the left. It was still plenty dark, but he knew the sunlight came quickly once it broke over the horizon. Picking up the pace, he moved up the side of the hill. For every one step he took, Jawaski had to take two and breathing hard, he fell behind.

"Don't leave me, Welch!" The little man whispered between breathes. Welch heard the plea and slowed his pace. Once they crested the ridge, they would rest in the rocks. From then on, the walking would be downhill. It was just a matter of getting over the top and Welch knew that. Raised in the Appalachian Mountains, it was up or downhill everywhere you went in West Virginia. Jawaski, on the other hand, was not up to the task. Welch slowed his pace even more to keep the shorter man close.

As he turned his head to check on Jawaski's progress, Welch saw flashlights moving parallel to their trail, below in the valley. The lights were about a half a mile behind them. Looking to the east he saw the sun breaking up from behind a peak, spreading light against the higher peak of the mountain ahead. He could see they weren't far enough around the hillside to make cover before the sun broke, and he was beginning to worry. If they were caught in the open on the mountainside by the sunlight they would be easily spotted by the patrol coming to their rear. He looked up and decided their only chance was to head straight up and over the ridge ahead of the sunlight. Grabbing Jawaski by the collar he pulled him up the hillside.

On the mountain above the ridge, the rocks and bushes were beginning to take form as the light crept downward. They had about two hundred yards to reach the crest, and the slope increased considerably as they drew nearer to the top.

A hundred yards now, Welch struggled ahead, pulling poor Jawaski along. The sun's rays were only a couple of hundred yards above the ridge now, lighting its way down the hillside like a wave coming toward a beach. The rocks and bushes were clearly visible. In a moment, the light would betray them to the patrol below. The ridge was just fifty more feet.

"Come on Jawaski, don't quit on me now, just fifty more feet, forty feet, thirty, ten!"

The light was almost on top of them now. Their shadows beginning to show as Welch gave one final jerk and hurled them both over the crest of the ridge. The sunlight broke over the mountain peak and the hillside lit up. Down below, a North Korean soldier looked up and watched the sunlight expose the crest of the shorter mountain. At a half of mile, he could clearly see the rocks and bushes intermingled with shadows. Satisfied nothing had gone that way, he turned and followed the patrol as it continued up the valley.

A few seconds later the sunlight peaked the ridge crest and cast a warm blanket of sunshine on Welch and Jawaski's outstretched bodies. The warmth was caressing, physically and mentally. In the heat of flight neither man noticed how cool the October night air had been. The field jackets that kept them warm were now unbuttoned to let in the air. They lay on the ground slowly catching their breath. Welch rolled over and patted Jawaski on the leg. Too breathless to speak, Jawaski smiled. His first since he and Inman had smiled at each other for the last time.

Sitting up, Welch scanned the valley that lay out in front of them. Several knolls were to either side with larger mountains to the right. Mentally picturing the contour map he had studied the day before at the command tent, he pointed his finger west and said, "There. That's where we'll find the brigade lines, on the other side of that mountain."

Jawaski sat up and pointed to the mountain and said, "Go west young man!"

Welch chuckled as he helped Jawaski to his feet, and they started down the hill at an angle, keeping their feet under them and maintaining a westerly direction. After three hours they approached a small village that rested in the valley between the mountains. Jawaski sat in the shade of a bush, while Welch kneeled and surveyed the village below. He saw mud huts, about ten by ten, with rice straw roofs. There was cloth hanging on most of the front doors and no windows, simple dwellings for a simple people. The village stirred with morning activity, workers headed for the fields, older women cleaned up after breakfast, and began to prepare lunch. It looked friendly, but Welch knew looks were deceiving. The villagers might be friendly and hide them out, but more likely they feared the ruthless North Koreans more than the South Koreans and Americans. Out of fear they would sound the alarm. There could also be North Korean agents there. Agents were everywhere and Koreans, north or south, looked like Koreans. Looking back into the shade, he saw a very pale and worn out Jawaski. Looking around he spotted several large boulders to their right where they could hide and rest.

"We'll move to that outcrop of rocks and wait for dark. It's too risky moving in daylight. We'll have to be patient and settle for a late-night supper back at camp."

Jawaski nodded in agreement, and they moved carefully toward the rocks. Crawling between two large ones they sat back in the coolness of the shade and relaxed. Jawaski's boyish face and blue eyes portrayed an air of innocence. His delicate hands still trembled from the swift flight over the mountain. His five-and-a-half-foot frame gave him the appearance of a choir boy. There was no outward indication of how efficient he could be at fighting the enemy, eyeball to eyeball, and killing them.

Welch, on the other hand, was large framed, tall and firm, like the yellow poplar tree that grew in his native West Virginia Mountains. He was nearly a foot taller than Jawaski. His face sported a two-day beard, his eyes were brown and steady, a face that could have easily been chiseled from granite. He was handsome in a reassuring kind of way. His hands were large and powerful, capable of delivering a man to his maker with one well-placed blow. The two soldiers were an odd pair, thrown together by a deadly moment in time.

"Where you from, Welch? Southeast, I'll bet. How'd you manage to escape the North Koreans? Do you have a girl? I've got a bunch of girls back home. When I get back, I'm going to pick out one and marry her. You married, Welch?"

Welch patiently listened to the little man jabber on. He had never had a conversation with Jawaski, but the word was he'd talk your head off. By the time you had a chance to answer his questions, you had forgotten most of them. Welch tried to speak, but was cut off.

"You making a career of the Army? I'm not. It's 1951, and I got better things to do with my life. My dad works on the docks and is in the union. He said he would get me on when I got back from the war. Hard work, but it pays, and if I'm going to get married and have a bunch of kids, I need a good job, don't you think? It's all union, so once I'm in, I'm set for life. What'd you do before the war?"

Welch gave the little man a look. The chatterbox had run out of questions and was ready to hear someone else's voice. Jawaski sat and stared at Welch, patiently awaiting his response.

"I worked in a coal mine in West Virginia. My family has worked in the mines far back as anyone can remember. Coal has been very hard on us."

Jawaski sat pondering what Welch had said. In Brooklyn you didn't have to face death two hundred feet underground. It usually came with a fire, ten stories above ground.

"You got a girl?"

"Welch smiled, "We married just before I left for Korea. The first time I saw her, I knew I had to marry her. It took a lot of courting and a lot of money, but she finally said yes."

Welch sat with his eyes closed leaning back against the boulder. He was back home now, remembering, daydreaming, and Jawaski was right there with him.

"We were married at the Elkins Baptist Church in Amelia's hometown. She arranged the whole wedding and it was the grandest thing Elkins had seen since the VJ day parade. You should have seen her perform as she walked down the aisle. She looked like the Queen of Sheba. I can still see her smile as she walked toward me."

"The Queen of Sheba? The King of Siam, I am!" Jawaski was hanging on every word, just like when he was riding the range with Cody Inman's stories.

"I rented the Elk's Hall in Elkins and hired a small band to play at the reception. For the bride and groom's dance Amelia's second cousin, Connie, sang Johnny Mercer's song, *And the Angels Sing.*"

"Was she as good as Martha Tilton?" Jawaski asked.

"Better."

Jawaski leaned forward, his interest peaking.

"The band wasn't up to the level of Benny Goodman's band, but they gave it their best."

Jawaski broke in, singing softly:

"We meet and the Angels sing, the Angels sing the sweetest song I ever heard."

Surprised, Welch listened as the little man sang the song from start to finish. He leaned back and remembered how Amelia floated across the dance floor, how light she felt in his arms, her beautiful smile.

"You speak and the Angels sing, or am I reading music into every word?"

Covering his mouth with both hands, Jawaski puffed out a quiet solo of whiney notes that sounded similar to the trumpet solo played at the end of Tilton's vocals by the song's co-writer, Ziggy Elman.

Welch leaned forward in amazement. "Man, where on earth did you learn to do that?" questioned Welch quietly.

"Ah, that ain't nutin'. You can learn a lot of stuff sitting at home listening to the radio all the time. I was always too little to get picked for stick ball games. I spent a lot of time by myself. Where did you go for your honeymoon?"

"I spent all my money on the wedding and the reception, so we couldn't go far. My Aunt Betsy invited us to come and spend a week at her home in Huttonsville. She took care of everything. All we had to do was enjoy ourselves. It was one of her wedding gifts. Aunt Betty took me in when mom died. Have you ever been to the mountains, Jawaski?"

Jawaski shook his head, no.

"From Aunt Betsy's front porch, you can see the Tygart Valley and the Laurel Mountains. Amelia and I married in the fall when the trees were in full color. We would sit on the porch swing and watch Canada Geese fly in "V" formations around the mountains and down through the valley. On our last day we were walking in the upper pasture when a red-tailed hawk glided over us. Amelia shouted, *'Wait for me!'* I wrote her last month and told her when I got home I would buy a small plane and fly her over the mountains and valleys. I miss her and write every week. I haven't got any letters back. I can understand her not having the time to write. God, I really miss her. You ever fly Jawaski? Jawaski?"

The little man was sound asleep. Welch eased over to the opening of the rocks, squatted, leaning against one of the boulders. Everything looked normal in the village below. He felt alert, but soon started to doze. He had gone thirty hours without sleep. Not a great length of time by combat standards, but the swift flight from the battle had taken its toll. He folded his arms and laid his head on his knees. He wasn't tried, but it would be good to rest a little. His thoughts were with Amelia as he fell asleep, holding her in his arms, dancing about in Aunt Betsy's leaf covered yard.

Welch woke startled by a howling dog below in the village. Easing over to the opening he peered out into the darkness. He couldn't see his watch, but from the look of things it was early evening. The rest was welcomed. They would miss supper, but he would settle for a hot cup of coffee and breakfast. He felt the hunger pains of not eating for nearly 40 hours. He tried to forget the pain in his stomach and reached over to wake Jawaski. Placing a hand over the little man's mouth he shook him gently.

"Wake up Jawaski! Wake up!" whispered Welch. Jawaski jerked awake and fought the hand over his mouth until Welch's calming voice reassured him he was safe for the moment.

Sensing a release of tension, Welch removed his hand.

"What time is it?" Jawaski asked, yawning.

"It's around twenty-hundred hours. We slept through the day. I dozed off and on until I finally gave in around eleven-hundred. Been awake about fifteen minutes. There's a dog howling up a storm down in the village. He must have got wind of our scent. We'll stick to the side of the mountain until we reach the rice fields. We should make good time along the roads in the dark."

"I'm hungry," said Jawaski.

"So am I, but it will have to wait until we reach brigade. Let's get to moving."

Welch eased from between the large boulders and started walking. Below, the dog continued its barking. They traveled a half mile along the hillside before Welch felt they were safe. Down below, the rice fields were barely visible in the starlight. Moving carefully down, they came to the flat hard surface of the dirt road. The rice fields were broken up into watery grids with narrow walkway dividers and access roads to either side. The men traveled along the road moving quickly, leaving the barking dog behind in the darkness. The rice fields stretched endlessly up the valley. Welch noticed faint lights on the right ahead. Motioning to Jawaski, he kneeled in the road and studied the surrounding landscape.

"Light up ahead," he whispered.

"What are we going to do?" questioned Jawaski. "Do you think it might be brigade? Do you want me to walk up there and see what it is? I'm cold and hungry"

Twisting around nearly face-to-face with the jabbering Jawaski, Welch said, *"Shush!"* Jawaski reeled backward and plopped down in the road. Welch frowned, feeling angry with himself for shushing so loudly.

"There's another village straight ahead. The two villages have adjoining rice fields, and I'm betting there's a road that crosses between the properties to the other side. It will be wider and safer to cross on. It must be along here somewhere."

Looking directly into the darkness, Welch allowed his eyes to adjust to night vision and slowly began scanning the landscape, not focusing directly on any one object, just scanning and taking in the landmarks, whispering softly as he scanned. "Mountain on the right, rice paddies down the valley, bigger mountain on the left, village behind and village ahead."

"Access road across the field, twenty yards ahead," whispered Jawaski from behind. "See the shadow line that travels right to left. It's thicker than the walkways."

Sure enough, the thicker pattern of a road was ahead. Welch had scanned across it several times without noticing its significance. He looked back into the bright smiling teeth and eyes of Jawaski's dirty face. Reaching back, he patted Jawaski on the shoulder and whispered, "We'll cross, circle the village on the side of that mountain. It's higher, but doesn't appear to be nearly as steep. Let's go, pal. Quickly!"

They trotted to the intersection, took a sharp left and headed out at double time. The rice field was a hundred yards wide, so they would cross it in about twenty seconds. They were vulnerable out in the middle of a flat area and needed to move quickly across and get up the side of the mountain. Half way across disaster struck as the road swallowed up Welch with no more noise than a soft, muted splash. Jawaski skidded to a stop and stood there in the darkness, staring down at the spot where Welch had dropped out of sight.

"Welch," whispered Jawaski—silence.

Ten more seconds. "Welch!" A little louder this time, with a hint of fear.

The surface of the road a few feet in front of Jawaski suddenly began churning. Welch reappeared, splashing, coughing and fighting to keep his head above the thick liquid substance that was sucking him back down. With no swimming skills and very little buoyancy he struggled to catch his breath, before sinking below the surface once more.

Jawaski stood engulfed in dark silence once again, but only for a second as he began looking frantically for something to extend out to the drowning man.

Several seconds later Welch resurfaced a second time, now in a dead panic. He was fighting for his life, but somehow maintaining enough of his senses to not scream out loud. He continued to do the only thing he knew to do and that was to flail about, catch a deep breath, drop down to the bottom and push off, attempting to draw himself closer to the edge. It was a good plan except for the two feet of mud on the bottom, which grabbed his feet and refused to let go without a struggle. Resurfacing again, he was no closer to the edge.

Jawaski moved as close to the edge of the mysterious pool as he dared, kneeled and reached out to grab Welch as he surfaced and flailed about. As Jawaski leaned out he felt the Garand sling tighten across his chest. Reacting instinctively, he pulled out his bayonet, cut the sling near the barrel's end and wrapped it twice around his hand. When Welch broke the surface again, he gripped the end of the sling tightly and tossed the rifle toward him.

Welch felt the impact of something against his shoulder and neck and instinctively grabbed hold, pulling it to his chest. Jawaski felt the strap go taunt and pulled in his big fish, grabbing him by the collar of his field jacket and wrestling him onto the road. Welch lay flat on his stomach, gasping for breath, throwing up the thick liquid and all the time, attempting to crawl away, trying to put as much distance between him and whatever it was he had just crawled out of.

Listening to Welch gasp and puke, Jawaski smelled for the first time the strong stench of human waste. The pool was about eight by eight and judging by the bouncing efforts of his friend, at least seven feet deep. A four hundred square foot pool of human waste in the middle of the road, thought Jawaski. Minus, of course, the square foot Welch had just recycled through his stomach and out on to the road.

Kneeling next to Welch, Jawaski whispered softly, "It's a croc, a trench where farmers store human waste to fertilize their fields. 'Waste not, want not' they say. You, my mammoth friend, have been swimming in human poo!"

Welch fought to gain control over his retching and spoke in the direction of the voice. "I fell in a pond of human crap?"

"*Shush!*" said Jawaski. The word was barely out of his mouth before Welch was silenced by his efforts to further empty his stomach on to the dirt road.

Jawaski stood, took Welch by the collar of his jacket and pulled the big man across the dirt road and down the bank. The thick slime that covered Welch's body provided a slick apron to easily move his large frame across the dirt.

"No! No! Not again. I will be quiet, I promise," Welch whispered in a scream. Too weak to resist he slid down the bank toward the water of the rice paddy.

Jawaski warned, "Hold your breath." They both entered the rice paddy together, Jawaski standing knee deep in the water, Welch just on the top of the surface. Half rolling the body and swishing him about, Jawaski moved around the paddy repeating the movements several times, before stopping and lifting Welch's head above the muddy water.

"More," Welch said taking a deep breath and dunking himself under the water. Jawaski repeated the rinsing action several times until Welch found his feet and stood, clinging to Jawaski's jacket. Soaking wet and exhausted, he stood facing the little man who saved him. In the dark, Welch reached out, grabbed Jawaski and hugged him. Jawaski attempted to pull away at first, but the big man held tight, so he hugged back. They stood for several seconds in the middle of the dark rice paddy, clinging to one another.

Grabbing the bigger man by the arms and pushing him to arm's length, Jawaski whispered, "You stink!" Laughing and sobbing Welch watched as Jawaski walk over to the bank and located his rifle. Stepping back into the water, he lowered it below the surface, rinsing it off.

"Sergeant Jetti is going to kill me for treating my weapon this way."

"At least, you have your rifle," responded Welch mournfully.

He continued to swish it about as they waded across the rice paddy and reached the road at the base of the mountain. Helping each other out, they began to climb. Jawaski led the way this time, with Welch holding onto the strap of the Garand for balance.

"God, I stink!"

"Yes, you do, Welch," said Jawaski, trying to hide a chuckle.

"I mean, I really stink to high heaven, Leo. Is this what it smells like in Brooklyn in the summer time? And it's Dan, Leo. My friends call me Dan."

"You smell worse, Dan!" Jawaski said, smiling in the darkness.

✱   ✱   ✱   ✱

The North Korean officer brought the bamboo stick down across the head of the farmer. Grimacing in pain he turned away, but was hit again in the side of the face. The officer drew up the stick to strike again, but the man fell to the floor, groveling and pleading. The farmer's wife, her mother, and their two children were pressed up against the outer wall of the hut, pleading for the officer to spare him from further beatings. The officer barked off quick orders to two soldiers, who bowed and lifted the man to his feet.

"You know and then you don't. You waste my time old man, and now you think maybe there was something in the dark the dog barked at. Maybe you think I should ask the dog, or maybe, I beat you some more and you recall even more. You take from me my time. What if I take something valuable from you? What if I . . ."

The officer reached down and grabbed the farmer's wife by the hair and pulled her across the floor. Terrified, the woman cried out, but there was no one to help.

"What if I take this woman from you to make up for the time you have wasted?"

The officer pulled the woman to her knees by the hair of her head, pulled out his pistol, cocked the hammer and put it to the side of her head. The woman, wide eyed in terror, was beyond crying out or pleading. She simply trembled and gasped, trying to catch her breath with the barrel of the pistol pressed against her temple.

"Tell me farmer. What is this woman worth to you, tonight?"

The farmer searched for some thread of information that would satisfy the officer and spare his wife.

"No! No! You must wait. I will tell you what you need to know. But you must give me time to think, to recall. Yes, there is much to recall."

The woman was released and her mother pulled her to her side. The officer stepped over to the man, squatted next to him and said, "Think carefully farmer. You take much care before you speak as this is last chance for you."

Struggling to give the officer something acceptable the farmer said, "When the dog barked, I lifted door to look out. I see an American Jeep traveling up the road, with three Americans in it. Yes, I am sure that Americans were traveling on the road."

Standing up the soldier placed the barrel of the pistol against his temple and pulled the trigger. The man's head jerked to the side violently, blood and skull fragments splattering across the small room. His body went limp, and dropped to the dirt floor. The women and children began screaming hysterically, clinging to one another in the corner.

The officer turned on his heels, lifted the cloth door of the hut and stepped outside. The villagers had remained in their huts, not interfering. They had experienced the ruthlessness of North Korean agents and knew that to resist the soldiers meant death. They recognized the report of the gunshot as the death of a neighbor. They would find out who soon enough. Life must go on.

The officer turned to his men.

"An example has been made. The next time this village will be more willing to talk about real Americans, in real jeeps! The rest of them are not worth wasting bullets on. Pour gasoline on the straw roof, and light it. They will scream and those hiding in their huts will remember that I am not a man of patience."

The officer walked to a small truck and lit a cigarette. One of the soldiers released the straps holding a gas can on the fender of the truck, carried it over and poured gasoline onto the low edge of the rice straw roof. The screaming grew louder as the gas saturated the inside of the hut. The soldier circled the hut and shuffled back over to the truck. The officer took one last draw off the cigarette and exhaled the smoke slowly through his nose as he flicked the burning butt toward the hut. A glowing tail of orange sparks traced through the air and landed on the edge of the straw roof. The gas drenched straw ignited.

One of the soldiers took out a lighter and started for the hut, but was stopped by the officer who knew from experience the fumes inside the hut would soon ignite with a flash. In another instant there was a loud, *poof,* and blue and yellow flames shot up from the edges of the roof. The soldier let out a surprised yelp, falling backwards onto the ground. Kicking vigorously with his feet, he managed to move across the dirt on his behind to a safe distance from the burning hut.

The North Korean captain laughed and calmly walked over to the entrance of the burning hut and waited. In a few moments a screaming child bolted through the door, straight into his waiting arms. Her clothing had already burned off and parts of her body were charred with black loose skin. What was left of her black hair was charred and matted to her head. The captain picked her up, took two steps and tossed her back into the burning inferno. He walked slowly over to the truck, picking the girl's charred skin off his uniform and the three of them climbed into the truck and drove down the road toward the rice fields. Behind them the hut was engulfed in flames. The villagers remained in their huts. The North Korean officer felt certain his next stop at the village would produce much more useful information.

✴   ✴   ✴   ✴

The two men had traveled for nearly an hour across the side of the mountain, well above the village in the valley.

"I'm tired Dan. Can we stop and take a break?"

"No, we have to," Welch thought for a second and said, "Sure, we can stop, Leo. We should be miles away from the North Koreans by now."

Jawaski sat down on the mountain, laid back and stared up at the stars. Welch looked around studying the area. The big man sat down and stretched his legs out, propping them up on top of a small rock.

"We should be close now, shouldn't we? How much further, Dan? I'm really tired and cold. Do you think we could rest some and build a fire?"

"Hard to say. It's strange we haven't seen some signs of American troops. We have to keep moving. We'll rest a little, but we can't have a fire, not in the dark. It's too easily seen and not in the daylight, either. Smoke is too easily noticed. We rest and keep moving until we find our guys."

"But, I'm hungry, Dan. I got to eat something soon. My stomach is really starting to hurt. My canteen is empty. I'm thirsty."

Welch took his canteen out of its pouch. "Sorry, little buddy. I've got this, but it's contaminated." Welch smelled the top of the canteen and drew his head back.

"See if you have enough in your canteen to rinse off the lid," and he tossed it over to Jawaski.

Jawaski unscrewed the lid of his canteen and held it upside down over the lid of Welch's canteen. The water that poured out did little to sanitize the lid, but it was enough to satisfy him. He took a long draw of water and sat staring into the darkness, waiting for the water to sooth the pain in his belly, but found no relief. He screwed the lid back on and held it out until Welch took it from his hand.

Jawaski reached into his pocket and pulled out the can of peaches. He rolled it around in his hand, patted it and stuck it back into the pocket. For the moment, friendship conquered hunger. It was the only thing he had left that was Cody's and he cherished it more than what it could do for his stomach.

Fifteen minutes and they were up moving again, picking their way across the mountainside. Lights began to materialize up ahead. Welch played it off, but a few steps later there came a whisper from behind, "Lights, Dan. We did it. I told you we'd make it, didn't I?"

Off to their right a vehicle traveled up the road toward the lights.

"You see. There's a patrol going in."

Welch rolled his eyes and smiled to himself. As they approached the lights multiplied. The nearer they got, the more obvious it became they were approaching a military encampment with tents and vehicles staged together. Their pace quickened as they made their way to the valley below. On flat ground, they doubled their efforts, stomachs bouncing up and down, growling, but the pain wasn't nearly as bad now with food just around the corner. Rounding the bend, they slowed, fearful of walking into a sentry with a quick trigger finger.

The closer they got the more unsettled Welch felt. In their excitement were they getting careless? When he was a kid and found himself in a mess, his father would shake his head and say, "Boy, your brain works well, but only when it's turned on." His brain had been drained and turned off for over a day, but suddenly he realized that something was definitely wrong with the surroundings. Jawaski was several steps ahead of him. The moment he realized things weren't right he realized it was too late to do anything about it.

To his left, he heard the faint click of a safety being released, followed by the soft jabbering of words that sounded Korean and then a faint, "Hey Joe!" Welch responded quickly with, "Hey, Kim!" His heart wanted him to believe it was South Korean guards on a battalion perimeter, but that didn't make sense. His instincts halted him in his tracks. Jawaski, now out of sight and earshot of a whisper, kept walking. The words came again, much louder and demanding, accompanied by the glare of a bright light. He stood there locked in place, unable to see. He slowly raised his arms. Up ahead there was loud angry shouting and two shots rang out.

✷   ✷   ✷   ✷

A little round woman stepped out the door on the stoop and checked her mailbox. Curlers clung tightly to her brown hair, covered by a scarf tied under her chin. She had refused to give up her natural color, even when it was clear her hair had turned gray. She simply wouldn't give in to the gray.

She grabbed the letters out of the box, and thumbed through them quickly. Taking one of the letters out, she kissed it, shook it in the air and hurried back into the apartment.

"Lenny! Lenny! It's Leo. We have a letter from our Leo. Wake up, Lenny."

Leonard Jawaski walked into the sitting room. A short, stocky man, he was dressed casually in slacks and a blue flannel shirt. Saturday was his day off, along with Sunday. He worked weekends at the docks when he was younger, but now he enjoyed them off. Besides, the younger dockworkers needed the overtime with their young families. The union found ways of taking care of its own.

And what a weekend it was, the New York Giants were playing the New York Yankees in Game One of the World Series at Yankee Stadium. The Bronx Bombers had a twenty-year-old kid named Mays who had hit twenty home runs since being called up in late May from the farm club in Minneapolis. The Yankee's Joe DiMaggio was probably in his last Series. The fans would miss Joltin' Joe, but they were excited about his heir-apparent, a nineteen-year-old kid from Oklahoma named Mickey Mantle.

What kind of baseball name is Mickey? thought Lenny. Mickey was a mouse, not a baseball player. Next thing you know the Yanks will have Donald Duck taking Berra's place behind the plate and Goofy on the mound. He chuckled to himself picturing the Disney cartoon characters playing for the Yankees.

Lenny felt good about his Giant's chances and had a couple of seats lined up for games three, four and five at the Polo Grounds. The seats were right behind the Giant's dugout, so he could watch the game up close and hear Manager Leo Durocher's tirades in the dugout. In an additional show of faith, he had a sawbuck down at Polanski's Deli riding on the Giants in Game One.

His son, Leo, grew up at the Giant's ballpark. He had spent lots of time with his son and they always seemed to have a good time, but he had given up a long time ago trying to figure out where he had gone wrong. A father could only do so much and had to let nature take its course. Leo had always been a good kid, but the day Lenny walked into his son's room and saw the corner of the Yankee pennant sticking out from under the pillow was the day he knew his son was his own man. They had talked and agreed Leo could hang the banner on his bedroom wall, if he hung a Giant pennant next to it. He couldn't stand the thought of having to look at the Yankee pennant, without a reminder of his beloved Giants.

Besides, he figured if Leo was reminded of his Giant roots enough, he might repent and mend his errant ways. Baseball took on a different perspective when Leo left for Korea. There would be plenty of sunny, summer afternoons for him and Leo to go see the Giants and the Yankees, when his son returned home.

The pre-game show was about to start on the radio, but it would have to wait. He walked over and turned the Motorola off.

"Leo, you say? Where is it, Irene?"

Irene excitingly held up the letter for Lenny to see. The return address was sure enough, Private Leo Jawaski.

"Ah, Lenny, I wonder how our Leo is doing. You think he is staying warm? You think they are feeding him good? You know what a sensitive boy he is. I just don't think he would be a good soldier. I don't know why the government wanted to make our Leo a soldier. Do you think he's okay, Lenny?"

Lenny Jawaski stood there looking at his wife for a couple of seconds, and smiled. "Well, we'll just have to open the letter and see, won't we?"

Irene handed the letter to her husband and they sat down on the sofa to read Leo's letter:

September 23, 1950

Dear Mom and Dad,

> *I am safe and well. The nights are cool here, but we stay warm. The food is okay. That's all I will say about that. Nothing is as good as your cooking, Mom, so it really wouldn't be fair for me to judge the Army cooks. I would be gaining weight if we didn't have so much to do and the workdays weren't so long. We get up early and go to bed late. Sorry, Dad, we can't have unions in the Army, we would never get anything done.*

> *We have been waiting to return to the front. It's been a week since our last engagement with the North Koreans, and we are anxious to get back at them. Cody and me are getting itchy sitting around. All the guys are great. They really treat me well. They're not like the guys in the neighborhood. They don't poke fun or shove me around. They are pretty square guys.*

> *Dad, I still want to work down at the docks, but I want to visit Cody's ranch out in Wyoming after I visit with you and Mom for a while. Cody has real horses out there, and he said he would teach me to ride and rope,*

and he and I would work on the ranch. Imagine that, a Jawaski riding the range out west like a real cowboy.

Don't worry, Dad. In a couple of months, I'll come back home and start at the docks. Cody wants to come and visit, if that's okay? I've told him all about Brooklyn and mom's cooking. He can't wait to meet you. He is my best friend.

I have to go now. Sergeant Jennings is hollering for a formation. We've got those North Koreans scared and running north. We'll have them whooped and I'll be back home in no time.

I love you Mom and Dad and I'll see you soon. I'm scheduled to come back home in three months, just in time for Christmas. I'll write again next week.

Love Leo

Mom, tell Constantine Wheeler hello, and Dad, "GO YANKS!"

CHAPTER 2

▼

Bacon sizzled in the skillet as pancake batter bubbled, cooking slowly in a pan. The pancakes were shaped like turtles, or maybe cows, depending on whose plate they were destined for. A stack of eggs sat in a small flat pan on the wood stove. On the back sat a pan of sausage gravy, while drop biscuits browned in the oven. Cooking on a wood stove took great skill, a combination of burning just the right amount of wood and timing out the meal.

Martha Lowe scooped the last piece of bacon from its grease, flipped the last pancake, emptied the gravy into a bowl, put the eggs on a platter with bacon and took the biscuits out of the oven.

Her husband, Howard, transferred the loaded dishes to the kitchen table. He buttered Amy Sue's turtles while Wanda Faye buttered her cows. He then generously poured maple syrup on both stacks.

At the same time, Martha was pouring fresh milk from the Long farm down the lane, and two hot cups of coffee for her and Howard. With everything on the table, Howard and Martha sat down with their daughters, and they all joined hands.

"Wanda Faye, it's your turn to say grace," Howard said to his oldest daughter. The ten-year-old closed her eyes and blessed the food.

"We thank thee Heavenly Father, for the blessings we are about to receive. Amen!"

Saturday morning breakfast was special at the Lowe home since no one was rushed. Weekdays, it was Cornflakes or Quaker Oats through the winter and the same on Sundays, as they got ready for Sunday school and church.

When they had finished cleaning their plates Howard asked, "So, young ladies, what are your plans for today?"

"I will put fresh water and dog food out for King. Then Amy Sue and I will go to the hen house and gather eggs. I will take a dozen over to Mrs. Long and clean and set the rest in the springhouse for Mrs. Katherine . . ."

"Oh! Oh! Mrs. Katherine. Mrs. Katherine visit today?" blurted out Amy Sue. Impulsiveness in a four-year-old was understandable, but never ignored.

"Amy Sue, Wanda Faye was speaking and you interrupted her," said Martha.

Howard turned away tickled, trying to hide his smile. Realizing it was futile trying to hide such behavior from the local schoolteacher, he turned and faced a stern look.

"Daddy, don't you think Amy Sue should allow her sister to continue, uninterrupted?"

"Why, of course, Mother. Wanda Faye you were saying?"

"After we clean Mrs. Katherine's eggs, I will dust mop the living room floor and help Mom finish in the kitchen and when we finish . . ."

"We go play with our tousins!" blurted out Amy Sue, whose happy face quickly changed to serious expression. "Sorry, Wanda Faye, I ruppted you again."

"Daddy, what are your plans today?" asked Wanda Faye.

"I will go to the barn and check on that young steer we are corn feeding for . . . feeding to," he looked quickly over to Martha.

"Feeding to help him grow big and strong, Daddy."

"Thank you, Mother."

Amy Sue giggled and said, "Blackie happy and biggest Angeese steer on farm."

"And then we'll have him slaughtered and have good meat to eat all winter."

"Now, Wanda Faye, you know your sister isn't old enough to understand such things."

"I not little! I too, understand. I too, like hamburger!"

Howard and Martha laughed while the girls giggled.

"Well then, after I fatten up Blackie with our corn, I will rake leaves, mow the yard, walk the fence lines and repair any problems and then . . ."

The girls looked on with anticipation.

"and then I'll come in, get cleaned up, help Mom get you two cleaned up, and then . . ."

"And den!" repeated Amy Sue.

"and then, I will help Mom fix a picnic basket supper, and we'll all go to the drive-in and see *Snow White and the Seven Dwarfs*."

"*Yeah!*" squealed both girls as Wanda Faye clapped her hands and Amy Sue waved her arms over her head.

"But it can't happen unless we do what."

"Get our chores done," said Wanda Faye.

"Chores done," repeated her little sister.

"May we be excused, Mom?"

"We be scused?" repeated Amy Sue.

"Yes, you may."

Both girls leaped down and went to the back porch where King's food was kept.

"I thought we were having a nice quiet evening at home tonight, Howard."

"We were, darling, but you know those Disney movies only come around every seven years or so. It looks like this evening will be a perfect drive-in night. We'll take the old quilt for the girls to sit on and sit beside the car in our lounge chairs. It's a perfect October night, and it will be fun for the girls and wonderful for us too."

"What's so wonderful for us?" Martha asked sheepishly.

"Why, popcorn and soft drinks, of course."

Howard dodged the flying dishtowel, grabbing it before it hit the kitchen floor.

"If you're going to take your girls out tonight, you had better get your chores done too, farm boy."

"Yes, Mrs. Lowe," said Howard as he followed the girl's path out the back door. As he passed, he tossed the dishtowel to his wife.

Howard loved doing things with his girls, and Martha loved him for it. Most Saturdays, he worked till dark, but tonight they were going to see *Snow White*.

"And you had better get to your chores, Martha Ann," she said out loud to herself as she started gathering the dishes off the table and stacking them on the counter.

The Chevrolet sedan was parked on the mound, front end pointed toward the big screen, as if preparing to take off and fly into the vast blueness of the October sky. A large quilt was spread out next to the automobile, with four aluminum lounge chairs. Howard gathered up their supper plates and soft drink bottles, placing them in a brown paper grocery sack. Martha and the girls were down at the playground. The drive-in lot was mostly empty but Howard knew it would start filling up before long. The warm Kentucky night and the Disney movie would bring out families. He finished up and walked down to the base of the screen.

"Watch me, Daddy!" yelled Wanda Faye swinging higher and higher.

"Oooh! You're going to touch the sky if you go any higher."

"Me too, Daddy! Me touch sky!" added Amy Sue who swung with pushes from her mother.

Howard began pushing Amy Sue, as Martha sat down in the swing next to her.

"Me too!" said Martha smiling over her shoulder. Howard positioned himself between her and Amy Sue and pushed each in turn, as they swung back to him. Martha's shoulder length, brown hair was down for the evening and cascaded back and forth across her shoulders as she swung. Her soft brown eyes complimented the tanned complexion of her skin. Her natural beauty was stunning and it never failed to take Howard's breath away when she wore her hair down.

Martha spoke to Howard in broken sentences as she swung back and forth.

"Now, Howard . . ."

"Not too high with Amy . . ."

"She's too young."

To which Amy Sue responded, "Me not too young . . ."

"Me hold tight . . ."

"Swing high, Daddy."

Howard gave a hefty push and Amy Sue responded with a squeal that grew with momentum and height.

She yelled, "*Higher!*" and Howard restrained his pushes although he knew Amy Sue had swung much higher at home on the tire swing.

"*Higher. Look Mommy. Look Wanda Faye.*"

Wanda Faye drug her feet and with each contact slowed till she bailed out on the upswing, sailing through the air and making a perfect landing. Without missing a step, she ran for the sliding board. Amy Sue called out to her dad to stop her, which he did, slowing her down so she too could leap out and run for the sliding boards. Howard then took the swing next to Martha.

Automobiles were starting to take their place on the rows of mounds. Some families remained in their cars, and others sat chairs outside. The sky dimmed in the east with hues of blue and gray, while behind the concession stand the setting sun lit the western horizon with shades of bright orange, yellow and red. As other children arrived on the playground, Howard and Martha moved and sat on a bench next to the slides. They sat quietly, close together, holding hands and watching the girls play on the slide.

Behind them the big screen came to life with a preview of the coming attractions:

> *"Judy Holiday is beautiful, blonde, brazey, and oh-h-brother!*
> *William Holden is smooth, smart, smitten, and smoochy!*
> *Broderick Crawford is rich, raucous, rowdy, and a riot!"*

"Oh, Howard, I think I would like to see that when it comes."

"That?"

"Behind you, ninny, the movie, *Born Yesterday*. I want to see it when it's showing at the Columbian next week."

Howard turned to face the screen as Holiday attempted to be affectionate with her millionaire boyfriend played by the gruff Crawford. Crawford fails to recognize her advances, but can't ignore her clever retort:

> *"What are you doing?"* bellowed Crawford.
> *"Well, if you don't know, I must be doing it wrong."*

Martha squeezed her nose and squawked out, "Well, if you don't know, I must be doing it wrong," giving a fair impression of Holiday's high pitched, comedic voice.

Howard laughed and kissed her on the forehead.

"She is beautiful and talented and so are you, sweetheart."

"Okay then, like old times, just you and me. Mrs. Katherine can watch the kids, and we'll have supper at Circle R."

Howard moved a little closer and put his arm around her shoulder, "Can we sit in the back row of the theater?"

"Mr. Lowe, are you suggesting something suggestive at the Columbian Theater?"

"Ma'am! You've clearly understood my intentions. If you feel too old for such, then I will, we will have to, just watch the movie."

"Scandalous, Mr. Lowe. People will talk!" laughed Martha.

"I will notify my booking agent immediately to cancel my engagements for next Friday. You make the arrangements with Mrs. Katherine and I'll pencil you in."

Howard hugged Martha and they got up and walked over to gather up the girls. Behind them, the movie previews continued as they walked to their automobile.

"Okay girls, bathroom break before the movie starts."

"Me no need to, Mommy," protested Amy Sue.

Martha took both girls by the hands and the four of them headed for the concession stand.

"The usual, girls?" asked their father.

"Yes!" responded both girls in unison.

"Martha?"

"Could you just, maybe get me one of those little tiny boxes of Tootsie Rolls?"

"Consider it done, me Lady."

Howard had beaten the rush; the line was short and he was pleased. He had gained a dislike for standing in lines like most veterans who served in World War II. Standing slightly over six feet, Howard was trim, but his muscled body was hard and powerful. Farming sixteen-hour days forged hard bodied men. His dark hair was trimmed tight around the ears and wavy on the top. His face was clean shaven. His eyes were grayish-green and most of the time they smiled along with his broad grin. He sported a dark farmer's tan from the long hours under the sun.

Leaving a couple of dollars at the cash register, he walked out of the concession stand leaving behind the strong smell of fresh popping popcorn, hotdogs and hamburgers. He balanced a small paper tray loaded with popcorn and candies. As he approached their car, the girls were laughing at the high jinks of Mickey, Goofy and Donald hunting a moose. By the time the moose found them out Howard was seated and had passed out the treats. The cartoon was followed by the feature length cartoon movie, and the girls sat thrilled and amazed as Snow White charmed a hunter, danced and sang with the dwarfs, and escaped death with a princely kiss.

On the drive home, the girls leaned over the seat between their mom and dad, talking about the movie. Amy Sue recited, "Mirwe, Mirwe on da wall, me da fairest of dem all," followed by giggles and laughs. Wanda Faye quizzed her mother on how the prince's kiss could wake Snow White from her enchanted sleep. They arrived home, had the girls in bed by nine and were sitting on the front porch swinging, by nine-fifteen. They sat quietly listening to distance dogs barking and bullfrogs croaking down at the spring. Martha slid a little closer as they gazed at the evening stars.

"Thank you for a fun evening, Daddy."

"You're welcome, darling. The girls seemed to enjoy everything, didn't they? They thanked me a dozen times as they went to bed."

"I fear Amy Sue will be reciting 'Mirwe, Mirwe' every time she sees a mirror, and Wanda Faye, Howard do you think she's growing up too fast with questions about things like kisses?"

"How old were you when you thought about your first kiss?"

"Why, the night you kissed me at my door after our first date, of course."

"And the month before that, and before that, and before that."

"Howard Lowe, the first thoughts I ever had in my head about kissing a boy were trying to figure out how to get you to pay attention to me. You wouldn't lay down your ball glove long enough to pay attention to any of the girls, let alone me."

"I had my eyes on you long before you noticed me."

"That's not true!" protested Martha. Crossing her arms and looking over at Howard, she blurted out, "When?"

"Tenth grade, Mrs. Goodman's English class. You sat two rows up from me and never turned around. I got a C because I couldn't keep my eyes off you. I had total loss of concentration every time I stepped foot in the room. You were more beautiful than anything I had ever seen, and every boy in the class was secretly in love with you. I didn't feel I had a chance, so I never found the courage to ask you out."

"Until when?"

"When we were paired on that FFA project. You remember, the livestock project our junior year. Who would have thought the Future Farmers of America and a passion for a Yorkshire hog would bring two people together for a lifetime."

"Oh! My Thomasine. What a wonderful friend she was. Smart as she could be and all those tricks we taught her to do. I cried all night after we weighed her and she had reached tops."

"I recall quite an argument as we weighed her. She was easily over two hundred pounds, and you swore she was a hundred and ninety-five. When we finally agreed she was close enough to two hundred to take to the stockyards, you ran into the house crying. That's when I realized she was more than just a pig to you."

"And you, you wonderful, irresistible romantic. You took money you were saving and bought her the next morning at the stockyards. I can see you now walking up the yard, Thomasine on a leash with a big pink ribbon around her neck. My hero in a John Deere cap and denim overalls."

Martha hugged Howard and kissed him on the cheek.

"You know I wasn't quite sure what to do after I asked your dad permission to buy you that pig. He looked at me all serious like, spit some tobacco juice down on the ground and asked, 'Just what are your intentions, boy? I don't see this being part of your FFA project.'"

"You talked to Dad about Thomasine?"

"Of course, I did."

"So, what did you tell him about your intentions?"

"I spit my tobacco a little further than he did and told him I intended to spend my life making his daughter happy."

"Your dad said, he'd been married to your mother for nearly twenty-five years and was still trying to figure out what made her happy. When he asked me how I thought I could make you happy, I told him I didn't know for sure, but I was going to start off with the hog and work my way from there. He slapped me on the back and said, 'You'll do fine, boy. You'll do fine.'"

"Oh, Howard! I didn't know you asked Dad permission to see me?"

"Sometimes odd situations work out for the best."

They sat, gently swinging back and forth, holding hands for several minutes.

"Howard?"

"Yes, dear."

"This Korean conflict thing. They're starting to draft young men into the Army. Is there a chance they would call you back up again?"

"I served my time in Europe, honey. I don't think it's bad enough to call veteran reservist back up, especially those of us who fought in the last war. Besides, it's just a small police action with the United Nations. It's not like fighting the Nazis in Europe and the Japs in the Pacific. That took every available man, and every man and woman back here in the states to win. We can lick those North

Koreans easy enough. General MacArthur's got them on the run and he won't stop till he chases them plum into China, if that's what it takes."

Howard placed his arm around Martha and pulled her even closer.

"No, dear. They won't need me for this one."

Howard lay asleep. Four o'clock came early on a farm. Martha sat in front of the vanity mirror that had belonged to her grandmother. She had spent hours in front of it brushing her grandmother's long silver hair. When Granny passed in '45, she left the vanity to her favorite granddaughter. It was H shaped with deep drawers on either side. The dark veneer wood was outlined with a lighter wood, giving the chest a delicate, attractive appearance. The middle was open, allowing one to scoot up under the small desk. The middle mirror was arched, as was the angled mirrors on either side. The girls liked looking into it because they could see three of themselves. Martha liked looking in it because she could see Granny looking back from the glass, smiling and chatting about the latest gossip.

Martha reached inside the right, bottom drawer and took out a small wooden box tied shut with a white silk ribbon. Undoing the ribbon, she lifted the lid and removed the top letter. It was postmarked September 25, 1945, and had "FREE MAIL" printed in large letters up in the top right-hand corner. The return address simply said, "Private Howard Lowe."

Opening the envelope, she took out the one-page letter, held it to her breast and closed her eyes.

After a moment she turned up the oil lamp and read Howard's last letter from Europe, at the end of World War II:

September 10, 1945

My Dearest Martha,

This will be a very short letter, my dear, as I just got word from the Old Man that I will be shipping out tomorrow for the States. I will spend a few weeks at Ft. Bliss, Texas, and then be discharged to come home. Some of the guys are going to stay on to help with the occupation of Berlin, but they're sending those of us who saw a lot of action on home.

Just think Martha, soon we will be together again. You, me, and little Wanda Faye. I can't wait to see her and give her a kiss and a big hug. This is it Martha. I made it. All that fighting and by the grace of God, I've survived and I'm coming home.

Kiss Wanda Faye for me and tell her that Daddy's coming home. My heart feels like it's about to jump out of my chest, I'm so excited about being with you again. I love you my dear and we will never be away from each other again.

Love always,

Howard

CHAPTER 3

▼

Welch lay on the ground, his hands tied behind his back with communication wire. The North Korean soldiers had been brutal after his capture. When Welch realized he and Jawaski were walking into the enemy's camp, he tried to back up, but the headlights from a truck came on and stopped him in his tracks like a deer caught in the middle of the road. If he had been struck down like a deer it would have been more merciful. He stood with his arms in the air, tense, bracing himself to block an oncoming bayonet. Instead, the butt of a rifle caved in his stomach, and left him doubled up and breathless on the ground. While he tried to catch his breath they tied his hands behind his back with the wire and took his boots. A soldier tugged at his jacket, but stepped back quickly when the stench reached his nose. A second soldier laughed, pointing at his friend. The disappointed soldier kicked Welch in the stomach sharply. He rolled over on the ground moaning. It was only the beginning.

Two new soldiers stepped forward kicking and hitting him with the butt of their rifles. The beating went on for several minutes with soldiers taking turns on him. Welch tried to stay on his stomach, but the powerful kicks rolled him about. Finally, one of the soldiers stepped back and aimed his rifle at the American. Welch heard the click of a safety release.

From behind the soldiers came an angry shout and they both quickly came to attention. A man approached and began kicking the soldiers in the seat of their pants, driving them away. The soldier knelt next to Welch and spoke in a language he had heard before, a language not at all like Korean. Welch struggled to look up and said, "Why are you here? They said there were no Chinese in Korea."

The Chinese officer looked down and responded in broken English, "It better to ask you, American. Why you in Korea?"

Welch started to answer, but the pain of the beating had overwhelmed his senses. His head was swimming and everything began spinning around as he drifted off into unconsciousness.

Welch awoke on the floor of a small mud hut. He was cold, his body ached, and he could barely see out of his right eye. His hands were still tied behind his back, numb from the tight wire. He was alone, disoriented, and confused. He struggled, and with considerable effort, pulled himself to a sitting position, leaning back against the wall. His mouth was parched and his stomach ached from hunger. It had been days since he had eaten. The cloth door of the hut opened and two soldiers came in, grabbed the shoulders of his jacket and stood him up. One of the soldiers blindfolded him and said, "Come with!"

Welch struggled to keep up. Every step was extremely painful. They finally grabbed him by the arms and half-led; half-dragged him over into a larger hut. They sat him in a chair, removed the blindfold and moved over to the door. Welch sat, trying to position his arms and hands so some bit of circulation would flow through them, but it was useless.

Through the door came the soldier who rescued him from the beating. The Chinese officer was dressed in a dull, gray, cotton-padded uniform. The little padded ball cap he wore had a red star centered on the front. The difference between him and the Chinese soldiers at the door was the leather, fur lined boots he wore and the pistol holstered on his hip. Holding his hands behind his back he walked a circle around Welch, stopping in front of him.

"You American commanders desert you in battle. They leave you to die. I keep North Koreans from killing you. I return you to Americans, but need unit you with? What you unit?"

Welch looked at the officer and said, "Daniel Welch, Private, Serial number 2165342, Valley Head, West Virgi . . ."

A hand shot out and caught Welch on the right side of his face.

"Do not try my patience, Welch! What you unit?"

"Under the Geneva Convention I don't hav . . ."

The right hand shot out again, this time knocking him from the chair. Unable to catch himself he hit the floor hard.

"The Peoples Republic of China not recognize Geneva Convention. You answer questions, or you die."

Welch braced himself with his legs and sat up. Blood was pouring from a new cut just above his left eye. He took a deep breath and said, "Daniel Welch, Private, 2165342."

The questions, the beatings and Welch's persistent resistance went on through the night. At times they would leave long enough for him to fall asleep, only to return, wake him and start into the questions and beatings again. He eventually passed out. The officer kicked him in the side as he lay there, yelled at the guards and walked out.

When Welch awoke, he thought it was daylight, but wasn't sure in the dark hut. He was aching all over and confused. Where was he? Why did he hurt so badly? Jawaski? He was safe back at the boulders. No! My God, he thought, they bayoneted him on the hill when he tried to surrender. The little guy who had saved his life was dead. But wait, didn't he walk into the camp with him? Was the little man dead? No, maybe not. Welch just wasn't sure of anything. His head hurt and his thoughts were a jumble of mixed memories. Blood and mud were matted on his left eye, distorting his vision. He couldn't see from the swollen right eye. He pulled himself into a sitting position and shrugged his left shoulder against the left side of his face, trying to wipe his eye. It worked a little. He stared about the mud hut. Two armed guards were at the door, and a chair was on its side in the center of the room. He eyed the chair remembering the brutal torture and his dogged effort to resist. He didn't talk, or did he?

Welch's hands were still tied behind his back, his arms and hands were numb. Lying on his side he grunted as he struggled to gain his balance and wiggle himself to his knees. He moved over to the chair and with his head and shoulders succeeded in standing it up, a minor triumph. He knelt on the dirt floor till he caught his breath, and slowly brought himself to his feet. His knees wobbled as he stepped around and eased himself down in the chair. He sat up straight as he could, and waited for the beating to commence.

They had left him alone for nearly an hour. He thought about his predicament, and home. Thoughts of Amelia gave him strength. He tried to reconstruct the last time he was with Jawaski. His thoughts went to his dad and how he had suffered the last year of his life, never complaining as the black coal dust destroyed his lungs. The night his dad died, he had held his hand as he slowly drowned in the fluid that filled his lungs. He lay there, fighting for each breath and finally let go. He left his worn-out body behind and his spirit went home. He did the same for his mom, who died a year later from the cancer. A small tear trickled down Welch's cheek. He loved and admired his parents. They were from strong stock. He hoped he could be as strong with his impending pain and death.

Outside an old truck pulled up in front of the hut. It rattled and popped, like most old trucks do. Two Chinese soldiers came in, blindfolded Welch, dragged him out and threw him into the back of the truck. They climbed in, banged on the fender and dropped the back tarp. The truck drove for an hour making several turns and stops as Welch bounced around on the wooden flatbed. When it finally stopped they rolled him out onto the ground and removed the blindfold. From there, one of the soldiers nudged him with his rifle barrel in the direction of a side road. There were no huts, no tents, just the dirt road and trees. Was he to be shot in the back on some deserted road, never to be heard of again? If so there wasn't a lot he could do about it. He walked on.

The soldier said nothing, now and then giving a nudge with his rifle to keep Welch moving ahead of him. His bare feet ached as he stepped on rocks hidden in the dust. It felt as if he was walking on glass, as he stumbled down the road. They rounded the corner and ahead was a small village. The inhabitants lined the narrow dirt road, armed with crude farm tools like wooden pitchforks and rakes. Most held sticks. At their feet were small children with rocks. At the sight of Welch, they began to shout angry threats, shaking their sticks and fists in the air.

Welch attempted to slow his walking, but the soldier struck him between the shoulder blades with his rifle butt. He lunged forward, falling in the dirt and rolled down the road to where the crowd stood. Their shouts were angry, and they struck him as he tried to crawl and roll down the road past them. The children hurled rocks as he passed, some striking with deadly accuracy. Welch struggled along the gauntlet, fearing that at any moment the crowd would pounce and rip him to pieces in the middle of the road. One older female villager ran at him, and got in a couple of good blows with her stick before being pushed back by the soldier. The crowd roared in approval as the old women danced about in triumph. Small children would run up and throw dirt in his face, as others leaned forward and spit on him. He crawled, kicked and rolled his way down the road, finally reaching the end of the village where he scrambled to his feet and stumbled down the road away from the mob.

As the noise of the angry villagers grew dim Welch grew weaker. Unable to walk any further he fell to the ground. The soldier prodded him with the rifle barrel, but he couldn't get up. If he were to die, it would have to be there in the road. His humiliation was complete. Lying on his back staring up at the clouds he drifted off into unconsciousness.

Welch woke with a start as water splashed in his face. His reaction to the water was instinctual, even in his semi-conscious state. He managed to wet his lips and the inside of his mouth, but got very little down his throat. He found himself once again in the mud hut. This time a different Chinese officer, much older, sat patiently in the chair watching him trying to catch some of the water with his tongue.

"Private Welch. You must let me help you. You should not have to struggle this way. It is not good for you. It is not good for us. We want to help."

Welch stared at the officer. He was not like the young officer who had beaten him relentlessly. He spoke with grace, and with better English than Welch himself. He might be a man to respect, but certainly not one to trust. Welch focused mentally and prepared himself.

The officer stood and walked over to him pulling a knife from his belt. Welch tensed as the knife carefully cut the wire that bound his hands. His arms fell free, useless appendages, hanging from his shoulders. He wondered if he would ever feel with them again.

The officer returned to his chair. "You see I can be very generous. We are not all cruel and mean. Where are you from Private Welch?"

Welch sat there giving no response.

"Oh, come now my American friend, everyone is from somewhere. My knowing about your hometown will not win or lose this war."

Welch quietly said, "West Virginia. Valley Head, West Virginia."

"Ah, wonderful! The Appalachians. The beautiful mountains along the eastern seaboard, unlike this miserable pile of rocks here in Korea. We also have beautiful mountains in China, but none as beautiful as the Appalachian Mountains in the fall. What brings you to Korea, Private Welch? I know you are not here of your own accord. No Americans are here because they want to be."

Welch thought for a moment and decided the questions were harmless. What could it hurt to talk to him about noncombatant things?

"I was drafted. A lot of us were drafted into the Army."

"Conscripted, were you? Unlike the proud young volunteers of the Peoples Republic of China, America must force its young men to fight an unpopular war, in a country far away." Seeing the dismay on Welch's face he quickly changed the subject to something more agreeable.

"You have family back home? A wife, maybe?"

"Yes, a wife."

"Children?"

"No, no children."

"What do you do back home in West Virginia, Private Welch? What do you do to make a . . . living?"

"I worked in the coal mines."

"Coal mines, marvelous!" The officer stood and walked over to Welch. Taking him by the arm he assisted him to his feet and over to the chair. "Mining for coal is a very noble occupation. There are many hard-working coal miners in the People's Republic of China. There is much coal in the West Virginia Mountains, I believe. You should be proud of your work in the mines. You should be back there in the mountains helping your people with coal to heat their homes and run their factories, coming home from work every day, kissing your wife and playing with your children. You should not be here, fighting a war for the Imperialist Wall Street Dogs who run your country. You and I, Private Welch have much in common. We are soldiers. We have family who work and die in the mines, and we miss our wives. We should not be killing each other in this miserable little war."

Welch sat there in the chair, his arms burning as the blood and nerve endings struggled to bring back feelings. He was starting to gain some control in them. He weakly held up his hands toward the officer and said, "Thank you."

The officer was walking toward the door, and stopped, "No! Thank you, Private Welch, from West Virginia. You have been most kind to talk with me. I know you must be thirsty and hungry. I will have food and water brought to you right away." He ducked his head under the low doorframe and walked out.

Welch carefully got to his feet and stretched. He still hurt all over, but stretching out his arms made a big difference. He slowly walked about the room, working out some of the soreness and finally went over and sat in the chair. Feeling guilty, he also felt a glimmer of hope for the first time in days, as he waited anxiously for the food and water.

It was just fifteen minutes, but it seemed like an hour. The cloth flap opened and Welch turned in anticipation to find the younger officer who had beat him. He was carrying a bowl and jar of water. The Chinaman stared at Welch, and dropped the bowl onto the dirt floor. He then dropped the water jug on top of it, and placed his boot on top of the food, twisting it about. A smile came over his face as he watched Welch's stunned reaction. He said something laughingly in Chinese to the two guards, who laughed as he left the hut.

Welch sat there for a second in disbelief, but only a second. He leaped from the chair to the spot where the food lay mingled in the dirt. His sudden movement startled the guards. He grabbed the water jug and drank what little was left. It slid down his parched throat. He then picked the chunks of rice out of the dirt. There was some sort of meat substance mixed with the rice, but it was now hard to distinguish from the globs of mud. He carefully picked through the mud with his fingers, managing to salvage most of the rice. He poured water in the bowl, and rinsed off the food as best he could before he ate it. When he could find no more food in the mud, he went over to the chair and sat down.

After about an hour he got down on the floor next to the wall, curled up and tried to sleep. He drifted off, his mind struggling to untangle the confusing mess of events of the past few days. There were days he and Jawaski traveled the mountains. There were days he had been held captive, interrogated and beaten. Was it five days or one? He couldn't remember. The days blended together like a horrible nightmare. It seemed like a month since he had talked to the First Sergeant about the impending attack that night. As things raced through his mind, he slowly drifted off to sleep.

✶   ✶   ✶   ✶

"Look at me!"

"No!"

"I say look, American Pig!"

"No!"

Jawaski kept his head turned away from the North Korean Officer who had been interrogating him for the past three days.

"If you not sign confession, you not useful. You waste my time. What if I take something valuable from you? What if I break good arm? What if," pulling his pistol from its holster, he put it against the side of Jawaski's head, cocked the hammer and said, "Now American! What you do on paper, signature or brains?"

The standoff between the sadistic officer and the young American had lasted three days. In the beginning Jawaski asked ten questions to his one. As the beatings continued the American had become more withdrawn. He was wearing down and although he was already physically broken, his spirit was still intact, but for how long?

He sat there in the chair, numb from the relentless beatings. His right elbow had been broken from the rifle shot when he was captured. When the guards grabbed him they had jerked him about by his arms, an intense and painful experience. The elbow joint was horribly dislocated, swollen and grotesque. They stripped him of his coat and boots. His feet were swollen, bruised and bleeding from a full day's march and miles of kicking and beating. He had survived only because his arm had gone numb, along with the rest of his body.

Now as he sat in the mud hut, he couldn't see out of his left eye. The Korean interrogator had struck him hard in the face so many times the left eye globe had split and ruptured. It had popped like a balloon, the vitreous liquid running down his cheek, mixing with the blood and dirt. The busted white membrane of the globe lay on his cheekbone and the spot where the eye had been was swollen, adding to its grotesqueness.

A large gash on his left cheek had stopped bleeding when it filled with mud from the ditch they forced his head down in. They nearly drown him, not once, but several times. He was a dreadful sight. The officer who had inflicted the pain and damage enjoyed his work, whether he was tormenting local farmers or torturing prisoners. He would remove a little more dignity and then finish the job with a bullet to Jawaski's head. He was enjoying the moment, so much so, he failed to notice the older Chinese officer who stepped in the room, followed by two armed Chinese soldiers.

Jawaski sat with his hands in his lap, holding his breath, waiting for the end. The barrel of the pistol was pressed against his left temple and when the trigger was pulled the hammer made a loud, *Click!* To Jawaski it sounded like a clap of thunder and he flinched so violently he jerked himself out of the chair onto the dirt floor. Unable to catch himself he crashed on his right side, screaming in pain. He lay there trembling, whimpering out loud. The North Korean holstered his pistol, reached down and lifted the little American up, putting him in the chair.

"Signature or brains, Private Jawaski. Which you choose?"

"I . . . *sniff* . . . I will . . . I will sign. I confess to it all, please don't hurt me anymore. Please let me sign."

The Korean smiled and handed the whimpering American a pen. Sniffling and snubbing Jawaski signed the confession paper with his left hand. The Korean officer showed excitement for the first time as he grabbed the confession, looking at the signature.

"What this, King of Si am?"

The split second of distraction was all Jawaski needed. He was up into the Korean officer driving the pen deep into his left eye. The Korean's scream was cut off by the little American's death grip on his throat. Jawaski squeezed and pressed down with his left hand as hard as he could, attempting to crush the windpipe and larynx—an eye for an eye and the throat for the kill.

The North Korean guards, intimidated by the presence of the Chinese officer and stunned by the swiftness of Jawaski's attack, stood watching. One of them finally ran over and kicked Jawaski, knocking him across the floor. Screaming and jumping to his feet, the Korean officer was gasping for breath. Drawing his pistol he turned to the guard who had kicked Jawaski and hit him in the side of the face, knocking him down. The other guard cowered and he brought the barrel of the pistol down on the top of his head, knocking him out. Coughing and gasping he turned and chambered a round in the pistol as he walked over to the American lying unconscious in the corner. He carefully aimed the pistol at his head.

"You would be wise not to pull that trigger, Comrade Jin," came a voice in Korean. The Korean officer snapped about to find the Chinese officer, flanked by his bodyguards, their weapons pointed at his chest.

"*This*" screamed Jin, "*Is of no concern to you, Colonel Hua. Do not interfere!*"

"Oh, but it is, Captain. I personally admire this little American and his, his strength of character. He is near death, yet he fights back against overwhelming odds. The wounds he carries are honorable. He had the best of you Captain Jin and because of that you must carry that shame with you the rest of your life, but, that is not why I showed up at such an opportune time. Concern brought me here because Americans are more valuable alive than dead. Torture is a science, not the sadistic art you practice. You kill more than not, and put me out of business. Can you not see my dilemma?"

Colonel Nam Hua motioned to his bodyguards, who walked past Jin, picked up Jawaski and carried him out of the hut to an awaiting truck.

"I must strongly protest! He is my prisoner. He has attacked and wounded me. I demand justice!"

Turning to the North Korean as he started to leave the hut, Colonel Hua said, "Think carefully about what justice you may receive, Captain Jin. A Chinese proverb tells the story of a beetle that felt wronged by an ox who stepped on a plant the bug was eating. The beetle sought revenge and as it stood behind the oxen, leaping to grab the tip of the animal's tail, the oxen released a pile of dung that engulfed the tiny bug and smothered it. The oxen finished his business and walked on, never knowing their paths had crossed."

With that said, Colonel Hua gave him a cold stare and left the hut.

✱   ✱   ✱   ✱

"Wakie! Wakie!"

Welch rolled over and looked up at the soldier standing above him.

"Wakie! Wakie!"

He slowly and painfully pulled himself to a sitting position, and focused his eyes to the sunlight coming through the door of the hut. Outside he heard a considerable amount of commotion.

"Come with!" The guard took Welch's arm and lifted him to his feet, leading him to the door. The sunshine warmed his body, but the light burned his eyes. Covering his eyes, he tried to look out the door as the soldier repeated the command.

"Come with!"

He was pulled by the arm to the road and lined up with several other soldiers, American soldiers! Welch looked around as his vision adjusted to the light. He noticed several mud huts with American soldiers coming out of them. There was an entire village of mud huts, but no villagers. The inhabitants had apparently been relocated to provide a place for the American prisoners.

Welch looked about the crowd hoping to see Jawaski. Had the little man made it? Had he survived? He walked about looking over each soldier. Up ahead a truck unloaded more Americans. As he walked forward, he stared at the occupants, one by one as they climbed down. They were battered, bruised and bloody. They helped each other down and melted into the crowd. Suddenly, Jawaski appeared, struggling as he tried to sit down on the tailgate and work his way off to the ground. No one helped him. He was visibly cleaner than the other Americans, with fresh bandages around his head covering his left eye, and his right arm was in a sling.

"Leo! Leo Jawaski!"

Jawaski turned his head to the left, so his right eye could see who was calling out his name. When he saw Welch, his face lit up with a smile.

"Dan! You're alive. You made it, old buddy!"

Welch walked up to help Jawaski down from the tailgate. When he took hold of Jawaski's arms the little man squawked.

"Diddly-damn! Go easy on that arm. It's liable to come right off in your hand."

Welch took his friend around the waist and helped him to the ground. Several prisoners were in as bad a shape, or worse, but Jawaski was the only one who had received medical treatment. The Americans looked at him with contempt on their faces. Some made remarks loud enough to be heard. It cut Jawaski to the quick.

"Dan, they think I'm a traitor. A guy on the truck wanted to know how I got medical treatment. He kept saying I must have cooperated with the enemy. They were angry and quit talking to me."

Looking up at Welch, Jawaski said, "Dan, it's not fair. I didn't tell them anything but my name, rank and serial number. I stood up to the bastard. When he gave me the pen to sign the confession, I jumped on him and stuck it in his eye. I was choking the life out of him, Dan, and one of his lackeys kicked me in the ribs. That was the last thing I remember. I woke up and somebody had fixed me up. I didn't tell 'em nothing, and I didn't sign nothing. I don't know why they looked after me, since they were the ones who beat me up—beat the hell out of you one minute, fix you up the next. Maybe they were using me for some kind of medical training or something. What do you think, Dan?"

"I don't know what they are up to, Leo, but if some of guys bother you, they'll have to deal with me."

The little man looked downcast for a moment and then perked up, "How did it go for you, Dan? You spit in their eye?"

Welch took off his belt and gently wrapped it around Jawaski's chest, under the good arm and around the upper end of the broken arm. The little man chattered away. Sliding the tip of the belt through the metal buckle, he tightened it a little, lifted Jawaski's hand and tucked it under the buckle. He then tightened it more. Jawaski grimaced a little, but allowed Welch to tighten the belt and secure his arm to his chest.

Up ahead a whistle shrilled and the crowd of Americans became quiet. Standing on the tailgate of a truck was a Chinese soldier preparing to address the crowd of captives.

"Dan! He's Chinese. There ain't no Chinese in Korea. Didn't the Old Man tell us there weren't no Chinese in Korea? I think that was his exact words, 'No Chi nese!' What the devil is he doing here? Didn't we liberate China from Japan? I think it's a bit ungrateful of them to be here helping the North Koreans fight us now, don't you? I'm hungry Dan. I mean really hungry."

"American soldiers! You line up on road and prepare to move. You run, you shot! You not keep up, you shot!"

"Plain enough," said Jawaski. "I guess we'd better get in line. How far do you think we are going, Dan? Why can't they ride us in those trucks? I'm hungry, Dan, I mean I'm really, really hungry!"

The two men hobbled to the center of the group. American soldiers pointed to them as quiet murmurs spread. Welch stood head and shoulders above everyone else. Jawaski was not visible as the crowd of men started up the road.

Sergeant Kenny Jennings focused on putting one foot in front of the other. The pain in his stomach was excruciating. Each step was a challenge and each step prolonged his life a step further. Weak from dysentery he struggled along. He fought hard to keep up the five days they had been marching, but there was no strength left to go on. With the next step his knee buckled and he fell to the ground. There was no struggle to get up this time. No agonizing efforts to rise. He lay there beside the road in the dust, eyes half open and glazed over. It was hard to know if he continued to struggle mentally, or was welcoming his impending death.

"You keep moving!" shouted the North Korean soldier in broken English. *"No Stop! No Stop!"* The American lay there motionless. The guard plunged his bayonet between the downed soldier's shoulder blades, withdrew it and plunged it again, the sound of muscle tissue and bone tearing with each plunge. The dust at Jennings's mouth fluttered once or twice as his heart and lungs struggled to continue. The chest cavity filled with blood as the heart pumped four or five more times and stopped. The pupils slowly dilated as the iris muscles relaxed and the body lay motionless. With the toe of his boot the North Korean nudged the body over and it rolled into the ditch.

The rest of the Americans kept walking. The first day of the march they were outraged when an American was executed. There was a yelling match with the guards. The senior American officer demanded to see the senior North Korean officer, Lieutenant Le. As the official complaint was verbalized, a gun was put to the officer's head and there was no more discussion. The complaints stopped, and the men kept moving or they died. Now, after five days of marching and death, they walked past Jennings's body in the ditch with numbed indifference, glad it wasn't them. Seventy-eight American soldiers started the march. Now they were down to sixty. No one had tried to escape. The dead were shot or bayoneted there on the road when they were too weak to continue. Some dropped from their wounds, others from their weakened state, brought on by the dysentery or beriberi. Others just gave up. Everyone had their breaking point and some broke earlier than others. The ditches along the route were filled up with bloody bodies.

"Dan. I'm tired. My feet hurt. Why did they take our boondockers? They have their own boots, why do they need ours? Can't we just sit down and rest a couple of minutes? Look at the guards. They're not looking. We could sit down there on that rock. Please Dan?"

"Nope! Ain't gonna happen, little fellow. We stop, they shoot both of us, and I don't think today is a good day to get shot. Yes, I'm sure of it. Today is not a good day. Come to think of it, I believe yesterday was our day and you wouldn't stop, so you blew your chance. You and I are getting a walking tour of the badlands. We're going somewhere and I'm inclined to see where that might be, and you, my little man shall see it with me. You never know when I might jump into another pool of poop and need you to pull me out."

Dan turned and looked at Jawaski, "So keep moving."

Welch had a tight grip on the back of Jawaski's trousers with his right hand and was holding his left arm with the other. They were moving slow, but keeping up. The march was in its sixth day. They had received no food and only small drinks of water from time to time. Every so often a shot would ring out, or a bayonet would pierce a lung or heart and another captive would be left beside the road. Welch was holding his own, but Jawaski was wearing down. Without Welch, he would have been dead in a ditch back down the road.

"Did I ever tell you about the White sisters who lived across the ridge from me when I was sixteen?"

"The White sisters? I think you told me about them when we were resting in the mountains, Dan. Weren't they fast and easy, and loved the smell of diesel fuel?"

Welch looked down at Jawaski and frowned.

"Hey, Dan! Did I ever talk about the Ogerman brothers who lived on our block?"

Looking at Jawaski, Welch said, "Ogerman brothers. Never heard of them. What did they ever do?"

"Exactly the point, my gentle giant. Every red-blooded American boy should know the story of Phil and Al Ogerman. There is an important lesson to learn from their tragic story."

Welch looked at Jawaski as they slowly made their way down the dirt road. "Well?"

"Phil and Al were identical twins with the uncanny ability to know and feel exactly what the other was feeling. Phil met and married Mary Kathryn Fields from Queens and immediately moved his new bride in with him, his brother and his parents. The four-room apartment was crowded, but the family was happy until the day Phil came home from work and accused Al of having carnal thoughts about his wife, Mary Kathryn. Are you with me so far big guy?"

Welch looked down at Jawaski and said, "Get on with your madness."

"The grand patriarch, Papa Joe Ogerman, in his wisdom determined that it wasn't healthy, or fair for Albert to have to live with Philbert's innermost thoughts about his wife, Mary Kathryn. He challenged Al to find his own wife to occupy those thoughts, and in short order he did. He found and married a dancer from the Milner Club over in the lower east side of the Bronx."

Welch looked down at Jawaski with bewilderment. The little man ignored him and continued.

"She was very healthy at five foot eleven, a natural redhead and went by the stage name of Crystal Chandelier, because of the things she could do while hanging from the brass pole there at the club. The Ogerman family was once again happy, until a hot day in June."

A shot rang out from the rear of the march, and then a second. Jawaski turned his head slowly until he looked up at Welch with his good right eye. "Don't let them shoot me, Dan."

"I won't, little buddy." They walked on a few more minutes without saying a word and came upon a long stretch of road with rice patties on either side. Height had its advantages and Dan saw up ahead that North Korean soldiers were bailing out of vehicles and quickly running for cover. He looked up in the sky and saw two aircraft coming out of the noonday sun. They were flying straight down on to the column. Welch was already moving quickly toward the rice paddy on the right, dragging a sputtering Jawaski with him. They slid down the short bank, and hit the water with a splash. The column of soldiers was now peeling off to either side of the road, from the front to the back, while the planes, American Mustangs, roared down strafing the stationary Chinese vehicles. One blew up in a large orange fireball. The American soldiers cheered as the planes flew over. The Mustangs circled and flew by once again, before flying out of sight over the mountains.

Welch helped Jawaski back up on the road, and they stood watching the truck burn. As the Korean guards rounded up prisoners, a young officer jumped on the back of a disabled truck and addressed the Americans.

"Travel in dark now. We go this way now." The prisoners were turned left toward the hills and in less than thirty minutes they came to a tunnel, entered, and were ordered to be seated. The rest was needed. Some slept, while others sat with a dazed look, afraid that sleep would be too difficult to wake from.

Welch sat Jawaski close to the entrance where there was light. He loosened the belt and checked his arm. It was now showing signs of infection. Without treatment, gangrene would set in and the arm would have to be taken off. Dan lifted the bandage on the eye and saw that the eye was gone. He had seen lots of battlefield injuries, but the brutality of Jawaski's lost eye set him back a moment.

"That handsome face looks fine, little man. That scar on your cheek will drive the ladies crazy."

Jawaski half smiled and almost laughed out loud for the first time in several days.

"The arm is looking kind of rough, though. Infection is setting in."

Leo reached into his pocket, pulled out a bottle filled with powder and gave it to Welch.

"They gave me this and told me to use it on the wound, if it got infected."

Welch opened the bottle and smelled it.

"Sulfur. It should help keep the infection down."

Welch sprinkled some of the powder on the wound and rewrapped Jawaski's arm. As he screwed the lid back on from behind him came an angry voice.

"There are others wounded here that need some of that sulfur. Why are you wasting it on that little shit of a traitor?"

Welch put the bottle in his pocket, stood and turned to face the man, an officer. Welch towered over the man, but that didn't deter him.

"Why are you messing with that collaborator? He should be left in the ditch to die."

Welch scolded the officer. "Who the hell are you to think you know what Jawaski went through, or did or didn't do."

Three men stepped in behind the officer and Welch braced himself. Behind him Jawaski said in a low voice. "No, Dan. It's okay. Give him the sulfur. Some of our guys need it worse than me. I'll be okay."

Welch turned and looked at Jawaski, who nodded his head.

"Okay, pal." He held the bottle out and when the officer took it Welch grabbed his wrist, closed his other hand over the hand gripping the bottle and forced it down and back. As the bones compressed in the upper hand, the officer went to his knees with a loud *"Ehaa!"*

The other men started to step in and Welch yelled, *"Back off!"* Turning his attention to the captain he said, "You go help the other soldiers and you tell them that Leo Jawaski insisted they have it. You got that? You tell them they might be a little confused about Leo. Tell them some asshole North Korean beat him until his eye exploded and popped right out of his head. Tell them that instead of signing a confession, he stuck the pen in the bastard's eye and was choking him to death when the guards jumped on him. If that's too much for your little brain to remember Captain, I'll go over it again!"

The officer looked up with tears running down his cheeks, and angrily mumbled something unintelligible. Welch pressed his hand back.

"Yes! Oh God, Yes! Please . . . please stop. I'll . . . I'll talk to the others."

Welch released the captain's hand and he dropped to the floor of the tunnel. The other soldiers gathered him up and they walked away.

"And if there is any of that sulfur left, I want it back," yelled Welch as the men disappeared down the tunnel.

"There won't be any left, Dan. You shouldn't have been so hard on that captain. He could make things hard on you."

"I hope he tries. I've killed better men than him who were trying to kill me."

"Dan, I'm tired. Can I sleep a little?"

"Sure Leo. I'll wake you when it's time to go."

Jawaski stretched out on the dirt floor and was asleep in seconds. Welch sat down next to him, with his back up against the tunnel wall. His feet were swollen and bloody with blisters and open wounds.

He closed his eyes and pictured himself back home sitting on a large granite rock in the middle of a mountain stream, his feet dangling down in the cold, swirling water. The water came from high above and traveled for miles down the mountain. He could feel the coolness on his feet, the warmth of the sun against his face, and the cool mist generated by the stream. In just a few moments he was asleep.

"You will go now!" shouted the guard. Walking down the tunnel the guard kicked the sleeping Americans as he went. Welch woke, reached over and shook Jawaski, who woke abruptly yelling out, *"No!"* They walked toward the mouth of the tunnel and lying near the entrance was an American curled up in a fetal position against the wall of the tunnel. Welch walked over and gave him a good shake. The soldier was dead. As they limped down the hill several gunshots rang out behind them. They didn't look back.

*   *   *   *

The reflection in the mirror was enchanting, the long eyelashes, the perfectly plucked eyebrows. Even perfection needed a little enhancement and she knew it. She rubbed a touch of rouge on the cheeks and then started on the lips. The red lipstick touched her full, puckered lips and shaped the angles that attracted. The lips were a masterpiece in the center of a beautiful, oval face that had enchanted boys and men for years.

The tight, red and white polka-dotted dress slid over her slip and down the nylon hose that covered her legs. The dress showed just enough cleavage to keep a man's attention, and the length was perfect for showing off her shapely legs, especially with a slit up the sides to her knees. The dress was as stunning as the woman who wore it. She slipped on her spike heeled shoes and sat down at the dresser mirror.

Her blond hair was curled in the popular wave that all the women wanted in 1951. Down at the beauty parlor, Sally had worked hard to make it picture perfect. Sally had an artistic eye and the ladies in Elkins knew it, tipping accordingly. She stared in the mirror and admired what she saw. It was Friday and before the night was over, she hoped her date would insist on messing up her hair.

As she admired her reflection, a knock came at the door. She stood and sashayed across the apartment taking her purse off the table as she went. Before opening the door, she attacked her gum with an exaggerated chewing fashion.

In the hallway stood a young man, staring wide-eyed at her.

After a couple of seconds of silence, she blurted out, *"Well!"*

"Aaaa, sorry, ma'am. Chris Peach, Western Union. I have a telegram from the War Department. Would you like for me to read . . . ?

Jerking the telegram from his hand she opened it, gave a sneer and read out loud:

"Government, Washington, D.C. 1951 October"

"Ah here it is:"

"From North Korea the name of your"

"Oh gee!" She mimicked a pouting face:

"your husband is missing in action, and has been mentioned in an enemy propaganda broadcast. Prisoner of War status is not officially established by this report.
Further information will be"

"Bla, bla, bla, bla, bla."

Rolling her eyes, she reached into her purse and handed the astonished young man a dime tip. His stare was void of the admiring look he had seconds earlier, because he didn't like what he saw. Not saying a word, he handed her a pen and a receipt to sign.

As she signed, footsteps could be heard coming up the hall. She leaned out and saw it was her date. His long dark hair was slicked back. A pencil mustache was neatly trimmed on his upper lip. His half jacket outfit was brown on tan, with checkered front panels, matching brown pleated pants, and shiny brown loafers. The jacket was unbuttoned and a flashy white tank undershirt was exposed. He moved gracefully as he walked, almost dancing with himself. His charming smile thrilled her. It was going to be a night of dancing and fun.

She tossed the telegram on a small table at the end of the hall, next to her apartment door. She turned to her handsome young date and said, "My goodness. Good evening, Kenny Hayes."

"Good evening to you, Amelia Welch."

She giggled as she took his arm and pulled the door closed. They walked down the hall, down the steps onto the street below.

The young Western Union man stood listening as the sound of their footsteps disappeared on the street below. He looked down at the pile of letters on the nightstand and he saw the telegram he had delivered a month earlier. He remembered her reaction at the time, but now he could see he had confused mild shock with indifference. Some letters were opened, some not. They all had the distinctive "FREE MAIL" written up in the right-hand corner. He reached down, picked up one of the opened envelopes, and gave a quick look down the hall. He removed the letter and read:

September 4, 1951

Dear Amelia,

I sat and watched the sunrise yesterday morning and suddenly felt that you might be watching it set there at home. The beauty of the day changing and the thought of us sharing the moment made me feel warm inside. Our world was beginning and ending all at the same time. Just as my love for you begins and ends my day.

I find it difficult to put in words how much I miss you. When the thought of not being home becomes too painful to bear, I think of things I miss the most and you are suddenly in my thoughts, giving me life and purpose. Your presence is always with me. I remember the smell of your hair every morning just as I wake up and then you are there, your soft brown hair against my face. I remember your smile as I left for work and there you are at the back door, kissing me goodbye, smiling and waving as I leave. Through my day there are constant reminders of you everywhere I go, in everything I do. I lay down every night and you are suddenly with me, talking about your day while I rub your back to relieve the stress of your day.

As I drift off to sleep, I dream of your warm body pressed against mine. Sharing the passion of the moment as love engulfs us, my fingers tracing the line of your eyebrow, the outline of your ear. That's what I miss the most. Oh, what I would give to be with you now for just one night. To caress, to touch, to love and be loved in return, to hold you tight as we fall asleep together.

I love you so much. The thought of being with you once again has pulled me from the depths of despair time after time. I love you Sweetheart, and live for the day we will be together again.

Dan

The young man placed the letter back down on the table, gently placed the dime on it, turned and walked away. The tears in his eyes may have been from the letter he had just read, or they may have been from the anger he felt. Most likely it was from both. It really didn't matter to anyone but him. He walked down the steps and onto the sidewalk.

It was Friday night and Main Street was busy with its usual Friday night traffic. People going about their lives as usual, no worries, children playing, people shopping. A flashy new white Studebaker rolled down the street, with its wide, white wall tires. Its radio was playing a bit too loud to suit some of the older folk, filling the street with Rosemary Clooney's, *Half As Much.*

Everything is wonderful in Elkins, USA he thought to himself. You would never know a war was raging on the other side of the world. He looked around, stuck his hands in his pockets, and headed back to the Western Union office

CHAPTER 4

▼

"Raymond Tracy, stop that this instant! Halloween is tonight, but the school day isn't over yet, young man. I've warned you to leave the girl's pigtails alone. Now you leave me no choice. Come up here to my desk, *Now!*"

As Mrs. Martha Lowe took the paddle from the nail that held it at the end of the chalkboard, Raymond Tracy stood and walked slowly to the front of the one room schoolhouse. No stranger to Mrs. Lowe's paddle, he walked with an air of confidence to let the rest of the class know he felt little intimidation from his teacher or her wooden paddle. An exhibition not lost on Mrs. Lowe. Reaching the front of the room he felt confident, but prepared for the worst. He indeed had a reputation for not fearing Mrs. Lowe's paddle. The image had been painful to develop. He encouraged the talk, but secretly it was hogwash. Secretly he would be the first to admit that the paddle stung like the dickens.

"You have been here before young man. Let's not waste any time."

Raymond Tracy walked to within a couple of feet of Mrs. Lowe's desk, leaned forward, placing his hands on the edge. As each moment passed his muscles tensed even more, a reaction that only intensified the effect when the wood met the behind. A reaction Mrs. Lowe used to her advantage when her boys appeared overconfident.

Raymond Tracy Collins and his best buddy, Steven Michael Trace were cousins. They managed to sneak Mrs. Lowe's paddle out of Tabor schoolhouse at the end of last year's session, convinced its disappearance would end the curse the wicked plank had at Tabor. The conspiracy to remove their dreaded antagonist was conceived one hot afternoon on the banks of Russell Creek. That very day both of their behinds had felt the harsh sting of its bite. They had played a messy trick on a studious underclassman named Allen Johnson. It can be said that a lit Cherry Bomb dropped through a crack in the back of a double seated outhouse far exceeded even Raymond Tracy's expectations, the mastermind of the prank. Even more so, when a tattletale like Johnson was doing his business in that outhouse. The result of the prank is better left buried, along with Johnson's clothing.

The boys' demise was the result of poor planning and unfortunate timing. Mrs. Lowe had witnessed their dash from behind the outhouse as she stood at the schoolhouse door, calling students in from recess. Their flight, the resulting muffled *"BANG"* and Johnson's rather quick and messy exit from the outhouse, with his pants down around his ankles may be circumstantial evidence in a court of law, but in Mrs. Lowe's classroom it was an overwhelming fact, and all she needed to hand down a guilty verdict. Besides having to wash down the outhouse, the prank warranted a triple nailing by the infamous paddle, but the lesson learned was not necessarily the one Mrs. Lowe had in mind for the boys. What they learned instead was planning and timing was crucial, and it was something they would not fail to discuss in detail that summer afternoon on the bank of Russell Creek. The conspiracy started with a simple, but painful proclamation by Raymond Tracy.

"That paddle has to go! We have suffered more whoopin's with it than is humanly possible to tolerate. Without it, Mrs. Lowe will have to, to keep us after school, or give extra homework, or surely something of a less painful nature."

"I'm with you, Ray!" said Steven Michael, turning his head sideways to spit a mouth full of tobacco juice into the creek.

"Besides! Don't we get our butts whooped good and proper when we get home after school? Why, why, that's bein' whooped twice for the same deed. Didn't we study something about that in Government this year?"

"Double jeopardy!" Steven Michael rang in.

Jumping up on a stump Raymond continued as if stumping for public office.

"That's right, Double Jeffrey! That's agin the law of nature, and me and you are going to put a stop to Mrs. Lowe's reign of terror. We're going to take that paddle and hide it where its evil can never be used on us again."

Still on his back, but now with a skeptical look on his face, Steven Michael asked, "Just how you going to do that, Ray? You know Mrs. Lowe has powers of reception normal people don't possess. How many times has she caught us before we even had time to do the bad thing we planned to do? I'm a tellin' you now

Ray, before I stick my neck out to do somethin' this serious, you had better have a good plan."

Sitting up Steven Michael continued, "You can't just walk up to the front of the classroom and say, 'Excuse me, ma'am. I'll be a taking that devilish thing off your hands now. Now, now Mrs. Lowe, I know you can't depreciate its loss in the here and now, but someday you're gonna be standing at the Pearly Gates and when St. Peter starts questioning you about all the pain you inflicted in the name of ed u cation, you're a gonna think back and say, 'Thank heavens for Ray and Steve. They have surely saved my hide!'"

Looking at Steven Michael, Raymond Tracy leaped down, lifted him by the collar of his shirt and kissed him on the top of the head.

"*That's it, Steve!* It's so simple I can't believe we didn't think of it before. The Sunday Meeting is the key. It'll be our crusade against evil, and doing it on Sunday will assure us of the Lord's blessing. You, my friend, must be one of them quiet geniuses Allen talks about all the time."

Steven Michael stood up in disbelief. "You kissed me, Ray! Guys don't kiss guys except for the father and son thing. You know that." Looking around quickly to be sure no one witnessed the indiscretion he pointed his finger at his friend and continued, "Don't you ever kiss me again. You hear?"

Raymond Tracy looked at Steven Michael for a second, nodded his head and leaped back up on the stump. Steven Michael accepted the unspoken apology and gave his friend his full attention.

"Here's the plan. This Sunday evenin' the Lowe family will be at the Hardscratch Christian Church, as I believe they always are for the six o'clock Sunday evenin' worship. At exactly six-thirty, when Brother Cook is in the height of his sermon, do you know where we, that bein' you and me, will be?"

"Where?"

"You and me, Mr. Trace, will be at Tabor, relieving the schoolhouse of that demon board."

"How we gettin' in the schoolhouse, Ray?"

"Good question my friend. A good question deserves a gooder answer and here it is. Tomorrow we stay after to help clean up the classroom. We tell Mrs. Lowe we are doing it because we disappointed her so badly when we blew up Allen and the outhouse. When we close the windows, we accidentally leave one unlocked, which, by a strange twist of fate, is the one we slip through Sunday night. We grab the paddle and slip back out, clean as a whistle."

"Not bad, Ray. Not bad at all, 'cept one thing, Mrs. Lowe's gonna know it was us who took it. Nobody at Tabor has the nerve or the genius to do it, 'cept you and me. You bein' the nerve and me bein' the genius, and there ain't nobody with as good a reason. I believe they call that motorvation, and you know it don't take much in the way of evidence for Mrs. Lowe to turn on us."

"Steve! Steve! You are such a nitwit. *Think!* What happens tomorrow?" Impatient and on a roll, Raymond Tracy answered before Steven Michael could respond. "Tomorrow is the last day of school. We're out for the summer. By the time we come back next fall she won't notice it's gone until she has to use it. Since we are the two she uses it on, we'll be extra careful and not give her reason to look for it. What's she going to do by then?"

"She'll just have to let it go, won't she, Ray? She'll be relieved it's been misplaced. We'll be in the clear, her conscience relieved, and no more whoopin's."

"Now you got the picture, my friend. Time has a way of fixing the problem— her guilt over swingin' that paddle and our pain for bein' in its way.

It was a sound plan and they pulled it off flawlessly. A great evil was exorcised from the Tabor Schoolhouse when the paddle was removed that Sunday night and it wasn't missed . . . until the next day. Mrs. Lowe stopped by the schoolhouse to complete the children's final report cards for mailing. She didn't notice its absence right away, but when she did, she smiled and said to herself, *"Boys, Boys!* So much energy put to so little good. Well now, we'll see how long it takes before my boys return our mutual friend to its proper place." Laughing to herself she walked around the classroom until she found and secured the unlocked window.

*   *   *   *

The children noticed the absence of the paddle the first few minutes of the first day back at school. Quiet murmurs spread around the room like an August fire on a broomsedge field. Mrs. Lowe quieted the disruption, but made no mention of the missing plank. Tabor was business as usual until two weeks later when the boys temporarily forgot their pledge of unobtrusiveness. In a moment of weakness they unwittingly tripped up Elizabeth Gail during recess. The skinned elbows and knees weren't serious, but nevertheless the act forced Mrs. Lowe to take action. After she doctored the girl's injuries and the recess ended, she called the two boys to the front of the classroom and directed them to assume the position.

Although puzzled by the order, they bent over the desk and were both gripped with fear when they heard a collective gasp fill the classroom. Looking quickly over to Steven Michael, Raymond Tracy saw fear in his friend's eyes as his head shook back and forth. Slowly looking back over his left shoulder, he caught a glimpse of a maple switch as it *swooshed* down and made contact with his behind. Unlike the flat paddle he was accustomed to, the pain from the switch was much more centered and twice as intense. Raymond Tracy yelped loudly and danced about, barely keeping contact with the desk. As a second *swoosh* filled the air, Raymond Tracy closed his eyes, tightened his bottom and prepared for the worst. He breathed a sigh of relief when a yelp came from Steven Michael, as he did his own little Buck dance.

One swing of the switch for each boy was all they needed. That night it took the boys several hours to locate and dig up the buried paddle, which was none the worse for being buried three feet deep for nearly four months on the bank of Russell Creek. As the boys searched the outside of the schoolhouse for a way in, they found to their amazement and bewilderment, the same window they had used four months earlier was left partly open. As best friends they were able to confide in one another their newfound respect for Mrs. Lowe. She had known all along, but had not called their parents or confronted them about the theft. She had a plan, had waited and got her revenge . . . and paddle back. She was the master. They were truly the students. They agreed then and there that night that Mrs. Lowe was not one to be trifled with on serious matters.

Now as the class looked on, Raymond Tracy leaned over the desk waiting patiently for the paddle to strike. Looking out across the classroom his eyes met Janice Sparks. She flipped her pigtails about and stuck out her tongue. As he smiled and winked at her a loud *Whack*, filled the classroom.

Each boy in the class, young and old cringed, and squirmed uncomfortably at their desk. Each girl tried to hide a little smile. They tried because Mrs. Lowe had often told them, "Girls, it's not proper to find joy in another's misfortune, no matter how gratifying it might be."

"Mrs. Lowe."

"Why, Beth," said Martha Lowe, looking up from the papers on her desk. "It's recess. Why aren't you outside with the rest of the children?"

"My momma got a letter from my big sister, May. She's a Lu ten . . ."

"Lieu ten ant?"

"Yes," smiled Beth proudly. "She's a Navy Lu ten ant. She's a nurse in a hospital in Korea, where that war is going on. Momma cried when she read her letter 'cause it's so sad over there. A lot of the soldiers she helps die, 'cause they're so messed up."

"War is a horrible thing, Beth. People die."

"Momma says I should write May a letter to cheer her up, but I don't know what to say."

"Would you like me to help you get started on it?"

"Oh, yes ma'am. Would you?"

"Of course. You get your writing paper and pencil, and we'll write her a nice letter to cheer her up."

Beth went back to her desk and got her tablet and a pencil. She returned to the front of the room and pulled up a chair.

"Now child, to cheer up your sister tell her you love her, you miss her, and you're very proud of what she's doing to help our men that are fighting. Tell her how things are going back home. When I wrote Mr. Lowe, when he was fighting the Germans in Europe, I would always tell him about the farm and how things were going. He loved to hear about the farm. What are the things your sister cares the most about here at home?"

"She really misses Big Fred, her cat. I'm taking care of him until she gets back. He's having a great time chasing birds and mice."

"Very good, Beth. Your sister would like that. Let's start the letter. Up in the left corner put your greeting, 'Dear May' and the date in the right corner."

Beth carefully wrote:

Dear May,   *October 31, 1951*

"That's good. Now skip a line and start the body of the letter, and remember, it's the little things she will enjoy reading about. Write it like your assignment papers you get A's on, and write like you are talking to her. When you get to the end, tell her again that you love her and miss her."

Martha got up and walked over to an open window to check on the children. Beth sat for a moment, staring down at the paper.

"Stephen Michael! You turn loose of Allen's ear! I do declare," Martha mumbled to herself as she headed out the door.

Beth watched as Mrs. Lowe took both boys by the ear and walked them over to a bench, where they would spend the rest of the recess. She giggled to herself, looked down at her paper and took a deep breath. With the heading already completed she put the pencil to the paper and wrote:

October 31, 1951

Dear May,

Momma got your letter and read it to us after supper. When she said, Lieutenant May Browning, US Army, little Bobby Joe jumped up and saluted. Daddy had to yell out, "At Ease" before he would sit down. He started school this fall and at recess he and Earl White play Army. I have personally been captured many times. Last week they took Mrs. Lowe prisoner at the end of recess and we got to play an extra five minutes.

We are all very proud of what you are doing to help the soldiers who are hurt. I think I might want to be a nurse someday. Maybe in the Navy like you, because I like those big boats. I could see the world and be an angel just like you. That's what Daddy says you are, an angel.

I have been taking good care of Big Fred. He and Dutch play sometimes under the porch, although I think Dutch gets angry and barks at him. Last week Big Fred brought a dead squirrel to the back door, and kept meowing till Momma went to see about him. When he laid it down, Momma bent over to look at it, and it up and ran off, with Big Fred chasing after it. Momma screamed and Dutch came running, a barking the whole way. Bobby and I laughed so hard, Daddy made us go sit on the porch, while Momma calmed down and caught her breath. Daddy said that Big Fred was proud of what he caught and just wanted to share it with us, but Momma didn't seem to care.

I saw Eddie Thompson the other day and he asked about you. I gave him your address. You always said you would like to go out with him, so I figured you wouldn't mind if I told him so.

I have to go now. It's almost time for recess to end and everyone will be coming back in. Being the oldest student at Tabor, I help Mrs. Lowe with the younger students, just like you did. They all listen to me, except for Bobby Joe, of course.

I love you and miss you very much. Mom says you will be home in six months. That will be wonderful. Bobby Joe and I pray every night for you to come home soon.

Love Beth

CHAPTER 5

▼

It was the tenth day of the march when the small group of Americans reached their destination, a small village evacuated by the North Koreans for American prisoners. The surviving Americans walked and carried each other into the village. There were forty-seven of them left. More than half had survived the ordeal, but more to the point, thirty-one had perished along the march route. When they became too weak to go on, they were bayoneted or shot where they lay. Some were beaten for whatever reasons the guards saw fit, kicked and hit until they were unable to get off the ground. A bayonet would finish them off. The ditches, tunnels and fields along the march route were littered with the bodies. They were Americans who would never be accounted for. They had families who would never know what happened to them. They were sons, husbands and fathers. They were gone forever.

As the column of prisoners came to a halt, North Korean guards took small groups to the different huts. Welch and Jawaski were led to a small eight by ten mud brick hut on a hillside, along with eight other soldiers. Tired from the walking and weak from hunger they collapsed on the dirt floor, shoulder-to-shoulder and slept. They covered the entire floor of the hut. They slept the rest of the morning and were awakened by a guard at the open door of the hut.

"You wake! You wake! Come!"

The men woke slowly. Some rose to their feet, stretched and followed the guard out the door. The others moved slowly, eventually standing and filing out the door. Welch and Jawaski were the last to stand. Welch helped Jawaski to his feet.

"What are they doing, Dan? Do you think we are moving on North? Maybe they will let us stay for a while. Watch your head Dan! That door is too low for you. You could really brain yourself on it, if you don't pay attention. These Koreans are little people, aren't they Dan?"

Welch looked at Jawaski, rolled his eyes and eased under the door header and in turn helped Jawaski out the door into the open air.

"Would you look at this? A village emptied so we would have a place to stay. Where are the people, Dan? Do you think they shot 'em? I wouldn't shoot 'em. I would give them back their home and send us back south. What do they need us for, we're just in the way? Don't you think we're in their way, Dan?"

"I'm not sure, Leo. I do know they don't want us to go back and end up fighting them again, which is what the Army would do with those who can still fight."

"I can fight, Dan. I can lick 'em with one arm and one eye."

Looking at Jawaski, half beaten to death, an arm virtually useless and blind in one eye, Welch knew he had the heart to fight, but his fighting days were over as far as Uncle Sam was concerned.

Down the road the prisoners were walking away from a line with tin cans in their hands.

"Chow time!" said Welch.

Jawaski's spirits seemed a little brighter as they waited in line, finally reaching the front where they received a tin can. The North Korean server dipped the ladle and it came up about half soup, half soybeans. They took their cans and walked back to their hut, sitting on the ground against the outside wall. With no eating utensils, they drank the soup from the can.

"Pretty tasty, if I may say so," said Welch.

"You may say so, Mr. Welch. Give my compliments to the chef."

"Eat it slow and chew up the beans as much as possible," came a voice from the hut next to theirs.

"Welcome to Bean Camp. My name is Slay. Corporal Ron Slay. I'd been here a couple of days when they moved the poor slobs out of their homes. I've never heard such wailing and carrying on in my life. I was grateful to have a place to rest, but it was shameful the way they treated the families who lived here."

Slay walked over to them, squatted and continued to eat his soup beans.

Welch extended his hand, "Private Dan Welch and this little maggot is Private Leo Jawaski. Glad to meet you."

Slay shook Welch's hand. Jawaski sat his can in the crook of his arm and extended his left hand.

Shaking it Slay said, "That arm looks pretty bad."

"I've been keeping an eye on it. We had sulfur to put on it several days ago, but nothing since."

"There's a medic down the road. I'll fetch him after I'm done eating and have him look at it."

"Thanks," said Welch.

"When you're done eating there is a wash point down near the mess hut. You can wash your can, and get fresh water to drink. They boil it at the mess." Slay stood and walked down the road to the mess hut chewing as he went.

As Welch finished off his soup, he noticed Jawaski had become quiet.

"You okay, little buddy?"

Jawaski looked up glassy eyed, "I want to lie down for a while. Can I go in the hut and lie down, Dan?"

When Welch got up to help him, he noticed Jawaski had eaten very little of the bean soup. He sat down next to him.

"You need to finish your soup. It's not your mother's sauerkraut soup, but it's nourishing and all we got. Come on now; turn it up, chew it up, and then we'll talk about a nap."

Jawaski looked at Welch and smiled, "Yes, mom."

He turned up the can several times, chewing after each drink. Finishing the last mouthful he handed the can to Welch, who helped him to his feet and into the hut.

"Could you get me a drink of water, Dan? I'm awful thirsty."

Welch eased him down to the floor. "I'll walk down to the mess and get us fresh water. I won't be gone long. Can you stay awake till I get back?"

"You bet, Dan."

Welch took the cans and headed down the road. Outside the mess hut on a makeshift stove were two pots of boiling water. He dipped the cans in the first pot and wiped them out with his hand. He rinsed them in the second pot, and the metal cans were burning hot, but cooled quickly. He took a ladle from the pot of cool water and filled his can several times, drinking the contents down. He then filled both cans as full as he could and made his way back to their hut. As he entered, two men kneeled next to Jawaski. The bandage was off his right arm, exposing the wound.

Jawaski looked up at Welch and half smiled, his eyes glassy with tears.

"Dan Welch," said Welch extending his hand.

"Corpsman Ed Sims, your friend here is holding up remarkably well, considering the damage to his arm. I had to maneuver it around a little to see what was going on with it. It had to be extremely painful, but he never made a peep. I'm afraid it's shattered pretty bad at the joint. There's a large amount of infection. We may need to lance and drain it to keep blood poisoning from settings in. We will see. Be sure and check him every half hour. Look for a red line up the underside of his arm toward the armpit. We'll need to intervene quickly, if poisoning sets up. If it reaches his heart it will kill him."

Jawaski lay motionless on the ground as the three men stood. After a few more words, the two were alone once more.

"Well, little buddy, I'm glad someone looked at that arm who knows what they are doing."

Jawaski nodded his head. "Can I sleep now, Dan?"

"Sure, Leo. Drink this water and you can take a good nap." Jawaski slowly drank one of the cans of water before lying back down. Welch sat with him until he was asleep, got up and left the hut.

"Tell the captain Dan Welch wishes to speak with him."

The soldier went into the hut, and Chambers emerged, followed by two other soldiers.

"What do you want, Welch?"

"I've come to get the sulfur."

"The sulfur was used up before we left the tunnel. If you weren't so absorbed with your little friend, you would have noticed others were hurting. Even if some was left, do you think I would let you use it on the collaborator?" Chambers tensed and prepared for an assault that never came. Welch stared at him for a moment, turned and walked away. He stopped after a couple of steps and turned to face the men.

"You're wrong about Jawaski. I hope he lives long enough for you to apologize to him."

Chambers started to speak, but Welch turned and walked away. Back at the hut Jawaski was sleeping soundly. Welch stepped back outside and sat down with the other men assigned to the hut.

"We need to talk, Welch," said a sergeant, who looked out of place in uniform with a two-week beard.

Welch looked at the sergeant and the other men, two of which were from his B Company.

"What's on your mind, Sergeant Harris?"

"The camp scuttlebutt is that Jawaski collaborated with the Chinese. That he received medical treatment when no one else could get it. Some of the guys here say they know Jawaski from B Company, and say he is a square guy. We've all been beat up pretty bad and it looks like he got the worst end of it. Nobody got training on what to do if we were captured, so the way I see it, we all do the best we can. I'm not going to judge a man and his breaking point 'cause God knows, I would have probably broken if they had continued to beat me. If we are going to stand up to the likes of Captain Chambers, we need to know what we are dealing with."

Welch looked at each one of the guys, sizing them up. Adams and Miller from B Company, he felt he could trust. The sergeant talked pretty square, but talk was cheap.

"Jawaski and I ran into each other about twenty minutes after we lost the hill." Welch relayed the story of their ordeal together, what Jawaski had told him of his interrogation and finished with the confrontation with Captain Chambers in the tunnel.

The men sat listening intently.

"If you're looking for the absolute truth about what Leo did when he was being beat by the North Koreans, I can't give you that. What I can say is that he saw I was drowning in that croc pit and saved me. He willingly shared his medicine with the other soldiers. I believe him and I trust him with my life."

The men looked at each other and nodded.

"I believe you Welch, and I'm going to believe Jawaski handled himself honorably until someone can prove otherwise. Captain Chambers will create problems for us, but I know how to deal with his kind."

Looking at the others the sergeant said, "Anyone who thinks they need to request a different hut over this needs to speak up now."

No one spoke. No one got up and left.

"All right then, we're in this together. Anyone speaks out against Jawaski we tell 'em to shove it. Anyone gets nasty with the little guy, we lock horns with them. I'll apprise Major Greivetti of the situation, and that's that."

Turning to Welch he said, "So the little Polock stuck a pen in the bastard's eye. I'd like to have seen that. He's got guts all right."

For the first time since the tunnel Welch didn't feel alone. He nodded to the men and said, "Thanks."

"Let's take a look at that arm," said Welch as he removed the bandages around Jawaski's elbow. The smell of infection filled the air as the wound was exposed. Welch, Sergeant Harris, and Miller stared down at the red and yellow festering hole just below the swollen elbow joint.

"What do you think, Dan? It's feeling much better today. Look, I can even move it around a bit." With considerable effort he moved the arm, bending it slightly at the elbow.

"See, lookie there. I haven't been able to bend it since we were captured."

Dan took the elbow and squeezed. Bloody, yellowish pus oozed from the bullet wound. As he slowly rotated the arm, Jawaski's jaw muscles tightened. There on the underside, halfway to the armpit was a distinctive red streak. Welch nodded to Sergeant Harris who got up and quickly left the hut.

"What's going on, Dan? Where is the Sarge going?" Jawaski looked down at the arm and back at Welch.

"Blood poisoning has set in, little buddy. We need to lance and clean it out. No time to waste. Sergeant Harris went to get the corpsman."

Miller gathered up the bandages and sling. "Dan, I'm going to run these down to the mess, borrow some boiling water and clean them up. They'll be nice and clean when they go back on."

"Let them soak and bring back some boiled water."

"Got it."

Sergeant Harris walked toward five men sitting under a small tree playing cards. They sat on rocks and logs. In the middle was a flat rock on a stump with five cigarettes on it.

"Three."

"I'm good," said a fat man, and on around the circle it went until each man sat and contemplated his chances of staying in, or folding.

"I'll raise two smokes." Three men tossed their cards face down onto the rock table, and the other two coughed up two more cigarettes.

"It'll cost you two more cigs to see these cards," said the fat man. Sims stared at his hand, a pair of Jacks and Eights, and tried to figure the odds of the fat man hitting a better hand straight up.

He sweetened the pot with two more smokes and said, "Okay, hot shot. Let's see 'em."

The man laid his hand down, and four Queens stared up at Sims.

"Horse apples! That's it for me, guys. I'm cleaned out."

"As always, it has been a pleasure, Sims," said the fat man as he gathered up his winnings and dropped them in his hat, already half full of cigarettes. Corporal Sims stood and noticed Sergeant Harris for the first time.

"Henderson never bluffs. If he bets it, he's got it."

"I know," said Sims. "I just couldn't let him walk away without seeing what was in his hand. What's up?

"It's Jawaski. Looks like blood poisoning, all right."

"Red streak?"

"Halfway to the armpit."

"Let's get on down there. My hut is on the way."

They stopped at a hut and Sims went in and came out with a small canvas bag, a tarnished red cross on it.

"I'm going to consult with our resident medical expert first. Then we'll take care of that arm." Sims walked off the road, up toward a hut that sat by itself.

"Yo, compadre! Señor Garcia!"

An older soldier stepped out of the hut, squinting in the daylight.

"Hello, my friend. What brings you to our hillside hacienda?" The man smiled as he shook hands with Sims and Harris.

"I come for a favor. I need your help to save a man's life. Blood poisoning has set up in his arm. I can lance it and drain the poison, but I need your help to calm the infection. Otherwise, it will continue to fester."

"He is the little man, Jawaski, is he not?"

"Yes, my friend. He is the one Captain Chambers refers to as traitor."

"Yes, Chambers. I am the one Chambers refers to as the Old Spic. The little Pole and I have much in common, I think. I will help you because Jawaski is one of God's children, and because it will give the captain much irritation."

Garcia stepped back in his hut and returned with a small box. The three men hurried on down the road and arrived as Miller was hanging the bandages on the low hanging limbs of a bush.

Entering, they were met with the strong scent of infection.

"What's up, Doc?" Jawaski joked as they kneeled next to him. Sims gently picked up the arm and rotated it slowly over to expose the soft underside.

"*Ai-yai-yai,*" said Garcia.

"*It is not good, is it?*" said Jawaski in Spanish. "*Do you think Señor Sims can save the arm? My friends are too kind and try to spare me bad news.*"

Garcia looked down at the little man, smiled and answered. "*I will examine and see Jawaski, but I must warn you, it will hurt. Can you stand the pain?*"

"*Si.*"

Garcia leaned forward, gripped the elbow with his right hand and rotated the wrist with his left. Feeling the joint in his hand and watching Jawaski's complexion turn to a chalky pale white, he released the elbow and sat back on his heels. In a moment, the color began to slowly return to Jawaski's face.

"*It is indeed bad, my little friend. We can stop the infection this time, but if you are not taken to a hospital soon; your arm must eventually come off at the elbow. I am sorry to tell you this, but this is your arm. You have a right to know.*"

"*Gracias, Señor.*"

As Sims laid out his medical instruments, Garcia set his box next to Jawaski's head, opened it and took two leaves from a small bottle.

"*Here, my friend. Chew the coca leaf, but do not swallow. Tuck it between your cheek and gum. It will ease the pain you must suffer to make the arm better.*"

Jawaski took the leaves into his mouth, chewing slowly. He quickly began to feel light headed and dizzy. At his elbow Sims placed a small pan and directed the men to brace different parts of Jawaski's body. He picked up a long narrow spike with a small sharp hook on the end that looked like a darning needle, but knitting wasn't what he had in mind. He took out a book of matches, lit one and began to sterilize the needle halfway up and down its ten-inch length. Garcia took a soft stick from his box that was about six inches long and placed it in Jawaski's mouth.

"*Bite down my friend. How are you doing?*"

"*Never better,*" said Jawaski, the stick slurring his Spanish. "*You know, my mom has a bunch of those darning needles. She makes sweaters for Dad and me. Sits around knitting all evening, while Dad and I listen to the Giants or the Yankees on the radio. You like baseball, compadre?*"

"*Si. Baseball, mucho grande. I spent many wondrous hours at the neighborhood ball park when I was young.*"

As Jawaski and Garcia discussed baseball in Spanish, Sims picked up Jawaski's elbow. Garcia continued talking baseball, but reached over and braced Jawaski's upper arm, holding it stationary. Sims set a visual mark at the bullet wound where the infection seemed to be the most prominent and rammed the needle deep into the soft puffy skin. Jawaski screamed a muffled scream that was more an inward grunt. His body arched upward and a mass of yellowish, white pus shot out from the hole as Sims churned the needle around inside the elbow.

The pus continued to flow as Sims withdrew the needle and started squeezing the elbow area with his hands. He compressed the joint until he was getting more blood than pus. Jawaski lay motionless on his back, his eyes glassy and tears rolling out of the corners, down his temples.

Garcia took a bottle filled with a white powdery substance and mixed it in a small bottle with sterile water. He put his thumb over the opening and shook. The powder mixed with the water, leaving it a milky white. Reaching down he inserted the neck of the bottle into the freshly made opening in Jawaski's arm and shook it until the liquid substance was emptied from the bottle into Jawaski's arm. He removed the bottle and placed his thumb over the wound. Sims massaged the elbow, rotating the forearm around several times, making sure the substance saturated the inside of the elbow.

Jawaski spit the stick out and spoke softly in Spanish, *"Hey compadre! You got any more coca leaves?"*

"You don't need any more leaves, my friend. You are feeling good now, are you not?"

"Si, amigo. I was hoping for some later when we could just sit and talk. When things are not so busy."

"Ah! I see, my little friend, but I must tell you no. Others will need its magic. I will come back and we will talk of life and the New York Yankees. Señor DiMaggio is one tough hombre and I need to hear about him from one who has seen him play. I will come back, my friend. When you are better."

Garcia released his thumb from the wound and the white liquid drained out into the pan. Blood and pus flowed out with it.

"Now I must pull the rest of the infection out. Bring me the bandages, Miller." Garcia took a folding knife from his pocket and opened it. From his box he took a potato and dropped it into the bucket of sterile water. Air-drying the potato, he cut it in half lengthwise and placed the freshly cut side over the wound on

Jawaski's arm. He took the bandage from Miller and wrapped the potato securely to the elbow.

Turning to Welch he said, "In the morning when you get up, cut the darker outer layer off of this and place the freshly cut side against the wound. The starch will pull out more infection."

Turning back to Jawaski, Garcia said, *"Now, my little brave lion, you must spit out the coca leaves and sleep. Your body will need rest to help heal the arm."*

Jawaski turned his head sideways and spit the mush out of his mouth into the pan. Welch took the pan and walked outside, along with Sims and Garcia.

"What do you think, Sergeant Garcia?"

"It is not good. The forearm bones are badly shattered at the joint. The arm cannot heal with bone fragments in it. Another infection and the forearm must go. Even if he were in a hospital, I doubt they could save the arm."

"Corporal Sims, Sergeant Garcia. Thank you for helping Leo. I know he will want to tell you so when he feels better." Welch shook their hands as he spoke.

"Not everyone can be cured, but everyone must be cared for," said Garcia as he shook Welch's hand. "We will help you care for your friend, and pray that Mary will watch over him. He is worn down and weak. The arm is the least of his worries as time goes on. In the morning get him up and take him for a walk. I've known many men to lie down and never get up. You must keep your friend from giving up."

✳   ✳   ✳   ✳

"Let's take a walk, Dan. You got time to walk with me? I want to see some of the camp. See if any more of B Company is here. Do you think very many survived, Dan? Maybe us four were the only ones to get caught. Come on Dan. Let's walk."

Welch was sitting in a makeshift chair, weaving a mat out of rice reeds he had found behind the hut. There was a partially completed mat left behind, which he had quickly figured the weave pattern from. He and Harris had already made mats for half of the guys in their hut. As a child he helped his grandmother weave cotton rugs. It was a pleasant activity to pass the time with, and the mats beat sleeping on the ground.

"Sure Leo, a stroll would be a good break from my weaving. You feel up to it?"

"You just watch me, big guy. I feel better every day. If I could just stop having to go to the bathroom all the time, I'd be fit as a fiddle, as you hillbillies are fond of saying up in them there hills."

A rice stalk came firmly down on top of Jawaski's head with a loud, *Thump!*

"*Ouch!*" Rubbing the top of his head, Jawaski looked at Welch and said, in a serious melodramatic voice, "Remember, my hillbilly friend. Sooner or later you must sleep and while you're in slumber land, dreaming of your mountains and moonshine, a one-eyed, one-armed nightmare may pay you a visit and . . ."

The rice stalk came down toward Jawaski's head again, but stopped just inches above it. Jawaski grabbed it, struggled to his knees and then to his feet. Welch stood, grabbed the water bucket, and the two men started down the hill toward the center of the village. Jawaski used a walking stick that Miller had carved out of a tree limb for balance, while Welch kept a firm grip on the back of his trousers.

The infection in his arm had cleared up thanks to Sims' field expedient, operative skills and Garcia's magic potion. The arm was still useless as it rested in a sling, but the danger of infection was quieted for the moment. Welch's belt was still used to keep the arm stationary, lessening the chances of the bone fragments inflaming the tissue and stirring up another bad infection.

As Welch and Jawaski walked, soldiers would throw up a hand in greeting, or speak. Others would turn away, or simply ignore the passing men. The ugly comments were few and far between, but occasionally someone would throw a cutting remark. It was always at a distance, as most cowardly remarks are. As they did on every walk, they turned and headed up the hill to the hut the Puerto Rican soldiers shared.

"*Ah! Amigo!*" shouted Jawaski, as they approached the hut.

"*Leonardo, my friend!*" came from within the hut, and Garcia would come to the door.

"Welcome to my home, Leonardo. Would you like to come in, or does the sun suit you today?"

"The sun is good today. We will join you on your stoop, Fernando Edwardo Garcia. We will sit and talk and watch who walks by. There is much gossip to share on such a sunny November day."

"Yes, and if baseball should be brought up, we might talk of it a little . . . *si?*"

"*Si.*"

"You two talk in your Spanish gibberish, and I'll go to the mess and get a fresh bucket of water," said Welch, as he turned and walked back down the hill.

"Daniel, is a good water boy, si?" whispered Jawaski in Spanish, giggling softly.

"I understood that!" yelled Welch, as he disappeared around the corner.

"How is the arm, Leonardo?"

"It is well. It still aches, but Dan keeps it firmly strapped to my waist. I'm slowly getting used to not having it around. When the time comes, this will make its loss easier to overcome, will it not?"

Eyeing Jawaski, Garcia chose his words wisely, "Let us pray that it will not come to that. There is always room for a miracle or two, especially in such misery. Good things come to compassionate people, my friend. God watches over his children."

"Yes, he does and I'm prepared to work with whatever he sends my way. We will see. But, in the meantime it is important to discuss what we know of this year's Pennant Race," pausing for a second and looking at Garcia, Jawaski saw a little smile curl up on the corners of his mouth, "Is it not?"

"It is indeed," replied Garcia.

The two men were still talking about the Yankees when Welch returned. Taking some cans from the hut, he poured water for the three of them.

"Muchas gracias, Daniel," said Garcia, taking a refreshing drink. "The water is good, but most of all, it is clean. There are some who still do not trust the North Korean's boiled water, and drink from the stream below the village. Their stomachs rage! They walk about with their trousers soiled, growing weaker by the day.

They will soon find themselves on the hill across the stream in a shallow grave. It is dangerous to mistrust beyond common reason. The North Koreans are animals and need little reason to kill us. They would certainly not poison the water they prepare for us to drink, when they simply have to let us drink from the stream and die a painful, runny death."

"Speaking of which, I have to go," said Jawaski, as he attempted to get to his feet. Garcia stood and helped him up as Welch started to rise.

"Dan, I don't think I can make it back to the hut."

"You will come with me, my little friend. We have the finest slit trench in the whole camp up behind our hut."

"Let's go," said Jawaski, a bit of urgency in his voice. "You know how quickly the runs come and then leave you." Moving quickly the two men reached the trench, some fifty feet and to the right above the hut. It was a simple hole in the ground, about four-foot-deep and two feet wide. There were two wide boards lying across the trench. Jawaski stepped out on the boards, a foot on each, dropped his pants to his ankles. Holding Garcia's hand, he squatted down and did his business and none too soon. Paper was out of the question, but there was a pile of leaves for such. Garcia stepped around and held Jawaski firmly by the shoulders as he attempted to clean himself.

"Clean yourself well, Amigo. This is no time to add rawness to your list of ailments."

Jawaski wiped himself as best he could and rose slowly, pulling his pants up with him. With help from Garcia he stepped off the planks and fastened his belt.

"I'm getting quite good at this, if I might say. Before long I should be able to go by myself and not have to burden others."

"Then my little friend, all we would have to do is come and fish you out of the trench," said Garcia laughing.

"I have caught such a smelly fish and it is very difficult to clean," laughed Jawaski.

They both laughed loudly walking down the hill as Jawaski related Welch's swim in the croc.

"We speak of catching great, smelly fish, Daniel, the kind that fall into deep smelly pits."

"Great!" mumbled Welch. "A fellow takes one bad step in the dark and he's the brunt of everyone's jokes. Well, so be it, little man. One of these days I'll let go of your shirt and you can fall backwards into one of those trenches. If I fish you out, and that is a big if, we will be even."

Jawaski was laughing so hard tears formed in his eyes, and his arm began to throb from his jerking movements.

"No more, *No Mas!* You're killing me. Oh! Oh! Please no more."

"Mostly everyone has the runs and smell as if they've been swimming in slit trenches, Leonardo. It can be turned to your advantage. Bottle the liquid from the trench and sell it to the healthy who feel left out. You could call it, '*Ode, Da Poop!*'"

Welch watched as Jawaski rolled over on his side laughing uncontrollably, hollering out, "No." with "Ohs" and "Ouches," thrown together. The laughter was good for the little guy and him too. Garcia knew the healing power of laughter. There had been so little to laugh about, with so much death.

But, not today, Welch thought to himself as he smiled watching Jawaski recover from the laughing spell.

★   ★   ★   ★

"You are now liberated from American capitalist," said the North Korean officer. "You have much to think and talk about."

"Let's talk about a bath. We need to wash these clothes to get the lice and lice eggs out of them. The lice are eating us up. When can we wash our clothes? And we need food that isn't going to rip us apart."

The North Korean officer looked at Sergeant Harris with disdain. He had visited the hut to lecture the men on the people of North Korea's great effort to free the South Koreans from the imperialist tyranny. He wasn't interested in being lectured on personal hygiene by a filthy American.

"You wise to listen what I say, American. I speak of freedom. You insult the people of Korea with talk of lice."

"It is your lice and we want to give it back to you," said Miller.

The officer snapped a look at Miller, turned and left the hut. Several minutes later two soldiers came and motioned for Harris to follow.

"Spit in their eye, Sarge," said Jawaski.

"Sarge will be okay. I haven't seen anyone around here that is tough enough to break him," said Welch.

The Americans had been at the Bean Camp for fifteen days. Over half of the soldiers suffered from dysentery. The soybeans from which the camp got its nickname was the only sustenance they were given. The North Korean cooks were indifferent to properly cooking the beans, and undercooked beans played hell with the prisoner's digestive systems. Diarrhea was taking its toll. It overwhelmed the intestinal system. Mucus and waste ran down the soldiers' legs as they walked around. If they were too weak to stand, they would just lay in their waste. The fluid loss left the body dehydrated. Those who had someone to look after them stood a chance, and those who had no one, died.

Sergeant Harris stood in a large building, a barn or storage house. Two guards stood at either end guarding the doors. After nearly two hours of standing he sat down on the floor.

"You stand!" ordered a guard.

"No, I won't. If you want to stand, go right ahead. I aim to sit, thank you!"

The guard brought his rifle barrel down across the side of Harris' face, knocking him over.

"Now, you sit," said the guard laughing.

Harris lay on the ground, blood flowing from his forehead. He wiped the blood from his eyes, and the rifle barrel came down across his head again. Dizzy and disoriented he lay there for several minutes before a guard walked over with a small stool, and placed it at his feet.

"You sit!"

Harris slowly pulled himself to a sitting position. A door at the end of the barn opened and a young North Korean officer walked in, followed by another soldier who stood in the shadows. The young officer approached Harris.

"Sergeant Harris, you bad attitude. You reactionary and cause other American to rebel. Not good. Not good for you. Not good for others. The people of North Korea . . . ."

"The people of North Korea are a bunch of murdering animals. We got lice sucking the blood out of us. We got people dying every day because of the conditions we live in. I request to bathe and wash our clothes, and you beat the crap out of me for trying to help my guys. You're damn right I'm a reactionary."

"You American pigs all alike," came a voice from the shadows. "You no position to demand anything." A North Korean officer walked over and stood over Harris. His left eye was bandaged and he wore heavy bruises on his neck.

"Well, I'll be damned!" said Harris, standing up to face Captain Jin. "The little guy was telling the truth. This is for Leo, you son-of-a-bitch," and he spit in Jin's face. The guard swung his rifle around knocking Harris to the floor. The beating went on for several minutes until Jin motioned for the guards to stop. Jin drew his pistol, cocked it, and placed it against the bridge of Harris' nose.

"Go to hell, you one-eyed bastard!"

"Another brave one," sneered Jin, wisely taking a couple of steps back. "We see how brave in front of other Americans." Jin ordered the guards to bring Harris and started out the door, walking up the trail to the huts. A guard ran up the hill and ordered the prisoners out of their huts. Harris was forced to his knees on the road. When Jin had a big enough audience, he began to perform.

Seeing the Korean with the patched-up eye and bruised throat, Welch turned and quietly said, "Keep Leo in the hut."

Miller moved swiftly to the hut and blocked Leo's exit.

"Sergeant Harris brave man. He complain about lice and disrupt lecture. He not invited here, but complain about anything. He no like living here, then he no stay. I send him on his way."

A cold chill went down Harris's spine as he realized Jin's intent. He slowly pulled himself to his feet and came to a position of attention.

Jin pulled the pistol from his holster, cocked the hammer and shot Harris in the back of the head. The bullet passed through his brain and out his forehead. Harris' body remained locked in a position of attention for several seconds before the knees buckled, and his lifeless body folded to the ground.

Looking down at Harris, Jin said, "Let them take body. We see what lesson they learn."

Welch and Adams had been standing in the crowd closest to Harris. When Adams started for Jin, Welch threw up an arm and held him back.

"There has been one killing today. Let's keep it that way."

Welch walked down to the road.

"You bury him and his lice now," said Jin.

"You had no right to execute him," said Welch angrily.

"He trouble maker. He spit in Captain Jin's face," said the young officer.

"Now he dead. You bury him now."

The North Koreans walked back down the road as Welch stood over Harris' body. He took a deep breath, turned to Adams and said, "Walk down to the mess shed and get a shovel. We'll need to get him in the ground before dark."

As Adams headed down the hill, Welch met Jawaski at the door of their hut.

"It's him, Dan!"

"I know, Leo."

"If I had known it would be him, I wouldn't have told Sarge to spit in his eye. He's mean and likes to hurt people," Jawaski said with tears in his eyes. "If I'd had my hands on his throat another 10 seconds, I'd a killed him and Sarge would still be alive."

"And you'd be dead. The Sarge did what he did. Now we have to get him over to Boot Hill and put him in the ground. And you, you need to stay out of sight. If that devil sees you, we'll be burying you next. Pay your respects and go sit in the hut." Jawaski stood silent over Harris' body for a moment and quickly made a cross on his chest. As he hobbled back to the hut, Miller came back around the hill carrying a shovel, followed by a guard.

Welch picked up Harris' limp body and threw it over his shoulder. They walked down the hill and crossed the stream to the grave covered hill. Welch laid Harris on the ground and he and Miller took turns digging. They were down about two feet when the guard motioned to put Harris' body in the hole.

"It's not deep enough," protested Miller.

"Enough!" declared the guard, motioning with his rifle toward Harris' body.

The two men lifted the body and laid it in the hole. Miller began shoveling dirt and rocks into the hole as Welch watched the dirt slowly swallow the sergeant's body. When the last bit of dirt was piled on the grave, they gathered rocks and placed them on the fresh mound of dirt. The guard took the shovel and left. By dark the shallow grave was covered by a mound of rocks, protecting the body from scavengers. Welch said a few words over the grave and they returned to the hut.

"He was a good man, Dan."

"I know, Leo."

"How long do you think I will have to hide out? Can I still take my walks? I want to still take my walks, Dan."

There was a sudden movement outside and Garcia entered.

"Qué pasa, my little friend. We saw the one-eyed devil murder Harris. He will be looking for you and if he finds you out, you will lay next to the brave sergeant. You must leave this hut. Come, stay with me and my friends."

Turning to Welch, Garcia said, "There is very little time, Daniel. Word travels quickly in camp. My friends and I can take care of Leonardo, but we must move quickly."

*　　　*　　　*　　　*

"Wakie! Wakie!" The guard poked the rifle barrel into the backs of the sleeping men.

"What! What is this about?" said Welch protecting his eyes from the lantern.

Captain Jin stepped forward, pistol in hand and said, "Where is the little toad, Jawaski?"

"Who?"

"Do not try patience. Give me Jawaski." Stepping forward Jin grabbed a small man with a head bandage and an arm sling, dragging him into the light.

"Don't hurt me," said the man.

Jin motioned for the lantern to come closer and stared at the man he had separated from the group. Reaching down he pulled the bandage from the man's head, exposing a badly swollen eye. Jin grabbed the arm that rested in the sling, and the man cursed out in pain. Jin studied him for a moment and stood.

"This not Jawaski."

"Jawaski!" Came a voice, "You're about twenty days late, pal! Leo Jawaski is dead, rotting in a ditch where he deserves to be for kissing the Chinese's ass. If the guards hadn't shot him on the march here, we'd have got him, sooner or later."

Showing intense anger at losing his opportunity for revenge against the little American, Jin backhanded Adams and stormed out of the hut. The young North Korean officer who was with him said, "You gather you things. You move to new camp. Long march. Begin in dark." He turned and followed Jin out the door.

"Damn right!" said Miller. We're finally going to a decent camp."

"Maybe. Maybe not, but first we need to get everyone there. Remember the first march. We need to pair off and watch out for each other on this one," said Welch as he reached out and patted Adams on the head, "Good show son, I believe you fooled him."

Holding the side of his head, Adams said, "Glad to help out Leo, but you owe me big time, Welch. First you talk me into this and then you talk me into letting you pop me in the eye. To top it all off, I get socked by that one-eyed devil. Geeze! My head is ringing."

"If I ever need a pop in the chops, you'll be the first in line," Welch said to Adams smiling.

Welch entered Garcia's hut and found Jawaski and Pinto teamed up against Garcia and Sims in a game of Spades. The cards were worn and tattered, just like the men, but just like them, the cards still had a lot of playing time left in them.

Pinto studied his hand, "A very weak three, Leonardo."

Looking at Sims, Jawaski said, "Five, we'll go five."

Sims studied his cards and said, "Four. Looks like a pretty solid four. Maybe five, but a strong four for sure."

"We need seven to go out my friend" said Garcia as he wrote a seven and a five in the dirt of the floor. He pulled a card from his hand and tossed it out in the middle of the table.

With his cards tucked between his arm and belly, Jawaski pulled out the nine of Spades and trumped Garcia's Ace of Hearts.

"Ay, caramba!" moaned Garcia, followed with several poetic words in the language of his father.

"You have ruined me, Leonardo. I thought you were my friend?"

"There are no friends in Spades. Only partners and opponents," said Jawaski. Taking the lead Jawaski tossed out one winning card after the other, as his partner pulled the tricks off the table and placed them on the stack in front of him.

"That's six, partner. One more and they are set."

"This sandbagging must stop," demanded Garcia.

"That is not what you say when we are partners," responded Jawaski, gleefully.

"That is different." Garcia rebuffed, as if offended. "You are no longer my friend. Do not talk to me again unless you want to confess and do penance for your sandbagging. I will grant temporary absolution if you are my partner, of course. The given name of brave lion will no longer be spoken in this home," Garcia proclaimed as he watched Jawaski toss the ace of spades down on the table. They were set. Garcia's shoulders slumped as he stared down at the ace.

"Finish your game ladies and pack your bags, we march to our new home at midnight," announced Welch.

"What else do you know?" quickly demanded Garcia.

"Only that we move and that we must somehow disguise Leo. We fooled him with Adams. He thinks Leo is dead in a ditch somewhere."

"Thanks a lot, pal," said Leo, trying to hide a smile.

"We fooled him, but you can bet he'll be watching us leave."

"Do you have a plan, Daniel? asked Garcia.

"Yes, and I think it will work, if we are careful and Leo is up to it."

It was a good hour before the prisoners assembled on the road in the center of the village. They carried very little, as they had very little.

The North Korean guards walked from hut to hut making sure everyone was out. During their search two shots rang out. Forty-seven men arrived at the village. Three weeks later there were thirty-three. The prospects of that number dropping drastically during the march were certain. The men standing on the road were survivors, but some had reached their limit and a grueling march would most likely do them in.

The men began to slowly move down the road, escorted by ten guards. On the hillside to the left stood Captain Jin and the young officer, surveying the Americans as they passed. Adams, his eye bandaged and arm in a sling, walked assisted by Welch. Jin stared intently at them as they passed.

Up ahead a group of seven Puerto Rican soldiers were moving slowly down the road, leading the march. Garcia walked with two soldiers at his side. The middle soldier, Leo Jawaski, wore a pair of thick eyeglasses and a soft cap. Both his arms swung freely at his side as he walked along. The pain in his right elbow was tolerable. Corporal Sims had fashioned a bent splint that fit snuggly to his arm at the joint, giving it a slight bend at the elbow and allowing it to bend slightly as the arm swung back and forth. The only real indication of his pain was an occasional grunt. The brace, hidden under the shirtsleeve allowed him to walk out of the village without bringing attention to himself.

As Chambers passed Jin, the American officer looked at the North Korean, his bandaged eye and the fading bruises on his neck. If there was anything to Jawaski's claim, he would be dead now, Chambers thought to himself, still confident he was right about Jawaski.

The march from the village to the permanent camp took eight days. The small band of prisoners that arrived numbered twenty-one, twelve had perished along the road.

The men took turns walking with Jawaski. Near the end, Welch had stuck by his side, bracing him, pulling him along. He had two rolled up mats under one arm and Jawaski on the other. They made it, their feet bloody and blistered, their bodies exhausted from the long days and nights of walking.

It was noon as they walked into the camp. Welch could see that it was another village where civilians were moved out, so they could move in. It was larger than the Bean Camp, but still a bunch of mud huts. With winter approaching Welch had an uneasy feeling of gloom. A village of mud huts, or a town of mud huts, you were still living in a mud hut, no different than the mud on top of a crawdad hole. At least the crawdad could crawl underground to hide.

"Dan! The guards are all Chinese. Dan! Hey, big guy!"

Welch turned to face Jawaski.

"The guards are Chinese. We've moved uptown, Dan."

Jawaski was forever the optimist, which is probably why he continued to survive under such horrible conditions, thought Welch. The little man saw the glass as being half full, where others saw it as half empty. Dan saw it as neither, since the glass was too big to begin with. They were a good combination, optimism and practicality.

Back down the road, seven days march, Lance Corporal Thomas Baker, U.S. Marine Corps, lay dead, face down in a muddy ditch. His body had been stripped of its clothing and a bloody bayonet wound was visible on his back.

Clutched in his hand was a tightly folded piece of paper. The North Korean soldier who took his clothes had failed to notice it. Even if he had, he wouldn't have been able to read it, or for that matter, cared about its content. In reality, no one had read the last formalized words of the young Marine, except the person his request was written to. For the day it was submitted, it had been reviewed, approved and forwarded to the High Command for immediate action. Baker's request for permanent transfer from his present assignment was implemented just moments after the North Korean bayonet was pulled from his body:

Dear Jesus,

> *Please help me. I am Lance Corporal Thomas Baker from Boise, Idaho. I am in the US Marine Corps and I was captured by the Devil sometime in August. I have tried to count the days, but I lost track because of the times he beat and locked me down in a hole in the ground. I hope you remember me. It's Tommy Baker and I was baptized when I was 12 at the First Baptist Church. It was in March of 1943. I'm sure you remember because I remember Brother Phillips saying he was baptizing me in your name. I have tried hard to do what you have asked of me since then. It has been hard and I have failed you several times, but please don't fail me. I'm trapped in an evil world.*

> *I'm writing so you can ask your father to allow my soul into heaven. My country has forgotten me and by this time tomorrow the Devil will have killed me. I remember you said somewhere in the bible that no one could go to heaven except by you, so could you put in a good word for me with your father? Tell him I have been loyal to you and the Corps and maybe he will think about allowing my soul to leave this horrible place and find peace in heaven. You are my last hope.*

Thank you, Sir.

Semper Fidelis,

Lance Corporal Thomas Baker
US Marine Corps
Somewhere in Hell

CHAPTER 6

▼

"Listen up, ladies!" cried out a husky voice. *"Enlisted on this side of the road, officers on that side, and coloreds over next to the hut."* The men began to separate into their groups, the larger number of enlisted to the left, three officers to the right side, and a lone colored soldier walked with great uncertainty toward the hut.

The enlisted men gathered around the tall, lanky First Shirt. His husky voice was more subdued now, less demanding. He wore a padded, cotton, pajama looking outfit, similar to what the Chinese wore. On his feet were canvas tennis shoes.

"Welcome to Camp One men, or as we fondly refer to it, Camp Won-ton. The town was called Changsong when the Koreans lived here. You'll be living in the Yongji River Valley. We're ten miles from the Yalu River. You've met our gracious host, the Chinese. There are some two hundred or so Chinese guards here. We are never quite sure of their number. The cruel reality is they have the guns, we don't. There are no fences. Escaping is easy, but you will find yourself in deep kimchi out there 'cause surviving ain't. The last two escapees turned themselves in. A white man wandering around the countryside stands out like a long horn steer in a hog lot. If you feel you must, come see me first. I can give you details on how far I got and why I came back. Remember, we still have a chain of command."

The First Sergeant continued in his slow, Texan drawl, waving his hand from one side to the other. "The Chinese have divided the camp with American on one side and British the other. They put the coloreds in their own compound, over yonder." The men looked over at the colored soldier standing by himself, still waiting by the hut.

"Don't worry 'bout him. They'll be by shortly to fetch him. Our side of the compound is divided in half between enlisted and officers. Everyone has their own side of town here just like back at home. Don't ask me why. Old Joe Chink has reasons for splitting everyone up. They can be fair at times, but most of the time they are meaner and more unpredictable than a spooked rattlesnake. I'm going to walk you down to your hut. The Old Man will work on getting you a bath and some student uniforms, or Cotton Pads." He posed for a second like a New York model. "Don't knock 'em. They're cleaner than what you got on now. You can't get rid of the lice and their eggs, unless you bathe and wash your clothes. With winter coming on I think you'll find the Cotton Pads will keep you a bit warmer."

"I'd rather keep the lice than wear them damn goony pajamas," cursed a man in front of the group.

"Suit yourself soldier. You'll have to discuss it with the men you'll be sleeping shoulder to shoulder with."

Once again addressing the rest of the men he said, "If you got any serious medical problems we'll try and get you in to see the Chinese doc at the camp hospital. Don't count on much help. We tend to take better care of our own here."

The sergeant looked at the men and explained, "You're a sorry bunch for sure, but welcome anyway . . . let's go," and he headed down the path into the center of the huts. The officers had long since departed. The colored soldier stood next to the hut, dejected and alone.

*   *   *   *

"Ah, wookie, big a ugee Amareakun," said Jawaski. He was wearing one of the student outfits, and some oversized tennis shoes. He had reached around with his left hand and was pulling the corner of his right eye up in a slant, biting down on his lower lip to expose his upper teeth.

"Wookie! Wookie, Amareakun pig."

Welch looked up at Jawaski standing there in his exaggerated Chinaman pose, "The doc must have dropped you on your little head when you were born."

"Oh! Big a ugee devil not likie Chinaman? No wonder big ugee, so ugee, he . . . *Ehhh!*"

Welch had moved quickly and had Jawaski in a headlock. Making a fist with his free hand he rubbed vigorously on top of the little man's head.

"Ouch! Ouch!" bellowed Jawaski as he was released.

"Oh! Chinaman see you in nightmare, big a ugee Amareakun capitalist. We play with you tiny widdle brain."

The men laughed as Jawaski danced around, imitating a Chinese soldier. The indoctrination had started almost immediately upon their arrival. They were in their hut, the ten of them, worn out and exhausted, when a Chinese officer entered and began blabbing about Imperialist Wall Street warmongers and the good people of the Republic of China.

On their second day, they were granted permission to bathe. There was one tub of water for the seventeen men. As each man bathed the water became darker. The men attempted to skim the slush off the top and the sediment of filth off the bottom, but the water remained dirty. A pair of cotton pajamas and tennis shoes was given to each man after they bathed. No one complained.

Jawaski was number sixteen in the tub and as Welch helped him get dressed, number seventeen, the soldier who had complained about wearing the padded pajamas climbed in. As Jawaski and Welch began walking up the hill Corporal Chris Hill climbed out of the tub and began washing his tattered uniform in the dirty water. After a bit of scrubbing and rinsing, he threw them over his shoulder and headed up the hill to his hut, naked as the moment he was born.

*   *   *   *

It was the first day of January, as much as they could make out. Some of the men were convinced it was as far along as January third, while others believed it to still be late December. The one thing they all agreed on was Christmas had indeed come and gone. It was a depressing time for the men and they wished it over quickly.

With the exception of the officer ranks, the Chinese soldiers spoke very little English. The guards did their job, but the officers were the least trustworthy of the bunch. They were sly and were constantly looking for ways to confuse and create discord in the prisoners. A little argument, some discontent, their efforts very seldom paid off, but they tried nevertheless.

It was early on a cold winter morning at the camp. The men were awakened at five-thirty in the morning and stood in line, waiting to enter a large building for their daily dose of indoctrination. They would attend all day, with only a short break so the Chinese could have their lunch. The sessions would last into the evening, the Chinese rambling on and the American's doing their best to stay awake. At the end of the day they were given an assignment, a "cognitive," related to their lesson. They were required to memorize and repeat it on demand. They suffered through the sessions at least once a week, sometimes more.

"Hello, my little friend."

"Fernando, come stand with Dan and me."

"*Gracias, amigo.* If we must listen to this lunacy all day, should we not at least enjoy one another's company?"

They were all dressed out in the Chinese padded outfits and canvas shoes. Their beards and long hair looked out of place.

Jawaski's stringy little beard gave him a creepy appearance. With his arm strapped to his side and the homemade patch over his eye, he looked like a character from a cheap horror movie. Being around him at times was like being in a cheap horror movie, or at least Welch had that feeling.

Misty clouds of vapor rose from the men's nostrils and mouths as their breath condensed in the frigid air. It was well below zero and the men shuffled their feet and huddled together to keep warm. The tennis shoes they were given offered very little protection from the extreme cold temperatures. There was already a number of men with frostbite on their toes and feet and the cold cut right through the padded uniforms, stinging the skin, causing the joints to stiffen up and ache. Welch knew cold, but not like this. When the wind was up it was unbearable. Two days ago, it was minus forty-five. In the huts at night they had laid as close together as possible, since they were issued only one blanket per two men. The shared body heat was helpful, but couldn't protect them against such intense cold. Nor could the limited fires they were allowed to have. The hut was designed with a small pit in the center of the floor where a fire was built. The Chinese allowed the men to burn wood for one hour at night. The coals provided some warmth for a while, but for the most part the men suffered through the night.

"What's on the agenda for today, boss?" asked Jawaski, looking up at Welch.

"I believe we're going to discuss why the Wall Street Dogs drive around in Buicks," said Welch, "Why they drive Buicks, while the dedicated and hard working people of the Republic of China ride in carts pulled by water buffalo."

"In Puerto Rico we have many Wall Street Dogs, but not many Buicks. There are some Fords, and a few corrupt government officials in used Chevrolets, but no Buicks, and in this there is an important lesson" said Garcia continuing his story and running in place for a moment to get some feeling back into his feet.

Entering the warm building they walked to the center of the room to sit down and Jawaski and Welch waited for Garcia to end his story. As with many times before, he started off with his usual closing question to the men, but this time he ended it with a twist.

"And now, my friends, it is time to teach you the lesson of this story. I will give you a cognitive that you will be expected to memorize and repeat tonight before you tuck each other in."

Jawaski giggled.

"Laugh now my little one-eyed friend, but remember this, 'The proletariat wants to look up to their comrade leaders, but they should not have to look too high. One must endeavor to act wisely when choosing between the People's Car and a Wall Street Dog's Car.'"

Over the next several seconds Jawaski, Miller and Welch spent a considerable amount of effort trying to restrain their smiles as a Chinese officer got everyone's attention in front of the room and began the morning lecture. They would settle down, until one of them would glance over at Garcia. The exaggerated look of superiority he would give would cause a loss of control all over again, igniting the others with the giggles. They finally settled down as the lessons carried on through the morning and like most school children, they struggled to stay awake. Just before the Chinese broke for lunch, a young officer stood in front of the room.

"Chairman Mao say, *'Without armed struggle neither proletariat, nor people, nor Communist Party have standing in China and would be impossible for revolution to triumph.'*"

The young man read passionately from a piece of paper he held in his hand. His English was fair, and although the Americans sitting on the floor understood most of the words, they daydreamed through their meaning.

"*. . . without armed struggle Communist Party would assuredly not be what is today. Comrades, throughout Party must never forget experience for which we have paid in blood.' Chairman Mao, 1939,*" finished the young officer.

"Now someone must share meaning and understanding of Chairman Mao's words. Who can share? You," pointing to a man sitting in the middle of the room, "You explain. Stand; give cognitive."

A skinny, bearded man stood up with the assistance of the men sitting around him. Taking his cap off he said, "The guys and I were discussing this very subject in the hut last night just before we went to sleep. We find that if we take turns quoting the Chairman, we can create enough hot air in the hut to keep us warm through the night." The man spoke very seriously, as if he was an authority on the subject at hand. No one laughed, out loud.

Mumbling on he continued, "It seems to me that this Chairman Mayor fellow is saying that the people with the most guns are going to whip the other feller's butt. He says that shooting and killing is good 'cause without it the pollymerriets and the commodist partiers forget about whatever they happen to be struggling about. That of course, is just my opinion."

Quiet and respectful applause broke around the room as the man sat back down. The officer struggled to understand the American soldier's response, but in the end felt reassured since the tone was respectful and certain words had been used.

"Now we break," said the officer as the Chinese left the building for lunch. The prisoners were not allowed food during the long hours of indoctrination. Those that had 'em went outside and smoked 'em. Others sat or stood in small groups chatting about camp life and back home, or chuckling over something witty someone had slipped into their cognitive. It was a dangerous game they played, a struggle similar to Mao's revolution. The people against those in control, only the Americans rebelled with their wits and words, not guns and bullets. It was a dangerous game indeed, as some had found out.

The Chinese came back after a short period and the lectures continued. That afternoon there was a movie about Joseph Stalin. The Chinese appeared to hold the Russian leader in great reverence. After the movie there were more lectures. Their theme was the reoccurring message that American soldiers were not to be blamed, because the capitalist warmongers had tricked them. The lectures also badmouthed Truman and MacArthur. The last topic of the evening was titled, *"Why America Aggressor in Korea,"* more Chinese babbling followed by the prisoner's mumbling cognitives.

By the end of the evening the men were exhausted. Before dismissing them the Chinese passed out pencils and paper and directed the prisoners to write down their views on communism. The men wrote on the paper, as a few murmurs of shared information rose here and there.

As the papers were turned in the men sat quietly, talking softy amongst themselves, waiting for their final task of the day. Eventually, a young Chinese soldier got up in front of the room and began to recite the cognitive they would be expected to memorize and recite on demand. Jawaski mumbled the words to himself as the soldier spoke.

"China advocates the abolition of war, we do not want war, but war can only be abolished through war, and in order to get rid of the gun it is necessary to take up the gun."

That night there was an intense wind, dropping the temperatures down into the minus-thirties. They had burned a fire in the floor for an hour or so, keeping them warm. When the wood burned down and the coals died away the men pressed against one another to stay warm. The five blankets did very little to keep the ten men warm. The air was painfully cold. As the warmth from the coals faded, Miller's teeth began to chatter, uncontrollably.

"Man," *clack, clack, clack,* "itsssss sooo cold," *clack, clack, clack, clack.*

"Just concentrate on being someplace where it's hot. Someplace really hot," advised Welch.

"I spent a year in North Africa during World War II," said McMeekin. In Egypt it got up to a hundred and thirty degrees in the summer. It was like standing next to a bon fire. You could feel the heat baking your skin."

"Wha . . . wha what was it like at ni . . . ni night?" Miller asked.

"It cooled down, but it was still hot, especially when the air was still. You'd lie there on your cot and just melt, the beads of sweat running down the sides of your body. After a while your clothes, your cot, everything was soaking wet, but that was a good thing. Just like during the heat of the day. You'd feel the sweat trickling down your spine and into the crack of your butt. It would keep you cool, a little, anyway."

The men pressed closer together under the blankets as McMeekin continued.

"I can't figure out who could be used to this kind of cold. It's been going on for a week now and I can't get used to it, it just hurts. My feet hurt. My fingers hurt. Everything hurts," said Jawaski.

"My feet quit hurting a couple of days ago. I think I'm getting used to it," said Martin, a young kid from Florida. He was lying on the outside of the pile of men, closest to the back wall of the hut.

"Your feet don't hurt anymore?" questioned Welch. "Have you looked at them lately? They may be frost bit and frozen over. We'll need to take a look at them in the morning."

"I'm fine Welch. Really, they don't hurt."

"Miller, remind me to take a look in the morning,"

"Got it!" responded a voice from beneath the blanket.

Two huts away three Chinese entered, waking those inside who had managed to fall asleep. Shining their flashlights about, the men shielded their eyes.

"Up! Up! Back up wall!" The men stood and moved away from the center of the room, their backs against the hut wall.

"Now you," shining the flashlight in the face of one of the soldiers, "You give cognitive of subject at end of day lesson."

"Man, do you know how late it is?" said the soldier.

"You recite cognitive!" the officer bellowed.

The man stood in deep thought, wishing he had paid attention during the last few minutes of the lecture. Finally realizing that he didn't have a clue, he started to double-talk his way through the recitation.

"The communist work together and again by the people and, of course for the working class and unions, and the way I see it when these things are used for the good of the working people, the working-class people and under the control of the proletariats."

"War! Do not want war," came a whisper close to him.

"And yes! Because of this, the Chinese hate war and feel it is not good, but sometimes Chinese people must fight to do, whatever."

The officer frowned, considering the recitation. Nodding his head, he said, "Next man!" and shined the flashlight in the next squinting face. On it went, each man doing his best to appease the officer by repeating a variation of the cognitive before them. Everything went as smooth as could be expected until the flashlight landed on Corporal Hill's face.

"You! You say cognitive."

"What the hell do you morons want? Don't you know we are trying to freeze to death in here," blurted out the rebellious American. "It's bad enough that you don't give us decent clothing, that you keep our mail, and feed us slop. You can at least let us freeze in peace."

"Hill, you bad example for men. You reactionary," said the officer.

"Yea, yea, yea!"

"You come with us now!"

"Are you nuts? It's too damn cold to be walking around at night. I got the night blindness, and so do half of your guards out there. Johnny Stuart went out to take a dump the other night and a guard with night blindness shot him. He wasn't doing anything wrong. Go back to your heated cabins and leave us alone."

"Hill, you had better do as they say. All they want to do is talk to you about your attitude," said a voice from the other side of the room. "You already know they can make it awful hard on you in the Hole."

Hill slowly moved forward and the Chinese officer reached out and grabbed his arm. Hill's hand shot out and slapped the officer on the side of his face.

"Don't touch me, you yellow piece of shit!"

A pistol shot up from the waist of the officer, followed by two rifles from behind him.

"You come!" shouted the officer.

Hill stepped around the fire pit and followed the Chinese out the small door. Darkness filled the room and a lone voice summed up their collective concerns for Hill.

"Damn!"

"We got to go gather some firewood, or we're going to freeze tonight. Besides, we'll feel warmer if we get up and move around," said Welch to the other nine men in the hut as they stirred in the early morning air. Each stretching and moving about trying to get the blood moving through their cold limbs.

"How about Martin?" said Miller.

"What about Martin?"

"Feet. His feet, Dan. Remember last night. He said his feet don't hurt no more. Frost bite!"

"Oh, yea," said Welch, finally remembering the young man's announcement the night before.

"Doesn't sound good," said Jawaski. "If he needs to go see the Doc, I'll walk him over while you all gather some wood."

"Let's have a look kid," said Welch.

"Really, I don't know what the big deal is. I'm fine."

"Off with the shoes and let's take a look," ordered the bigger Welch.

The young man sat up, unlacing the shoestrings and pulled the tennis shoe off his right foot.

"The sock too," demanded Welch.

He pulled the sock down over his ankle and yanked it off. The foot was brown and swollen. The toes were black. The middle toe had exposed bone sticking out of its tip, the hunk of skin and meat that belonged there, most likely somewhere inside of the sock.

"We don't need to see the other foot. Miller, help him with his sock and shoe, and take him to see the Doc. He'll need two good arms to help him there and back, if the Doc lets him come back. Jawaski, you can help us with the firewood."

Jawaski nodded his head and as he passed Martin, he patted him on the head and said a few words of encouragement. The young man sat sobbing, staring at his foot.

A half-mile down the road the men began to warm up. Welch carried a tote with eight strands of braided reed rope, each about ten feet long. Each man would bind the wood he gathered with the strap and carry it over his back. When they reached the woods he passed out the straps.

"You know the game plan. We're going to have to go deeper in the woods, since things have been picked over pretty good. Remember, the Chinese take most of it from us, so pick up good stuff. Anything left over will be heating the hut tonight."

The men paired off and headed into the woods. Welch and Jawaski veered off to the left and walked up a gentle slope. Welch took the large woven tote he had carried the straps in and tied it around Jawaski's waist. As they walked Welch would pick up a stick and hold it under his arm. Jawaski would place his in the sack.

"Dan, do you think we will ever get out of this mess?"

Welch continued to pick up sticks. "Yes, I believe we will."

Jawaski smiled. After a few sticks he asked, "Why do you think they are so mean to us? The guys I talked to who were prisoners in the Second World War say this is worse. What have we done to deserve this?"

"I wish I knew the answer. God knows they treat their own people horribly. They don't seem to put much value on life over here anyway, and then you got this communism thing that teaches it's okay to do anything that suits your purpose. Did you pay attention to that young officer last night when he was talking about war?"

"*'China advocates the abolition of war, we do not want war, but war can only be abolished through war, and in order to get rid of the gun it is necessary to take up the gun,*'" quoted Jawaski.

"See what I mean, war and killing is okay if it gets them what they want. I'm just not sure who they are doing it for. We fight for the folks back home. Over here they think nothing of sacrificing their own people if it helps their cause. And look how they live. My kinfolk up in the West Virginia Mountains live like kings and queens compared to these folks. It's a strange place over here. People like us can't begin to understand these people, and why they do what they do. It's just hard to figure."

They continued to scavenge through the woods, picking up sticks as they went. Occasionally, Welch would break a long, thick stick over his knee, or lay it on a tree and stomp it in half. As they moved on the bundle he carried under his arm grew larger and the sack strapped to Jawaski's waist sagged under the weight of the wood.

"Look here, Dan!"

Welch turned to see Jawaski limping toward him with a forked limb under his arm. "Look what I found for Martin."

"Not bad, Leo. Looks like the right length. Aren't you two about the same height? We need to find another, so he'll have a pair." Welch watched Leo waddle along with the forked limb under his arm.

"How's the arm. Are you wiggling those fingers like Sims told you to do? You don't want the cold to freeze them off."

"All the time. Dan, can we go see Fernando after breakfast?"

"Sure. We'll take a walk and stop by. Maybe they will invite you to stay and play some cards. You know, every now and then you could lose a game and make them feel like they have a chance."

Jawaski giggled.

"When I drop you off, I'll walk over and see the Doc. The quick step had me up all night running to the trench. I'm running a little more than usual, so maybe he can give me something for it."

With full loads of firewood and a second forked stick, they headed back to the starting point to meet up with the rest of the men.

*   *   *   *

"What is problem?" The Chinese doctor looked at the young American.

"My feet Doc, I think they're frostbit," said Martin.

"Off shoes, off socks, please." The doctor watched the young man carefully take the shoe and sock off one foot and then the other.

"Yes. I see. We must scrape dead skin off and medicate. Put foot here." The doctor sat a stool in front of his chair and motioned for Martin to put his foot up on it. Reaching over to a table covered with medical instruments, he picked up a small scraping knife, took a firm hold of the boy's foot and began to scrape off the dead skin on his toes and feet. Miller watched from across the room with great interest. Treating the raw wounds on the feet with sulfur powder, he then wrapped them in bandages.

"Put shoes back on. No socks. Have someone wash out first." He said looking over at Miller who nodded in acknowledgment. "You come back tomorrow for more medication. Clean bandages. Maybe skin grow back over bone, maybe not. We must wait, see."

Martin got his shoes back on and got up. He threw his arm over Miller's shoulder and they started out of the room. Stopping at the door, Martin turned and said, "Thanks Doc."

The Chinese doctor looked up and nodded. Motioning for an American orderly to clean up the pile of dead skin, he called for the next patient to come forward.

✴   ✴   ✴   ✴

"You Wake! You Wake!"

"Go to hell!" came a shaky voice from down in the hole.

The Chinese guard took a long bamboo pole and poked it through the bamboo grate that covered the top of the hole in the center of the hut. The blunt tip of the pole jabbed the man in the ribs. He grabbed the pole and shoved it up through the grate, knocking the guard off balance. The next poke struck him in the head, shoving his face down into the urine-soaked mud at the bottom of the hole.

"You bastard!" Hill screamed out, holding the side of his head. "Let me out of here and we'll see how brave you are."

As Hill spoke, two guards came into the hut along with the officer Hill had slapped the night before.

"How you now, Corporal Hill? You think about you attitude. You stay warm down in hole?"

Hill cursed, grabbed the bamboo grate and gave it a good shake. It rattled, but didn't budge. A pole came down across his knuckles breaking the two middle fingers on his right hand. As he grabbed his hand, a pole shot down between the bars and jabbed him in the throat, another struck him in the ribs, still another hit him on the back. The blows came now in rapid succession, each inflicting pain, each drawing blood or cracking bones. The assault continued until Hill's profanities turned into groans and screams of pain. After ten minutes of being jabbed by the poles his screams turned to pleas for mercy, yet the assault continued. After twenty minutes the officer signaled for the guards to stop. The whimpering that had been heard minutes before had been replaced by the thumps of the poles striking the American's body. After the guards stopped there was silence.

The officer spoke briefly and left leaving one guard to watch over the Hole.

*   *   *   *

The men stood in line awaiting their breakfast meal. Actually, it could have been lunch, just as easily. The food resembled neither, but it helped to refer to the meal as something. So, they called it breakfast.

The food was a mixture of sorghum and millet, with a little rice. It tasted horrible, but they stood in line waiting to be served. They would eat it because they knew what it was like to go days and weeks without food. Life in a prison camp was all relative to something worse. They had seen the worst, so they ate the food, attended classes, suffered humiliation from their captors, and survived.

Near the front of the line stood Welch, Jawaski, Miller and Martin, leaning on his new crutches. Welch had fitted the length and wrapped some old cloth around the fork to act as a cushion for Martin's armpits. They were already aching, but he was okay with it.

"What's for breakfast this morning, Martin?" asked Jawaski.

"Let's see. I smell fried eggs and sausage patties, and wait a minute. That smell, I believe there might be, yes, I see it now, some biscuits and red eye gravy."

"I can smell it," said Welch, "and bless me, if it doesn't smell good."

"Orange juice, do you see any orange juice?" asked Miller.

"Yes, I do believe there is some fresh squeezed Florida orange juice, and can you smell that hot steaming coffee?"

The men stood there with their eyes closed, letting their imaginations feed their senses. The memories of smells and tastes caused their mouths to water. Miller helped Martin manage his bowl as they walked over to the side of the road to stand and eat. Some walked in place as they stood. The air was frigid, but out in the sun it was a few degrees warmer.

There were heavy clouds moving in from the east and Welch watched them closely. He knew about winter storms back in West Virginia. They would blow in off the Atlantic with strong winds, plummeting temperatures and sending the thermometers dipping into the minus degrees. As he drank his breakfast and studied the eastern sky a voice came from his right.

"Well, if it isn't the Lame Squad. You seem to attract the sick, the wounded and the traitors, Welch." Captain Chambers stood in the middle of the road with his hands on his hips, staring at Welch and the rest of the men.

"You have no business here, so keep moving Chambers," Welch said with a hint of threat in his voice.

"I'll move when I'm good and ready. Your little turncoat can hide behind your skirt for now, but sooner or later we'll go home and he'll face a court martial like the rest of the traitors in camp. I'll see to that."

"That's what the Chinese want, Chambers. They want discontent and hatred. They want us to go after each other. You're a bigger stooge than you accuse Leo of being. It's a shame you don't have the smarts to see it."

Welch's comment flustered Chambers. Unable to come up with an insult that would shoot down Welch's remark, he turned and headed down the road.

Miller started to follow, but with Welch's words ringing in his mind, he stood his ground with the group. Little white grains of ice began to bounce off of them as they stood and looked skyward.

"Sleet. We had better head back to the hut. I've got Dennis, the rest of you get on back," said Adams, volunteering to help Martin along the road toward their hut. As they moved along Welch and Jawaski turned right and walked down a lane to a small hut by a large tree. There was smoke coming out of a small crack in the wall. Welch knocked on the door and a voice invited them to come in.

"*Bienvenido, me amigos*. What brings you by our humble home on such a fine day?"

Garcia sat in a small, homemade wooden chair, next to a small, mud brick fireplace. In the middle of its back was the crack leading to the outside.

"Come, sit by my fire and warm yourself. We have much warmth to share. Carmen. Get our friends something to sit on."

Turning to them he asked, "Did I hear the sound of sleet on our roof a few minutes ago?"

"*Si, Fernando*, but now if you listen more carefully you will hear the sound of snow as it piles up outside."

"Ah, Leonardo. Sleet, snow, it is all a wonder of God to us, as we do not see such in Puerto Rico. We would truly enjoy it if it weren't so dependent on the cold. Daniel. What do you read in the sky?"

"Can't be sure. We haven't had much snow so far, so we'll just have to wait and see what she dumps on us. It doesn't look good."

"Indeed, it doesn't my friend."

The men sat and talked for several hours. Welch made several trips to the trench, which didn't go unnoticed by Garcia. After his return from the most recent trip he announced that they had better head back to their hut.

"The snow is starting to come down heavy, now. The wind is making some sizeable drifts. We had better go or you may have company for the night, Fernando."

"We would be honored by your presence, but as you can see, we would have no place for you. When Luis and Roberto return from gathering wood it will become very crowded. Our hearts are big, but our hut is small."

"*No es mucho*," said Jawaski. "It is indeed much smaller than our hut. We have ten, you have only six. We must find our way home before it becomes *muy frio.*"

"It is most cold indeed. God go with you my friends. Daniel, one moment, please." Garcia took something from the shelf next to him and handed it to Welch.

"This will help your runs. The doctor's heart is in the right place, but his potion is useless. This will slow you down."

"*Mochas gracias, amigo*," said Welch making Garcia break into a big smile.

"We'll make an hombre out of him yet, will we not, Leonardo?" Jawaski hugged Garcia and the two men headed out the door into the whiteness of the storm.

✴   ✴   ✴   ✴

Corporal Hill's eyes adjusted to the dark, but only found darkness. Liquid waste had frozen to his pants and body, freezing him to the ground. The pit Hill had been thrown into twenty-four hours ago smelled of human waste and urine when he entered it. The stench was much stronger now as he had soiled his pants at some point during the beatings.

Was it dark or was the night blindness affecting his ability to see in a very poorly lit room? He had awakened to a strong urge to go again, but had fought it. Realizing that at some point he had already, he lay there and released his bowels. The back of his pants and between his legs warmed as the liquid spread. His dysentery had been acting up the last couple of days and he was in no position to fight the pressure and impulses his body was having. He lay there in the bottom of the pit feeling the few moments of warmth it provided.

The pit was three feet square, by two feet deep. His legs ached, as he lay doubled in a fetal position on his side. Unable to stretch out, he could only change position from side to side, or sit up and bend over his knees. In order to change his position he had to twist and pull to break his clothing and skin loose from the frozen ground. Patches of clothing tore loose, as well as skin.

Movement caused his rib cage to throb. He reached around and felt two broken ribs that pressed outward against the skin. Each breath brought excruciating pain.

In the darkness of the pit his will power was weakening. He could confess to something, he thought. He could apologize for his bad attitude. The Chinese would forgive almost anything with a proper apology. They didn't like rude, difficult people. He had been a bad ass, but he felt it was his duty to antagonize the enemy. Create problems for them. It was easy since he had a deep hatred for them anyway. He could give in, to come back another day, or he could stick it out and hope his body wouldn't give out before the Chinese. He gave serious thought on what to do as he lay caged in the Hole.

✸   ✸   ✸   ✸

In the middle of the night Jawaski woke Welch with an elbow to the back.

"I need to go take a leak. I'll be back in a jiffy." Welch groaned acknowledgement as Jawaski rose and stepped out the front door. Welch sat up and waited. They had certain rules in the hut, one being if you left in the middle of the night you let someone know, especially during extreme cold periods. He fought to keep his eyes open. As time passed, concern overwhelmed his drowsiness. He hopped up and stepped out the door. The air was thin, and the wind blistered the skin. The snow was already over ten inches deep and piling up. The fresh tracks Jawaski had made were easy to follow and as Welch stepped in the footprints and rounded the corner, he found Jawaski on the ground, trying to back out of a snowdrift. Only his legs were visible. He was grunting and struggling with his one hand and knees, fighting to get to his feet. Stepping forward quickly Welch grabbed Jawaski around the waist and picked him up. As he did, he heard a deep moan come from the little man. Within seconds Welch had him back inside the hut.

Jawaski was gasping and fighting to keep his pain within, but it found its way out. Holding his left arm tightly against his body he started to sob. In the darkness of the hut Welch gently felt the length of the arm and found a sharp bone tip protruding through the skin just below the elbow. The damaged bone in the lower arm had shattered on the fall, slicing its way through the skin.

"Adams!" shouted Welch. Adams popped up to his knees, suddenly wide-awake from the urgency of Welch's voice. The other men also woke and rose to their feet.

"Leo has fallen and bone is sticking out of his skin below the elbow. Run and get Sims. Miller, we need Garcia here as quick as possible. Both of you tell them what happened so they will know what to bring. And be careful, for Christ sake!" Miller and Adams sprinted out the door.

Jawaski was now trying to speak between sobs. Welch started a small fire in the hole in the center of the room to provide some light and warmth. As light filled the room the men gazed upon Jawaski's ghostly appearance. His face was covered with snow from where he had gone down face first in the drift. Ice balls were sticking to his hair and around his nostrils and beard.

"I . . . mmmmm . . . sss . . . slipped and fell innnn the snow drift," Jawaski got out between sobs. "I ta . . . ta . . . tried to ca . . . ca . . . catch myself with both hands. I for . . . forgot, Dan. I'm sss . . . sorry."

"That's okay, little buddy. Sims and Fernando are on the way to help you. You just hang on. Fernando will have something for the pain." Welch took a rag from his pocket and wiped the snow and ice from Jawaski's beard and hair. Martin continued to throw wood on the fire as the light and warmth increased in the small room, Welch could see that Jawaski's complexion was pale and chalky. His eyes were beginning to take on the shallow look of someone beginning to lose consciousness. Grabbing two blankets he wrapped him up, eased him to the floor, elevating his feet above his head.

In a matter of minutes, Garcia arrived covered with snow and shivering. He brushed himself off and went immediately to Jawaski. Throwing the blanket back he examined the arm and felt the bone sticking out at the elbow. He reached up and stroked Jawaski on the cheek.

"Take this mi amigo," and he put two leaves in Jawaski's mouth. *"Chew now. Put the magic in your body. We are going to need mucho magic before this night is over."*

Unable to speak, Jawaski chewed up the leaves and parked them under his lip. He looked at Garcia through his tears and half smiled, but the pain in his eyes was unmistakable.

Sims entered the hut, quickly examined Jawaski and started barking out orders.

"Welch, get him to the camp hospital as quick as possible. Fernando, we will need strong painkiller for what we will have to do. The Chinese will not waste any of their morphine on him. I'm going to run ahead and get the Doc up. Fernando, you help Dan, it's really slick out there." Sims headed out the door, followed by Garcia and Welch, who carried Jawaski. The wind and snow were blinding. Garcia shielded his eyes and pulled Welch along.

The camp hospital was a tenth of a mile from their hut. The snow had drifted to nearly four feet in some places. Garcia plowed through the lane Sims had already cleared. They entered the hospital, walking through the patient area where several prisoners lay, to a middle room where they found Sims in a deep discussion with the Chinese doctor.

They both turned and walked over as Welch laid Jawaski on a small wooden table. Examining the elbow carefully Doctor Wong turned to Sims.

"Watch tonight. Take arm off in the morning. One stay, rest back to hut."

Sims and Welch agreed that Garcia would stay over with Jawaski. He had the coca leaves and knew how to administer them. Jawaski was already groggy from the effects of the drug, slipping in and out of consciousness through the night, waking abruptly at times wanting to know where Welch was.

Just before sunrise Jawaski awoke with a loud gasp and cried out, *"Cody, watch out!"* reliving the night he watched the North Koreans murder his friend.

Garcia sat with him holding his hand, "It is okay my little friend. I am here, you are safe."

"Dan, they've killed Cody and they're coming after me. Hide, we need to hide. They will kill us too. They're killing everybody."

"Hold my hand Leo and close your eye. We are hiding now. We are safe."

"Thank you, Dan."

Jawaski lay there sweating in the thirty-degree temperatures of the building. Garcia had laid an additional blanket on him and had wrapped one around himself. Sometime around two-thirty he had become drowsy and tore off a small tip of a coca leaf and stuffed it down between his lower lip and teeth. He was alert the rest of the night, without the over drugged effect of a full leaf. He thought of home and he thought of his friend lying on the small table. He thought about what the coming day would bring.

At daybreak, Welch showed up followed shortly by Sims. They sat and discussed the night's events with Garcia, and the likelihood the Chinese doctor would give Jawaski his best.

"He is a combat surgeon with years of experience. I've seen him show considerable care for our men," said Sims.

"But, will he give it his best?" demanded Welch.

"I never give less," came Wong's voice from the back of the room. "Question. Is patient stable to do surgery?"

The doctor walked over to Jawaski and examined his eyes, felt his brow and studied the damaged elbow. Turning to Sims, he asked, "You assist?"

"Yes."

As they prepared Jawaski a Chinese officer walked briskly through the front door, came to attention and addressed the doctor. They conversed and the soldier retreated to the front door and waited. Turning to the prisoners the doctor paused for several seconds in thought, and sighed deeply before speaking.

"A horrible accident. A crash, near division headquarters. Truck turn over. Five Chinese dead, twenty hurt. Most serious. Must go now. Car waits."

Leading Sims by the arm they walked over to Jawaski.

"You must do this. Must not wait," and then he told Sims the procedures for removing the arm. He then went back into the back of the building and gathered the things he would need for the trip.

Stopping next to Jawaski with his medical bag in hand he turned to the men and said, "Little American very brave warrior. Colonel Hua tell me of brave attack on Korean turtle, Jin. Little man sign confession with "King Siam." Wong's face broke a smile. "'Eye for eye,' Colonel Hua say." He hesitated, looking sad, "I must apologize I cannot help such brave man. It would be honor, but countrymen come first."

Putting on his heavy fur lined coat and hat as he walked across the floor, he turned and said, "Sims. You do fine job. Remember. Important to get all bone fragment. Must not leave even small bit, and leave good flap. Easier to trim skin flap, than cut more muscle and bone. I return in week. Patient stay in hospital until I return."

He turned and looked at the officer at the door and spoke in Chinese. The officer nodded his head and Colonel Wong left.

It was a group effort. Martin and Adams gathered firewood and got the temperature of the room up to a tolerable level. Not too hot, but enough to where Sims felt he could feel with his fingertips. The Chinese officer Colonel Wong had left in charge sat behind the doctor's desk and watched as the men prepared for the surgery. They were ready by mid-morning. Sims scrubbed up the best he could, as did Garcia and Welch, who would assist him.

Per Doctor Wong's instructions, an hour before surgery Garcia removed the coca leaves from under Jawaski's lip. Doctor Wong had left Sims enough morphine to get Jawaski through the surgery.

Sims had removed limbs the hard way, on the battlefield, under fire. Those procedures were designed to extract a soldier who might be pinned down, or to remove a limb that was hanging on by a piece of skin. In combat he worked with confidence knowing a surgeon in the rear would clean up after him. Here with Jawaski, there was no rear. Nobody back there to tidy up his temporary fix.

Jawaski was down from the effects of the coca and the morphine was administered. A tourniquet had been placed half way up the upper arm. Jawaski looked up at Welch, eyes teary, half open, and tried to speak, but no sound came from his lips.

"You're going to be fine, little buddy. Just relax and Sims will fix you up good and proper."

Jawaski gave a little half smile, nodded his head and slowly closed his eyes.

Sims took the scalpel in his hand and envisioned the line the doctor had traced with his finger across his arm. He could see the muscle, the tendons and bone under the skin. He took a deep breath and nodded to Welch, who tightened the tourniquet. Laying the knife against the skin, he began to cut.

*   *   *   *

The sunlight ran through the opened door with a vengeance, searching out the dark corners of the small hut. The brightness was intensified by the sun's reflection off the white blanket of snow on the ground outside. Hill stirred and tried to open his eyes, but the light that made its way down into the pit was unbearably bright.

The savage attacks with the poles had been carried out with regularity through the night, but they had not bothered him for what seemed like several hours. Hill wasn't sure how many times he was beat, or how long he had been in the pit. Time deserted a man when he entered it. There was suddenly a noise from above and he tried to squeeze his body up against the side and hide. If he hid, he thought, they would leave and go beat on someone else. He lay still and waited.

The pin was pulled that held the metal slide bar in place over the bamboo grate. The grate was lifted and muffled voices spoke. Hill felt a hand on his shoulder pulling him from the pit and he understood the guard's voice this time.

"You go now."

As the guard spoke Hill heard another voice coming from the Hole, encouraging him to stay.

"No Chris. You can stay. It's safe down here with me. We can hide here and they can't hurt us. We're invisible down here."

He broke away from the guard's grip and plunged head first back into the pit. Curling up into a tight ball he squeezed himself up against the cold dirt wall and became invisible. The guard turned and shrugged his shoulders.

"Go away and leave us alone," came Hill's voice from down in the pit.

Confused, the guards talked briefly and one left to search out the Lieutenant who had ordered the American's release. Hill continued to babble from down in the hole, a conversation where only one side could be heard by the sane mind.

*   *   *   *

Private Leo Jawaski stood at the bottom of the stoop, in front of his home. The one he had lived in with his mom and dad before he left for military service. The homes up and down the street were identical to his. Two story houses with ten steps to the front door. Cars lined the street and kids played stickball, stopping only when an errant car or truck had the nerve to drive down the middle of their playing field. Other children played hopscotch and jumped rope on the sidewalk. Families sat out on their stoops enjoying a warm summer day.

Jawaski was dressed smartly in his brown army dress uniform, a service cap on his head. There was a row of colorful ribbons on his chest above the left pocket. A duffel bag was slung over his shoulder.

"Leo! Leo! We're so glad to see you're home safe from that war," shouted Katen`ka Pierwszy from her stoop next door. Her husband, Adok, a veteran of World War One, stood and gave him a sharp salute, which Jawaski returned smartly with a smile.

He started up the steps and just as he reached halfway his mother burst through the front door. Her hair was done up, she was dressed like it was Sunday, and an apron was around her waist. She stood there on the stoop with tears in her eyes, looking down at him.

"My little Leo," she said as his dad appeared behind her and gave him a smile.

Jawaski took another step and from behind him came a loud shout.

"Leo!"

He turned, but found no one was there. Turning back to his parents he was surprised to find them hugging each other, their smiles replaced with sadness.

"Leo!" Came the voice again, but this time from above. He looked up at the windows and then into the bright blue New York sky and back to his parents. His dad was now helping his mother back through the front door.

In anger he looked up and shouted, *"No!"*

"Leonardo, mi amigo."

"Home, I want to visit home for a while," said Jawaski softly, his eye shut, his body wrapped in several blankets. A small tear escaped the corner of his eye and trickled down his cheek.

"Just visit for a while longer. Let me tell them I'm going to be okay," he whispered.

Welch nodded to Garcia who sat across the bed from him.

"Si, mi amigo. Visit your madre and el papa. We will wait here for you."

Jawaski's troubled face suddenly became peaceful. His breathing slowed and he lay there quietly.

Welch stood, walked over to the door and stepped outside into the cold air. It had been two days since they had removed Jawaski's left arm. Sims had done as good a job as possible. Without the guidance from Doctor Wong it would have been messy. Welch had been with Sims that morning when he checked the stump and was surprised to find it in relatively good shape. There was some swelling, but that was expected. It would be easier on Jawaski now, not having to carry and protect a useless arm around.

Welch looked out over the camp. The serene blanket of snow that had fallen a couple of days before was now a quagmire of mud and frozen slush. After the storm had dumped a foot and a half of snow, the sun came out the next day and temperatures climbed to the high twenties. It wasn't warm enough to melt the snow, but the heavy foot traffic on the roads and paths mixed the snow and frozen dirt into brown trails that contrasted heavily with the whiteness of the surrounding areas.

Movement caught Welch's attention over in the graveyard across the valley. Two men half carried; half pulled a dead body down the road that led up to the site. Weak themselves, they struggled along, doing their best to keep the body off the ground. Weight wasn't a real issue as the body was emaciated to the point it was just skin and bones. Weight was never an issue. It was the men themselves who were not much better off than the body they were carrying. They reached the graveyard and lifted the stiff body onto a stack of bodies. The ground had been frozen hard for so long that it was very taxing trying to dig graves. He could see the bodies of the men who had died over the past two weeks stacked up like a cord of firewood. Snow lay on top of the bodies and there were fresh ones being added every day.

Turning, Welch went back inside the hospital to his seat next to Jawaski.

"He is doing fine, Daniel. We will let him dream of home and he will come back to us when he is ready. In a prison camp a man must dream of home when he can. It is powerful magic for the soul."

Welch nodded in agreement, "The bodies are piling up across the hill. The cold is picking us off one at a time."

"Yes, the cold is an icy devil, preying on the weak and those who give up, but the weak can survive with hope. We must help them find hope."

"I saw a new group of men coming in this morning as I left the hut. I believe two of them were Puerto Rican brothers."

Garcia's eyebrows lifted.

"I stopped by the hut and told Luis. He went right away to see about them."

"*Gracias,* Daniel. Luis will handle it. We will make room somehow."

"Fernando."

"Yes, Daniel."

"How . . . I mean, what is it that you . . . I mean you and your Puerto Rican buddies do to stay so healthy? Well, not healthy. No one here is really healthy, but you even manage to help others in need, like Leo."

Garcia smiled a gentle smile as Welch stumbled around words, trying to pick them carefully so as not to offend. He knew Welch to be an honest and caring man. He answered his question just as thoughtfully.

"There is much magic in giving people hope, Daniel. My brothers and I come from the many towns and villages on our island. The 65th Infantry Regiment has fought bravely in this country forgotten by God. Some of us have been unlucky and now we are here with our American and British brothers from across the water. We are all God's children."

Garcia reached out and stroked Jawaski's hair and felt his brow.

"Yes, we are all God's children," he said staring down at Jawaski.

"Because we are his children, he commands us to care for one another. A man without hope is mostly dead already. You look around, you see the walking dead. It is easy to tell which men, which huts the dead come from. We have mucho magic, my friend. The magic of the heart, like the magic of our little friend. He not only has the strong heart of the brave lion, but also the compassionate heart of a lamb. When one shares the magic Leonardo has, one has purpose and will to survive."

Looking Welch in the eyes he said, "The magic is also strong in your heart, Daniel my friend."

✳   ✳   ✳   ✳

Walking quietly down the road, sloshing through mud and ice, Hill walked up to the guard shack, hesitated a moment and continued on past. He had the thousand-yard stare, his eyes open wide, staring out beyond his immediate space and time. It was the look of the lost. He continued to walk and slowly disappeared into the evening snowstorm.

✳   ✳   ✳   ✳

"And I'm telling you what I heard Colonel Wong say. You can believe it or not. It's your business if you choose to continue to make an ass out of yourself, Captain. I don't give a damn one way or the other, just back off. Leave Jawaski alone. Hell, the kid will probably get a medal."

Chambers stood there staring at the major who had just returned from the hospital with a serious bout of food poisoning. There had been other things and people that contradicted his feelings toward Jawaski. He had dealings with Doctor Wong. The doctor had saved his foot from sure amputation. He remembered seeing Captain Jin at the Bean Camp. His eye patched, the marks on his throat. His anger and obsession, focused on finding Jawaski, and now the story that Colonel Hua witnessed the attack. It made perfectly good sense. The Chinese were ruthless, but they admired courage and honor. As much as they tried to break the Americans, they respected those who kept their honor, even to their death. Colonel Hua saw Jawaski not only as an honorable man, but a great warrior. Because of that he must have ordered he be given special medical treatment. As much as he hated to admit it, he had been wrong about Jawaski and it troubled him deeply that the little man might die before he had a chance to make things right with him.

Chambers turned and walked down the muddy road. He certainly didn't want to carry that kind of guilt around. He would have to find a way to make amends. He would find a way to make Jawaski forgive him.

"Good morning, Dan," said a very weak voice. It was the third day since the surgery and Jawaski had been in and out of consciousness. They had watched him closely and someone had been with him at all times. Welch sat up straight in his chair.

"Good morning, Leo." There was great relief in his voice and on his face.

"I'm thirsty, Dan. I mean really thirsty. Can I have a drink of water?"

"You bet, little buddy." Welch was up and in moments had a cup of water back over to the bed. He reached under the pillow and lifted Jawaski's head and put the water to his lips. Jawaski drank some, but not much, and nodded his head. Before he could lay Jawaski back down he spoke.

"I'd like to sit up some. Can I sit up, Dan?" Looking around he said, "Where are we?" Looking to Welch he asked, "Is this an American hospital? Are we free?"

"No." Welch said sadly. "We are still at Camp One."

"How long have I been out? How is everyone else doing? Is it still snowing? I'm hungry, Dan. I mean, I'm really hungry."

Welch grinned from ear to ear as he propped Jawaski's head up with another pillow.

"You have been out for three days. You fell four nights ago and badly damaged your arm. Sims, Sims had to take it off." Welch said quietly.

Lying there, Jawaski looked down at his arm under the blanket and looked back at Welch with puzzlement.

"But I can feel my hand down there. I can move my fingers."

Welch reached down and pulled the blanket back to reveal the bandaged stump. Jawaski stared down at it for several seconds before speaking.

"What did you do with it, Dan?"

"I thought you would want to see it, so I laid it outside in a snow bank. It's probably frozen stiff by now."

"Can you get it, Dan? I'd like to see it."

Obediently, Welch got up and walked out the front door. In a few moments he came back in with the arm wrapped in a cloth. He pulled the cloth off slowly revealing a clinched hand and forearm. It was light blue and had a thin layer of ice on it. The nails were dark. Welch held it out for him to see.

Jawaski sat quietly, staring at the arm and down at his left stump.

"You know, one of these days I bet they will be able to sew one of these back on. Someone will figure out how to do it. Wouldn't that be something, Dan?"

Welch nodded his head.

"I think I want to rest now, Dan. You can throw that thing away. Thanks for saving it for me. It looked better on me, but since it didn't work anymore, I'm better off without it.

Welch helped shift Jawaski down, and covered him with the blanket. As he turned to take the arm back outside Jawaski said softly as if he didn't want anyone to hear, "Life will be much easier without it," and he closed his eyes and went to sleep.

"Did I ever tell you about running shine for my Uncle Mack?"

"Didn't you get chased by the County Sheriff on your first trip and swear never to do it again?"

Welch stared at Jawaski. "When did I tell you that?"

"A couple of months ago. If you had helped your uncle make that moonshine, we could live like kings in this camp."

Jawaski was propped up in his bed, pillow against the wall. Colonel Wong had returned and examined his arm. He was impressed with the work Sims had done, and told him so. He would have released Jawaski except he was concerned about a low-grade fever he was running. He watched after him as a favor for his friend, Hua.

"Did I ever finish telling you about the Ogerman Brothers?"

"No, you didn't."

"Didn't mention it while I was delirious from the surgery?"

"Nope."

"I could have sworn I told you about it."

"No, you didn't."

"Could you have forgotten?"

"Never."

"Are you sure?"

"Bet my life on it."

Welch sat looking at Jawaski, waiting for the little man to end his stalling tactics, his tormenting. Jawaski looked away and began speaking to other patients as they shuffled by. He finally turned his attention back to Welch.

"Would you like to know how that ended?"

"Please."

Jawaski giggled and Welch attempted to sustain his frown, but a little smile slipped out.

"Let's see. Where were we? Ah, yes! The carnal thoughts of Philibert and Albert Ogerman came to a head one afternoon over a Sunday dinner when their verbal assaults on each other escalated into a fist fight right there in Mama Overman's dining room. They had locked on to each other and rolled into the living room. Albert thumbed Philibert's eyes leaving him temporarily blinded, so he had no choice but to retaliate by biting off a piece of Albert's ear.

Mama Ogerman pleaded with her husband to stop the boys, but he knew there was bad blood that needed to be let, so he refused to interfere. Mary Kathryn and Crystal hugged each other, watching in horror as their husbands wrestled across the floor, blinded, bloody and slugging it out."

Jawaski coughed, his throat was becoming scratchy from talking. Welch handed him a cup of water, which he drank slowly. Clearing his throat, he continued with a slight pain in his throat and hoarseness in his voice.

"When the two boys rolled over and tipped over the family's two hundred year old grandfather clock, Papa Ogerman had suddenly seen enough. His grandfather had brought the clock with him when he fled Poland. It had survived crossing the Atlantic. It had survived the boy's childhood. Now it lay on the floor in pieces. Taking his walking cane, he struck the boys repeatedly until they fled the home screaming profanities at each other and angry words at their father."

Jawaski coughed again, only this time he grabbed his throat and grimaced in pain. Welch leaned forward.

"You okay, Leo?"

"Fine," whispered Jawaski, his voice barely audible. He took another drink and sat there for a moment trying to swallow. Each time he would make a pained face. After several drinks the spasms went away. He sat silently for several seconds and finally continued. "Philibert, Albert, Papa Joe and Mama Ogerman eventually reconciled their differences. Papa Joe knew an old Polish clock maker who repaired the family heirloom and the boys reluctantly footed the bill. In days things were back to an uneasy truce at the Ogerman home except, Mary Kathryn and Crystal had seen enough. A month later to the day, while their husbands were at work they quietly packed their bags, withdrew their savings from the bank and got on a southbound train. Apparently, something more than the horror of watching their husbands in a fistfight, stirred in them the afternoon they stood in the dining room hugging. Rumor has it they can both be found dancing at a nude club down in Havana for a hundred bucks a week. With their departure, peace returned to the Ogerman home."

Finished with the story Jawaski took a long drink of water while Welch chuckled out loud.

"Is that a true story?"

"Do you want it to be true?"

"Well, yes."

"Then it's true."

Welch sat there, a half serious look on his face looking at Jawaski smiling.

"But, is it true?"

"No!"

Welch threw up his arms in defeat. Confused he sat there staring at Jawaski, seeking clarification.

"Second cousins on my mother's side. Every word of it is true."

They both had a good laugh.

"Garcia." Garcia turned to see Captain Chambers walk toward him.

"Yes, Captain?"

Chambers stopped a few feet from Garcia with a strained look on his face.

"I have learned through a fairly reliable source that I didn't have the correct information on Private Jawaski. It appears that I have misjudged him."

"It appears? Either you have or you have not, Captain. A man's reputation leaves little room for doubt. What is it you want?"

"Could you get a message to Jawaski that I don't intend to push a court martial."

Garcia shook his head in disgust, "It would better suit the situation and your past conduct, for you to go to Leo and ask his forgiveness," Garcia said as sternly as he could without being disrespectful of Chambers' rank.

Chambers' shoulders slumped. "Yes, you are right, of course. I have made an ass of myself and I owe Jawaski an apology. I will try to take care of that when I can get to it."

"There is a great distance between said and done," Garcia said with clinched teeth.

Chambers looked at Garcia, turned and walked off.

Garcia watched him walk away, shook his head in disgust and walked down the path toward the hospital.

"We look. Wide, please."

Jawaski opened his mouth as wide as he could, gagging from the pressure of the tongue suppressor on the back of his tongue.

"*Aaaaaa.*"

"*Mmmmm*, not good," said Colonel Wong sitting up. He placed his finger just below Jawaski's eye and pulled down the skin.

"*Mmmmm.*"

Welch and Garcia sat on the edge of their chairs watching. It had been a week since the amputation and although the stump was healing nicely, Jawaski's health continued to deteriorate. His throat was raw and he had been spitting up bloody, yellow mucus. He could barely speak. He had been running a degree or two of fever off and on for some time. Welch and Garcia were worried. They had witnessed how fast one's health could fade under the camp conditions. A man was walking around one day and found dead the next morning, passing sometime in the night.

"Dan, Fernando. *Buenos tar . . .*" swallowing deeply he repeated, "*Buenos tardes, mis amigos,*" and finished in a whisper.

"You must rest my friend," said Garcia as Welch got up and followed the doctor into his office. "Colonel Wong will take very good care of you. He's a man of integrity and is giving you his best care."

Sweat was beading up on Jawaski's forehead, running down his face. Garcia felt his forehead with the back of his hand.

"You are burning up, *amigo*. We will cool you down a bit," and he pulled the blankets down.

Inside the doctor's office Welch and Doctor Wong discussed the results of his examination.

"Very bad throat infection. Supplies are very low. I have nothing to treat with. Unfortunately, must let infection run its course. Very sorry."

Welch sat there with his head hanging down listening to suggestions on making Jawaski comfortable.

Late in the evening Jawaski's breathing became irregular and strained. Talking was very difficult, but he did talk as he had things that needed to be said. Welch sat on one side of the bed and Garcia on the other.

"Ah, compadre," Jawaski said in a very weak and raspy voice.

"I am here, mi amigo."

"Dan," he said in almost a whisper.

Welch reached out and took his hand.

"I'm not feeling so good. I mean I'm really feeling bad. If I don't make it, promise me you'll tell my parents that I did my best. That I fought them all the way."

"You are going to be fine Leo," said Welch, unconvincingly.

Jawaski repeated, "Promise me you'll tell them."

"You can count on me, little buddy," said Welch sadly. His expression suddenly changing to a sad smile he said, "Look at what I got here for you. I traded one of my braided ropes for it." He took a small green can of peaches out of his pocket and held it up for Jawaski to see. A slight grin came over his face.

"I think I would like to have some of Cody's peaches now. I won them fair and square, you know. Could we have some, Dan?"

"Sure, buddy. Got my P38 right here in my pocket." Taking the little metal can opener out he opened the tiny blade, poked its point down through the top of the peaches and began to slowly work his way around the top edge of the can.

"I want you guys to help me eat them. Cody would have really liked you both," Jawaski whispered painfully, barely loud enough to be understood.

Welch took a mess kit spoon from his pocket, wiped it off with the inside of his shirt and spooned out some of the peach juice. He put it over Jawaski's lips and the juice dripped into his mouth, settled on his taste buds for a second and ran down his throat.

Jawaski nodded to Welch and whispered, "The King of Siam I am, if that ain't the sweetest tasting peaches I ever ate. You all help yourselves."

Welch spooned out one of the peach slices and ate it. After so many months of eating the bland, tasteless food the Chinese gave them, the sweetness of the juice and the peach tasted wonderful. He handed the can across to Garcia who put a slice in his mouth, closed his eyes, chewed and said, *"Bello!"*

Jawaski smiled. Garcia spooned out some more juice and fed it to him.

Licking his lips Jawaski whispered, *"Bello, indeed, amigo."* Turning to Welch he said, "Dan. I'm tired. Can we rest now for a while?"

"Yes, Leo, you can rest."

"Thank you, Dan," and he closed his eyes and slept. Those were the last words Private Leo Jawaski said. In the night he lay with his two friends on either side of him, fighting for each breath. The strep throat had quickly brought on pneumonia and with no resistance to fight the infection, Jawaski's lungs rapidly filled with fluid, but Leo kept right on fighting. Each breath was a struggle as gargling sounds came from deep in his chest. Welch and Garcia watched, as he would take a deep breath, exhale and his chest would stop moving for a couple of seconds, and then a deep inhale as he fought back death. His body would shake and tremble with each struggle.

"It's the death rattle, my friend. It will not be much longer and our little friend will fly with the Angels."

Welch knew the sound and knew how a strong-willed person could hang on for some time. He leaned over close to Jawaski and gently squeezed his hand.

"It's okay to let go, Leo. We'll be fine. I'll go see your parents when I get home. Just let go and go to Cody. He's been waiting for you." Welch sat there, tears running down his cheeks.

Jawaski took a deep gargling breath. His body shook and fell silent. Welch and Garcia sat quietly for several seconds waiting and finally realized the deep inhale was not going to come. Leo was gone.

Welch sat holding his hand for several minutes. Garcia made the cross on his chest and said a quiet prayer for his friend.

Welch finally stood, leaned over and kissed the little man on the forehead and then pulled the blanket up over his face. He took two steps toward the door, stopped and began crying, his large body trembling. Garcia walked up to him, his hand on the taller man's shoulder.

"Come Daniel, we must go rest now. We will bury Leonardo in the morning."

✳   ✳   ✳   ✳

As daylight broke, it was snowing heavily and visibility was poor. Squinting to see through the falling snow the guard thought he spotted something unusual in the road down from his post. Up the road from the camp came his replacement and as they exchanged casual pleasantries, the guard kept looking back over his shoulder at an object. His replacement being much more alert, looked down the road and agreed that whatever it was, it warranted investigation.

The Chinese soldier carefully walked down the road, his rifle at the ready, his replacement at the guard shack, covering his back. Close enough now to see through the falling snow, he slung the weapon on his shoulder and motioned to the soldier behind him that there was no danger.

There sitting on the ground on the edge of the road was a man. An American soldier, sitting with his legs crossed, his arms crossed on his chest. The soldier put his foot out and shoved the body. Stiff and frozen to the ground, it wavered, but didn't tip over. The layer of snow that covered him fell to the ground leaving a ghostly figure. Squatting for a better look, the guard saw the American uniform, the face and realized it was the crazy one. Icicles hung from his hair and beard. His eyes were frozen open, his mouth was open as if to speak. He stared into the bush in front of him as if he had been frozen instantly as he was talking to someone.

Since his release from the Hole, Hill had quickly gone from camp grouch to camp nut. The Chinese guards liked to yell, "You nut," as he walked about talking to himself. They enjoyed his carrying on and at the same time feared him. They allowed him to come and go as he pleased. It was the sane they needed to keep an eye on. Hill had fought back. He had resisted beyond his own capabilities. He had paid a high price. The other prisoners had tried to help him, but he was lost in a place where there was no return.

The guard stood and shaking his head in disgust walked back up the road to the shack. It would be a lonely outpost now without the crazy American to entertain him.

★   ★   ★   ★

Welch, Miller, Martin and Allen walked down the snow-covered road. It was early morning and the snow was now coming down in flurries. Up ahead, Garcia stood walking in place. As they passed, he fell in place with the men and they continued on down the hill to the hospital.

"It is a beautiful morning my friends," said Garcia as they walked.

"*Si, amigo.* It is indeed a beautiful day," replied Welch.

"I will miss our Brave Lion, Little Leonardo very much. There will come a time soon, when we will speak of him with great joy and respect, but today we are sad and must bury our friend."

Welch looked at Garcia, teary eyed and with a half-smile said, "I will miss him more than I can say."

Garcia nodded as they walked up to the front door of the hospital. Welch and Garcia walked on in to retrieve Jawaski's body.

Inside both men stopped half way across the room and stared at an empty bed.

Welch motioned for the orderly, who came walking over.

"Where's Leo Jawaski?"

"I had a couple of guys take the dead over to the grave yard earlier. He must be over there on the stack of bodies."

"You what?" screamed Welch in the man's face.

The orderly jumped back two steps.

"No one said anything to the otherwise. It's that way every morning here," shouted the orderly defensively.

Garcia stepped between them and faced Welch.

"He has done his difficult job, as he does every morning, Daniel. We were tired and not thinking ahead to morning. He is not to blame."

Welch looked at the orderly, clinched his jaw and lowered his brow. The orderly cowered back another step. Garcia was right of course, but that didn't excuse the man's lack of consideration for Leo. Someone had sat with him the entire time he was there. He should have known that they would be back for his body.

Welch turned and walked back out the front door.

"What's his problem? People die every day in this place."

"A estupido," sneered Garcia to the surprised man. "I should have let him squash you like the cockroach you are."

"They took . . ."

"We heard Dan. It's okay. There are two shovels and a pick at the graveyard. We should be able to do a proper job," said Miller as the five men started down the hill. They walked quietly, reverently as if they were actually carrying Jawaski with them, which in fact they were, each in his own way.

Halfway down the hill they met Captain Chambers coming up toward them. Garcia guessed his purpose and prepared for what was about to be unleashed on the captain. He couldn't stop Welch, he only hoped he could convince him to spare the captain's life.

"Good morning men," said Chambers. No one spoke. Chambers was oblivious. Garcia looked up into Welch's face, which had turned crimson.

"Garcia, I have decided to take your advice. I owe Jawaski an apology and I'm going to ask him to forgive, me." Chambers looked at the men and sensed danger. He looked over his shoulder for someone, anyone, but he was alone. He took a half step backwards.

"I, ah, I thought I would visit him now, if," he took another step backward, "if he feels up to company."

Chambers saw it coming, but could do little to avoid the big man's lunge. Welch pushed the startled man down and as he attempted to crawl away, Welch grabbed his collar and shoved him down hard, face first in the ice and snow.

"You want to apologize to Leo?" Welch yelled as he brought the captain up in the air by his collar and the seat of his pants and flung him down the hill. The men watched, relieved that Welch had not killed him on the spot.

Welch moved quickly down the hill and caught up with Chambers just as he rolled to a stop and was attempting to get to his feet.

"You want to apologize. Well, I'll take you to him to apologize, you bastard!" Welch pushed the captain forward, sending him head over heels down the hill and so it went down the hill and up the other side to the graveyard, and the stack of snow-covered bodies.

Grabbing him by the shirt, Welch gave one last fling, sending him up against the stack of the dead bodies.

"There he is, asshole! Make your apology and get the hell out of my sight before I put you on that stack!"

Chambers turned to face the bodies. The stack was nearly forty feet long, four to five bodies high. They were covered with body waste, blood and mucus. At the end were the three bodies from that morning. Jawaski was there, partly covered with fresh snow, his eye was frozen open, staring at Chambers, who reeled backwards in horror.

Welch lifted him up to his feet and screamed, *"Say it, damn you!"*

With a trembling voice Chambers turned to the men and tried to speak.

Welch leaned over and with restraint in his voice said, "Not them! To Leo!"

Chambers turned and faced Jawaski's body. The little man's face was not etched with a look of terror like most of the bodies on the stack. His mouth was closed, his eye staring at Chambers, waiting. His expression was almost compassionate.

Garcia finally stepped forward and said, "Captain, Private Jawaski is waiting for your apology."

Chambers slowly stood up straight and brought himself to attention.

"I . . . I am sorry Private Jawaski. I was wrong about you. I was wrong to have treated you the way I did."

"He forgives you, now get out of my sight!" Welch grabbed Chambers and flung him down the hill.

Watching Chambers tumble down the slope and scramble to gain his footing, Welch turned and looked down at Jawaski's body for the first time. The little man was lying on the pile of dead men staring back at him. His complexion was an icy light blue. His eye patch was still in place and little crystals of ice were shining on his face.

Welch walked up and brushed the snow from Jawaski's face and hair. He picked him up and started walking across the hill to a barren area, just under a large tree. Garcia grabbed the shovels and pick, and Martin hobbled behind on his crutches, with a blanket over his shoulder. Stopping under the tree Welch stood and waited for Martin, who arrived and laid the blanket on the ground. Welch gently laid Jawaski down. He took the pick and began to dig. Garcia moved in periodically to shovel out the loose chunks of dirt and rock.

They worked for an hour in the frozen ground and managed about a foot. The shovels chipped away at the frozen dirt and rocks. Effort, persistence and love made its way down, inch by inch.

Down below stood Chambers watching them dig the grave. Staring at Jawaski lying on the blanket, his fear had slowly changed to sorrow and remorse. The pathetic existence of all the men in the camp rushed through his mind, and he remembered Welch's accusations about how he was unintentionally the real collaborator. That he was the one who was playing into the Chinese hands with hate and discord. He went to his knees and feeling intense shame, placed his hands over his face and cried.

Welch and Garcia heard his moans and stopped digging.

"Go to him Daniel. He is remorseful and needs to make penance for his wrongdoing. You know Leonardo would want you to."

Welch turned and looked at Garcia, who nodded and motioned down the hill. Taking the pick, he walked down to Chambers.

"Come up and take a turn at digging, Captain. Leo would want you to," said Welch in a calm voice.

His hands trembling, tears rolling down his cheeks, Chambers took the pick and walked back up the hill with Welch. He stepped down in the grave and began to swing the pick, with Allen manning the shovel. At two feet they got below the freeze line and with the exception of an occasional rock, the digging became much easier.

At five feet they lifted Jawaski from the blanket and laid him in the bottom of the hole, covering his face with a piece of cloth. Martin and Miller refilled the hole with dirt. The rest walked around and gathered what rocks they could find in the loose snow to pile on top of the grave. When they were done, they stood around the grave, heads bowed as Garcia said the Lord's Prayer, and one by one they said goodbye to their friend.

*   *   *   *

Welch sat at Doctor Wong's desk. The day after his friend died, he sat down and wrote a letter to Leo's parents. He was careful not to put anything in it that would offend, or give the Chinese any reason not to mail it. He took it to the camp commandant's office and asked politely if they would mail it, and he watched the Chinese officer take the letter and toss it into the belly of the stove that sat in the middle of the room.

As he sat there at the doctor's desk, he didn't find it any easier writing it the second time. They had received word that several of the enlisted men were being transferred to another camp that day and Welch knew of one last chance to get the letter mailed out before he left. Once he arrived at the new camp, he couldn't be sure of anything. He sat there deep in thought and began writing:

January 1952

Dear Mr. and Mrs. Jawaski,

> *I am writing to let you know of the death of your son Leo to pneumonia. He was a prisoner here at a Chinese prisoner of war camp. He asked me to write you on his deathbed. He wanted you to know that he did the best he could and fought to the very end. He died peacefully in the camp hospital.*
> *Leo saved my life while we were trying to escape the North Koreans. He was a very brave soldier and I consider it an honor to have known him,*

as do the rest of the men at the camp. I am very sorry to have to be the one to bring you such bad news, but Leo wanted you to know.

Sincerely,

Private Dan Welch

"It's a letter to Jawaski's parents. I want them to know about his death. I promised him I would let them know," Welch said as he handed the letter to Doctor Wong.

"Very difficult to get letter out of camp now," said Wong as he paced back and forth across his office floor. "But," and he turned quickly to face Welch with a smile on his face, "can write friend, Colonel Hua. He hold Jawaski in high regard. He maybe send to parents."

"Thank you." Welch turned and walked out of the building.

*   *   *   *

Leonard and Irene Jawaski sat together on their living room couch. They had received a telegram from the War Department several weeks ago informing them of Leo's death. The letter they had received from Leo's friend had touched their heart. The letter from the Chinese Colonel had at first stunned them, until they read its kind, compassionate words:

January 25, 1952

Mr. and Mrs. Jawaski,

> *It is with considerable honor that I have been entrusted to forward you this letter from your son's friend. Your son and my path crossed shortly after his capture by the North Korean Army. Private Jawaski was seriously wounded and weak from several days of evading capture. During his questioning, I witnessed him conducting himself honorably and at one point attacking and wounding his North Korean interrogator.*
> *Although I feel considerable opposition to the American intervention in Korea, I also find myself having great admiration for Private Jawaski's courage and honor. I was deeply saddened by the news of his death at our detention camp and had the Camp Commander report his passing to the*

Red Cross immediately, along with statements of his courage and loyalty to his country.

Please accept my deepest sympathy.

Respectfully,

Colonel Nam Hua
People's Republic of China

CHAPTER 7

▼

"Can we stack seven high?" Silas yelled over the deafening noise of the John Deere tractor and the baler.

"Maybe, throttle down a notch."

"Stack seven high and . . ." Silas looked up and down the field at the alfalfa hay still laying in rows on the ground, *"one more trip will do it."*

Howard Lowe stood on the front end of the hay wagon catching the bales of alfalfa with a metal hook as they came out of the back end of the baler. Pulling up and swinging the bale around, it would land on the stack of bales behind him. The wagon was half full and was ready to start the fifth row. There was nothing difficult about stacking seven bales high, unless you were working on the wagon all by yourself. It took effort to work fast enough to stay ahead of the baler and to position bales tight enough to keep them on the wagon on the rough ride to the barn. A loose stack usually left bales along the road, extra work and extra effort.

Driving the tractor was Silas Long, Lowe's neighbor. The white stubble of a two-day-old beard accented the wrinkles on his tanned, weathered face. White hair peeped out from under the old tattered cap that protected a bald head from the sun. The bib overalls he wore over a white T-shirt were worn and faded. The left galluses strap was unhooked, allowing air in under the denim. A man of short stature and pushing his mid-seventies, he could work with men half his age.

Howard and Silas traded out work, as most farm neighbors do. Usually there was a second man on the wagon, but the August hay was on the ground and neighbors were busy in their own fields. When hay is on the ground, you'd didn't leave it long for fear of an August thunderstorm ruining it.

The wagon was three quarters of the way full now and Howard was running out of space to operate. Silas notched down the fuel lever on the steering column of the A60 and the tractor slowed to a crawl.

"Putt, putt, putt," purred the engine as it pulled the baler and wagon across the field. Silas kept one eye focused on the row of raked alfalfa, the other on Howard.

At thirty, Howard was strong and agile. He had been lucky during World War II. He had been awarded two Purple Hearts, but the wounds were not life threatening. He had fought his way through North Africa, on through Italy and then the fields of France to Berlin.

When he finally got home, Wanda Faye was three years old. He had missed her birth and first steps, as did many fathers who had served. Now there was little Amy Sue. Four years old and full of spit and vinegar. Wanda Faye would teach like her mother, but Amy Sue already showed more interest in the farm than boys twice her age. Howard didn't have to encourage her. Martha saw it and had her hopes on a veterinarian or agricultural degree from the state university in Lexington. They would have to see. A lot could change, especially if she met the right boy, as her mother had.

As the last bale edged up the chute Howard hooked it, swung it out and around, over his head and locked it into place. The baled alfalfa sat on the wagon tighter than a cow's belly ready to calve. The trip to the barn would be uneventful.

Silas stopped the tractor as Howard hopped down and pulled the pin on the wagon tongue. Silas drove about fifty more feet and shut the tractor off leaving it on the line of raked alfalfa.

The baler sat there frozen in motion. The steel rakes stationary with a blanket of alfalfa partially lifted off the ground, flowing over the rakes and into the mouth of the beast. The large steel arm protruding from the top of the machine hung in the air, ready to swipe the alfalfa into the compacting chamber once the tractor moved again. The two pieces of farm equipment were a picture frozen in time, sitting alone in the middle of the field, waiting for the return of their masters.

Silas, now on a red McCormick, backed the tractor up to the loaded wagon. Howard positioned the tongue, dropped the pin in place and moved over to a second wagon sitting at the edge of the field. Silas swung the tractor around and backed the hitched wagon up to the second wagon, a skill honed by decades of practice. Howard picked the tongue up, swung it around to the hitch on the back end of the first wagon and dropped the pin in. He ran and hopped on the tongue of the McCormick and got a tight grip on the seat Silas was sitting on, as Silas shifted into low gear and let out the clutch. The tractor and its tandem load crept forward.

Looking up at the evening sky, Howard shouted at Silas, *"Sky looks clear."*
"Yup!"
"But no sense taking chances with that much alfalfa on the ground."
"Nope!"
"You free after supper?"
"Yup!"

Up ahead Martha stood next to the barn door with two baskets, covered with dishtowels. Silas drove the tractor and wagons in through the barn hall and stopped. Howard had hopped off the tractor and was taking a long drink of cool water from the jar Martha gave him. As Silas walked up, Martha gave him a jar. He drained it, took the ladle from the gallon bucket and refilled.

"Thank you, Martha."

The two men washed their hands in a separate bucket, and Martha walked to the east side of the barn where two straight back chairs sat in the evening shade.

"Gentleman, I leave you to your supper. I have two hungry girls down at the house that need to be fed and prepared for bed. Leave everything in the baskets and I will fetch them when I hear the tractor leave."

"Child, you are an angel, and oh my, is that fried chicken I smell coming from this basket?"

"It is, Brother Long, as I know your passion for things fried. It is the least I can do. There are also fried potatoes and squash."

Silas dug into the basket, placed the plate on his lap and began eating.

"Thank you, dear. We should be done around ten. It won't take long to get this stacked in the loft. We'll go back out and bale whatever is left and park it in the barn for the night."

Martha leaned over and kissed Howard on the top of the head and as she walked by Silas she gave him a quick peck on the top of his head. Grinning ear to ear with a chicken leg in his mouth, his eyes twinkled as she headed down the small path to the house. As she approached the screen door, she could hear Wanda Faye lecturing her younger sister in the kitchen.

"The fork goes on the napkin on the left side of the plate. No, the left side, this side, your left-hand side," and Wanda Faye moved the napkin and flatware to the left side of the plate.

"Me like this side, use right hand."

"No, no, no. It's not proper to put it there."

"Me not proper. Me just me."

Wanda Faye rolled her eyes and walked over to the stove to check on the boiling corn on the cob. Amy Sue went around the table arranging two more place settings. She climbed in a chair and carefully placed the knife, fork and spoon in their proper place. When she was done, she climbed up in her chair and moved her utensils to the right side of her plate. Crossing her arms in defiance, a triumphant look spread across her face.

Martha entered the kitchen, surveyed the table and the meal cooking on the stove.

"My goodness girls, what a beautifully prepared table." The place settings really look nice." Amy Sue smiled and sat up in her chair.

"Wanda Faye, is everything ready for the table?"

"Yes, ma'am."

"Take your seat girls. I'll set things on the table and we'll give thanks and eat."

Outside Howard and Silas were making short order of their supper. Between bites Silas yupped an occasional "Yup" to Harold's speculation on why the tobacco crop looked poorly.

"If it had just rained a little in June. I'll be lucky to make twelve hundred pounds this year. I'm afraid it will have to be a light Christmas."

"Howard! You have never had a light Christmas, even in the worst of times. You won't let those girls get up on Christmas morning without something special under that tree. That tobacco will sell. It ain't the best, but I've seen worse patches."

Howard smiled knowing he was right on both accounts. He dropped the plate and fork in the basket and finished his water. Setting the jar in the basket, he walked into the barn hall and surveyed the tobacco hanging from the rafters and the two wagons of alfalfa.

"You're right. I've seen worse. I've just never seen it hanging in my barn. I'll tell you this though, I don't think I've ever seen as good a field of alfalfa." Howard hopped up on the first wagon and began to roll the bales off onto the ground.

"Yup!"

The other side of the aisle was already stacked up to about a foot of the hanging burley.

In short order Howard had the two wagons emptied and hopped down to help Silas stack the bales. As he dropped the last bale in place the McCormick roared to life, was shifted into gear and starting out of the barn hall. Howard hopped on the tongue and the tractor rolled around the side of the barn and down the lane past the house. Up on the front porch stood Martha and the girls waving. Silas threw up a hand and waved. Howard hopped on the wagon, turned to the house and placed both hands over his heart, tilting his head sideways, signaling his love for his girls. Both girls threw kisses to their dad. When the tractor was out of sight, they ran down the steps toward the barn to fetch the two baskets. Martha returned to the kitchen to start cleaning up the supper mess.

Out in the field the men were hitching a wagon to the back of the baler when they heard loud frantic barking take up just over the hill. Howard cupped an ear in the direction of the barking.

"King has got something cornered over there. Let's take a minute and see what he's up to," said Howard and they walked to the crest of the hill. Down below a standoff was taking place between the Lowe's mixed collie and a mature groundhog. King stood with his head down, crouched, ready to spring to either side as the large reddish-brown groundhog crouched about six feet away. Behind King was a series of holes the groundhog called home. Caught out in the middle of the field grazing, the groundhog was in a perilous position with the dog blocking his escape route to the nearest hole and safety. His short legs were no match in a foot race with the dog.

Howard had made a mental note of the fresh holes yesterday as he mowed the field. Groundhogs were harmless for the most part, if they kept their burrows in the rocky ledges at the edges of the woods. They grazed on grass, clover and alfalfa. A clean animal, the young ones were good eating. But, unchecked and allowed to proliferate, they could make a mess out of a field or fence row.

"Wonder how long that dog's been tormenting that animal?" Howard questioned out loud.

"He's just having some fun." Silas took a pouch of chewing tobacco from his bib pocket, raised the pouch to his mouth and scooped in two fingers worth. Between chews he continued. "That collie is worth his weight in tobacco seed Howard. There's no telling how many groundhogs he's killed this year. I've seen hog holes big enough to flip a tractor. I'm told that last month a young man over in Russell County shot a hog in a fence row, crawled head first up to his waist in the hole to trying to fetch the animal out and got stuck. They found him around midnight with his feet sticking up out of the ground, none the worse for the ordeal."

"It's time King made short order of this one." Placing his fingers in his mouth, Howard let out a loud shrill of a whistle. King looked up the hill and when Howard motioned with his hand toward the groundhog, the dog charged. The hog struck out at King, who dodged and grabbed the smaller animal by the nape of the neck. Shaking viciously, he snapped the small animal's neck. Releasing his bite the dead animal was tossed through the air and rolled to a stop in the dust. Instantly King was upon it again, taking it in his jaws and repeating the game of shake and toss.

"He's just playing with it now," said Howard. "He'll chew on it a bit, roll around on it and maybe even eat a little of it. If he doesn't bring it to the back porch tonight to show it to the girls, a possum or fox will finish the rest overnight."

Turning, the two men walked back to the tractor. By nightfall two wagonloads of alfalfa were parked in the barn hall with the McCormick parked ahead of it. The John Deere and baler were parked alongside of the barn.

Walking to the truck with Silas, Howard said, "I'll have them stacked after breakfast and meet you at your barn around noon with the baler and two wagons. The rows should be dry by then. Thanks for today, Silas."

"Yup! It's been a good day for working in the hay. God willing, we'll get my field up tomorrow. It's been cut, Ed raked and conditioned it today. It should be ready to bale tomorrow after lunch. I'll see you then."

The old truck drove off down the lane, its taillights disappearing around the bend in the road. Howard walked from the barn to the house and found Martha in the kitchen sitting at the table. A stack of unopened mail sat in front of her as she went through the family ledger book, balancing accounts, and posting the different expenses in their appropriate columns. Howard went on the back porch and washed up. When he came back in, he stopped at the counter, dipped himself a glass of water and sat down at the table. Taking the mail, he thumbed through it one at a time reading aloud.

"Something from the Bank of Columbia, a letter from your Aunt Jewell, a couple of letters from the Agricultural Department, a letter from the Board of Education, some sort of advertisement from Western Auto and the September issue of the *Progressive Farmer*."

"Why don't you take care of the two Ag letters and see if Western Auto has anything we need. I'll look at the rest in a minute."

Howard glanced at the Western Auto flyer: tires, toys, furniture, tools and auto parts. He studied the tools and determined that there was nothing he didn't already have in the tool shed or couldn't borrow. He glanced at the toys and tossed the flyer to the side.

He thumbed through the *Progressive Farmer* and saw a couple of interesting articles on planting corn and Black Angus cattle, made a mental note to read them and laid it aside.

One letter, a burley tobacco survey, was from the County Agent's office. He laid it with the *Progressive Farmer* and opened the second Ag letter. Glancing over it he reached to lay it with the other, but slowly withdrew his hand and stared down at the letter. After reading it over carefully he laid it down on the table and sat quietly watching Martha make the last entry in the ledger. She reached for the letter from her aunt and began to open it. Looking up and smiling at Howard her expression changed to a look of concern.

"Howard, what's wrong?"

Howard sat there for a moment looking at Martha and finally said, "I've been called back into service. The Army has called me back up. I report to Fort Knox on the first of November."

Martha sat speechless as Howard got up and walked around the table, took her hand, pulling her to her feet and hugged her tightly. She cried softly in his arms as they stood there.

"You've already served in the big war, Howard," she said between sobs. "It's not fair to ask you to go through that again. Who will see to the farm while you're gone? What will the girls do without their dad?"

The two of them walked to the living room and sat on the sofa. They tried to talk about the impending separation, but only managed to sit, holding each other with only the sound of the mantel clock pendulum swinging. Mentally exhausted they finally retired to the bedroom to prepare for bed. Martha's work lay on the kitchen table and would wait until the morning.

Little was said between them as Martha sat at her vanity and brushed her hair. In front of her was the photograph of Howard in his army uniform, the sergeant stripes on his sleeves, a row of ribbons worn proudly on his chest. As she brushed her hair she gazed down at the picture and began to cry.

Howard sat on the edge of the girl's bed and stared down at them as they slept. Tears rolled down his cheeks. He knew what the impact of his recall would mean to the girls and Martha. He knew the drastic affect it would have on the upkeep of the farm. He felt the saddest about being away from Martha.

From behind, Martha walked up and placed her arms around his neck running her fingers through his hair.

"My sweet Howard. My poor sweet Howard."

✱   ✱   ✱   ✱

The duffel bag lay next to the front door. In it were uniforms and some field gear. On the bag was stenciled:

LOWE, HOWARD
1725416

Martha sat at her vanity brushing her hair. Howard walked into the room, sat down on the edge of the bed and slipped off his house shoes. He had been with the girls, reading them a story, listening to their prayers and kissing them good night. When he got to kiss them good night again, they would be much older.

Oh, Wanda Faye had prayed that he would be safe on his trip and God would protect him. But in her innocence, she couldn't understand the horrors and the danger of war. That was good, he had thought to himself. It was good that his children should not have to understand the horrors of war, as so many around the world did.

Sitting there on the edge of the bed he watched Martha gently brush her hair. He would miss the girls, but he would be lonely without her, his friend, his companion, and his lover. When he left for training and North Africa in 1942, he and Martha had been married for only a month. They had decided the thing to do was to get married before he got called to go. All the young men were getting the call, and most joined up. It was just a matter of time.

They had married on a Saturday evening at the Hardscratch Christian Church. Everyone they knew was there. With the war going on it was something to be happy about, so everyone came.

The reception was in the church basement decorated by Martha's closest friends. The tables were covered with dishes of food and desserts.

During the reception the young couple could hardly take their eyes off each other as they moved around the room thanking everyone who came. Martha's sister, Karen, had finally taken them aside and suggested that they should appear to want to leave or people would talk. She pointed out that they had thanked everyone for coming, and without acting too eager, they should jump in the truck and get going. Looking at each other they smiled and nodded in agreement. They both hugged their parents and walked out to Howard's old '38 Ford pickup truck.

The truck wasn't much for looks, as farm trucks weren't meant to be, but it was reliable and since they had done most of their dating in it, Martha had insisted on taking it on their honeymoon. Howard looked at it and shook his head in disbelief. It was covered with white streamers and someone had written messages in white shoe polish all over the glass, a sight sure to scare the cattle, if it were left on there. Martha, on the other hand, was tickled by the decorations and hugged Howard with one arm and pointed gleefully at the truck as they walked across the lawn. Behind the truck were several old tin cans tied to strings.

Helping Martha in and shutting the door, Howard ran around to the driver's side and jumped in. They waved as they drove off, amongst the revelry and noise of the well-wishers and the racket of the cans trailing behind them.

Howard had made arrangements to spend their honeymoon at a small Hotel in Glasgow, just fifty miles or so, west of Columbia. He had, of course kept the location secret for fear friends would choose to show up and raise them in the middle of the night in an old fashion charivari, and his suspicions were correct. On the square in Columbia he turned onto Campbellsville Street. Since it went in the opposite direction from Glasgow he circled quickly back up through Lindsey Wilson College and eventually got back around to the street headed to Glasgow. The maneuvering and speeding around the curves had thrilled Martha and she kept her eyes peeled behind them for Joey Houseman's old gray Plymouth.

The Houseman boy's car hadn't been seen since they had turned onto the square, where Howard had motioned to the Deputy Sheriff's car that sat in front of Long's Department Store. Leslie Rudolph, one of Howard's baseball teammates from high school flipped his red lights on, got out and motioned for Houseman and the two cars behind him to pull over. There were many accusations made, laughter exchanged, and Deputy Sheriff Rudolph finally let the group go with an official, but half-hearted warning to drive carefully on the curves and hills going toward Campbellsville.

The final effect was that Tony Houseman and several of Howard and Martha's friends spent the night driving around Campbellsville looking for Howard's truck. They had a fun time of it, but failed to find the newlyweds.

Later that night at the hotel Howard had sat and watched Martha brush her hair for the first time. The long gentle strokes, one hundred in all, carried the brush through her hair like it was silk. He walked over and kissed her lightly on the shoulder as he took the brush from her hand and continued the brushing. She sat there watching his face in the mirror as he lovingly brushed, stroke after stroke. She looked in the mirror and studied his face, the line of his nose and the wavy hair, his handsome chin and those bedroom eyes. His body was hardened from the years of farming.

She had told him how handsome he was that first night they were together in Glasgow and it had embarrassed him. Sitting in front of her mirror almost ten years later, she looked up at his reflection as he walked up behind her, took the brush and brushed her hair. He was just as handsome now, as then. She looked at him in the mirror and tears began to run down her cheeks.

"You've made me lose count, Howard," she said between sobs.

"Please don't cry, darling. I don't think I can stand it if you cry."

"I will miss you so," she said sobbing softly. She stood up and they held each other close. She cried while tears trickled down his face. He walked her over to the bed and helped her under the covers. He finished undressing himself, blew out the coal oil lamp and eased into the bed beside her.

Through the darkness came, "Howard, promise me you will be careful. You were careful in Africa and Europe. It won't be much different in Korea, will it? Promise you will come back to me."

"I promise, dear. I won't take chances. I will be careful."

He rolled over against Martha and found that she had taken her gown off. Her body was just as soft, just as firm as that first night in Glasgow on their honeymoon. He took her in his arms, laid his cheek between her breasts and held her tight. In the quietness of the house he could hear the soft pounding of her heart as it beat in her chest. She held him close, stroking his hair into the night.

Breakfast that morning was unusually quiet at the Lowe home. Martha had taken a leave day from school. A substitute would see to the kids that day. The girls sat quietly playing with their pancakes. Even Amy Sue was subdued.

"Would you look at my three girls, it's sad to think that my last little bit of time with them has to be so sad."

"Oh, Dad!" said Wanda Faye.

"Dad!" repeated Amy Sue.

Martha made an honest effort to perk herself and the girls up for Howard's sake, and her own.

"Girls your Dad will be back before we know it. He will come walking down the lane carrying his bag and he will never have to leave us again."

"Never again?" asked Amy Sue, looking at her dad.

"Never in a million years," said Howard to both his daughters. Wanda Faye and Amy Sue hopped out of their chairs, went and sat down in their dad's lap.

"Dad, why are we fighting in Korea?"

"Why we fight Korina?"

"Girls, we are trying to stop the bad guys from taking over the little country of Korea. They are very bad and they want to be mean to all of the people who live there. If we don't stop the bad guys in Korea, they will continue to spread their meanness to other countries like Japan. They are doing some bad things and we are going to make them stop."

"Who this J pan, Daddy?"

"They are one of the countries America had to fight when your father fought in the Second World War. Now we are helping them to be good neighbors," said Martha trying to help Howard explain the complexity of world politics to the girls.

"You be nice to them like Jesus says, Daddy, and they be nice to you," said Amy Sue.

"Yes, darling. I will remember what Jesus has taught me. I will try hard to think about him while I'm away."

Amy Sue hugged her dad tight as he stood, holding both girls in his arms and carried them into the living room, followed by Martha. The four of them sat on the couch talking and waiting for Silas to come. Silas was always on time and this morning was no exception. The Waterbury Clock on the fireplace mantel in the living room struck seven o'clock and before it chimed the seventh chime, Silas pulled up into the front yard and parked. With him were Samuel Woods and Mrs. Katharine Newhouse. At the sound of slamming car doors, the girls hopped off their dad's lap and raced to the front door.

"It Mrs. Katharine! It Mrs. Katharine!" announced Amy Sue jumping up and down.

"Mrs. Katharine has come to see you off, Howard, and Sam is going to keep Silas company on the trip back."

Howard smiled, already knowing who was going to be in the car with Silas. Martha was right, except for Mrs. Katharine. Her visit was so Martha would not have to be by herself after he drove off. He would have friends to talk with on the trip and now that Mrs. Katharine was there, so would Martha.

Dashing out the front door, the girls ran down the steps and grabbed Mrs. Katharine. Howard and Martha stood alone in the living room watching the girls hug Mrs. Katharine's legs. Turning to Martha, Howard took hold of her arms and looked deeply into her eyes as they began to fill with tears.

"I will write when I can."

"I will too," sobbed Martha. "You be careful and don't try being a hero. You already are in the eyes of your girls. We just want you back. We need you back. The girls and I," she looked at Howard, "I just don't think I could stand it if anything were to happen to you, Howard."

"I will be fine, darling, and I will be home before you know it."

"Welcome friends," said Howard as he and Martha walked out on the porch.

Wanda Faye and Amy Sue broke away from Mrs. Katharine's legs and ran to Howard, who knelt to hug them.

"I will miss you, Daddy," said Wanda Faye as she gave her father a kiss on the cheek.

"I miss too," repeated Amy Sue, kissing him on the other cheek.

"Don't forget me girls. No matter how long I'm gone, don't forget me and that I love you very much."

The girls hugged their father until he kissed them both and sent them running to Mrs. Katharine. Standing, he turned to Martha.

"Don't forget that I love you. I always have and always will, no matter what. Never forget that."

Martha wrapped her arms around Howard and hugged him hard. "I love you Howard Lowe," she said with tears in her eyes. They stood there embracing as the others tried to give them as much space and time as they needed. Behind them Silas carried Howard's duffel bag to the car and put it in the trunk.

Taking Martha's chin in his hand, he took his handkerchief and wiped the tears from her eyes and face, kissed her on the forehead and turned to walk to the car where Silas and Sam waited patiently. As Howard opened the passenger side door to get in, the girls waved and yelled at their father, blowing kisses down the hill to him. He stood there for a second looking at his daughters, placed his hands over his heart and tilted his head sideways. He then looked up at Martha and blew a single kiss her way. With tears streaming down her cheeks, she smiled and whispered, "I love you."

Howard lovingly nodded his head to her and climbed in the car. The girls continued their waving and blowing kisses until the car drove out of sight around the bend in the road.

✶   ✶   ✶   ✶

"All right you maggots, rise and shine!" rang through the barracks as the lights came on in the bay. The loud, gravelly voice was followed by the sound of a lead pipe beating against a garbage can lid.

"Up, up!" came another voice in unison with the staff sergeant. *"Formation in forty-five minutes."*

"You don't understand Corporal; the sun isn't up yet and I don't want to eat breakfast." Smelling blood in the air, the sergeant moved over to devour the new recruit as the rest of the men moved about the bay getting ready.

"What have we here, Corporal Lewis," shouted the Staff Sergeant.

"It appears the private prefers to wait until the sun is up before ending his night of slumber, Sarge."

"So it seems. Well, seeing that this is his first day in this man's Army, should we let him sleep in?"

"I concur, Sergeant Bowser, anyone can see he needs his beauty sleep."

The recruit smiled, rolled over and pulled the dark green wool army blanket up over his head. Sergeant Bowser, a short, stocky, powerful man took one step forward, grabbed the side of the mattress with both hands and flipped the recruit and mattress out on to the wooden floor between the bunks.

Corporal Lewis jumped immediately into the young man's face, yelling, *"Get off my floor, Judd. Move! Move! Move!"*

Wide eyed, the recruit came out from under the mattress like a rabbit from a brush pile. Grabbing his shaving kit and towel from his locker, he ran for the bathroom not looking back. Trailing behind him were Bowser and Lewis, who turned at the bathroom door and headed up the steps.

The first floor was a beehive of activity, busy with men scurrying back and forth, making their bunks and squaring away their areas. From upstairs came the sound of the sergeant's voice as he roused an unlucky recruit who still remained in bed.

"I can't believe what I'm seeing Corporal! Where do they find these slugs?"

"Maybe McClarney needs a few more minutes of sleep, Sarge!"

"Not in my Army!" A loud thud was heard, as another sleeping beauty hit the floor.

Lowe looked up at the ceiling and smiled to himself. He had been up since four-thirty, had shaved, showered and put on his uniform. His green fatigues still fit and with a little polish and spit, his boots came to a high state of shine. The sergeant stripes on his sleeve had caught the attention of all those on his floor who took the time to notice. Staff Sergeant Bowser and Corporal Lewis came thundering down the steps and stopped at the bottom to survey the men and their progress. Noticing the stripes on both arms, the 1st Cavalry Division patch on Lowe's right upper sleeve, and the Combat Infantry Badge above his left shirt pocket, the sergeant walked briskly over and shook hands.

"Staff Sergeant Marshall Bowser. This wart on my butt is Corporal Derrick Lewis. You must be the Howard Lowe the First Sergeant mentioned this morning in his meeting. Top wants you to take these maggots under your wing. Fall them out for formation at zero-five-forty-five in front of your barracks. March them to chow and back, then report to Top's office at zero-seven-hundred."

"Yes, Staff Sergeant."

"Sergeant Lowe reporting as ordered, First Sergeant."

"Sit. I can guarantee my clerk's coffee is better than that swill you had in the mess hall, if you would like to try it."

"Yes, First Sergeant. Thank you."

"Mitchell! Two cups of Joe. Black!" A shuffling noise was heard outside the office as the company clerk poured two cups coffee.

The top sergeant eyed the combat patch on Lowe's sleeve. "Pacific or Europe?"

"Europe."

"Where and when?"

"North Africa in '44, and on through Italy, France and the Rhineland. Came home in '45 just after Berlin was split up. I've been farming ever since, until I got my letter."

"You want to be here."

"No, First Sergeant."

"Good. Most don't." He nodded his approval. "I'm a career man. Why they would bother a man who paid his dues against the Nazis is beyond me." The sergeant hesitated and continued, "But, I'm not one to wonder why. Until you get your permanent orders, I want to use you to move and baby-sit my recruits.

Nothing has really changed, a lot of hurry up and wait to get them through processing and over to training. Move yourself into the cadre room at the end of the bay. The building and its contents are yours. I have a cadre meeting every morning at zero-five-hundred. Get with Staff Sergeant Bowser for your roster and the training schedule.

Deal with your problems. Anything serious happens let me know about it.

Don't be afraid to ask for help. Make good use of your spare time. Anything you can teach those boys will make your life a lot easier, and make theirs last a little longer."

Mitchell came in with two cups of hot coffee.

"Now, tell me about North Africa."

✱   ✱   ✱   ✱

"Make way!" shouted one of the young men and the recruits stepped aside and allowed Lowe to move to the front of the chow line. The supper meal was usually the better meal of the day and always seemed to be more enjoyable, less stressful or rushed. The phrase "Eat it now, chew it later," was reserved for breakfast and lunch. Of course, that would change once the men got to their combat training unit. The days would be longer and more intense.

Lowe grabbed a couple of glasses of cold milk and carried his shiny metal tray back to the cadre section of the mess hall and took a seat. It was Saturday evening and most of the other cadre had departed. He sat at the table alone and picked through his meal.

The Reception Center commander and executive officer sat two tables over. The XO suddenly shouted, *"DRO, more tea!"*

The dining room orderly, a recruit standing off to the side, quickly walked over with a pitcher of tea and refilled their glasses. He just as quickly returned to his position off to the side.

Lowe gazed about the mess hall eyeing his recruits and wondered how many would still be alive after a year in Korea. They were young and anxious to get in to the action, just as he was in '42. War was so deceiving, so misleading. He supposed that it always had been. Those that needed young men to fight made it so.

And with that thought, anguish suddenly engulfed him. Creeping up from his stomach to his throat, an empty feeling grabbed him, the first attack of homesickness since he had left home two weeks earlier. He sat there fighting, trying to resist, trying to push the monster back down where it belonged, but it overwhelmed his thoughts. His heart ached and the tears welled in his eyes. Standing, he walked over, took his hat from the rack and made his way out the door of the mess hall. Behind him the D.R.O. quickly policed up his tray and took it to the tray drop window.

Outside he started to walk, tears flowing down his cheeks. Knowing how awful he felt at that moment he knew it had to be twice as hard for Martha. He had walked this road ten years before and knew his heart would eventually accept the separation. It was just difficult in the beginning. He told himself not to think of Martha and the girls, to get them out of his mind and focus on his job. After three laps round the block he finally gained control of himself and slowly walked back to fetch his boys at the mess hall.

"Fall out! Smoke 'em if you got 'em," barked Lowe as he walked over to the shade of a large maple tree, took a pack of Camels from his shirt pocket and lit one up. He hadn't smoked since '45. He had promised himself that he would not smoke around Martha and Wanda Faye, and had quit when he returned to the states. Now that he was back in, it seemed like the thing to do.

Several of his men sat around on the ground or stood, smoking and talking. They had just finished their series of shots. Some sat with their white T-shirt sleeves rolled up, blood trickling down their arms. They were the ones who flinched when the needle went in the muscle. They sat rubbing their sore arms. The group was not scheduled to continue evaluations till zero-nine-hundred, another forty minutes.

"What's it like in combat, Sarge?" asked a young recruit who couldn't have been much more than eighteen. The rest of the men looked on anxiously awaiting his answer.

Lowe inhaled a long draw from the unfiltered Camel and exhaled, pondering the boy's question. He had faced the dragon and knew that words could never effectively describe the life and death struggle on a battlefield. Words always came up short, next to the real thing.

"Stand up Henderson and put out your smoke," said Lowe, his cigarette hanging out of his mouth. The young man stood and flipped off the ash on the tip of his cigarette, twisted the end and put the short smoke quickly back in the pack.

Before the recruit could look up, Lowe lunged forward and tackled him, slamming his body to the ground in the leaves under the tree. The rest of the men jumped up or flinched, backing off in shocked silence, horrified by the suddenness of the attack. With the wind knocked out of him, Henderson lay on his back, gasping for breath, his eyes wide with fear. Grabbing a large stone from the ground, Lowe lifted it above his head and with deadly force slammed it down toward Henderson's face, diverting it into the ground at the last second. The young recruit screamed out in terror.

Standing up, Lowe brushed the dirt and leaves off his fatigues and offered a hand to the trembling boy on the ground, lifting him to his feet. Turning to the men, he took the Camel cigarette from his mouth and blew smoke from his nose. They looked in amazement at the ashes still clinging to the end of his smoke.

Lowe looked them over for a second before he spoke. His cold intimidating stare kept their attention as they sat motionless.

"Combat means killing your fellow man. It means shooting, stabbing, choking, crushing or doing whatever it takes to kill him . . . before he kills you. And trust me, he will kill you if you don't kill him first. It means watching your buddies get their arms and legs blown off. It means listening to them scream as they die. It means picking up their body parts and putting them in a bag or crawling over them as you move on. There is nothing romantic about it. It's nothing like what you've seen in the movies."

Taking another puff off his cigarette, he flipped the ash to the ground and put it out with the sole of his boot. He field-stripped what was left, letting the wind spread the tobacco out in the grass, wadded up the paper and stuck it in his pocket.

Returning his attention to the boys he said, "You sat and watched me attack Henderson. Not a one of you reacted, or even made a sound in his defense."

Many of the young men hung their heads in shame, as Lowe let the moment sink in.

"By the time you complete your training, you won't sit by while someone attacks your buddy, but you still won't have that instant connection between knowing and reacting. If you survive your first combat experience, you'll understand. When Henderson here quits shaking, he can tell you what it felt like."

First Sergeant Drumwright stood at the orderly room window, listening to Lowe talk to his soldiers. The half-smile on his face was betrayed by the sadness in his eyes. He too, had faced the dragon and survived. He knew all too well what Lowe was talking about. In his hand were the orders that would send the young sergeant to Korea. He had hoped to keep him at Knox, safe and close to home, assisting with the reception recruits, protected from the reservist recall mess the brass had created, but it wasn't meant to be. In his twenty-five years of soldiering he had never heard or read anything in an Army manual, or ever expected to read anything that made reference to the military service being fair.

Turning he walked slowly across to his desk. His boots felt unusually heavy. This would be a tough one. Sending young men off to die was starting to get to him.

"It's time to retire, old man," he said to himself in a whisper and then shouted, *"Mitchell get in here!"*

★　　★　　★　　★

"Incoming!" shouted the sergeant, as he dove headfirst into the foxhole. The whistling of the dropping mortar round tightened to a near painful pitch, just before it impacted the ground and exploded, heaving mounds of earth skyward. The concussion from the explosion moved the air out from the center of impact with deadly force, only to be sucked back in to fill the void of the vacuum that was created. The air pressure moved painfully around and down into the foxholes of Delta Company. Even the bunny holes in the bottom of the trenches offered little protection. The soldier's inner ears ached as their eardrums vibrated with the moving air and intense noise. Chest muscles constricted tightly against lungs from the physical and mental stress of the battle. Soldiers sat in the bottom of their foxholes, hands pressed against their ears trying desperately to catch their breath, screaming silently for the onslaught to stop.

Helmeted heads would stick up and pop off as many rounds as possible until the mortar barrage forced them back down. *"Pop, pop, pop!"* The sound of a shrill *"Whissstle"* and quickly down to the bottom of the hole.

"Boom," and the dirt would rain down.

Up again, *"Pop, pop, pop, pling,"* as the metal clip pops out of a M1 Garand receiver. Back down into the hole to feed another clip of .30-06 caliber ammo into the weapon, and come up shooting. There was no rhythm or pattern to combat, just general mayhem. Hugging the bottom of the foxhole kept you from getting blown apart, unless your number was up and the hole took a direct hit. In any event, just being in the vicinity where mortar rounds impacted the earth blurred the vision and set the ears to ringing.

After fifteen minutes of the barrage, a twenty second period of silence was shattered by the sounds of bugles, blowing whistles and the screaming of the human sea of a thousand Chinese regulars, as they charged up the north side of the slope toward the American defensive perimeter. They kept charging, climbing over piles of their dead comrades, trying to get to the American lines. It was the third such attack that evening and each time there were twenty seconds of silence, followed by a screaming charge into the American machine guns and rifles.

The number of Chinese casualties grew with each successive wave of the attack, but their numbers never seemed to diminish. The number of fighting American soldiers did, and when a combat unit's strength dropped below seventy percent, the unit became ineffective in battle. The number of D Company soldiers that were still fighting was tragically at the other end, at less than thirty percent of the unit's authorized strength. The company had taken heavy casualties in each wave of the attack. There was only one machine gun position still operating and with over two thirds of the men dead or wounded, there was a massacre in the making.

Two hours ago, Lieutenant Eugene Allen had become the new D Company Commander, by default. His rise to lead the company had been confusing and swift. He had arrived in country yesterday. On his arrival he was immediately driven to the front and designated the Second Platoon Leader.

Fresh out of Officers Candidate School he jumped headlong into his duties with the intention of making his mark. The months of leadership training poorly prepared him for the intense chaos of combat. The sights and sounds overwhelmed his senses. He was fully aware of his confusion and pushed back the fear that pressed to overwhelm his consciousness. At times he felt as if he were under a very heavy blanket, accompanied by a strangling feeling that would suffocate and leave him fighting for self-control. With each successive wave of attack, his feeling of helplessness grew stronger along with the suffocating strangulation associated with fear. He needed to feel order, but all those months of training and discipline did little to teach him to restore order in his mind.

Allen had radioed for reinforcements on his PRC-6 two hours ago, just after the first wave of attack, just after the death of his commander, just after he had assumed command of the company.

The Artillery is known for eating its children. His crusty Battalion Commander, Lieutenant Colonel Billy Ahern was a legend for such. He had politely informed the young Lieutenant in so many words that everyone was being hit hard and to do what he could to hold the position. Unsure that his Battalion Commander understood the helplessness of his situation, he repeated his request. As Lieutenant Colonel Ahern exploded into a tirade of abusive adjectives, the line went dead. Standing next to his jeep the Lieutenant Colonel slammed down the receiver on his AN/GR-9, but not before making a mental note of the belligerent Lieutenant's name. He then went back to the business of saving his command center.

At the other end of the line the Lieutenant was ready to push the panic button when suddenly the need was no longer there. The radio and command bunker had taken direct artillery hit. It happened that quickly. His second day in country, a few hours into combat, just hours into his first command, Lieutenant Eugene Allen, Commander of D Company, no longer existed. His life and bright military career ended on the Korean hilltop.

For those left behind the chaos continued. With the officers and nearly all of the sergeants dead no one knew who was in charge, nor really had time to figure it out as the attack continued. A total collapse of the position was inevitable and the remaining soldiers kept fighting because there was nothing else to do.

Sergeant Howard Lowe peered over the earthen mound of his fighting position, firing his M1 Garand rifle indiscriminately into the charging horde. His legs and hip were pinned against the right side of the foxhole by the body of a D Company soldier. The soldier had tumbled down into the hole with a fatal chest wound just after the latest attack had started. With night flares above, Lowe could see the bubbling red blood pouring from the wounded soldier's chest with each successive breath. He instinctively knew there was nothing he could do except keep firing at the charging enemy and hope he didn't end up the same way.

Battle hardened once again from three months of combat, Lowe had thought little about who the dead soldier might be. His only focus was that of surviving the deadly chaos that surrounded him. Killing the enemy accomplished that, and kill them he did.

The semi-automatic fire from his rifle paused as he grabbed at his ammo pouch to reload, nothing! He quickly slapped his ammo pouches one by one in desperation. Nothing! Nothing! Nothing! The realization that he was out of ammo with a thousand charging Chinese running up the hill, hell bent on killing him, hit his gut hard. But he checked his panic and reacted the only way possible.

Time and movement seemed to slow down as he set the weapon aside, twisted to his left and squatted in the foxhole, bringing the dead soldier's body across his knees. Frantically he rifled through the man's ammo pouches, taking loaded clips and placing them on the foxhole ledge. Grabbing the man's M1 Carbine from the bottom of the hole, he fired off four rounds, dropped the clip and rammed a full fifteen round clip into the weapon.

As he pulled back the bolt with his right index finger to chamber a new round from the new clip, he half heard, half sensed a soft thump on the sandbag above his head. Looking up he caught a glimpse of a wooden hand grenade, as it hovered for a split second and gently tumbled down the far side of the foxhole. With reflexes honed by weeks of combat, but fatigued from the hours of fighting, he reached up to catch the grenade in midair. He only had a few seconds, if he was lucky, to catch and toss it back out of the hole before the charge exploded. He grabbed at it, and missed.

In the split second after the charge in the grenade exploded, several deadly forces interacted instantly within the tight confines of the hole. The concussion was as deafening as the bright flash was blinding.

Deadly air pressure and shrapnel blew in all directions. Lowe's steel helmet flew up and out of the hole, snapping the helmet strap as it left his head and fracturing his lower jaw. The dead body that had rested across his legs was slammed into his chest and face, knocking out his front upper teeth and fracturing his nose. The concussion forced deadly air pressure down the right ear canal bursting his eardrum.

The physical impact on his body was devastating. The mental impact was numbing and fortunately for Lowe his brain shifted into overdrive. The human brain is a complex organ made up of millions of cells. It can not only store and recall, it can also repress events which overload and break down the body's systems. Lowe's brain instantly triggered a mechanism for dealing with his catastrophic pain, simply by shutting itself down. Howard Lowe saw the grenade flash, felt a numb sting of pain and was engulfed in total blackness.

The last wave of Chinese soldiers came over the hill, through the American line shouting, screaming and killing. Their intent was to take no prisoners. Their young leader had insinuated as much with his inspiring speech. They were to overrun the American line and continue on over the hill to the company headquarters and supply lines below. To accomplish that they had to kill the Americans as they went. They couldn't leave anyone at their backs.

Their numbers were overwhelming for those defenders still alive. Some of the Americans fought on bravely, taking several of the enemy with them before they were killed. Others, realizing the futility of the situation dropped their weapons, raised their hands in surrender, only to be shot to death in their foxholes. The wave of death continued over the hill and down in the valley on the other side.

When the senior Chinese Army officer arrived at the top of the hill, the slaughter was over. With jaw clinched, he walked about the American position with the officer who was in charge of the attack, surveying the carnage. He would lecture on some issue of combat, or point at the dead bodies and issue a loud reprimand.

When his tour of the battlefield was complete, it became clear that despite his previous orders, he had no prisoners to interrogate. Gazing about at the slaughter, he lost all self-control and angrily threw himself into a frenzied fit, arms flailing about, screaming a torrent mixture of obscenities and threats, even beating one of the young Chinese officers with a long bamboo stick he carried. The officer stood subserviently absorbing the tongue lashing and beating, while his men kept their focus and attention on searching the dead American bodies, feeling lucky that they were not the object of the beating.

Fifty feet down the line, a pale bloody face rose from a foxhole as an American GI attempted to climb out of his fighting position. A streak of blood ran down his jaw line from the right ear. His right hand and forearm were a bloody mess of skin and muscle, shredded from a grenade blast. The futile attempts to extract himself from the foxhole caught the nearest Chinese soldier off guard. Startled, the Chinaman began yelling, hopping up and down around the foxhole. His excitement quickly caught the attention of his fellow soldiers. The wounded American soldier remained indifferent to the bouncing Chinaman. His blank stare was unfocused as he struggled to pull himself out of the foxhole, with his one good arm. Reacting to the taunts of his fellow soldiers, the Chinese soldier stuck his bayonet into the American's upper chest. The long knife passed through the left shoulder and exited out the back, slamming the soldier up against the wall of the foxhole.

The taunts and laughter grew louder from the surrounding soldiers, until the soldier assumed a forceful thrust position and prepared to run the American through the center of his chest with the bayonet. He turned and smiled at his cheering comrades for only a brief second. When he turned to the foxhole and drew back his bayonet a shot rang out and the back of his head exploded in a fine red mist. His body went limp and tumbled into the foxhole.

Nearby the senior Chinese officer shouted at frightened soldiers, while he slowly swung his pistol around toward them. After several seconds of silence, he was confident there would be no challenges and holstered his pistol. Walking briskly over to the foxhole he reached down, grabbed at the unconscious American, attempting to pull him out. The American, now wedged in the hole by two dead bodies, wouldn't budge. The junior officer ran over to assist and in a short time the American was stretched out on the ground next to the foxhole. A series of loud barking orders and a swat across the back sent the young officer dashing down the hill and within minutes he returned with two stretcher-bearers and a medical assistant, who immediately started treating the American's wounds.

Turning to the winded officer the senior Chinese officer patted him on the back and said, "Now, Comrade Sun! You have learned important lesson, have you not? Large body count commendable, but a prisoner," and looking down at the wounded American soldier and back up at the young man, he smiled for the first time, "especially, American prisoner counts in war of propaganda."

Clouds, maybe? His eyes wouldn't focus. Images would clear and then become fuzzy. There were the clouds again. He was definitely floating in the clouds. There were sounds. He could hear a muted squeaking noise coming from his right. He slowly rolled his head over to the right and could see the spokes of a wheel squeaking and grinding as they passed by his face. He rolled his head to the left and an identical wheel was rolling along, getting louder as his head rolled over. Staring hypnotically at the spokes as they spun, he lay there trying to absorb the meaning of floating in the clouds and the slowly spinning wheels. It was all very surreal, the clouds, the wheels and the noise. He felt he was in a dream, witnessing it from another place.

The cart stopped and his dreamlike state was interrupted by sounds from a different direction. He heard yelling and screaming. A word here and there he felt he knew, but in a language he couldn't understand. He rolled his head to the left and focused his eyes on a small group of soldiers, Chinese soldiers, being reprimanded and beaten by a Chinese officer. Next to them in a ditch, a small anti-aircraft cannon lay upside down, its double barrels submerged in mud and water. The officer beat and kicked the soldiers unmercifully as they attempted to drag the weapon out of the ditch. Despite his continual interference they managed to drag it out, turn it upon its wheels and continue down the road.

"You disapprove of his methods?"

Lowe rolled his head back to the other side of the cart and stared into the face of a Chinese officer. Too weak to speak he mouthed a couple of painful words that were best left unsaid, but his facial expression got his point across.

"Sergeant Lowe! You know nothing of Asian culture. The end justify means. The weapon more important than soldiers. Soldiers can be replaced. Weapon cannot. Sometime it become necessary to do what takes to achieve end. If beating soldiers save weapon, officer achieve end. If shooting soldier help rest to understand, then soldier must be shot. How else we maintain culture that survive many thousand year. You travel ten thousand-mile, fight for people you no understand, or care for, because imperialist leaders say it must be so. They are mere lackeys for Wall Street. They care nothing about you and you friends dead on hill. They care about money, and war is money. You kill thousands women and children, who don't want you in country. And now look at you. Shot up, torn in pieces. You barely able to hold eyes open. Had I not intervened, you stabbed dead in foxhole by soldier, like rest of comrades."

Walking beside the cart the officer sidestepped a large mud hole. The cart dipped down and bumped up with a jolt.

"You tore up pretty bad, I think," he continued. "Medic sewed you together for trip north. Give praise to you god, Sergeant Lowe. If comrade had not been in the fighting position with you to catch grenade blast, we also find you dead in bottom of hole."

Lowe stared glassy eyed at the Chinese soldier, comprehending, but confused as he had very little memory of the day's events.

The more serious wounds on his legs were open to the air and covered with small squirming maggots. As gross as it may have appeared, the maggots served a purpose, eating bacteria and cleansing the wound. Field expedient and effective.

"Is that what America expect of you? Kill innocent women, children? You have lot to learn about Korea and China. Indeed, you have lot to learn about America. You lucky to have me for comrade, Sergeant Lowe. I save you from assassin bayonet and when you recover from wounds, I teach you truth about war mongering Wall Street dogs and hardworking, dedicated peoples of Korea and China. But first, let us ponder what we must write to wife."

Howard rolled his head over and stared up at Captain Lin.

"Yes, you married, as letter in pocket indicate." Lin took Martha's letter from his shirt pocket and waved it about. "Oh, you will get letter back in time. I am married also and know letter important. Martha and two daughters will want to know you safe. You can't expect me to do such important thing for you. It must come from you, but I will help."

"We start with 'Dear Martha' or you prefer 'Sweetheart' or 'Darling', as her letter to you. You not sure? Then we say 'Darling' as I see she special."

"Darling, I have been bad wounded in big battle. Chinese officer save my life and take good care me. I be in prisoner camp for while where People's Republic of China treat injuries. Please not to worry."

Lin continued to walk beside the cart dodging mud holes and loudly composing the letter to Martha. Howard stared at the Chinaman and tried to stay focused on what was being said.

"Please not to worry, I treated fairly. I now know I should not fight in country who not want me. It is mistake for America to stay. The peoples of Korea not need us. I fear President Truman being misguided by capitalist and imperialist, who desire money from war. I am sorry I have hurt peoples of Korea and have apologized to them. I will be home soon. Love, Howard."

"What do you think? I write for you. You sign and I mail to Martha. She anxious to hear from you after War Department report you missing. You sign letter and I see that you get good care. Better than other Americans who do not cooperate. Better food. Better place to live. No lice, no rats to bite you. I take good care of you."

Howard looked up at Lin. Through his swollen jaw and clinched teeth, he called on enough strength to speak the few words he felt he had to speak, and said, "You go to hell!"

"Oh, Sergeant Lowe! I not one who go to hell. You one who go to live in hell!" Looking down at Lowe he added, "And you see hell, very soon now."

CHAPTER 8

▼

Julius Alfred was a dedicated Western Union employee. A company man, Western Union's President, W.P. Marshall, would be proud of. He had devoted thirty-six years of his life to Western Union's telegraph office in Columbia, Kentucky. He could retire with full benefits, but had no intentions of doing so anytime soon. He was dressed in a white, long sleeve shirt, and a smart yellow bowtie. In the pocket of his shirt was a Western Union penholder containing a red, blue and black pen. There were also two yellow, wooden number two pencils. He liked to be prepared.

The pleated black wool pants were cuffed. His hair had a neat part down the left side and was neatly trimmed. He had a reputation for looking and dressing smart. Since he represented Western Union, he felt he had a duty to present himself well in the eyes of the public. It was quite a contrast to the old days when he wore the garters on the sleeves and the bank teller clerk hat with the open top. That was then. This was 1952, and times had changed.

On the other hand, Johnny Roberts, the young telegraph operator dressed like any young nineteen-year-old with white socks and black loafers. His tie was always loose and his sleeves rolled up. His hair was a little long and slicked back, but he did keep it neat. He was the spitting image of Julius when he started with the company. Oh, the clothes where different, but the spirit was the same and that's why Julius tolerated the touch of sloppiness.

Fresh out of Adair County High School, he was bright, innovative and took a lot of initiative in the daily operations of the small office. A local boy, Julius had interviewed and hired him on the spot the day after he graduated from high school. He had known both the boy's parents and grandparents. Good people, the Roberts and Morris families. Someday, if Johnny worked hard, he might take his rightful place as office manager. But not today.

As Julius continued his silent debate over contentment and job security, the sleeping telegraph machine woke up and began chattering. Johnny waited tentatively as the machine printed out its message, took the completed telegram in hand and read. He handed the telegram to Julius, sniffed a couple of times and walked over to get his cap from the coat rack. Julius read in stunned silence.

"Gees Louise, Mr. Alfred, I had Mrs. Lowe for a teacher up through the eighth grade. I don't know if I've got what it takes to do this to her."

Looking up from the telegram, Julius responded, "Hang your cap back up, son. I'll deliver this one myself. I've known Howard and Martha since they were kids in my Sunday school class. She's going to take this hard."

Glancing down at his Timex, Julius figured Martha would be home from the Tabor schoolhouse by now, and well into the evening chores. Gadberry was only fifteen minutes from town and Henry Cook's place was on the way. Taking his brown felt hat and jacket from the coat rack he started for the door.

"Ring up Brother Cook and tell him what's going on. He's their minister and will want to be with me when I break the news to Mrs. Lowe. Tell him to be waiting at the end of his lane."

Johnny obediently picked up the telephone and rang up the operator. Outside it was one of those early October, Indian Summer days that encouraged young boys to skip school and go fishing in Russell Creek. The town square was as busy as one would expect for a Tuesday in October. Julius eyed the two trucks parked in front of the Bank of Columbia. Most likely farmers signing for a short-term note to hold them over till their tobacco sold. There were other cars and trucks parked here and there around the square, people in town to shop, others visiting the County Court House in the middle of the square. Julius walked halfway around and down Greensburg Street where his car, a black 1949 Ford Coupe was parked next to the County Jail House. As he approached his car, he was hailed from across the street.

"Afternoon, Julius!"

Turning about he shouted, *"Mayor Olsen, really good to see ya."* Julius had responded as cheerfully as he could. *"How are Mrs. Olsen and the children?"*

The Mayor walked across the street toward Julius, hand stuck out to shake, but pulled up short. "There must be a bad telegraph, because bad news is written all over your face, Julius. Is there anything I can help you with?"

"I'll be picking up Brother Cook on the way out to Gadberry, Mayor. He's the kind of help I need for this one," patting the breast pocket of his coat. "Thanks for asking though. I'm afraid it's bad news from the war. I've got to tell the family before I can publicly discuss it, so I need to rush along. Bad news can't wait you know."

"Come now Julius, a telegraph with bad news from the war! Picking up Brother Cook, heading to Gadberry to tell the family! I don't have to use much brain power to figure your visit will be to the Tabor schoolmarm, Mrs. Martha Lowe." Julius turned and continued to walk to his car.

"And, I would expect you not to indulge any of that information until you hear it from someone else this evening, Mayor," Julius said over his shoulder.

"Why, Julius! You cut me to the quick."

Julius climbed into his car, started the engine and drove off. The Mayor was trustworthy or he wouldn't have shared any of the information with him, but word traveled fast and Martha needed to hear the news first before word got around town. Recipient first, was company policy and the decent thing to do. Martha would have to be told as soon as possible.

Driving back toward the Courthouse, Julius slowed to downshift the Ford, yielding to the circling traffic. Seeing three of the more eminent town loafers seated next to the Courthouse door, he raised two fingers of his left hand from their grip on top of the steering wheel.

A cone shaped pile of reddish-white cedar shavings lay at each man's feet as their Buck and Old Henry knives whittled a cedar stick into something unidentifiable and useless. The County Sheriff provided the cedar whittling sticks for the men for reasons no one could derive. The Mayor himself had been known at times to sit with the men, pulling from his pocket a stag handled XX, Case knife to whittle his cedar stick. Lots of good information, gossip if you will, made its rounds over the cedar shavings.

Hearing the approaching car downshift, the three men looked up from their shavings and stared at the black Ford. Julius knew the game was at hand, as he held the clutch in with his left foot, his two fingers frozen motionless above the steering wheel, while his right hand nervously gripped the gear shift stick, waiting to shove it up into second gear, once the men acknowledged his wave. The Ford coasted slowly on to the square as the momentary standoff continued. Finally, the loafers blinked. All three shot up their hands, simultaneously, in acknowledgment to his wave. Julius smiled and nodded his head in hollow victory. They had waved, but only after stalling long enough to slow him down and force a downshift to keep the car from stalling. One of these days they would cause him to misread his timing and the engine would stall. That would make their day, and give them something to crow about, and crow they would, if that day ever came.

If they had known the seriousness of his mission, they would have solemnly waved and let him proceed. The three of them had lost family and friends in the first two World Wars and old man Kent, had himself fought in the muddy fields in France. Of course, they had no way of knowing, so they played their little game.

Julius let out the clutch and the Ford lunged forward, around to the other side of the Courthouse where he took an immediate right turn on to Jamestown Street. Down the hill he went, past the pool hall and the Dairy Whip, back up the hill again, past the old Trabue House on the left. As the Ford crested the hill and rounded the curve it drove past Campbell's Feed Store and slowed, pulling off onto the gravel shoulder. A few feet in front of the car at the corner of a gravel road stood Henry Wesley Cook, with determined eyes and a compassionate expression. A worn King James Bible in hand, the minister had studied the Word at Johnson Bible College, down below Knoxville. Julius immediately felt reassured in his decision to invite the young minister to call on Mrs. Lowe.

Brother Cook stepped over to the car and got in. The two men rode quietly as the Ford slowly pulled out on to the road and continued toward Gadberry. After a short five miles they turned left on the Long Cemetery Road and carefully maneuvered around potholes, making their way slowly down the gravel road. The mile and half lane was inhabited by five farms, five families scratching out a living on the rocky central Kentucky land. The gently rolling fields were now brown. In the distance a field of corn stood half harvested, the neatly clipped rows of stalk stubs in direct contrast to the tall, unpicked rows of standing corn. Fencerows, some clean, some overgrown, broke the fields up into brown squares. The heavily timbered woods in the background offered a patchwork of oranges, yellows and reds to complete the earthen quilt. Mother Nature's bed was topped with distant pillows of white clouds and a bright blue, autumn sky. The color patterns on the fields, woods and sky changed from farm to farm, just like walking through the quilt displays at the County Fair. The farms were all of Blue-Ribbon quality.

Bordering on the left of the second sharp bend in the lane was a barnyard full of Red Poll milk cows lined up at the barn door, udders bulging with milk. Several young calves fed from teats, periodically butting their heads into the bottom of their mother's udders in an attempt to gain an advantage over the milk inside.

Other more mature calves pranced about the yard, hopping and kicking their legs high behind them, as if dancing to some silent happy melody.

The milk barn sat on a slope in the lot. You could walk into the upper part of the barn, making for easy storage of the baled hay. The milk cows could easily walk into the lower part, where the milking parlor was. The barn was nothing fancy, your basic oak siding, running vertical up the sides, with the half to one inch crack between the boards. It sat on a cinder block foundation that was partly exposed by the slope of the hill. The wood siding had been painted black sometime ago, giving it a dull blackish-gray tint. The whole structure was covered with a corrugated tin roof, freshly painted silver gray to match the corncrib, stock barn and equipment shed, all located in the barn lot.

Next to the lot was an orchard with several different fruit trees and a couple of mature Chinese chestnut trees. The brooder house, smokehouse and woodshed were located outside the barn lot, easily accessible to the woman of the house. They were all painted white to match the weatherboard home.

In the midst of this barnyard opera, the main character entered stage right. Dressed in gum boots, overalls, flannel shirt and cap, Jordan Long appeared carrying two shiny milk buckets. As he approached the gate, he recognized the inhabitants of the black Ford and threw up a concerned hand. Julius and Brother Cook returned the wave as they drove on down the gravel road. The farmer turned and walked briskly back up to the house. In less than a minute he was back outside, going through the gate toward the cows and the milking barn, followed by two young girls, who skipped and hop scotched in and about the cow piles that littered the lot. One of the girls carried a big Tomcat dressed uncomfortably in doll's clothing. The cat harmlessly struggled to ease the death grip the little girl had on it, knowing that squirts of fresh milk from the cow's teats would be a reward for his humiliation.

The milk cows gathered around the farmer as he approached the barn, quietly mooing, flipping their heads about. Happy to see him, they were grateful that their evening load of milk would soon be drained.

About a mile still further down the lane sat a mailbox with "HOWARD LOWE" painted on its side. The mailbox stood on the left side of the road, its base surrounded by tall, Black-Eyed Susan wildflowers. The road continued on up the hill where a barn stood and still further to the Long Cemetery. Across the road from the mailbox was a white weatherboard home sitting on a small hill, facing the cemetery. A porch swing hung on a large porch that dominated the front of the story and half country home. To the right and below the home, a solitary figure worked vigorously with a garden hoe, grubbing up the summer garden. Between the garden and the house two small children played in the dirt.

Martha Lowe was dressed in a white ankle length, heavy cotton skirt that continued to be useful because of the many patches that held it together. Under the rim of the skirt could be seen the cuffs of a pair of blue jeans, resting on a pair of brown brogan boots. She wore a large, long sleeve, plaid shirt that no doubt belonged to her husband. Her long, brown hair was tied up in a bun and hidden under a large off-white bonnet, which shaded her tan face and soft brown eyes. The leather gloves on her hands and the work clothes failed to conceal the natural beauty that lay beneath. Standing up and resting her hands on the end of the hoe handle she watched the dust covered Ford carefully turn and pull up into her yard, stopping in front of the stone steps below the porch. As Brother Cook climbed from the car, Bible in hand, she smiled and waved in acknowledgment. When Julius Alfred appeared from the driver's side, her jaw tightened and the smile faded. The two somber men walked to the garden without speaking and met her as she made her way to the end of the row.

Martha glanced to her right at Wanda Fay and Amy Sue playing in the dirt, her grip on the handle of the hoe tightened as she nodded and spoke to the men, "Brother Henry, Mr. Alfred, I was just in need of a break from my grubbing. Let us cross the road and rest in the shade of the trees. The spring will be running cool on a hot day like today. Would you accompany me down to the spring?"

Smiling, Brother Cook responded, "Martha, there is nothing I would like better than a long cool draw of fresh water from your spring." Turning toward the road he offered his arm for support, so Martha set the hoe aside and hooked her arm around his. Julius followed as they walked quietly down the hill, across the gravel lane and down a short path to the shade of the woods and the spring, out of earshot of the children.

"Gentlemen, God has blessed our boiling spring with a freshness that is hard to find in an area of so much hard water. Howard . . ." Martha's voice wavered, but quickly found strength on her minister's arm, "my Howard says his grandfather settled here after the Civil War and built his home on that little hill so he could be close to this spring. He lived, coon hunted and worked this farm into his late eighties." Looking toward Julius, Martha said, "Mr. Alfred, I don't believe I have ever had the pleasure of seeing you outside of church. You have much to learn from Brother Henry's ability to deal out bad news with a comforting smile."

Julius, humbled by the woman's strength was unable to respond, so he simply kept quiet.

The small group reached the spring and Brother Cook, laying his Bible aside on the grass, took the ladle from a tree limb, filled and rinsed out two one-pint Ball jars that lay in the grass beside the spring. Filling the jars, he handed one to Martha, the other to Julius and scooped up a ladle full of the water for himself. The spring water boiled up from the ground under the springhouse and flowed down a small brook that disappeared into the woods. Even the air around the spring was cool. They all drank quietly. The metal ladle felt cool against Julius' lips the water cold as promised as it slid down his throat. He needed to feel refreshed, clear headed for what was to come next.

Turning to Martha, Brother Cook took her hand in his and said, "Martha, I'm afraid we have some very bad news. It's Howard."

The Ball jar dropped from Martha's hand, bounced and tumbled down into the spring. Brother Cook hesitated, searching for words. It was his job to find words at a time like this, but it never came easy, especially when the words were to comfort someone he felt very close to. Reaching out he took her other hand and could feel the tension building up in her body. Her soft brown eyes were demanding, but at the same time laced with fear.

Julius slipped the telegram out of his coat pocket and began to read as Martha continued to face Brother Cook:

P B 45 GOVERNMENT WASHINGTON DC OCTOBER 10, 1952 4:35 PM
MRS MARTHA LOWE
LONG CEMETERY RD GADBERRY KY

THE SECRETARY OF THE ARMY HAS ASKED ME TO EXPRESS HIS DEEP REGRETS THAT YOUR HUSBAND SERGEANT HOWARD LOWE HAS BEEN MISSING IN ACTION IN KOREA SINCE 25 SEPTEMBER 1952 UPON RECEIPT OF FURTHER INFORMATION IN THIS OFFICE YOU WILL BE ADVISED IMMEDIATELY CONFIRMING LETTER FOLLOWS

WILLIAM E BERGIN MAJ. GENERAL USA
ACTING THE ADJUTANT GENERAL OF
THE ARMY

Julius' voice trailed off as Martha, visibly shaking now, turned to him and said, "What does this mean, Julius? Is my Howard alive, or is he dead?"

"We can't be sure, Martha. All the Army can confirm at this moment is that Howard is missing."

Turning to Brother Cook and tightening her grip on his hands Martha whispered, "My God, Henry, is there a chance Howard is still alive?" Having said that her legs buckled and she went down to her knees on the soft grass. Brother Cook, kneeling with her, maintained a firm hold on both her hands.

Sobbing softly, she whispered, "I thought you had come to tell me he was dead. Oh, Howard! My dear sweet Howard may still be alive." Overwhelmed, she collapsed into Brother Cook's arms and he laid her gently on the soft grass, in the shade of the trees, next to Grandpa Lowe's cool spring.

Martha was sitting up with Brother Cook, Julius and her two daughters, when May Long and Mrs. Katherine came driving down the road in Jordan's old flatbed truck. She pulled up next to Julius' car and parked. May called Mrs. Katherine, right after Jordan had bounced back through the door and informed her that Mr. Alfred, from the Western Union and Brother Cook had driven down the road. A combination that could only mean something had happened to Howard in Korea.

May sent Elizabeth and Rebecca out to stay with their dad and tried to ring up Mrs. Katherine. Since the whole neighborhood was on a single party line, she very politely, but firmly asked Flo Owens and the forever nosy, Annetta Gardner, to relinquish the line so she could make an important call. They did, she did and as she hurried off to fetch up Mrs. Katherine, she bristled, knowing that Annetta had probably listened in on the call and the whole Gadberry community would quickly know that something was up with the Lowe's.

When Martha had fainted, the girls had come running to aid their mother. Now that Mrs. Katherine was there, the crisis was over in their minds. The girls walked back up to their earth works in the garden, while Mrs. Katherine kneeled next to Martha.

"Child, I want you to drink some water and then we're going to walk up to the house. It's time to call it a day."

"I'm fine now, Mrs. Katherine," and Martha proved it by standing up. Unsteady at first, she braced herself by putting a hand on May's shoulder. As she stood May took one arm, while Mrs. Katherine held the other. Together they led her up the hill to the shade of the porch, where she sat down on the swing, with

Mrs. Katherine at her side. May brought two thatched shaker chairs out from the house for the men, and then went straight to the kitchen to start preparing supper.

Looking at Julius, Martha said, "You have proved yourself to be a kind and compassionate man by coming out to deliver the telegram to me personally, Julius. I know the young Roberts boy usually delivers telegrams, and I appreciate your personal attention."

Speechless, Julius humbly bowed his head in recognition of her kind words. Turning to Brother Cook she continued, "Henry, everyone would expect your visit under these circumstances, but I still deeply appreciate your being with me through this."

Pausing for a moment to glance down the hill at the girls still playing at the edge of the garden, her eyes moistened. She watched the girls, but continued talking, "Julius, when I saw you get out of the car, I convinced myself that Howard had been killed in the war, a fear that I live with daily. I'm afraid that comprehending the good news that he was just missing and may still be alive was a bit overwhelming for me."

Although she continued to stare at the girls, only she could see the illusion of Howard working diligently in the garden behind them. The image in her mind was so distinct and clear a warm feeling swept over her body.

"Yes, gentleman, my Howard is very much alive."

"And the Lord will carry him through this misfortune, Martha."

Warmly smiling, Martha stood and both men quickly rose from their chairs. "He will indeed, Henry. Gentlemen, you must stay for supper. We would be honored by your presence."

Brother Cook said softly, "Gracie would be very disappointed if I didn't eat the supper she has prepared for me at home."

"The same here Mrs. Lowe, but thanks for asking," added Julius.

Martha walked with Brother Cook and Julius to the porch steps and taking their hands said, "Bless you. God bless you both. My Howard is still alive. I feel it deep in my soul. We must pray for his safety and quick return," and bowing their heads, Brother Cook, the Bible clutched to his chest and still holding Martha's hand, did just that.

Martha sat in one of the thatched chairs at the kitchen table, her sewing box open before her, patching a fresh tear in Amy Sue's dress. An oil lamp burned in the middle of the table providing enough light to sufficiently light the kitchen. Wanda Faye sat at the table reading her homework assignment. The fifth grade could be very demanding when your mom was also your teacher. On the countertop sat a galvanized tub, half full of warm water and half full of Amy Sue. Mrs. Katherine stood at the tub rubbing here, scrubbing there, trying to remove an afternoon's worth of dirt from Amy Sue's skin. The child had tolerated the scrubbing, but was quickly becoming impatient. Mrs. Katherine had her stand up in the tub and started rinsing the soap off with clean, warm water.

Without loosening her grip, or taking her eyes off the fidgeting child, Mrs. Katherine said, "I remember when my Monty was off to the The Great War. There wasn't a day went by that I didn't have thoughts he would not be coming back. Some days I would let it cover me like a dark cloud. President Wilson promised he would keep our boys out of that war because it had nothing to do with us. He promised and then turned right around and broke his promise. I was angry with the President and the Draft Board, but mostly at Monty for going. Oh, I kept up the good image of a woman waiting for her man to come home from war, but underneath I was brooding and miserable. I kept myself fairly miserable until the day I realized that Monty was really the one who had reason to be miserable. Over there living in God only knows what kind of conditions, people getting killed every day, watching his buddies getting blown up all around him. He never talked much about the death in his letters. I guess he wanted to spare me the worry, but I read the newspapers. I knew what was happening over there. Monty liked to say 'being artillery don't protect you from the enemy artillery!'"

Wrapping a towel around the child's shoulders, grabbing her by the arms and digging both index fingers into her ribs, Mrs. Katherine lifted a giggling Amy Sue out of the water and carried her, wiggling, over to a chair at the table. The drying process was the most fun, especially when it came time to towel off her hair. Amy Sue wiggled about on Mrs. Katherine's lap singing a warbled version of *"Jesus Loves Me"* as the towel vigorously rubbed her head, drying her blond hair.

"I suppose it's the same for those of us who stay behind," Martha said. "I've blamed Truman a hundred times for taking Howard away from me and the girls. I understand why we have to fight the communist, I just wish my Howard didn't have to be the one to do it. He fought the Nazis and deserves to be here with me and the girls, working his farm."

Mrs. Katherine nodded her head in agreement. "It's foolishness for our boys to have to run off and fight a war in some foreign country every twenty or so years. In 1917, and again in the 1940's, I suspect we will have to do it a couple of more times before the turn of the century. I saw the eighteen hundred's roll over to the nineteen hundred's. Thank God I won't have to live long enough to see it roll over to the twenty hun . . . dred's? Land sakes child! What on earth do you think they'll be a calling it after nineteen ninety-nine?"

Smiling, Martha said, "I'll need you here for some time yet to come, Mrs. Katherine, so don't go making plans to leave me anytime soon. Uncle Monty can wait a little longer for you to join him." To which Mrs. Katherine smiled a big smile.

"I remember when Daddy took Uncle Monty to the VA Hospital in Lexington. He seemed so tired and worn out all the time. I felt sorry for him, and you with the kids. Was he wounded in the War?"

"My Monty came back with nothing more than a scar from where a bullet hit his left leg. They just left the fool thing in there. It would move around like a jellybean. He was young and strong, ready to take on the world. Later the seizures came and slowly took more and more control of his life. I remember the evening he failed to come home from stripping tobacco at Fred McAlister's place. I called Fred and he said Monty had left before dark. It didn't take the men long to find him a lying over in the seat of his car, a bump on his forehead. He had driven through the curve there in Fred's lane, straight into a big white oak tree. Monty felt real bad about messing up Fred's oak tree, but fortunately he never was one to drive too fast. Neither he, nor Fred's tree were hurt too bad. That was the last time he drove a car and he so loved driving his cars." Mrs. Katherine stared into space as if catching long lost memories of Monty and holding on to them for a precious few moments.

"Poor Monty, he never knew when the fits would come over him. The VA doctor said it was shell shock from the endless artillery rounds he fired and the enemy's artillery rounds landing all around him. His wounds didn't come from the fighting, he just carried them home hidden inside, to come out later and cripple him up. He never was the same after he stopped driving. He was in and out of the hospital in Lexington, and he finally got the cancer and died in December of '42. Your daddy and I sat up with him that night. He went peacefully and he didn't die alone. My, but I do look forward to being with that man again someday, God willing."

Martha knotted the last stitch, bit the thread off at the knot and put the needle back in the sewing box. Standing she said, "Come girls, it's time to say our prayers and get in bed." Amy Sue, half dressed in her tiny, white panties, broke away from Mrs. Katherine and ran for the stairs, followed by Wanda Faye. Martha got up, took Amy Sue's nightgown from a tickled Mrs. Katherine and followed the girls up the steep, narrow staircase to their upstairs bedroom.

Mrs. Katherine had pitched the bath water out the back door, tidied up the kitchen and retired. Martha sat at her desk staring at the eight by ten photograph of Howard in his army uniform, so handsome and brave looking. He was wearing the smile that had charmed her the first day she had started looking at him as more than just a neighborhood playmate. They were pals through childhood, but had drifted apart during their early high school days at Adair County High School. She couldn't remember at what point during their junior year she had set her hat for him, but it wasn't long after he had brought her hog, Thomasina, back home. After that they became inseparable. Her leaving to attend Campbellsville College, an hour drive from Columbia, was difficult on both of them. Howard proposed during the Christmas break of her freshman year. He worked his family farm and she worked at becoming a teacher. They were married the summer after she completed her teaching certificate and returned to Gadberry, just before he left for the Army.

Martha's brown eyes moistened as she stared at her husband's picture. Reaching into the desk drawer, she got out writing paper and pen, and began to write Howard his weekly letter. She didn't know if, or when he would be able to receive letters, but she would write it anyway, once a week with news from home, with unending love. It was her way of helping her man to hold on and survive the madness of the war raging on the Korean peninsula. Her letters were always neatly hand written. They always started out the same and ended the same. The fact that Howard was missing couldn't, and wouldn't change that. Some things would never change:

October 10, 1952

My Dearest Howard,

> *I am doing well. The girls are growing like weeds and miss their father very much. They ask daily about you and want to know when you are coming home. Wanda Faye got up in front of the class last Friday and gave a report on how the war was going. She was very brave about it and*

wants to do it every Friday as a Current Events report. Her report was well received by the rest of the class.

The children in class always mention you in the Morning Prayer and talk of the war every day. There has been great competition over who gets to lead the morning Pledge of Allegiance.

I nearly finished cleaning out the garden today. Silas and Carl came by Saturday and finished harvesting the corn. The rains have made it impossible to use the corn picker, so they picked the whole barn field by hand. It's now safely in the corn crib, less for you to do when you get home, my dear.

I don't know what I would have done without everyone's help with the crops. The whole community has pitched in to help. The hay is nearly all up and the tobacco is hanging in the barn waiting for a few cool, damp days, so it can be stripped.

I find it to be increasingly more difficult to see to everything as I move further along with our unborn child. I have been showing for about a month now, but have managed to hide it with clothing. Mrs. Katherine has been a tremendous help, coming down twice a week to wash clothes and prepare things in the kitchen. She turned to me from the stove last week and asked when the baby was due. I was dumbfounded for several seconds, but finally gained my senses. She believes it to be a boy. I sense that you may finally have a son to keep you company on the farm. At my checkup yesterday, Doc Slaton commented that it was acting more and more like a boy every time he sees me. It will not be much longer and we will know for sure. He has set the date for the end of March.

Just think Howard, a son! Everyone will look at him and say, "There goes young Howard Lowe, my but doesn't he look just like his father," or "Why look at that Lowe boy hit that ball and run, just like his dad did on the '40 Indian team that beat Campbellsville." A boy, Howard! Oh, how I wish you were here to share the excitement the girls and I feel.

Brother Cook and Julius Alfred came this evening with a telegram from the War Department informing me that you have gone missing. I feared the worst when they drove up and was overcome with joy when Julius read the telegram and I realized that you were still alive.

God has granted me the strength to carry on without you for a while and it's written in the Bible that He will only place on me that which I can bear. Believing that and knowing that I could not go on if you were permanently taken from me, gives me the divine belief that you are still alive. You are, I can feel it, but my heart does break knowing that you may be in great peril at the hands of the North Koreans.

I told the girls the news tonight after they went to bed, just before they said their prayers. Wanda Faye asked God to keep you in the palm of His hand and to smite the Koreans if they were mean to you. I don't believe they can truly understand at their age what you might be going though. They do know you are far away and they miss you.

I must go now darling. Know that I will hold you safely in my heart until you return. Sweet Dreams.

Martha

CHAPTER 9

▼

The prisoners were lined up along the outside wall of their barracks, seated with hands cupped, awaiting their daily ration of rice. Their clothes were tattered and torn, some wore boots, and some were barefoot. All were malnourished. The rice balls were bland and tasteless, but provided nourishment. An individual ration was small, never enough to satisfy the hunger pains the men felt. The server dropped the rice ball into cupped hands as he walked down the line of seated men. The men sat subserviently, until the last man was served.

Slowly, some of them stood and walked to their favorite eating spot. Three men sitting next to each other remained seated, the two on either side slowly ate their rice. The man in the middle sat indifferently with a wide-eyed stare. Finishing his rice the man on the right took a tin from his pocket, reached over, took the rice ball out of the cupped hands of the man in the middle and dropped it into the tin. He then very carefully picked each grain of rice out of the cupped hands and placed them in the tin also. The man sitting in the middle appeared not to notice as the thief placed the tin back into his pocket and stood, using his neighbor's shoulder to steady himself.

"How ba . . . ba . . . 'bout a hand, Bob," said Earl Davenport.

The standing man extended a hand down to the other outside man, who pulled himself up to a standing position. The middle man, without side support began to lean to his left, but was quickly steadied by Davenport.

"Oh, hey! Sorry, Jim. Let me help you up. Little help here, Earl."

Both men reached down and brought Jim to his feet. Two other men came over and walked with the group to the barracks door, one in front, and one behind.

At the steps the men stood and talked, intentionally blocking the guard's view as they walked up the steps and entered the old schoolhouse building.

Inside, a hallway went to the back of the building where a longer hall went right and left with doors to the individual rooms. There were ten all together, approximately twenty by thirty feet in size. At either end of the hall were side doors. On the west end of the schoolhouse there was a large library for the men. There were books, magazines and newspapers, all selected for their slant on communism. The men would attend indoctrination classes in the library, when bad weather kept them inside. In the middle of the building was a large latrine that no longer worked.

Earl Davenport and Bob Green carried the man down the hall, his feet dragging limp along the floor. They took a left, walked half way down and entered the third squad room, gently laying Jim Fort down on a bamboo mat on the floor.

"I think that will probably be the only ration we'll get from Jim. The dust does a good job of covering his complexion, but he'll be too stiff by tomorrow to fool the chinks. We'll bury him in the morning."

Davenport nodded and reached out to gently caress the man's hair. Placing his thumb and fingertip on Fort's eyelids, he pushed them closed and quietly said, "Thanks Jim. God bl . . . bless you."

Turning, the two men walked to the back of the squad room where a man lay on a thin bamboo mat, once used by children at the school. The man's complexion was pale yellow. His eyes appeared sunken, his cheekbones protruded under the flesh. His head turned to greet them as they approached and his lips moved to speak, but no sound came out. Green sat down on the floor next to him and pulled the tin can from his pocket. He sat it on a box next to a small tin pan of freshly boiled water. Green vigorously washed his hands in the pan. Letting them air dry for a few seconds, he dipped his fingers in the water once again and pinched off two or three gains of rice. Rolling them in his fingertips, he smashed the grains flat several times and placed them in the sick man's mouth. The man slowly chewed and struggled to swallow. The Chinese had a simple way of thinning the ranks of the prisoners at Camp Two. If a man was too ill to sit in the ration line, he was not fed. Green patiently and compassionately repeated the procedure of dipping his fingers in the warm water, smashing the rice and feeding the ill man, compliments of their deceased friend, Jim Fort.

Leaning against the back wall, Dan Welch watched expressionlessly as the soldier struggled to chew and swallow the rice. Welch had lost over fifty pounds since his capture a year ago. Since arriving at Camp Two he had avoided close contact with the other prisoners, preferring to do odd jobs around the camp, helping in a way that didn't involve friendships with the other men. When the camp transfer occurred, he was forced to leave behind several close friends in Garcia, Allen, Miller and some of the others. Although it had been several months, he had still not come to grips with losing his friend Leo Jawaski. His way of dealing with the loss was to push Jawaski out of his mind and avoid any close contact with other soldiers who would likely die.

Earl Davenport and Bob Green were good men. Like Welch, they worked hard at helping those who needed help. Davenport had taken a bullet in the lower leg, just before he was captured. Fortunately, he had enough excess fat and meat in his calf to allow the bullet to pass without hitting bone, tendon or artery. His medium height, coupled with his excess weight gave him the appearance of being as round as he was tall. But that was before he was captured. Now he was lucky to push a hundred and twenty pounds. His wild, blond hair and thick beard shielded a compassionate face.

Bob Green, on the other hand was a career man, once fit and powerful. His tight crew cut was replaced with long stringy black hair. He had lost a lot of muscle mass, but his body was still as fit as he could keep it under the circumstances. They could have passed for Laurel and Hardy prior to being captured. Now it was hard to tell them apart. Their bodies were wasting away as they struggled to keep themselves and their friends alive.

Green lifted the small tin of water to the man's lips periodically to wash down the rice and provide needed hydration. He spoke quietly, but assertively while feeding the sick man.

"You're not going to let those bastards kill you, Les. No, you're not. We're going to cheat them out of another day, and tomorrow we'll steal another day, and do you know why, Les? 'Cause you and me, buddy, we're going to paint Nor 'lans red when we get home." The man's face remained expressionless, but his eyes turned to meet Green's and smiled.

"Yeah! You and me kid. We're going to have the damn'st week that ever was," said Green with considerably more excitement. "We're going to start off at Arnaud's with two big plates piled high with crawfish. We're going to strip and eat those tails, and suck the juice out of their beady-eyed little heads. And all the time we'll be drinking big mugs of ice-cold beer. They'll just keep'em coming.

Then that pretty waitress is going to bring us two of the biggest, juiciest T-Bone steaks that ever come out of Texas."

The corner of Les' mouth turned upward, agreeing with the smile in his eyes.

"That chef is going to cook those steaks so hot and fast that the grill is going to look like one of our flamethrowers lighting up. Those big thick slabs of Texas beef are going to be sizzling on the plate when they arrive at our table, and when we cut into 'em Les, *mmmm, mm*! They're going to be so pink and tender inside, we won't even have to chew them. They'll melt in our mouths. I tell ya Les, ol' buddy, nobody, and I mean nobody, grows steaks like those boys in the land of the Lone Star."

"Damn," exclaimed Davenport, "Ca . . . ca . . . can I go with you guys?"

"Go with us. Why, all three of us will go together."

A smile slipped from Welch's face as he listened to Davenport's excited endorsement and request to join his buddies on their night in New Orleans. He turned and walked out of the squad room leaving them to their near impossible task of trying to save the dying man with grains of rice and words. He wished them well. Les Wheatley was a good man, a husband and father. He deserved to live if any one of them did.

Stepping outside he sat down on the wooden stoop and watched the sun as it slowly sank behind a distant cloud. Eventually the rays of light bled through the lower clouds giving off a yellowish orange lining. The mountain range was similar to the ones back home in West Virginia with one exception. There were no trees. Just ridge after ridge of barren rock and scrub brush. He stared teary eyed at the God forsaken landscape and wondered for the hundredth time why he was there? Why he couldn't be at home with his wife, having children and building a future?

As the sun set behind a distant mountain and the darkness approached, a guard bellowed out something in Chinese. Welch stood and stared at the guard tower in defiance for a couple of seconds, before slowly turning and walking back into the barracks. Behind him darkness swallowed up the horizon and covered the camp.

*   *   *   *

"The dialectic logical in matter! Chairman Mao state so, many time," cried out Lieutenant Le.

"I just can't quite understand the all and all of it. I'm not trying to be difficult mind you, it's just a matter of how you communicate it. Could you possibly reword it? Maybe phrase it in a different way. Give a bloody example." Standing, the British officer waited patiently for a response.

Le, the officer giving the class on Mao's communism, stared out across the seated POWs at Captain Hayes. The Chinese officers' face was tense and his body was twitching.

"It is as it is! If six-year-old child understand, why you not understand?"

"Well! I don't think it's necessary to start putting me down because I ask a question. I know how important this class is, and I'm trying to understand the point Chairman Mao is trying to make. Frankly, Lieutenant Le, you sometimes fail to make much sense of this Mao fellow and his witty little sayings."

Lieutenant Le stared blankly at Hayes for a few seconds, turned to the rest of the class, started to speak and stopped. There were several more seconds of silence before he finally spoke.

"Read next chapter for lesson tomorrow. Captain Hayes, teach class tomorrow." Looking at Hayes with a look of superiority he added. "Class dismissed."

The young Chinese propaganda officer left the hut and stormed down the yard, through the gate, to the camp commandant's office.

"Well, there you have it lads. Go back to your rooms and study your little red book. You can bloody well expect me to quiz the bunch of you on my lecture tomorrow."

The class of a hundred or so POWs burst into laughter, and those around Hayes jumped to their feet and pounded him on the back. Cheerfully talking to each other as they left the building, the soldiers went back to their daily routines.

"Jolly good show, Clyde," said Commander Simon Fletcher. "It's a fine line you walk between frustrating these buggers without setting them off. Keep it up, but do be careful not to push too hard. Life is easier when the Chinese think we are cooperating."

"Aye, sir! If I can lift the men's spirits and rub those little yellow noses in the dirt at the same time, all the better. If they ever figure me out, it's a week in the box for sure."

"Right there, lad. Keep it up. The men need a good laugh occasionally, and there is nothing I enjoy more than a frustrated Chinaman. Now get back to your barracks, Captain and prepare for your lecture. Cambridge it's not, but you'll need to understand that book if you are going to duel with the Lieutenant."

"Sir!" Hayes snapped to attention and quickly stepped out of the room, followed slowly by Commander Fletcher.

Outside the air was nippy, but the sky was blue, spotted with white clouds. The fenced in camp area was about two acres in size. There were several smaller buildings scattered about the main building, the schoolhouse. Down a small slope was a flat area where the men had roll call formations, exercised and played games. At that moment the yard was full of men busily occupying themselves. For two men, working diligently behind the barracks on the honey bucket detail, it was emptying the latrine pots. A roaring fire was off to their left where human waste burned.

In the yard area two men vigorously played a tennis game without the benefit of a net, rackets, or ball. Sitting on the slope, several men moved their heads back and forth in sequence with the player's movements, following an imaginary ball in an imaginary game. A serve was returned with a blazing backhand, followed by a sliding forehand and a difficult passing shot that could not be returned. The player threw up his hands in victory as the tennis fans politely applauded his efforts. From out in the yard two Chinese guards watched in puzzlement, speaking quietly to one another. The next serve was a blistering shot with no chance for return, causing the opponent to fall and roll on the ground as he attempted to reach for the ball. There was more polite applause. Getting up and dusting himself off, the young Australian soldier pointed to the ground immediately in front of the two guards and yelled, "'Ows about a little 'elp, mate."

The guards looked at the ground and back at the soldier as he approached.

"Eh! A little 'elp wouldn't 'urt, now would it? See 'ere now, I'll just 'ave to fetch it me self." Bending over in front of the guards he picked up the imaginary ball, tossed it up and down a couple of times and walked away whistling. The tennis crowd politely applauded as he returned to the court.

Commander Fletcher walked across the yard, pipe clenched between his teeth. He was tall and distinguished looking, despite the obvious effects of months in a POW camp and walked with an air of command and control. His silver hair was neatly combed, a heavy mustache sat comfortably across the pipe stem. Dark, piercing eyes took in everything around him, but never deviated from their narrowed stare at the gate down at the foot of the hill. He walked around the tennis court that was scratched out in the dirt, and the match stopped momentarily as the fans recognized the commander with polite applause. He granted them a slight smile, tipped his cap acknowledging their recognition, and continued down the yard toward the compound gate. It wasn't Wimbledon and he wasn't royalty, but the fans didn't care. A custom was a custom.

As Fletcher approached the gate one of the guards stepped forward blocking his way with a bayoneted rifle.

"I intend to see the Camp Commandant, Colonel Ling. Tell him Commander Fletcher would like a word with him, if you please."

The guard turned to his companion and spoke briefly. The younger guard left his post and ran down the hill. Several minutes later he returned.

"No can see now. Tomorrow. Come tomorrow."

"He bloody well can see me now!" exclaimed Fletcher as he stepped around the young soldier, only to be blocked by the more senior guard. He stopped and announced loudly. "I demand to see the Colonel immediately. It is my right under the Geneva Convention to have any grievance heard without delay."

Both guards were now yelling frantically at the British Officer as he stood his ground between them. The men inside the compound continued their activities, but kept a worried eye on their commander. As Lieutenant Le approached, the guards became calm, glad to turn the problem over to an officer.

"Commander Fletcher, Colonel Ling understand need to meet, but very busy now. You come back later. Let us say hour, maybe?"

"Lieutenant Le, I will wait here until the Colonel is prepared to meet with me. Please relay that message to him, if you would."

Nodding, Le turned and walked back down the road. The guards returned to their post on either side of the steps. Five, ten, twenty minutes went by, before Le reappeared.

"Colonel Ling see you now."

Fletcher went through the gate and followed the young officer, thankful for the opportunity to finally stretch his legs.

"Yes, Commander Fletcher. What do you want . . . today?"

"Colonel Ling, I've come to protest the living conditions of the men. They need better food, if they are expected to survive. They need competent medical treatment. Right now, you have two of my men in your tin boxes who have been there over a week. I must protest and demand their release. Their punishment is far too severe for their crime."

"Commander! You protest same every week. If I grow tired of complaining, you may end up in box with men. Go back to your foolishness in the yard and let us not play this game today. I have more important issues that need attention. New commandant to run camp. He not listen to complaints. He shoot you in head in front of men and toss you in latrine pit. I must prepare for arrival. Leave now. Go back to men."

"I insist once again that you release my two men, Colonel Ling. It wouldn't do either one of us any good for the new commandant to find two dead prisoners in the Box on his arrival."

Staring at Fletcher, Ling pondered his remarks for a few seconds and said, "Very well. Lieutenant Le, take Commander Fletcher to retrieve men."

Fletcher snapped to attention and bowed slightly to the Colonel, who dismissed him with a flip of his hand. Fletcher did a snappy about-face and went through the front doors, followed by Lieutenant Le. With his pipe back in his mouth, Fletcher marched across the yard as he did every week. Up in the compound the men continued their busy activities, but stared silently from their spots throughout the camp. Halfway to the gate, Fletcher and Le turned and as they approached the tin boxes, the men stopped what they were doing and slowly moved to the fence along the front gate.

Down below Fletcher stood patiently and waited for Le to open the first box. The door swung open and inside a soldier jerked to life, startled by the sudden intrusion of light into his dark world.

"Come out now Corporal. It's time to come out and walk with me to your squad room where your mates will see to you. Come now."

A hand slowly came out of the box into the sunlight.

"That's the stuff, lad."

A head followed a hand as the soldier crawled out of the tiny door of the tin box. Squinting his eyes, trying to adjust to the bright sunlight he groped about, attempting to stand. Muscles ached from being bent and unused after several days of confinement, but the man moved his stiff joints with slow determination, came to a position of attention, clicked his heels together and saluted the Commander.

"That's it, Corporal! Stretch those limbs. Look sharp. Now let's get your American friend out of his box. Le had already unlocked the other box and was standing next to it.

"Come now, lad! Let's move out of it now."

A hand came out, but with much more difficulty than the first man. Barely moving, the second man tried to crawl out of the box, but was too worn down to make it over the wooden board at the base of the door.

"That's it now, Corporal Staley. Help Roberts out of that hellish box."

The corporal reached down and assisted the younger soldier out and to his feet. The boy's pale, chalky complexion belayed a serious health condition. Another day in the box would have brought an end to his life.

"Here we go now, lads. The compound is just a brisk walk up the hill where your mates can lend you a hand. Chins high! Mustn't let the bastards think they've broken you. Look sharp now."

As best they could the men struggled to march together up the hill behind Fletcher. As they wobbled through, the camp broke into a roar of whistles and cheers, and the two men were absorbed into the crowd. The soldiers across the yard shouted words of thanks and praise to Fletcher as he walked toward his building.

"*Sergeant Major!*"

"*Sir?*"

"Committee, ten minutes, room seven."

"*Sir!*" snapped Sergeant Major Roberson, and disappeared into the crowd of cheering men.

"You shouldn't let him pressure you like that. He should rot in the box or be shot like any other foreign dog. The people of China do not have to tolerate such arrogance. Chairman Mao says, 'It is . . . .'"

"*Enough!* shouted Colonel Ling. "Sometimes you forget your place, Lieutenant. Your role as Propaganda Chief continues because you are good for little else.

If you are not careful you may end up in a box. Now, *sit!*"

Stunned by his commander's strong words, Le stepped back and passively sat in a chair in front of the commandant's desk.

"I have run a strong camp for the American and British dogs. No escapes. No riots. There are many deaths, but they have been the weak and foolish. They disgraced their country and families by allowing themselves to be captured alive. It should not be China's responsibility to care for those who came from far away and choose not to die in battle. They are weak and should have been shot."

The Lieutenant sat motionless as his commander spoke.

"Now, other Chinese come to take over my camp. They come to teach, but they are as imperialist as the foreign dogs." Hesitating, the commandant stared at the young propaganda officer, who shifted uncomfortably in his chair.

"Lieutenant Le! When you lick the new commandant's boots, try to remember that soon he will see your incompetence. Now, leave my office."

Le jumped up and snapped to attention. "I am . . . ."

"Get out!"

Gentlemen, I've just been informed the Chinese are sending a new commandant to take over the whip here at Camp Two."

The men stirred. In the room was the senior representative from each country imprisoned at the camp. Fletcher was the senior most officer and British. There was an Australian sergeant major, the senior noncom representing the enlisted ranks. There was a Turk and Filipino captain, and two Americans who represented the vast majority of the men.

"What do you make of it Commander?" asked the senior American officer, Lieutenant Colonel Paul Cruz.

"Colonel Ling just informed, or shall I say warned me that the new man is on his way. He gave no explanation. I must say he didn't seem pleased. Spread the word. See if anyone has over heard anything from the little yellow buggers."

"Honestly, sir," responded a young U.S. Army Air Force captain, "Could it be any worse? No food or medical, no clothing, and winter coming on. The sick will be dropping like flies. Do you think there is any chance things will improve with a change in camp authority?"

"Maybe, Captain O'Brian. God willing, the new man will view us as useful tools. Sergeant Major put the word out. We will meet again tomorrow night, eighteen-hundred, room four."

"Sir!"

Sitting on a box, Welch took a folded piece of paper and a short stubby pencil from his shirt pocket. The paper had been lifted from the camp cook's desk. The pencil had been lifted from the commandant clerk's desk by a crafty prisoner and traded for cigarettes in two-inch stubs. Five cigarettes were a bit high since no mail was allowed out, but Welch felt a great need to write Amelia. The price of paper and the short life of his pencil limited him to one letter per month. Safely stashed away in the straw mattress of his bunk were letters he had written over the past year.

Examining the pencil, he took a small, rough stone from his pocket and gently rubbed the end of the pencil against it. Careful manipulation was required to file down the wood, without harming the valuable lead tip. With just two inches, one could not be wasteful.

Welch's monthly letter was one of the things that kept him going. It would momentarily lift him from the confines of the prison camp. Chaplain Burns had suggested it to combat his depression and he looked forward to the first of each month with great anticipation. He loved to write. He loved Amelia.

Relaxing on the stoop Welch chatted with an American and British soldier. Down at the camp gate two Chinese trucks and a staff car pulled up. Ten soldiers piled out of the back of the second truck and surrounded the first as its human cargo unloaded. Two officers stepped out of the staff car. Both were older soldiers, but one was much more senior to the other. They stood talking, pointing to various locations throughout the camp, and just as quickly the senior of the two turned, and headed down the road to the commandant's office.

The new prisoners looked to be in pitiful shape. Ragged and emaciated, it was clear they were transfers from another camp. The men began to gather down at the gate to welcome their fellow countrymen. The new prisoners consisted of two Turks, a Brit and fifteen Americans.

Welch watched from the stoop, his companions having gone down to the gate with the crowd. Two British soldiers quietly helped their countryman up the hill to the schoolhouse. The Turks hugged and slapped each other on the backs, as if they were long lost family. The Americans were herded off to the side and assigned to prospective squad rooms. The eighteen new bodies failed to replace the men who had been buried over the last couple of days. Given the theory of diminishing returns, the camp would be empty by Christmas.

The commotion at the gate had settled down when something down at the trucks caught Welch's attention. On the back tailgate lay a soldier on a stretcher. Apparently forgotten by the Chinese, the man slowly propped up on one elbow and looked around. His head was bandaged, as well as his arms and one leg. Seeing that no one paid him any attention, he slowly sat up and swung his legs out and over the tailgate. His movements were very slow. Most likely painful, Welch guessed, as the bandages suggested he had been seriously wounded.

The man rolled on his stomach, eased his legs over the back of the tailgate and dropped to the ground. The drop was only about four feet, but the impact with the ground folded him over like a pocketknife. He lay there for several seconds before he rolled under the front end of the second truck. If the trucks moved, the man could be crushed under the wheels. Welch grimaced, jumped to his feet and moved quickly down the hill. As he walked, he motioned to Captain Hayes and they met halfway down the slope. Welch started to speak, but noticed movement under the truck, so he directed the Brit to the truck and they watched the events unfold outside the fence. Sure enough, the man appeared from under the back end of the second truck crawling along on all fours.

"Well, I'll be! He's trying to escape. The bugger can barely move and he's bloody well trying to escape, and in broad daylight," explained Hayes, astonished at what he was seeing.

Reaching the back end of the staff car, the man slowly pulled himself up and walked down the road. From behind, at the gate, the officer who had arrived in the staff car swiftly walked after the man, overtaking him easily. Without a struggle the officer led him back to the gate and into the compound.

"That is one determined son-of-a-gun," said Welch as he and Hayes watched the man being led up the hill and into the schoolhouse.

"Crazy. I doubt that he will even remember the episode when he feels better. Odd that," said Hayes rubbing his chin. "Why wouldn't that officer send one of his goon squad to fetch him?"

"Commander Fletcher. Colonel Pol, new camp commandant. This Captain Lin, propaganda, or I should say education specialist. They wish to meet senior ranking prisoner, you."

Casting a respectful nod toward the Chinese colonel, Fletcher responded, "Colonel Pol. We appreciate the medical attention the new lads received. I do feel I must point out that the medical needs of the men at this camp have been neglected for quite some time. If you could spare your medical man to examine them, I would appreciate it."

"That I regret, I cannot do, Commander. He is only borrowed and must return to the battlefield without delay. He managed to get your men here. The camp doctor and your men, Commander Fletcher, must do rest. There will be more time to discuss these and other matters, later. Captain Lin will escort you back to compound."

Fletcher came to attention, nodded to Colonel Pol and followed Lin out the door without acknowledging Ling's presence.

Walking up the road to the compound Fletcher pondered the events of the last few minutes.

"You will find Colonel Pol a fair man, to those who show proper respect and patience."

"Yes. That I can sense." Fletcher stopped and turned to Lin. "Tell me, Captain. How go the peace talks in Panmunjom?"

"Very slow, very difficult. Much to be determined before talking begin. They talk in earnest soon."

"I've a mind that healthy prisoners being repatriated would make a strong bargaining tool and would foster better world opinion than a bunch of undernourished, walking skeletons. And, if that were the case, Colonel Pol has much work to do here at Camp Two," said Fletcher.

"We, Commander," said Lin looking up into Fletcher's face. "We, have much work to do."

Lowe lay on the bamboo mat staring at the ceiling. He felt considerable pain in several parts of his body, especially in and around his right leg and hand. He closed his eyes and tried to remember the last time he had eaten.

"Sergeant Lowe."

He opened his eyes and above were two faces staring down at him.

"How goes it, partner?"

Lowe smiled and spoke, asking the men where he was, and if he were free. Bent over with their hands on their knees, they listened, looked at each other, and looked back down at him.

"What'd he say? His jaw is so swollen, I couldn't make it out."

"Sounded like, 'var amma' and 'ema mee.'"

"That's what I heard too, but it was more like 'emma three' at the end."

"You heard a number there at the end?"

"Yea, a three."

"That weren't a number, you nimrod."

"What was it then?"

"It was a word."

"Yea, the word three."

"That's a number."

"It's a word."

"This poor man has been blown up, shot and he's got something important to say and you're talking like an idiot," said the taller man as he reached over and lightly cuffed the shorter man on the forehead.

"Two idiots, I'd say."

"What?"

"Nutin'."

"*Ahhhh!*" shouted the tall man in frustration. Giving his companion a mean look, he stood and walked around to the other side, where he bent over and put his hands on his knees once again. The shorter man followed and assumed an identical position. Realizing his attempt to get away had turned futile the man raised his hand, causing the shorter man to flinch and cover his head with his arms. Saying something under his breath, he moved back around to the other side.

Looking down at Lowe, the taller man continued his attempts to communicate.

"Take your time man, and tell us what you've got to say."

The floor was spinning around and the light in the room burned his eyes. The more he tried to talk the more his jaw ached. He hurt all over, but most of all he was confused about where he was, and as luck would have it, he was trying to find out from Abbott and Costello. Any other time he would have seen the humor, but not now. Looking up at them, Lowe tried one more time to find out where he was.

"Bear, var arrr vee."

"There! There it is again. Just like I said, the number three."

The man stood ignoring his friend. As he learned over again a sad look came over his face. He lowered himself to one knee and began to remove the bandages on Lowe's leg.

"I'm going to take a look at your wounds. See how you're doing."

"Fee? Fee?" repeated Lowe.

"No, buddy, you're not, free. None of us are free. We are in a Chinese prisoner of war camp. Camp Two. No, I'm sorry, pal. We are far from being free."

Lowe moaned, closed his eyes and lay there. Looking up from the bandages the man saw a small tear roll out of the corner of Lowe's eye and down the side of his face.

∗   ∗   ∗   ∗

"That sums up today's lecture on the eleven ways liberalism manifests itself. Any questions, lads?" asked Captain Hayes as he scanned the room. "Oh surely someone has a question. I've talked a bloody hour."

An older soldier stood in the front of the room, as if by design.

"Captain, you said something a while back about taking part in personal attacks, quarrels and revenge."

"Yes, Sergeant Jansen. I believe that to be the fifth type of liberalism."

"Yes, sir. I've never met a fifth, a quart, or a pint for that matter that I couldn't find something good to say about."

The prisoners snickered as a smile came over the captain's face.

"Well, I feel the same about a good gin and tonic, but be that as it may, Jansen, we're discussing liberalism, not social . . . ism. Do you have a question related to the lecture?"

"Why yes, Captain, I do. It's really a comment about these little yellow fellows that watch over us. It seems to me that they are always trying to get us mad at each other, us Yanks against you Brits, Aussies a fighting Abduls, whites again' colored. They make a big deal of trying to get us to understand and accept their way of thinking, yet they sneak around pitting us against each other. It don't seem right."

"Well spoken, Jansen. I guess it's just a case of 'What's good for the goose, isn't necessarily good for the gander' here at Camp Two. Mao talks about unity, about working together for the common good. The fifth type of liberalism he refers to is destructive. Never lending itself to progress. Arguing and struggle can be good, if it is constructive. Turning brother against brother has a different goal behind it that we are all aware of. We should all remember that we, as prisoners, should get along and work together. Help each other get through this hell and, God willing, go home someday. Good comment Jansen, thank you."

The soldier looked around the room and nodded his head as he slowly sat back down.

A hand shot up in the back of the room.

"Yes? That's it, lad. Let's have it."

A considerable amount of mumbling came from the back of the room until Captain Hayes interrupted.

"Hold a moment there! You're going to have to speak up if anyone's to hear you. Stand and speak up now. Pretend you're the sergeant major."

Restrained snickering spread throughout the room.

"That's it McCollum, pretend you're a man for once," boomed Sergeant Major Roberson from the back. Open laughter filled the room.

Captain Lin leaned forward at his table, but before he could intercede, Hayes took charge.

"See here now," warned Hayes concealing his appreciation of the sergeant major's comment. "I'll not tolerate interruptions in my lecture." Silence crept across the room.

"All that sounds mighty fancy, sir. All he, Mao is saying, I mean, he must be quite the talker 'cause that's all we've heard about since we were captured. There must be a platoon of fellers swarming around him to write down everything he says. He is a man, isn't he?"

"Yes, Private. Mao is quite certainly a man."

"All we hear is Mao said this, Mao said that. Mao, Mao, Mao. I thought Joe Stalin was the head man in this communism thing, and we hear very little about him, other than seeing him in a film, waving as his armies march by." Taking a deep breath the young soldier continued, "But, I just had a small thought about that ninth liberal type."

"You're always having small thoughts," came a voice close to McCollum, instigating a few chuckles across the room.

"Here now. Give the lad your attention."

Giving the heckler a glare, the boy continued, "I was wondering about that ninth one, sir. The one about that monk a ringing his bell."

"Ah, yes! Very good, lad. Actually, the ninth is my favorite. I believe it says 'To work half-heartedly without a definite plan or direction: to work perfunctorily and muddle along' and then it goes on to refer to your monk, 'So long as one remains a monk, one goes on tolling the bell. This is a ninth type of liberalism.'"

"Yes, sir. That's it. I was just a wondering. If that's how the communist look at things, then what kind a plan do they have for us? It seems to me that all they do here is, what's that word you used, muddle, yea, they just kind a muddle along looking the other way while we die off one at a time. If that were really their plan, it'd be a might easier to kill us and get it over with, so I figure they got something else in mind for us."

*   *   *   *

"Welch, Lieutenant Le has a letter from your wife," said Sergeant Major Roberson. "He's down in the library, but I suspect . . ."

Welch was on his feet jogging up the steps and into the schoolhouse.

"Welch, damn it, boy!" bellowed out Roberson as he wheeled about and headed across the yard.

Welch found the lieutenant sitting at a table waiting, with an armed guard behind him. The letter lay on the table. Welch reached for it and the lieutenant snatched it up quickly.

"You very rude person, Welch. I try to be nice and you forget manners."

Welch gathered himself, came to attention and bowed.

"Lieutenant Le, I was told you have a letter for me."

"Difficult get mail at camp. No mail from America. Nobody write. When arrive, prisoners have mail. Is this you on envelope?"

Welch leaned over and read the front of the envelope.

Amelia Welch
P.O. Box 102
Elkin, West Virginia

>Private Dan Welch
>POW Camp # 2, 0/0
>Chinese People's Committee for World Peace
>Peking, China

It was definitely Amelia's writing.

"You love wife, Private Welch?"

Welch stared at Le, his excitement suddenly overtaken by a combination of fear and suspicion.

"Yes. I love my wife very much."

"You write her letters?"

"Yes, many letters, before I was captured."

"When last time you receive letter from," Le looked at the envelope. "A-meal-ya?"

"I haven't received any since I arrived in Korea."

"Then maybe best you don't get letter." Le withdrew the letter as if doing Welch a favor and began to put it in his jacket pocket. Looking to Welch for a reaction he got a gasp and a grief-stricken look.

"Well, guess I must let you have it. It say, 'Private Dan Welch' and you Private Dan Welch."

"Yes. It is my mail," said Welch sincerely adding, "Thank you Lieutenant Le. It was kind of you to personally bring my letter to me," as if the officer had done him a big favor.

"Yes. Take letter. Sit down and read."

Becoming even more suspicious, Welch stood for a moment looking at the letter in the outstretched hand.

"Well, I not have all day. You want letter or maybe not?"

Welch reached out and took the letter and sat down at the library table.

The envelope was already open, which was expected. The Chinese read all mail, coming and going. Welch slowly slid the letter out of the envelope and read to himself:

September 1, 1952

Dan,

> *I'm really sorry to have to write this letter to you, but it is just as well that I go ahead and get it over with. I have met someone else and feel that I don't want to be married to you any longer. Please try to put yourself in my place. I am growing old and you are sitting in that prison camp and will probably never get out. I have myself to think about now and as long as I'm married to you, most men will not go out with me. I filed for divorce last week. If you ever get out, it would be best if you didn't try to look me up. I have my life to live and rebuild.*

> *Amelia*

As he read the end of the letter, Welch became conscious of the tightening in his chest. He struggled to catch his breath, but the pressure was so intense he felt he would suffocate. His eyes blurred with tears as he slowly looked up at Le, realizing his motives. Overwhelmed he turned his head and looked out the window so he wouldn't have to look at Le.

"Something wrong back home, Private Welch?"

"You know damn well what's wrong," said Welch gritting his teeth, but not turning to face Le.

"I feel you needed letter. You should know truth. America forsaken you. Now wife, as well. The People's Republic of . . ."

"The People's Republic of China can . . ."

"What is the meaning of this?" roared Commander Fletcher as he stormed into the library, followed by the American chaplain, Lieutenant Colonel Burns.

Welch slowly turned to look at Fletcher, the letter slipping out of his hand and falling to the floor. Judging by his crushed appearance, Fletcher sensed correctly the news from home was not good. He picked up the letter and read it.

"Commander, I deliver Private Welch letter. You complain about no mail. Here I give soldier letter and you barge in like stampeding water buffalo."

Looking up from the letter his eyes narrowed and he snarled, "This is outrageous Le. You never give out a post unless it contains bad news. Do you get some kind of sadistic pleasure out of destroying this man's spirit?" Hesitating for a moment Fletcher added, "By thunder, I wonder what Colonel Pol will say about your cruel tactics."

Realizing he was unsure how the new Camp Commandant would feel, Le stood up and snapped at Fletcher.

"You give me the letter, Commander."

As Fletcher and Le squared off in a verbal duel across the library table, Chaplain Burns pulled Welch up from his seat and helped him toward the door. He was a defeated man. Sergeant Major Roberson met them at the door and the three men walked out of the building.

"No! You will not have it, you little yellow turtle."

Le reacted abruptly to the severe insult by slapping his holster, but restrained his impulse to draw the weapon on the senior prisoner of the camp.

"If you must shoot me, then bloody well get on with it. This post belongs to Private Welch. Not you. Not the People's Republic of China, or anyone else in this God forsaken place." Fletcher turned on his heels and stormed out of the room.

Welch sat on the hillside just down from the schoolhouse. His shoulders were slumped and his arms rested on his knees. He stared straight ahead, looking at nothing in particular, tears rolled down his cheeks. The sergeant major quietly sat next to him as the shadows crawled across the valley below.

In a deep discussion, Fletcher and the chaplain stood up on the hill behind them. Off to their left the front door of the schoolhouse swung open, banging up against the side of the building. Le and his armed escort stormed down the steps, walking swiftly toward the gate. Seeing them, Welch made a move to get to his feet, but the strong hand of the sergeant major quickly forced him back down.

"Not today, lad. It's the wife you're upset with, not that whiny little rat. Let 'em go. His cruelty is not worth a month in the hole, or getting yourself shot over. Besides, his days are numbered. He's Ling's lackey. He'll soon find himself in a line unit where he'll end up being another body for his mates to scramble over."

Welch turned and looked at the Australian and nodded. "What am I to do, Sergeant Major?"

"The sun will come up tomorrow, just like it did today, lad. It'll come up and you'll struggle, and you'll fight these bastards the best you can. Don't let Le get the satisfaction of beating you. When he sees you walk across the yard tomorrow, he'll know he lost. Keep your chin up and mind focused on the day you and your mates walk out of this dung heap."

Welch looked at the sergeant major and gave him a sad smile. Roberson patted him on the back, stood and walked back up the hill to Fletcher and Burns. Fletcher still held the letter in his hand.

"Damn it! Damn it all to hell! That skinny little twit likes to find ways to kill a man, without getting his hands bloody. Damn the little bugger," Fletcher hesitated and turned to Roberson. How is he doing, Sergeant Major?"

"Not well, I'm afraid, devastated, of course. I would have wagered he would have told Le to piss off, if it had been something else, but we all have our breaking point, and she is his. We all know that when you care for someone back home, they give you the will to go on. I'm afraid he is a lost man now."

"That's it, Sergeant Major! Jolly good show," expounded Fletcher. "The word is Welch took exceptionally good care of a young soldier in his previous camp."

"The boy died just before Welch was transferred here," said Chaplain Burns. "Welch told me about him. A brave little man named Jawaski. Don't let Welch's size fool you. He has a compassionate heart, as big as they come. That's why that letter is destroying him. He writes his wife once a month and saves the letters to mail when they start letting the mail out. My doing, I'm afraid. I thought it would give him hope, and it has. Who would have expected her to betray him? Very sad for both of them."

"Sad for the both of them? You may think that if you wish, you're a man of the cloth. I say there is no excuse for her actions. I believe she was a little short on the loyalty to begin with and I believe he'll realize that if he survives. He is sitting down there right now making excuses for her not writing him a single letter since he left the states. She's a loose filly and he's better off rid of her."

"That's strong opinion, Sergeant Major. I won't disagree, but it would better suit the lad's situation if we kept our feelings to ourselves. Even if he brings it up, we keep things positive." Fletcher took out his pipe and clenched it between his teeth. There hadn't been tobacco in it for months, but its presence still stimulated thought.

"We need to use that strong character trait you mentioned, Chaplain, his compassion for others. Let's have him take care of one of our seriously wounded."

"How about that new chap that came in all blown up?"

"That's right on it, Chaplain."

"It may be just the thing to help get him through this bit of nasty business with his wife, and I agree, Sergeant Major, later he will see her for what she really is, and I would wager, what she has been all along."

Chaplain Burns and Welch stood over the soldier lying on the bamboo mat.

"Sergeant Lowe here arrived last week and needs constant attention, Welch. I know you are very capable of providing it, from what you told me about taking care of Jawaski."

"Thank you, Chaplain, but I just don't feel up to it. Leo Jawaski was a good friend. Part of me died the day we lost him. I just don't think I can go through that again. I'm tired of caring for someone and them dying on me. I guess you could say I've hit a string of bad luck with people deserting me."

"Well, be that as it may, Welch, this man still needs someone to look after him and I have no one else to turn to. I'm afraid you are stuck with him."

Welch looked at Burns, downcast and nodded his head.

"I'll do my best, Chaplain."

"Good. Start right now. He needs his wounds checked and bandages replaced. We're out of sulfur powder for the wounds, so you will have to use your own urine to disinfect. After you're finished, figure out something he can eat and make him eat it. He hasn't been eating with that broken jaw. Good luck. I know you will do your best."

The chaplain left and Welch stood there looking at Lowe. He was tired, more tired than he had ever felt. He knew he would get attached to Lowe only to lose him, but not like he did with Leo, and that thought gave him encouragement. He would do as the chaplain asked, but it would take a miracle for the man to survive with the wounds he had.

Welch walked over to a small table in the corner of the room and rinsed out a tin can with water from the pan of boiled water. Unbuttoning his trousers, he relieved himself, nearly filling the can. Urine fresh from the body was germ free and a reliable disinfectant when nothing else was available. He then rinsed out a rag and draped it over the top of the can.

Walking over to Lowe, he kneeled, setting the can of urine next to him and began to slowly unwrap the bandages on the left leg. The wounds were deep. Grenade, he guessed. He'd seen it before. The lacerations had been crudely stitched back together, leaving large chunks of meat either missing or knotted up. He tossed the soiled wraps into a can to be washed. He then took the clean rag and dipped it in the urine, swabbing the wounds thoroughly, before rewrapping the leg with fresh bandages. He repeated the procedure on the right leg, and then on the right hand and forearm.

"What do you think, pal? Am I going to survive?" said Lowe quietly, painfully, almost in a whisper, his words lisping through the gap where his front teeth used to be. The question startled Welch.

"The camp book has you going off three-to-one, dead by morning."

Lowe smiled. "I can beat that lying down. Put a sawbuck on me and I'll do my best to hang on."

Welch laughed. "I don't think the camp bookie would hold kindly to me betting with inside information, he's a naturally suspicious fellow."

Welch reached his hand over and gripped Lowe's left hand, the only thing on his body that hadn't taken any shrapnel from the grenade.

"Dan Welch, West Virginia."

"Howard Lowe, Kentucky."

"Eastern Kentucky?"

"Central. No mountains, just rolling hills, knobs and sinkholes."

"I'm kind of partial to mountains myself. Not this barren rock they have here. Give me real hills, with trees and streams. Deer, coon and trout."

"Neighbors, are we? Well," Lowe flinched in pain as Welch lifted him a bit to remove the bandage around his upper chest. "I'm glad to meet you." Lowe spoke, with great difficulty, his breathing showing stress from the few words he had said.

"Sit back and keep quiet for a while. You're wearing yourself out. I'll take care of you and when you get some strength back, we can swap hunting stories."

"A letter, I need to write my wife and girls, let them know I'm alive."

Welch sat motionless, his hands on his knees, the look of deep pain in his eyes.

"Maybe we could write one when you get better."

"I need to try now, I might not get better. Please."

"How old are your girls?" asked Welch as he finished the chest wrap.

"Ten and four."

No, thought Welch. Don't ask personal questions. As soon as you get too really like this guy, you'll lose him.

"What's your wife's name?"

"Martha."

Welch pulled a piece of paper and his stubby little pencil from his pocket. Looking at his last piece of paper, it occurred to him that it was good that he hadn't wasted it on Amelia like the others. This one would be written to someone who cared. He spun around and sat down on the floor next to Lowe. He would help Lowe to write his letter and do his best to get it mailed. It was the least he could do for a neighbor.

"Start off with, I'm okay. Don't mention that I'm, that I am badly wounded." Lowe swallowed and hesitated a few seconds.

"Take your time, pal."

"Tell her that my right hand is hurt and my friend, Dan Welch, is writing the letter for me."

Welch felt a lump in his throat and tried to swallow.

"Start with 'My Dearest Martha.'"

Welch began to write.

"Tell her I think of her constantly and pray to God," Lowe's voice cracked a little at the thought of his family. "Pray to God that she and the girls, that they are well and not worrying too much about me. Ask them to write, Wanda Faye and Amy Sue. Tell the girls I am saving lots of kisses for them. Tell them to trust the Lord to deliver me." Lowe lay on the mat with an ache in the pit of his stomach that was far more painful than the wounds throbbing throughout his body.

Welch wrote, taking his time. He had to be careful with the last sheet of paper. His heart ached for the man next to him, as thoughts of the letter he carried in his pocket faded. Lying on the mat beside him was a man who, despite his horrible wounds, had thoughts only of his family. The notion started to take hold that he had to keep Lowe alive, to help him survive to go home to his family. Welch's future, the one he lost that day, now lay there on the ground next to him. After several minutes of careful deliberations and writing he read the letter to Lowe:

October 29, 1952

My Dearest Martha,

By now you should have received word that I am missing. I am okay. I survived the fighting, but got captured. I'm in a Chinese POW camp. I am in good hands with the men here at the camp. They will take care of me, so you and the girls must not worry. Pray for me and I will pray for you.

Darling, you and the girls are in my thoughts every moment and those thoughts will pull me through this. The girls will have their father back and I will be in your arms again.

I have injured my right hand and a friend, Dan Welch, is writing this letter for me. You must have faith that the Lord will deliver me to you. Please write soon. I need to hear from all of you. Saving kisses for the girls.

Love Always,

Howard

✱   ✱   ✱   ✱

Martha Lowe sat on the couch in her living room, the girls in her lap. She had read Howard's letter at least ten times since Mr. Wilkerson, the local postmaster had burst into Tabor School House, disrupting class to hand deliver it to her. She had asked Sherrie Goode, an eighth grader to watch the class. She walked from the schoolhouse, to the Tabor Community Church next door, and sat down in the quietness of the sanctuary, and read. The first reading was very difficult, as she wept with joy before, during and after each sentence. Now as she sat on the couch at home she felt she could read the letter with the girls without breaking down.

"Mommy, what surprise?"

"We have a letter from your dad." The girls squealed and bounced in her lap with excitement.

"Now, now! Sit quietly and I will read it to you."

CHAPTER 10

▼

"Children, history period will continue with a discussion on the Founding Fathers of our country. Who was considered to be the Father of our Country?"

Hands shot up across the classroom. Quickly calculating who would benefit the most from answering the question, Mrs. Lowe announced, "Winnie Baumgartner."

Standing up Winnie pointed to a portrait on the wall behind Mrs. Lowe's desk and said, "The Father of our Country be him, I mean was him, Mrs. Lowe, George Washington."

"Yes Winnie, very good. Class, George Washington was a farmer, statesman and military leader. History tells us he had the single most dramatic impact on our young nation, and for that he is fondly referred to as the 'Father of our Country.' As a farmer he ran a very successful plantation that covered nearly eight thousand acres. Otha Burton, your grandfather has one of the larger farms in Adair County. Do you know how many acres he owns?"

Otha stood and recited just as he had heard his grandfather recite many times before, "Three hundred and ten acres, more or less, ma'am. One hundred and sixty-five acres of the finest yellow poplar, white oak and mature walnut trees in the whole county. Grandpa says that timber will make my pa rich someday. Grandpa don't need money, he just likes to walk in the woods looking at his trees and looking for squirrels to shoot with his old Stevens Favorite, .22 caliber rifle. Grandma says he curses like a sailor 'cause he can't see to hit anything anymore. Mrs. Lowe, how does a sailor curse?" Laughter erupted from the rest of the children.

"Thank you Otha. Class, Mr. Burton's farm is much like George Washington's. He raises crops, livestock and when he needs timber to build, he logs it from his land. Washington's plantation, Mount Vernon, provided everything that the Washington family needed to survive." Recognizing a raised hand, she continued, "Yes, Dorothy?"

"Are you kin to George . . ."

"Dorothy, please stand when you speak."

"Yes, ma'am. That paper on the wall behind your desk that says you are a daughter of the American Revolution. Does that make you kin to George Washington?"

Soft giggles broke out once again amongst the older children in the class.

"Quiet now! That's a very good question Dorothy. President, or General Washington, whichever you prefer, and his wife, Martha had no children of their own. Washington did have stepchildren from Martha's first marriage that he loved dearly. I am a 'Daughter of the American Revolution' because a long time ago my great, great, great grandpa McClister fought in the Revolutionary War. As a matter of fact, Private McClister wintered with General Washington at Valley Forge. When he was home General Washington enjoyed entertaining guests at Mount Vernon most any day of the week. He enjoyed dancing with the young ladies and even had a ballroom built on the side of his home for the large gatherings. As the evening progressed the furniture was moved aside and the dancing would begin."

"Raymond Tracy, why do we refer to Washington as General Washington at times?"

Raymond Tracy looked up at Mrs. Lowe with an appreciative look.

"George Washington was the general of our Con-ti-nent-al Army during the War for Independence from England. My dad says he was a great general and our best president 'cause he was the first and everyone that came along later would say, 'Hey, good ol' George did it this way, so we will too.' Some people wanted to make him King and he said 'No, sir! Not me! I fought to be free of tyranny and free people don't have to bow down to a mon-arch-kin-y.'" Raymond Tracy stopped his swaggering from side-to-side and said, "Mrs. Lowe, is it true that General Washington never got shot in the war?"

"As a matter of fact, the General had horses shot out from under him and his uniform torn several times from bullets. He was very brave and was quick to ride forward into battle with his men. Sitting atop a horse with bullets flying all around is a dangerous place to be, but you are right, Raymond Tracy. General Washington was never wounded in battle."

Carol Phillips' hand shot up from the back of the classroom. "He was very lucky."

"Very lucky indeed," said Mrs. Lowe. "Many feel General Washington received divine guidance and protection during the war. His little army of ragtag colonialists took on the mighty British Army, the most powerful and professional army of its time. Although General Washington lost most of his battles, quickly retreating to come back and fight another day, he outlasted five British generals. The Lord was certainly watching over him."

A small hand shot up in the front of the room, "Wanda Faye?"

"My daddy has a guardian angel watching over him in the war like General Washington did. Daddy was missing and now he has been found in a war camp. He is hurt and the doctor in the camp is taking care of him. Brother Henry says that God has truly blessed my daddy."

"Thank you, Wanda Faye. Class, we received a letter yesterday from Mr. Lowe informing us that he was located in a prisoner of war camp in North Korea. Chinese soldiers from the People's Republic of China run the camp. He has been wounded, but we don't know how seriously. He has received medical attention. God has answered our prayers and just like General Washington, God is keeping him alive for us. Thank you for keeping him in your prayers."

Looking teary eyed around the classroom Martha Lowe saw several children with tears in their eyes, to include Raymond Tracy who started clapping his hands together, quickly followed by the rest of the class.

Looking about for a way to show her appreciation for their support, she regrouped quickly and said, "To celebrate this blessing and Mr. Lowe's good fortune we are going to dismiss class early today and have an extended recess until Mr. Burns arrives with his bus."

A cheer went up from the students as they began gathering up their books, papers and copying their homework assignments from the chalkboard. Mrs. Lowe walked to her desk, sat down and took a lace handkerchief from her purse and wiped the tears from her eyes. It truly was a glorious day she thought to herself, as she watched the children put on their heavy clothing to go outside and play.

*   *   *   *

West of Columbia, in the tiny community of Knifley, a knock came on Gladys Henry's wood paneled kitchen door. The forty-year-old farm wife and mother of six stepped away from the white enamel coated pan she was rinsing and drying the morning breakfast dishes in and walked over and opened the back door. On the other side of the door were two strangers standing in the screened-in porch.

"May I help you, gentlemen?"

"Ma'am. My name is Johnny Roberts, Western Union Telegraph in Columbia. This is my supervisor Mr. Julius Alfred. May we come in, ma'am?"

"Most certainly, gentlemen. Come inside and warm yourselves by the cook stove. It's not much, but it does keep the kitchen warmed."

Both men stepped into the kitchen and stood grim faced. Johnny Roberts stepped forward and said, "Mrs. Henry, I've come here to deliver the worst kind of news. News about your son Terrance who is fighting in the war," and he handed her the telegram.

Without looking at the telegram she said, "There must be some mistake, Mr. Roberts. My Terrance is fine. I received a letter from him yesterday. Come see for yourself. He said he'd be home by Christmas. My Terrance is fine, gentleman, come and look at his letter for yourselves."

Taking Roberts by the hand she led him to the kitchen table.

"You see right here he says . . ."

"Please, Mrs. Henry. Please sit down for a moment." Taking her arm Johnny pulled one of the chrome kitchen chairs out from the table and moved it in behind the confused woman.

"Mrs. Henry, Terrance's letter is dated over a month ago. This telegram is from the War Department. Terrance was killed by enemy fire yesterday morning. Your son is dead," said Julius Alfred with as much compassion as he could muster.

Gladys brought the dishtowel she had been carrying in her hands to her breast and Johnny supported her weight as she slowly sat in the chair. Her eyes filled with helplessness, and grew wide with fear as the realization of their visit began to sink in. She looked up at both of them hoping for some sort of words that would rectify the situation and undo the awful mistake they had made, but none came. She looked down at the telegram. Unable to clearly see the print now she wiped the tears from her eyes with one hand while the other hand trembled, shaking the letter about. The only words she could clearly see through her tears she softly read out loud, "Killed in Action." Her shoulders slumped and she gazed toward the kitchen door.

"Terranccce!"

Sitting in the sofa chair, Douglas Henry stared out the living room window. The yard was full of cars. Gladys worked in the kitchen trying to give some order to feeding the fifty or so friends and neighbors that had dropped by after Terrance's funeral. The kitchen and dining room was piled high with hams, fried chicken, vegetable dishes, casseroles and every other imaginable configuration of food. Gladys had always been the first to show up with a dish of food at a friend or neighbor's house during their time of sorrow. Now it was their turn and with the food spread about she was occupied doing what she had done best nearly all of her adult life, taking care of family and friends.

Douglas himself had helped sick and grieving neighbors lots of times with necessary chores. Even a death in a family didn't bring things on a farm to a stop. Chores had to be done. Neighbors in Knifley helped one another in hard times.

Across the road in front of his home, Douglas could see Roy Appleton and his two teenage sons moving in and out of Douglas' milking parlor and barn, their breath steaming in the cool crisp November air. One son brought grain and hay into the milk parlor to feed his twenty-five Holstein cows, as Mr. Appleton and his other son worked vigorously on the cow's teats, emptying their udders. That's where he needed to be. The work would help numb the pain he felt in his heart. He hadn't cried when Mr. Alfred came down to the barn to get him that day. He had rushed up to the house to be with Gladys. He hadn't cried at the funeral parlor that first day Terrance was back. If he had been able to see Terrance's body, he may have folded, but viewing was impossible due to the massive injuries and the length of time it took for the Army to get Terrance home from Korea. He busied himself greeting his friends and neighbors as they came to pay their respects. He talked with the Army boys who were there as Terrance's Honor Guard. Nice young men, all Terrance's age. They were too young for World War II and hadn't been to Korea yet, but they acted like they couldn't wait to get in the action. He prayed the war would end before they came home in a body bag, their parents devastated and brokenhearted like he and Gladys.

That morning as he and Gladys, and the kids sat at the grave side, he watched as the Army boys in their dress uniforms and white gloves, took the American flag from the coffin and folded it neatly into a triangle with nothing but the blue field and white stars exposed. The sergeant turned and slowly rotated the flag over and into the hands of a captain. Douglas was proud that the Army thought enough of his son to send an officer to head up the Honor Guard. As the captain handed Gladys the flag and him the box with a Purple Heart in it, the first volley of the Twenty-One Gun Salute was fired on the hill above the grave by seven soldiers. Gladys and the children jumped. He sat motionless and nodded his appreciation to the officer. As the second volley of gunfire reverberated off the hill, Douglas reached over and took his wife's hand. The third and final volley completed the twenty-one reports and silence fell on the group of people gathered around the grave.

From up on the hill near the riflemen came the slow, methodic tones of a bugle as it wailed out the notes of Taps, slow and deliberate. Each note was blown out and blended to the next, carrying the sad message from beginning to end. There were no words to the notes. There wasn't meant to be. No words were necessary. The wailing bugle conveyed the intense grief associated with the loss of a loved one, the loss of a fellow soldier. Intertwined with the grief there was the proud message of comrades and family standing faithfully with their buddy and loved one until his mission was done. Just as Terrance had played and worked across the hills and valleys, pastures and woods, the bugle notes drifted with the wind and settled on the land.

When the last note faded away and the bugle fell silent, the Baptist minister stepped over, shook Douglas' hand and walked down the line of chairs shaking hands and giving words of encouragement.

As the crowd left the gravesite, two men stood silently waiting to shovel dirt, rock and slate back into the hole where Terrance lay. Douglas walked over and took a shovel from one of the men and began filling the hole. His next oldest son, Derrick took up the other shovel and took turns with his younger brother Phillip, helping their father do the last thing for Terrance they could do on this earth. Gladys and the girls stood patiently waiting for them along with several close friends. When the task was complete, Douglas and his sons handed the shovels back to the workmen, shook their hands and walked down the hill to the car.

Douglas hadn't cried a single tear since he got the news about Terrance. He had cried all day, when they buried his mother. He was thirty-one. He had wiped the tears from his eyes each time the announcement of the birth of one of his children came, as Dr. Hall stuck his head out of the bedroom door and called out, "Douglas, Gladys is fine and you got a fine healthy baby here!"

Douglas wasn't afraid to cry, but for some reason he couldn't find it in himself this time. Maybe it was the numbing shock of losing Terrance the way he was lost. Maybe he wasn't ready yet. He didn't know as he sat there in his chair and stared out the front window.

The last guest left around 6:30 that evening. Ray Appleton had offered to come again the next morning to milk, but Douglas had thanked and assured him he and his boys would see to the chores. He had gone to bed at his usual eight o'clock that evening because four came early. Gladys settled in next to him and went quietly to sleep. She was exhausted, physically and mentally. The rest of the children were in bed and sound asleep by nine o'clock.

At one AM the Henry house was calm as usual. Fester, the house cat, was asleep in his spot on the couch and the bell clock ticked rhythmically away on the marble top dresser in the living room. Somewhere around a quarter past one the sudden, intense wailing of unleashed grief shattered the stillness of the house. The Henry children sat up startled in their beds. Realizing the mournful weeping was coming from their parent's room, they all sprang from their beds and dashed to their parent's aid. Entering the room, they found their father sitting on the edge of the bed rocking back and forth, in their mother's consoling arms.

Douglas Henry had not slept since lying down a little after eight o'clock. His emotions had come to a head in the middle of the night and exploded, as he sat there on the edge of his bed fighting to repress the flood of emotion that was boiling inside of him. When his anguish released it was intense and unrestrained. The loud wails were coming from deep in the heart of a man who was coming to terms with the loss of his oldest son, his best friend and the one who would most certainly have taken over the farm someday, for Terrance had been everything Douglas had hoped he would be. There was no place his son would rather be than out working on the farm.

The children ran to his side. They cried and hugged their father tightly, trying to comfort him in his grief. Douglas' wails drowned out their weeping as the family grieved together into the morning.

*   *   *   *

The four men and two women stood in the barn hall stripping the Lowe's burley tobacco. A potbelly, wood-burning stove sat in the middle of them providing warmth to those who stood within its circle of heat. It was a cold enough day. The tobacco leaf had come into case earlier in the week. Silas and Jordon had theirs stripped and booked down, ready for the market. Samuel Woods' was also ready for the market. Ed Parker leased his tobacco to the Hamilton brothers. At seventy-eight he no longer desired to work it. Dorothy and May Long were there, both good hands when it came to stripping the burley leaf off the stalks. The six had accomplished quite a bit that morning and would likely finish up that evening. By the end of next week, the burley would be sitting on the warehouse floor in Greensburg, providing Martha a much-needed tobacco check.

The leaf that hung in the barn loft was partly gone now, tied in hands, stacked and covered by a heavy tarp at the end of the hall. A large pile of leaf, still on the stalks lay in the middle of the hall to one side or the other of the workers. Occasionally Jordon would climb up in the barn tiers, straddle the lateral poles and hand sticks loaded with tobacco stalks down to Samuel, replenishing the pile.

Samuel stayed busy grabbing the loaded sticks and pulling an armful of leafy stalks off and depositing the stalks next to each worker around the circle.

"You wanna know what I think?" exclaimed Samuel. "I think that Wilkerson woman has a lot of nerve showing her face around town after walking out on her husband and four little children."

"Disgraceful," added Silas as he tore the four or five bottom leaves off the tobacco plant and laid the stalk with its remaining leaves over to his right. He continued to tear the trash leaves off of several stalks, gathering the leaves from the plant in his left hand as he went. When he had a hand full, he took a single leaf and twisted it around the base of the leaves several times. On the last twist he took the last few inches of the leaf base and threaded it through the middle of the hand of leaves and out the other side. Placing the hand of tobacco in the pile behind him he started on a new hand. Jordon, May and Dorothy tied the lugs or reds—the middle leaves. Ed and Samuel tied the tips, the top and less desirable grade of leaf. The stripped stalks were tied in bundles of twenty or so with grass strings, saved from bales of hay. The bundles of stalks would find their way out into the fields, where they would rot over the winter, providing nutrients to the soil. Nothing was wasted on the farm.

"So, you think she has a lot of nerve, do you? You want to know what I think, Silas Long?" May glared at Silas, his head suddenly down focusing on his stripping. "I think you know nothing of what that woman has gone through at the hands of that no-good, drunk husband of hers." May looked across the cast iron stove, eyes glowing.

Jordon smiled. "Don't get that woman started," he laughed. "She'll heat up like that stove and there are way too many loose tobacco sticks around here for any of us to be safe."

May's eyebrows lowered as she pointed a stalk tip at Silas.

"She shouldn't have left her children with that man, I'll grant you that. He's mean as a rattlesnake and he's beat on those children, just like he's beat her. I ask you, Silas Long, what kind of man gets liquored up and beats his wife and kids?"

Silas raised his hands in front of his chest in a sign of surrender. The thick brown gum from the tobacco leaves was caked on his palms and fingertips.

"You're right! You're right! I know'd he was a drinker when I opened my big mouth. There are two sides to everything. I guess, ah, I know there is, and that poor woman probably put up with four kinds of h . . ."

Dorothy cut him off. "The whole community knew and never raised a hand to help her. It's a dry county, for heaven sakes!"

"Now Dorothy, you know if a man is weak to drink, there is not a whole lot anyone can do about it," interjected Silas. "All he has to do is visit that colored bootlegger in town and refuel himself."

Stripping faster now Dorothy glared at her husband. "You're one to talk. Didn't Wilber Sutton visit you last Friday night on his tractor, so drunk he could barely sit up straight, much less keep it on the road? He near fell off the tractor right there in our yard."

"Woman, you'd do well to hold your tongue, but since you can't, I'll say he did, and I'll say that I had him park that tractor, and I took him home."

Dorothy glared at her husband across the stove realizing she erred in mentioning old man Sutton's visit.

"Well, isn't it about time for lunch," cut in Jordon. "I'm starving." Grabbing his lunch tote he sat down on a bale of hay and gave May a knowing nod.

"Lunch? Lunch! Of course." May grabbed her tote, walked over and sat next to her husband.

By the end of the day the loft was empty of tobacco. The different grades of leaf were on tobacco sticks, booked down in separate piles and covered with the canvas tarp, which helped retain the moisture in the leaf. The two women had gone home around four to prepare supper for their families and get a head start on tomorrow's Thanksgiving meal. It was questionable as to what kind of supper Silas would get that night.

Jordon knocked on the Lowe front door.

The door opened, "Oh Jordon, won't you come in for supper?"

"No thank you, Martha, but it's kind of you to offer. The burley is stripped and booked down. I can see it to the market next Thursday, when I take mine, if it suits you?"

"Jordon, I can't tell you what it means to have it out of the way. Howard would be so pleased to know everyone helped out."

"He's done the same for me and would do it again. You and the girls have a happy Thanksgiving tomorrow Martha."

"God bless you Jordon, and give my thanks to May."

Jordon nodded his head, turned and briskly walked down the steps, as he still had cows to milk before he could settle down for supper. Climbing into his flatbed truck he headed up the lane.

Tomorrow is Thanksgiving, Mom," said Wanda Faye, as Martha and Mrs. Katherine busied themselves in the kitchen.

"Yes indeed, young lady and we have much to be thankful for, especially this wonderful meal Mrs. Katherine is cooking for our company."

"Mom, can Nelly and Coral bring their bicycles? We would like to ride up and play dolls with Elizabeth and Rebecca."

"No, honey, they'll be expecting company, also. Just plan on playing here, and Nelly and Coral will bring their dolls, but not their bicycles."

"Mom!" whined Amy Sue.

"That will be enough young lady. No bike riding and that's final."

"But Mom, I!"

"Amy Sue!"

"Mom," interceded Wanda Faye. "I think she has to go to the bathroom."

Turning from the kitchen counter, Martha looked down at her youngest and found her standing with her legs held tightly together, and a pained look on her face.

"Child, when are you going to learn not to put off nature? Wanda Faye, get the flashlight and walk with your sister to the outhouse."

"Yes, ma'am."

Wanda Faye took her younger sister by the hand and led her waddling out of the kitchen. They grabbed their heavy coats from the wardrobe in the hall, slipped into them, and donned their stocking caps. Wanda Faye picked up the flashlight from the red cedar, library table and headed out the front door, flashlight in one hand, Amy Sue in the other. The path to the outhouse was thirty or so yards from the front porch, but to two young children traveling after dark, it seemed considerably longer. Every trip was an adventure.

"I'm telling you those girls just tickle me to death."

"Mrs. Katherine, I doubt that you would feel that way if you had to put up with their shenanigan's day in and day out. They're at that busy age, you know."

"Get yourself and your big belly over to that chair and get off your feet. I'll finish up what needs to get done tonight. Do I need to constantly remind you that Dr. Slaton told you to stay off your feet? Seems to me you're the one fighting nature!"

Sitting down, Martha said, "I don't know how he expects me to do so."

"He expects it, because he remembers the difficult time you had with Amy Sue. He expects it because he knows I'm here to help. Now get those feet up. The girls will be happier than kittens at milking time, helping me get the rest of these dishes ready for tomorrow."

Mrs. Katherine was up at six the next morning finishing this and that in the kitchen, straightening up the house, and laying out clean clothes for the girls. The guests would arrive around ten.

"God Bless this home," said Brother Cook as he and Gracie entered the Lowe home.

"Let me take your wraps," said Martha. "Silas and Dorothy are here, when Karen and the girls arrive we'll sit down to dinner. Henry, why don't you take the pumpkin pie to the kitchen."

Relieved of his coat and hat Brother Cook smiled and disappeared into the kitchen.

"Well, Padre! I've never seen a good meal that there wasn't a man of the cloth lurking in the shadows, trying to get his fingers in it before a proper blessing could be said. Shouldn't you be out somewhere wrestling with Lucifer?"

"Indeed, Mrs. Katherine, I should be doing just that, as God's work is never done with the Devil on the loose. But mortal man must pause occasionally for nourishment and my, my, what is that glorious smell?" Brother Cook watched as Mrs. Katherine took a large baking pan from the wood stove oven and sat it on a heat pad. As she turned her back to stir the beans, he quietly lifted the pan lid and tore a strip off the turkey's breast. Carefully replacing the lid, he sat down at the table. Smiling to herself, Mrs. Katherine tasted a green bean and dropped another pinch of salt into the pot.

"I don't think you fooled Mrs. Katherine for a second with your sneaking around," whispered Silas as he leaned toward Brother Cook.

"I don't foresee the day when I, or anyone on God's green earth will get the best of Mrs. Katherine, so my goal is simple. Snatch a pinch here and there, and avoid a whack from her wicked stirring spoon." Taking a bite of the turkey he closed his eyes and praised the cook, "It tastes as if the angels in heaven themselves have cooked the bird."

"Angels, indeed! You take far too many liberties with that religion of yours, Padre! Enjoy what you got there, 'cause you'll be waiting with the rest of us sinners to taste the rest of it."

Laughing uproariously, Silas slapped his friend on the back. Enjoying the moment Brother Cook finished the turkey strip and continued the harmless bantering with his favorite cook. The laughter in the kitchen turned heads for only a moment in the living room, where more serious conversations were taking place.

"Honestly, Martha, you need to ask Mr. Moreman to assign a substitute at Tabor until you've had the child and recovered. It wouldn't hurt to sit out the rest of the school year and spend your time loving that new baby, anyway. It's all too much without Howard here to help you."

"I know you're probably right, Gracie, but working keeps my thoughts occupied."

Martha walked over and hung the two coats in the wardrobe and placed the hats on the top shelf. Turning, she took Gracie by the hand as they walked over to the sofa and sat down.

"I do need to get off my feet more and more lately. Look at these ankles. Aren't they a sight?"

The swollen ankles were well below the hem of her mid-calf dress. She kicked off her house slippers and swung both feet up to the round vinyl ottoman.

"I thank my lucky stars I've got Mrs. Katherine."

"You're lucky and she's lucky to have you. Otherwise, she would be alone in that big old home of hers. It keeps her young, having someone to take care of. She's been lonely without Monty. It's been some time since he passed, but I don't think she'll ever get used to being without him, oh dear me! I'm so sorry, Martha. There I go putting my foot in my mouth."

Taking Gracie by the hand Martha said, "It's the honesty of our friends that get us through such trying times. Don't start tiptoeing around Howard. He is still very much a part of our lives and will always be, no matter what."

"Mom! It's Nelly and Coral. They're coming up the yard and Nelly's carrying her new doll," announced Wanda Faye.

"Well, don't stand there child, go let them in." Martha swung her feet around into the slippers, stood and walked to the front door.

Wanda Faye was already out the door, down the steps and hugging Nelly. Amy Sue and Coral were dashing about the yard in a frantic game of tag. Karen carried a large basket covered with a dishtowel in one hand, and a pie in the other. She held two dolls under her right arm. She wore a heavy woven, dark brown wool coat. A long tan scarf warmed her neck, while a dark brown derby hat sat on her head, held in place with a shiny hatpin. She smiled at Martha, as she stepped out on the porch.

"Happy Thanksgiving, Martha. We're pleased to be able to share this day with you and the girls."

"What a crisp fall day it is," said Martha as she met Karen at the top of the steps and gave her sister a hug.

Gracie stepped out the front door and relieved Karen of the basket and apple pie. In the kitchen she dropped off the basket with Mrs. Katherine and dodged her husband's out-stretched hands on the way to the screened in back porch with the pie.

"Girls! Girls! In the house, now! We'll be eating directly." As the girls ran past, Coral grabbed her two dolls and handed one to Amy Sue. Neither girl missed a step as they followed Wanda Faye and Nelly through the living room and into the side bedroom. No sooner inside, Amy Sue ran back out and into the kitchen clutching one of Coral's dolls. *"Mrs. Katherine, our tousins are here!"*

"Not so loud child. I'm not deaf, yet!" Holding the doll to her cheek, Amy Sue whispered, "Mrs. Katherine, our tousins are here." She smiled and skipped back into the bedroom. The noise level in the bedroom remained tolerable, confirming what Mrs. Katherine once said to Martha, "When you don't hear 'em, you'd better check 'em."

Mrs. Katherine put the final touches on the dishes as Brother Cook and Silas set the table. Wanda Faye appeared briefly in the kitchen to get coloring books and crayons, gave one look at the place settings, rolled her eyes and walked out, shaking her head and mumbling to herself.

Martha returned to the sofa to prop up her feet, joined by Karen. Gracie went into the kitchen to help Mrs. Katherine.

"Mathew still not feeling well?

With a pained look Karen replied, "He seemed to be better when he first got up, but I'm afraid it just got worse as the morning went on . . ." Karen hesitated for a moment and said, "It was best for him not to come."

Martha laid a sympathetic hand on Karen's arm, but said nothing, as nothing needed to be said.

"I'm on a mission to gather the flock," said Brother Cook as he walked through the kitchen door. "The table's set and the feast is ready. If you don't hear from me in a few minutes, call the County Sheriff's office to send help."

Chuckling, Martha and Karen got up and walked to the kitchen, as Brother Cook disappeared into the bedroom.

The kitchen table was crowded with place settings to serve all seven adults. Karen and Gracie were busy in the living room setting up a card table and four chairs for the children. The food was lined up on the wood stove and counter top in buffet fashion, ready to be served.

Although two minutes had come and gone, no call was made to the Sheriff's office. Just as the place settings on the card table were complete, Brother Cook appeared leading the girls, hand-in-hand, into the kitchen. As was the custom in the Lowe house, everyone formed a circle around the kitchen table and held hands, young and old, big and small.

Martha addressed the gathering, "It is a very special occasion when close friends can get together and share Thanksgiving. The girls and I have much to be thankful for, especially with such special friends that have come to share with us today. Brother Cook, if you will give the blessing, we will all serve ourselves, sit down and enjoy the wonderful meal Mrs. Katherine has prepared for us."

Holding Martha's hand on one side and Amy Sue on the other, Brother Cook bowed his head and said, "Children let us find strength in the Lord's word. *'And we rejoice in the hope of the glory of God. Not only so, but we also rejoice in our suffering, because we know that suffering produces perseverance, perseverance, character, and character hope. And hope does not disappoint us, because God has poured out his love into our hearts by the Holy Spirit, whom he has given us.'* Lord, bless this food that has been prepared to nourish us today. We give thanks for the Lowe family and ask a special blessing for Howard as he perseveres in Korea. It's in your son's name we pray, Amen."

＊   ＊   ＊   ＊

The Friday after Thanksgiving Day had always held special meaning to Douglas and Gladys Henry. Douglas and the boys would take the family beagle hounds out for a day of chasing rabbits on the back of the Henry farm. The thick fence rows and briar patches around the fields of harvested corn and soy beans were sanctuaries for small Kentucky cottontails.

Gladys and the girls would rise just as early and drive to Louisville to get an early start on the Christmas shopping season. The Christmas Holiday window displays at the Sears and Roebuck Department Store on Broadway were always a highlight for the children. The mechanical reindeer, Santa and Mrs. Claus, and elves moved about doing their holiday business. It was magical in the crisp November air. Inside the holiday smells filled the air. Roasted cashews, warm sugar cookies, and the aroma of eggnog drifted throughout the large store. Elevators were mysterious, but a ride up and down the escalator was thrilling for children from a rural community.

Back on the farm Douglas, the boys and the hounds where having a good day. The cool temperatures were perfect for the hunt. The tri-colored hounds had dashed around excited, knowing full well the significance of the shotguns being carried. Duke was wetting down a fence post when Jack jumped a rabbit from the fence row in the back of the smokehouse. Duke quickly joined the chase as the rabbit took them down through the barnyard and into the woods. Douglas stayed by the smokehouse, Derrick and Phillip positioned themselves on either side of the barn lot. Douglas and the boys followed the hound's progress by their frantic baying and yelping. The short-legged beagles took their time and pushed the rabbit full circle back around the north side of the lot. With skillful accuracy and his grandfather's old Winchester Model 12, Derrick made good his first shot. Holding the rabbit by its hind legs he allowed the dogs to leap up and get just a taste of the blood-covered head. With fur lined mouths the happy hounds went back to the business of sniffing and working their way up the fence row.

At noon the hunting party sat on a rock fence next to a stream that split the farm in half. They nourished themselves with bologna on crackers, and tea left over from supper the night before. The dogs drank from the stream and milled about waiting for the signal to return to the hunt. The count of rabbits in game pouches were: Derrick three, Phillip two and Douglas one. The competition between the two boys was traditionally fearsome. Had Douglas not passed on several shots his boys would have just one cottontail apiece. The kill was an important part of the hunt and Gladys' rabbit stew was delicious, but Douglas had learned over time, as his boys would eventually learn, the fellowship of the hunt, father to sons, and master to hounds, made a day in the field special. The number would go up as the best rabbit country was yet to come after they crossed the stream and worked the honeysuckle fence row that edged a freshly cut soy bean field.

The last twenty-five miles of their return trip, through Campbellsville to Knifley, was after dark. Gladys and the girls enjoyed seeing the colored Christmas lights on the scattered homes through Campbellsville and a few here and there along the country road. When they pulled into their gravel driveway the back porch light was on, giving them safe passage from the garage to the back door. Jack and Duke had greeted them with barks as they pulled up the drive, but made no effort to leave their doghouse. Gladys' knew that tired hounds meant the hunt had been successful.

Leaving the gifts in the back end of the station wagon, they carefully picked their way to the house and entered through the screened in porch. Sitting at the kitchen table was Douglas. A sad expression covered his face as he held in his hand a letter, and an unopened envelope.

Staring at his wife and daughters he said, "We received a letter from one of Terrance's buddies in Korea. Terrance asked him to mail us this letter," Douglas held up an envelope with "Mom, Dad and Family" written on it. "Blake says Terrance had a bad feeling about how things were going and wrote it after breakfast the day he was killed. He asked Blake to make sure we got it, if anything happened to him. Susan, fetch Derrick and Phillip from upstairs and we will see what your brother had to say."

The Henry family gathered in the living room. Douglas and Gladys sat on the couch, with twelve-year-old Susan. Derrick sat in one of the Queen Ann chairs with Barbara in his lap. Phillip was in the other, sharing the large chair with Cynthia, his twin. Each family member had someone to sit close to, to hold on to while they listened to Terrance's letter.

Douglas wiped the tears from his eyes, pulled himself up straight on the couch and opened the envelope. Susan clung to his arm as he began to read:

November 5, 1952
South Korea

Mom, Dad and Kids,

If you receive this letter the worst possible thing has happened to me. I know it has been very difficult for all of you and I don't want this letter to add to your grief, but I feel it's important for you to know how much I love all of you. Time, distance and separation have helped me to understand the great gift God gave us in each other. I feel a great pain in my heart as I write this and think that I may not be there with you to watch the family grow up. I feel a greater pain when I think of the loss all of you must feel each day. Please know that my love for you all did not end with my life here in Korea. My love is with you now, there in the living room as you have this family meeting. My love will be with you tomorrow and the next day and the next, until we meet again someday. That will never change.

I suspect it must be close to Thanksgiving. Remember how much we have to be thankful for as Christmas approaches. Always remember the wonderful times we had together and value the time you will continue to have together.

As I sit here in my tent, I have much to be thankful for and it gives me a considerable amount of peace. I am thankful that I had such a special baby sister like you, Barbara. The rides I gave you on my back and shoulders were all special. You are going to grow up to be big and beautiful someday.

I am thankful to have two very special people for a brother and sister, like you Cynthia and Phillip. I never could figure out if I wanted a brother or sister when mom was carrying you, so imagine my excitement when Dad told me we got both. You two have a very special relationship and that will always be with you as you grow up and have your own families.

I am thankful to have a sweet and considerate sister like you, Susan. When I needed someone to talk to about special things, you were always there for me, just as I tried to be there for you. You have been such a big help to Mom around the house and Dad with the farm work. There will be someone out there for you, trust me. It will happen one day and you'll get to spend the rest of your life with him.

I am thankful for having a wonderful, younger brother like you, Derrick, who was my little pal, my wrestling buddy, my farmhand to order around. You were always a big help to me with all of your hard work.

I am so thankful for having loving parents, parents who didn't always let me have my way, but who were always there when I needed someone to help me through difficult times. Mom, I have missed you so much. Your home cooked meals. When you are sitting at the piano, singing a hymn or telling the kids a bedtime story, I will be standing next to you, listening, watching and loving.

Dad, I'm so sorry. All I ever wanted to do was work with you on the farm. Nothing can change the fact that I'm gone, but always remember that when you are plowing the Shady Grove field, I will be on the John Deere beside you just like I was when I was little. When you're milking late at night, I will be there in the barn beside you. I am part of the farm now and everywhere you go, in everything you do I will be there beside you.

Enough of this sad stuff! The holidays are on the way and Christmas at the Henry House is always a happy and joyful occasion. When you reach the end of this letter I want to see a big family hug just like the old days. I will be right there with you, my arms around all of you, hugging away.

Love,

Terrance

CHAPTER 11

▼

"Well, I for one can't say as I miss the bastards. Noncoms been picking on me since I got in this man's Army and them officers are a bunch of stuck up rich kids who don't know shit from Shinola away from their golf courses and tennis courts. Can't say as I'll miss any of 'em."

Welch listened to the cocky soldier talking to two younger soldiers.

"But who's going to watch out for us? They moved the officers and then the non-coms. Commander Fletcher stood up to them. The goonies will do whatever they want to with us now."

"Hey! You're not listening kid. I said we don't need 'em. We're all equal now. Rank means nothing. Hey, you gonna give me the damn smoke, or do I have to kick your ass and take it from you?"

The soldier was uncertain, scared and with good reason. The absence of leadership had an unsettling effect on the remaining prisoners. Know-it-all, loud talking bullies had come out of the woodwork, taking advantage of the weak, preying on the discord and uncertainty. Camp discipline had gone to hell.

Welch and his squad maintained their group and self-discipline, despite the morale decay around them. They understood the importance of military discipline, especially in chaotic times.

"Apparently we're not all equal, pal," said Welch. "You've proven that since the sergeants left by your bullying and smart-ass attitude."

The men turned to face Welch. The two younger boys took a step back, leaving the loud mouth to face the larger Welch.

"You got some kind of problem, buddy?"

Welch took three quick steps and got right up into the man's face, violating his personal space, but more importantly, changing the distance between the two from striking to grabbing. Welch's size and quickness unsettled the man and his loud, bullish voice became less threatening.

"I got no beef with you."

Welch leaned down, nose to nose with the bully.

"Ah . . . there's no sense in anybody getting hurt here. I . . . ahh . . . gotta get down to the kitchen," and he turned and hustled away.

The two boys looked at Welch.

"Guys like that are all bark and no bite. If he gives you any more trouble, tell 'em to get lost."

As the boys nodded and walked away, Bob Green walked up and grunted, "You're too damn nice. You should've pinched his miserable little head off. What a waste of bone and flesh."

Green took a pocket-sized Old Testament Bible from his shirt pocket and read, "*And the Lord hardened the heart of the Pharaoh king of Egypt, and he pursued after the children of Israel.*' Well, we know how that ends." Green tore out the page and from another pocket took a package of ration tobacco, sprinkled some on *Exodus 14: 8–31*, rolled it neatly into a cigarette, lit the tip and inhaled deeply.

"Those things are going to kill you."

"If they don't, the chinks will. There's plenty of ration tobacco and I'm learning some of the Bible. I just can't figure out what I'm going to do when I run out of scripture."

"The Lord will provide, Bob. Didn't he deliver you a pocket-sized New Testament," said Welch smiling.

Green laughed and patted Welch on the back. "Indeed, he did, brother. Indeed, he did."

Welch looked thoughtfully at Green and asked, "Didn't you tell me you had a sergeant's stripe in forty-four?"

"I've been up the ranks more than once. Those extra stripes get awful heavy at times. Poor self-control and guys like Wylie with a little rank usually landed me in the stockade, minus a chevron or two. Our squad is hanging in there, we just need to step on guys like him when they get out of control, but be careful. As soon as someone steps forward to show some leadership, the chinks send him off to another camp. Keep it low profile."

"You're right, we've got to be careful."

Despite the drop-in discipline, the living conditions had gotten better at Camp Two. Word was the peace talks were moving along and the Chinese realized they had to start fattening the prisoners up, physically and mentally. The food was still pitiful, but considerably better than it had been.

The Geneva Convention on Prisoners of War stated that food rations given to prisoners had to be equal in quantity and quality to the rations given to the detaining power's soldiers. Since the Chinese and North Koreans had refused to sign the Geneva Accord, food for prisoners was not a strong issue for them. Even if it had been, the meager amounts of food they gave their own soldiers would have been difficult for most prisoners to survive on.

The Chinese were now allowing the prisoners to do their own cooking. Volunteers were working in the kitchen doing the cooking and manning the details. Rice was more frequent and occasionally meat and fish found its way into their diet.

Although the improvement in food lifted morale considerably, it didn't have nearly the impact the release of mail had for the men. Nothing elevates a soldier's spirits like Mail Call. The Chinese had used mail to reward and punish, but now all the letters seemed to be coming through. Incoming letters took months to arrive. The men had no idea if their letters were reaching home.

During the early stages of the war, food dominated the thoughts of the prisoners. The pain of hunger was with them when they woke up in the morning, and stayed with them throughout the day. They dreamed of hamburgers, steaks and milkshakes at night. Their stomachs ached constantly and the rations they received were barely enough to keep them alive.

Most of the American POWs had survived the Great Depression as their families scratched out a living. Being physically and mentally beaten down by the cruelty of the Chinese wasn't the same as Depression deprivation. Some survived. Some died. For those who had managed to hang on, things were looking up. They were still prisoners, but at least the Chinese weren't trying to starve them to death.

"How does baked chicken sound for supper?"

Welch looked up at Green with humorous disbelief. "You get caught stealing chickens from the Chinese mess again and they are going to be rough on you. You know they don't like it when you don't learn from your mistakes."

"Thirty days in solitary taught me a newfound respect for the guards. Remember my public confession? I said I wouldn't get caught stealing Chinese chickens again. I said nothing about Korean chickens," and Green pointed to the village outside the prison fence.

"What do you have in mind, professor?"

"It's done, Danny Boy, and in an hour, it will be ready to take out of the oven."

Welch smiled as a warm feeling came over his stomach.

"Earl and I were down at the fence this morning, gambling on those chickens that scratch around all the time out on the road. We would each pick a hen and I would toss a small pebble through the fence. Chickens think everything that hits the ground is something to eat, you know, so if the hen you picked grabbed the pebble, you won. We bet a smoke each time. If an unclaimed hen got the pebble the pot builds up."

Welch stared at Green, attempting to express disapproval.

"Hey! It's boring around here. Anyway, as one hen pecked at the pebble it occurred to me it's a damn shame to let all that eatin' go to waste just because it's on the wrong side of a big fence. I thought on it a bit and realized I could stretch a hole in the fence, lay a small pile of rice on this side and when the hen stuck her head through, I'd yank a noose around her neck. Sort a like fishing. The guards see us down there all the time and don't give us any mind."

"So, the chicken sticks her head in the noose and says, 'Well, you got me Imperialist Pig, give me a sec to quietly step through the hole in the fence.'"

"If I could talk chicken, I'd charm them into jumping over the fence and climbing under my jacket. Until then, I'll yank 'em through, and wring their necks. We got three this morning, cleaned and packed them in mud and stuck 'em in the coals under the wash drums in the back of the kitchen. One of them is yours and Howard's. Drop by the kitchen in about an hour. I don't deliver."

Welch walked across the yard toward the School House carrying a bag of clean clothes. The mud packed hen was wrapped in a towel, concealed under his jacket. The bag of clothes concealed the bulge. In his free hand was a large pail of boiled water.

It was cold and the baked ball of mud kept his stomach warm. A little too warm at first and he had a slight burn on his side to prove it. In his squad room he found Howard Lowe lying on his mat staring at the ceiling. Lowe had had lots of ups and downs since arriving at the camp. At that moment he was on an upswing which allowed him to venture out of the School House once a day. He spent most of his waking hours sitting at a table in the squad room. He was waking from his afternoon nap when Welch walked in.

"Chop, chop!" quipped Welch.

"I don't need a menu, Dan. Just bring me the special. There's something about that purple mush that whets my appetite."

"Maize it is, governor. Let me get it set up and I'll help you over to the table."

Welch took two handmade, metallic forks out of his pocket and laid them down on the table next to two small pans. He poured water in the tin cups, and placed the mud ball at the center of the table.

"Will we be dressing for dinner, or are we dining casual tonight?"

"Casual, if you please. My tux is still at Goonies' Dry Cleaning after last week's dinner party."

Welch assisted Lowe off the mat and walked with him over to the table. The room was cold, despite the presence of a fire burning in the barrel stove in the hall. A blanket was draped across Lowe's shoulders. His gait was wobbly from avoiding pressure on his bad leg. As good as he felt, he still couldn't walk on his own. There had been times when he had gone in his pants as he struggled to get help to get to the latrine. As dysentery came and went, so did your bowels. Everyone always had a touch of it. Welch was always there to help him clean up.

It was a great puzzlement to Lowe that Dan Welch helped him so much. He would feed him when he didn't have the strength to feed himself. He would change his bandages, clean his wounds, read to him and write his letters. Someday soon he would have to ask him why, before he up and died.

Sitting at the table they rinsed their hands in a small pan of boiled water and air-dried them. Looking down, Lowe noticed the dried mud ball sitting in the middle of the table.

"Nice center piece. You take up ceramics at the camp craft shop?"

"Yes. I call it 'Dirt Ball', after the camp commandant."

Lowe chuckled as he picked up the fork and gazed around the table for the maize. Looking at Welch he shrugged his shoulders.

"Special meal tonight, compliments of Bob and Earl's Korean Carry-out.

Close your eyes and see if you can guess the mystery meat."

Lowe closed his eyes as Welch picked the mud ball up and banged it down on the table. It cracked like an egg and the smell of baked chicken filled the air. Lowe's eyes shot open and he stared down at the baked hen.

"Bob stealing Chinese laying hens again?"

"Nope. This is wild chicken. Well, almost wild. Let's just call it 'Baked Town Chicken and Rice,' compliments of the people of North Korea."

Welch began to pull chunks of chicken off the hen and place it in their pans. The cavity of the hen was packed with rice, chopped chicken livers and gizzards.

The men ate quietly, savoring each bite. In a short time, there was nothing left on the carcass but bones and tiny pieces of meat here and there. Tomorrow's supper would be chicken soup. It was just a week before Christmas, but neither man brought it up. Christmas in the prison camp was too painful to discuss.

Welch picked up his tin cup and held it up for a toast, as did Lowe.

"To your recovery, Howard."

"To the end of the war and home, Dan."

Welch smiled, saluted, and turned up the cup.

*   *   *   *

Martha sat quietly at the table with the girls. They were having meatloaf, mashed potatoes, green beans and cornbread sticks, the girl's favorite meal, as well as Howard's. She had eaten barely half of her meal. As Christmas grew near she missed Howard all the more. Her heart couldn't seem to grasp the idea of the holidays being happy holidays without Howard by her side.

The girls were pleading for a tree to decorate. By this time in December they would have gone with their dad to fetch one. She couldn't see to it with Dr. Slaton's orders to stay off her feet. Mrs. Katherine was taking a few days off to see to her own home. Martha wasn't sure she wanted a tree anyway. It just wasn't the same without Howard.

The girls had nearly cleaned their plates when Amy Sue bounced down to the floor with an "Extuse me a couple of whiles! I get my wings," and off to her room she ran.

Martha put the leftovers in the icebox and went to get the girl's coats. They were dressed and everything was ready to go to the Tabor School House where the children would present their annual Christmas Play. All of the costume preparations were made in the classroom and the children would march next door to the Tabor Community Church to put on their annual show. The church pews would be packed. The Tabor School's presentation of the "Christmas Story" was pretty much your standard birth of the Christ child play with one exception, something catastrophic could always be expected to occur during the course of the play.

Last year, old man Burton's donkey took a mind to walk down the middle of the pews and out the front door with Mary, Beth Ann Browning, perched on its back, heavy with child, or in this case, heavy with sofa pillow. The donkey dragged a hollering Joseph, Bo Redman, out the door with it. That, in itself, was not a show stopper. When the two sheep followed, one of the shepherds, Allen Johnson, remembered the teachings of Jesus from Sunday school class and followed his lost sheep. The pigeons went airborne and flew around the sanctuary while the baby calf bawled. Chaos ensued and Raymond Tracy declared it an animal conspiracy. Whatever it was, it stopped the play for a good twenty minutes.

Year after year catastrophic events had doomed the play for the few seriously minded patrons, but Martha always saw past the imperfections and saw the real meaning of the Christmas play. The children enjoyed preparing and performing it, and the family members looked forward to each holiday with great anticipation of a new, unusual showstopper.

After last year's animal uprising Martha had considered going on without real animals and substituting the children in animal outfits, but decided against it. The animal-child relationship was what made the program special, despite its spontaneity and unpredictability. They had used real animals when she and Howard attended Tabor, and without them it wouldn't be the same.

At the schoolhouse the students were milling around reading their lines, very controlled and professional as any acting troupe. Mothers were arranging angel's wings, shepherd's robes and make-up. Rebecca Long had volunteered her father, Jordan, to manage the livestock. "Daddy has a way with animals," Rebecca had said. Exactly what Martha was counting on to get her through the play without anyone getting scratched, kicked or bitten.

The livestock were in their pens behind the church. The pews were full of parents, grandparents and those members of the community who came to support the children's efforts. Martha, Mrs. Katherine, May Long and Pate Goode rounded up the children and marched them over to the rear of the church. Standing at the back-door Martha looked to the heavens, said a quick prayer, and entered.

"And it came to pass in those days, that there went out a decree from Caesar Augustus that all the world should be taxed. And all went to be taxed, every one into his own city. And Joseph also went up from Galilee, out of the city of David, which is called Bethlehem, to be taxed with Mary his espoused wife, being great with child.

And so it was, that, while they were there, the days were accomplished that she should be delivered, and she brought forth her first born son, and wrapped him in swaddling clothes, and laid him in a manger, because there was no room for them in the inn."

Raymond Tracy took a deep breath and smiled. He had gotten through the play's opening lines without stammering, saying "ah" or repeating himself. He was pleased. He had practiced long hours, standing in the barn hall at home reading and reciting to an unappreciative mule named Susie.

In the back of the sanctuary standing on several bales of hay an angel of the Lord, Rebecca Long, addressed a group of shepherds, *"Fear not, for behold, I bring you good tidings of great joy, which shall be to all people. For unto you is born this day in the city of David a Saviour, which is Christ the Lord. And this shall be a sign unto you, Ye shall find the babe wrapped in swaddling clothes, lying in a manger."*

Behind Rebecca Lynn appeared a multitude of heavenly host in the form of her sister Elizabeth Gail, Amy Sue, Wanda Faye, Janice Sparks and Winnie Todd Baumgartner, all praising God.

"Glory to God in the highest, and on earth peace, good will toward men," and so it went through the evening.

The children hit their marks and remembered their lines. The only adlib occurred when Ty Clark, the innkeeper, "Hey manned," Joseph and told him to "beat it," before relinquishing and allowing the couple to stay in the manger. Ty had always been somewhat of a free spirit.

A real breath hanger did occur when the three kings visited the Christ Child in the manger and Stephen Michael's Billy goat decided to start munching on Amy Sue's angel wing. She would wiggle it off, but the goat was persistent. Amy Sue remained patient, with her mother's words ringing in her ears, "Behave yourself, just like rehearsal, nothing else."

Unfortunately, during rehearsal there were no goats eating angel wings, so this was new ground for the young lady. As chuckles started to build in the audience, Jordan noticed her dilemma. He knew both the goat and Amy Sue's temperament were similar, so he slowly made his way around the back of the set to intervene, which, he had no doubt, would soon become necessary. Nature soon took its course as cause and effect instantly led the situation out of control. The goat took a mouth full of wing and jerked it off, which led Amy Sue to turn and punch the goat in the nose. The goat kicked the bale of hay the shepherds were seated on and Stephen Michael, Otha Burton and Earl White went over backwards into the choir pit. Jordan quickly restrained the goat and moved it to its pen in the back lot of the church. The good shepherds were unhurt and returned to their seat on the bale of hay.

Amy Sue was a trooper and continued her angelic role through the rest of the play, short one wing. When Martha introduced each student before the closing prayer, Amy Sue received a standing ovation. The crowd of farming folks understood patience and admired the young girl. They also appreciated the need for action when all else fails, and they let Amy Sue know they whole heartily agreed with her actions.

The Christmas play was a success. The parents pitched in with the clean up and had the church and school house back in order in no time. Jordan managed the livestock until owners claimed their animals, and everyone wished one another a Merry Christmas as they parted for the holidays.

Martha was pleased and proud of the children. The Tabor School tradition of spontaneous entertainment to start the holidays lived on, as did most things in America the Christmas of 1952.

*   *   *   *

"I don't know. Looks kind of puny to me."

"It's not even a cedar or spruce. I'm not sure it's actually a tree," added Dale French.

"Well, I think it has potential. It's the best we can do, so let's add some Christmas cheer to it."

Les Wheatley stood in the corner of the room surveying the tree, or bush, he wasn't really sure either. Last year the Chinese had refused to allow the men to celebrate the holiday. This year the men were going to let it slide by until Howard Lowe said what he said. They were eating dinner one evening and the issue of Christmas came up.

"Are we going to celebrate Christmas?" asked Bob Green.

"Why bother. The chinks will just make us take everything down."

"You're probably right, Earl."

Forced to consider Christmas, there were several seconds of silence as the men sat dejected, their spirits beat down another notch.

"Why let them have their way? It's Christmas!"

The men turned to Lowe, who seldom participated in squad discussions. He was still the new kid on the block, and had a lot to learn about the way things had to be.

Welch looked around and felt ashamed. Sometimes you needed to do more than just survive. It was Christmas and a week of holiday cheer would be great for the men. He stood and dramatically threw his arms up in the air.

"Gentlemen, our pale friend is obviously delirious, racked with fever. Everyone can see he is not in his right mind. Only those of us who are losing all hope can understand the control the Chinese have over us. Let me apologize for Howard's outburst. His hope is admirable, but he knows not what he says."

Welch looked down at Lowe and winked.

"After he has been here for a year, he will be just as whipped as the rest of us. What the new kid doesn't understand is that we would rather not even try. We prefer to roll over, face the wall and give up." Welch passed a glance at Lowe.

"No, Howard! The Chinese say there is no Santa Claus, no Christ Child. We as prisoners have worked long and hard to sink to this level of misery and I, for one, say we don't need any of your good holiday cheer lifting our spirits."

The men looked at one another in silence until Bob Green stood up.

"I'll start scouting out a tree, guys, start thinking about decorations." There were murmurs of agreement amongst the men as Green scurried out of the room.

That evening Dale stood looking at the tree and smiled. "It's a good . . . tree, I think, and it's going to get better. Bob and I will do ornaments, or something that can pass for ornaments. Earl, find an angel thingy for the top. Dan and Howard make some stringy things to wrap around it. Everyone think about something personal they can put on the tree."

Welch and Lowe sat at the table in the squad room folding small pieces of aluminum foil into a chain. The foil pieces had fallen from the sky several weeks earlier as B-29 Bombers flew over on their way to bombsites in the north. The aircraft dropped the foil to interfere with the Chinese radar. There had been thousands of small two by two-inch pieces floating down like snow. The Chinese viewed the raining foil with great apprehension. Two soldiers had walked about with facemasks, collecting samples of the foil with tweezers to have them analyzed. Germ warfare remained a big concern for the Chinese. They were convinced America meant to harm them with chemical or biological agents.

When the Chinese felt confident it was nothing more than foil, they sent prisoners out to gather it up. Welch saw fit to save a box of it, and it turned out to be just the thing to string around the tree. He and Lowe had woven five ten-foot ropes. They had enough foil left for one more rope.

"You know this reminds me of stringing popcorn when I was little," Welch said. "Of course, more went into our bellies than on the tree."

"My girls and I string popcorn every Christmas. Martha makes double the amount, one bag of plain to string, another bag of caramel coated for eating."

"You won't find anything to eat on this tree. We'll be lucky if the guys don't eat the tree."

Lowe laughed, smiling one of his unusual smiles. They sat there folding the foil over and over again until they had a two by one-quarter-inch piece. Connecting and folding the piece onto the chain they moved to the next sheet, and on it went.

"You like farming?"

"Ever since I can remember. Grandpa got land in Arkansas for fighting in the Civil War and traded it for land in Kentucky. Been in the family ever since. Dad farmed until he had a stroke in '39 and I dropped out of college to keep things running. I went to play baseball, so it was no big deal. Farming was what the good Lord always meant for me to do."

"How many acres?"

"A bit under a hundred and seventy-one, half in timber, but it all lays good for the most part. My plan was to clear it all off, but I don't know now. If you can't hire out, clearing land for farming is back breaking work, moving rocks never ends, cutting down the timber, blowing out stumps and burning them with the laps and tree tops. It'll be impossible work for a cripple like me."

"Howard, old buddy! You got eighty-five acres to work. In West Virginia you would have to own three mountains to get eighty-five acres of farmable land. Besides, you can clear off a little at a time. Trade work with your neighbors."

Lowe sat contemplating a future in farming. He could barely walk now, but with proper medical care when he got back to the states, who knows what he could do.

"You're forgetting your pension, too. Why, you could save and pay some poor mindless fellow to do the hard work for you."

Lowe looked at Welch knowing he'd made good points, but also knowing his friend from West Virginia didn't really understand. He was from the mountains and coal mining was all he knew.

"It's not just about making a living, Dan. It's working the land," Lowe gazed past Welch as he talked. "A man works hard on his land from before sunup till after sundown. He scratches out a living and loves every minute of it. It's getting up before sunrise to feed your livestock. It's turning over your land in the spring and watching something grow that you put in the ground. You spend the summer weeding and keeping the bugs off it and you harvest it in the fall. It's raising steers and hogs to slaughter, putting food on the table that you don't have to buy at some supermarket. When you sit down at supper you eat things you grew right there on the farm with your own two hands, just like the Lord intended for you to do. Farming is being out in the winter, cleaning fence rows so your fence won't rust and you can squeeze a few more tillable feet out of a field. It's keeping outbuildings maintained and things around the house and barn lot neat and clean so you can look at it every evening when you go in to your wife and children knowing that you provide them with a place they can be proud of. You work for no man, Dan. You decide when and where you do things and when the day is done and the crops are in you sit back knowing that you're living with God's grace and blessing. Living like a man was intended to live. It's not just farming, Dan, never was, never will be."

Welch sat looking at Lowe silently, envying what he had and a newfound respect toward the man, the farmer. Welch's life back at home had been nothing more than working all day so Amelia could spend all night. He had no future other than Amelia and her needs. His whole life had revolved around her. He bowed his head in shame, reflecting that he never really did understand her. What she wanted. What she needed. She certainly didn't need him, just his money.

"If something happens, if I don't make it home, I want you to get a message to Martha that I want her to stay on the farm. I think she knows that already. I just want her to know it was my final wish that she keep the farm in the family."

"You tell her yourself when you get home," said Welch, smiling and patting Lowe on the shoulder. "Now, enough of this dribble. Let's get these ropes done for the tree."

The men sat and stood around their tree as Wheatley directed the trimming. The first to go on were the foil ropes. They were distinct, with detailed braids.

Welch once again impressed the men with his ability to weave. He and Lowe stood on either side of the tree and strung the shiny ropes.

Next came French and Green's ornaments. French stood, walked over to the tree and sat a box at its base. Green reached in and took out three wooden ornaments, each about two inches in size, a circle, a square and a triangle. Each painted a distinctively holiday color, red, green and gold. No one ever questioned Green on his resourcefulness. It was an accepted thing. The box contained about twenty ornaments, one for each man in the squad to hang on the tree.

The men stood around the room and gazed at the tree. The foil chains and brightly colored ornaments sparkled in the dim light hanging from the ceiling.

"Anyone who wants to place something personal can come and place it on the tree, now." The men came up one at a time. There were photographs of family members. One man drew stick figures of a man, woman, child and family dog, the names neatly printed below each person. There were letters from home, while others placed a paper with a flag drawn on it, or the name of a home state, or town. Morrison Turner stepped up and carefully dangled the dog tags of twelve men from the squad who had died over the past month. He quietly called out their names as he hung each chain on a limb. The men sat for several seconds quietly remembering their lost comrades.

"Okay, Earl. What ya got for the top?" asked Wheatley, interrupting the silence.

Earl Davenport walked over to the tree. Reaching inside his jacket he pulled out a rag doll angel. The body, arms and head were made from white cloth that was stitched together. She had a long gown of gold that dangled down in strands. Her arms were made from forked sticks and were covered with flowing, open sleeves. Her head was a ball of twine, with an angelic face drawn on it. Her hair was fashioned from thin red strings. The halo was formed from a copper wire and her wings, her wings were real pigeon wings, opened wide and nearly, perfectly white. He held it up for the men to admire.

"M . . . m . . . my mom has red hair," stammered Davenport.

"Earl, you old devil. I didn't know you played with dolls," said French to the laughter of the men.

"It was a difficult project. Give me a sta . . . sta . . . sta . . ." The men waited patiently as Earl struggled to form the word. "stack of lumber and a box of nails and I'll build you a house. I'd never bu . . . built an angel be . . . before. Her name is Angel Number Six. She's a bea . . . beauty, isn't she?"

The men sat starring at the cloth angel in wonder of its delicate design.

"I bu . . . built it, bu . . . but I want Howard to place it a top of the tree. Without him we wouldn't have done this. How . . . Howard."

Howard stood and with the help of one of the men, moved slowly over to the tree. Setting on the floor it was barely over five feet tall. He took Angel Number Six and placed her on the point of the tree. Reached out and shook Earl's hand.

"Merry Christmas, Earl."

"Merry Christmas, How . . . Howard."

The handshake led into a hug. The men around the room began wishing each other a Merry Christmas, shaking hands and hugging one another as the tears flowed down their cheeks.

$$\ast \qquad \ast \qquad \ast \qquad \ast$$

Wanda Faye and Amy Sue stood at the front window, fully clothed for the outdoors. Amy Sue looked like a little Eskimo child. It was the twenty-second day of December, 1952.

"There Rebecca and Elizabeth, Mommy."

Martha came from the kitchen and met the Longs at the front door.

"Well, Jordan, are you sure you're up to this. You want to take on these four girls all by yourself? I'm told there is a little goat fighter amongst them."

"Me not little," protested Amy Sue, crossing her arms and nodding her head, "and goat start fight!"

Amy Sue had always tickled Jordan, so he responded, "Well, young ladies there are no goats where we are going. Let's go find a Christmas tree."

The girls cheered and headed out the door on a dead run to the truck. The sideboards were on the flat bed, and Jordan had stacked several bales of hay to create a windbreak for the girls to ride in. May stayed with Martha to visit and help out with a few of the chores, while Mrs. Katherine was away for a couple of days visiting her great nephew in Bowling Green. The truck drove up the hill past the house, headed for the back fields of the Lowe farm, in search of the perfect Christmas tree.

Jordan had a keen eye for cedars that produced good holiday trees. Every December, he took his girls over to his old home place to cut down a tree for the living room. During November he would usually scout out several to choose from, come Christmas. The best trees stood by themselves, out away from fence rows and other cedars. They were full all the way around and grew straight, not needing to lean to get the sun they needed. A straight trunk was important for a tree to stand straight and tall, when it was loaded with decorations.

The day before he'd overheard Wanda Faye bravely telling his Rebecca that they couldn't have a tree this year. He could have kicked himself for not realizing they needed help to get one. The little things always seemed to get overlooked. Of course, little things to adults were big things to children.

The truck pulled up into the middle of a field and stopped. Hopping out, Jordan walked to the back and helped the girls down. Reaching between the sideboards and a bale of hay he got his double-headed ax, and the five of them walked into the middle of the cedar thicket. There were little cedars a few inches to a couple of feet tall. There were tall ones, some ten to fifteen feet. There were fat ones, as big around as the cab of his truck and skinny ones no bigger than a bushel basket.

The girls paired off and dashed around, sizing up the different cedars. Rebecca picked out one that could have easily been set out and decorated on the County courthouse lawn.

"Oh, Rebecca Lynn! That one is too big."

"Too big, too big," yelled Rebecca as she zipped in and out of the cedars.

Jordan noticed Amy Sue squatting next to a two-footer and walked over to see what she was up to.

"Nice little tree, Amy Sue. Well-rounded and straight."

"Too little. Too little like me."

Jordan squatted next to her and studied the tree.

"But you know what, Amy?" said Jordan as he took a strip of white cloth out of his coat pocket and loosely tied it to the trunk of the tree. "Someday you and your daddy can come back here to get this tree. It will have grown and will be just right for Christmas. Just remember this white cloth and that it's in the corner of this field."

Amy Sue smiled, "Just like me. I be just right someday."

"Yes, honey. Someday you will be just right."

Amy Sue hopped up, hugged Jordan around the neck, and zipped off to check out other little trees.

"Daddy, Daddy, over here," called Elizabeth.

"Mmmm, a nice one Elizabeth Gail. Let me see." Jordan walked around the tree and stopped on the backside.

"Oh, my. Look here. Look at the backside. There is a big bare spot. That won't decorate well."

Over behind a group of large cedars Wanda Fay spotted the right tree. It was perfect, sitting in the middle of a large opening all by itself, surrounded by patches of broomsedge. She walked slowly around it and every side was full and thick. It seemed to be the right height. She walked up close to it and extended her hand up in the air. It was just right, about as tall as her dad. She put her face up close and smelled the fresh cedar. A smell that reminded her of Christmas' past and Christmas' to come.

"Over here! Over here!" she yelled. The girls came running and by the time Jordan got there they had paired off, arm-in-arm and were skipping around the tree.

Jordan looked the tree over and smiled. The girl had her father's eye. The tree was about six feet tall, maybe four feet across at the bottom. It was perfectly shaped and the trunk was straight as a hickory sapling.

"All right girls, step back and let's get this beauty cut and on to the back of the truck. I believe there may be some hot chocolate waiting for us back at the house."

The girls cheered and stepped back to watch the tree come down.

Jordan studied the base of the tree for a moment, kneeled on one knee and with one light stroke of the ax the tree fell over. The girls cheered loudly, dancing about. Jordan reached his gloved hand into the middle of the tree to pick it up and noticed a white strip of cloth tied to the trunk. To his amazement he realized that Howard had probably marked it for future use as a holiday tree, a common practice in those parts. It would surely be a special treat for Martha and the girls when he showed them that Howard had handpicked their tree. Picking it up he headed for the truck, with the girls dancing and running about, all around him.

*   *   *   *

"It's the holidays. I saw it last year. Guys just curl up in the corner and will themselves to die. They want to be home with their families and can't. The homesickness overwhelms them. Once they're down, all the encouragement in the world won't bring them back. He laid down this morning and hasn't moved since."

Bob Green listened to Morrison Turner discuss the plight of the young boy that lay in the corner.

"His name is Alex McBride. The men call him Scooter. Just yesterday he was talking about what he was going to do when he gets home. He's just eighteen, a tough age in this place."

"I really like this boy," said Green anxiously as Turner kneeled down next to McBride and talked gently to him, trying to encourage him to not give up, to continue to fight. The boy stared, glassy eyed past him into space, unresponsive.

Turner stood and shook his head. "I don't know what else to do. He'll be dead, come morning."

"No, he won't," said Green. Stepping forward he knelt down and grabbed the boy by the collar. Lifting him off the floor he smacked him as hard as he could across the face.

"Get up, damn it," yelled Green in the boy's face. And he smacked him again.

Turner reeled back in surprise as Green continued to scream into the boy's face.

"You're not going to let these ungodly sons-of-bitches beat you Scooter! Think of your mother. Think about your family, son! Get up damn it!"

He smacked McBride again and the boy began to cry. Sobbing incoherently he cried, "Mommy, Mommy." Green sat on the floor next to him and the boy threw his arms around his neck, laying his face on his chest, crying uncontrollably.

"I'm sorry Mommy. I'm sorry."

Green grabbed both arms and pushed the boy back, to where he could look him in the face.

"Look at me, boy. Look at me. Who am I?"

McBride looked up and through his sobbing he said, "Bob Green."

"Right boy, and are you going to give up and die? Are you going to do that to your mother back there in Texas? Make her spend the rest of her life without ever seeing you again? Wondering what happened to you over here? Wondering why you gave up."

"No, nooo, Mr. Green. I want to see my mom again."

"Then get yourself up! Morrison here is going to look after you for a couple of days. If I hear you try some more crap like this, I'm going to come looking for you. You understand me boy?"

McBride slowly nodded his head. "Now that's what I want to see. Get him down to the kitchen and get some food in him. Tonight, is the Christmas dinner, but it's okay for him to eat early. Tell Billy I said it was okay."

Turner nodded, put his arm around McBride's shoulder and Green watched them walk out of the room. By himself now he stared down at his hands and saw that they were shaking uncontrollably. Tears began to run down his cheeks and he quietly wept as he sat in the room by himself.

"I heard what you did to McBride. Never thought of that. We'll have to keep it in mind."

"It might work on some and not on others, Dan. Who's to know? Strange how a man is on his feet and okay one day, and the next he lies down and dies. Should have thought of it sooner."

"You did in time to save McBride. Shocked him right back to this world."

"How's the pig coming?" asked Green changing the subject.

"Shouldn't be much longer. I wonder what the chinks are up to? They'll be singing Christmas carols with us next."

"Propaganda. They don't do anything without a reason."

"Well, I don't care what their reasons are. If they feed us better, treat us better, more guys survive. The peace talks must be going good. We've seen more bombers and fighters flying around up there. We must be gaining an edge."

"Let's go check on the pig. Howard, I'll be back in a little bit."

"I'll take a little nap. Take your time Dan," Lowe said, carefully settling down on his mat.

Welch and Green walked across the yard to the kitchen shed. Each squad or company had its own shed. Mo Richards was chief cook, Allen Nichols and Mouse Atkins were his kitchen crew. The team was rounded out with Will Post as water carrier, Juan Chavez as woodchopper, and Fred Eastman was the fireman. The men worked hard to make the food taste good and go as far as possible, which was no small task.

The pork supper was an example of their resourcefulness. They had one of the camp doctors check the pig for trichinosis, a parasite as big as a grain of rice that lived in the animal's blood. When the doc stuck the pig, parasites poured out with the blood.

"Won't hurt. Must cook good," was the doc's advice

The cooks boiled the whole pig and then processed the entire carcass. Tonight the men would have rice, potatoes and Chinese cabbage that were cooked and seasoned with pork strips. It was Christmas Eve.

"Damn, that smells good," said Welch.

"It is good, man," said Mo Richards. "I call it, Piggy Went to Market."

"You call it anything you want, Mo. It smells delicious." Welch lifted the lid on the pot and the steam lifted, filling his nostrils.

"This time last year, Leo and I were eating grubs and insects trying to stay alive. We've come a long way."

"It's all relative, baby," quipped the head cook. "If I were back home in Swingtown I'd be sharing ham and turkey with my lady. Things are better, but we're still just making it. Now, if you cats will motor on out of my kitchen, me and my boys will get this slop ready to serve."

"Go Big Mo!" responded Green as he walked out of the shed dragging Welch behind him.

"Jack Gillispie!"

"Jack Gillispie! Somebody go get Jack!"

"Jack's dead!" came a shout, *"Died this morning!"*

Slivken placed the letter in a small box he carried.

"Bob Green!"

Welch nudged his friend in the ribs. "That's you, Bob."

"What's me?"

"Bob Green! Louie just called out, Bob Green. You've got a letter."

Green stood staring up at Louie Slivken, the camp mail clerk. He had stood in the crowd of men for months, hoping to hear "Bob Green" called out and now that it finally had, he didn't hear it.

Green raised his hand and shouted out, *"Here! I'm Bob Green!"*

"Well, Bob Green, go get your letter," shouted someone in the crowd.

Bob made his way up to retrieve his letter. The crowd of men parted making way for him. The Chinese control of the mail had eased and letters were coming through. Welch stuck close to Green as he got his letter and walked toward the School House. The two men reached the front steps and sat down. It was a cold December day and snow flurries had begun to drift down.

Green gave Welch a look.

"You want me to get lost?"

"No Dan, it's not that. You'd better stick around until I find out what's in here. You know firsthand how these yellow bastards operate. It could be a 'Dear John' letter from Doris, or something may have happened to Pa or Ma. If you don't mind, can you stay with me a couple of minutes?"

"You bet, pal."

The envelope was dated August 19th. The letter was four months old. Green's hands shook as he unfolded it.

"It's from Doris and, "Green quickly scanned its contents, "and everything is okay." Catching his breath and fighting back tears Green began to read to himself as Welch stood, patted him on the shoulder and entered the School House:

August 18, 1952

Dear Bob,

> *I pray that this is not just another letter you will never receive. I write regularly with no way of knowing if you are getting my letters. My hope is that sooner or later one will get through to you.*
>
> *We are all fine here. The children are preparing to start school. Little Bobby has been practicing football every day for two weeks now. His first game is next week. You would be proud of him. He has grown quite a bit the two years you have been gone. I am confident that God will get you home by next fall to watch him his senior year. He loves you and misses you dearly.*
>
> *Peggy starts Junior High. It's hard to believe our little baby is thirteen years old. She has blossomed over the last year. You would hardly recognize her. You won't have to worry about boys coming to the front door for a while. She says her heart belongs only to her daddy.*
>
> *Your mom and dad are doing well. The uncertainty during the period of time you were missing was very difficult on them, but over the past year they have done much better. Your dad retired from the plant and they have already visited us twice. You know how your mom loves to travel.*
>
> *I am doing okay. The neighbors here at Ft. Hood have been great. They have kept an eye on us and visit often. The other day the Post Sergeant Major's wife came by for coffee. Her husband was a POW in the Pacific in '44. We talked all morning.*
>
> *The days are long when I allow myself to worry, but for the most part I stay busy. When the kids are at school it's very lonely, but I know in my heart you'll be coming home to me soon.*

Loving you Always,

Doris

The men ate well that night and retired to their squad rooms to talk and socialize a bit before lights-out. Occasionally each man would steal a glance at the tree and sigh. It gave them hope. Hope that they would make it another day.

At the appropriate time the light went out in the squad room, as did the light in each room of the School House. Each heart ached for a time when innocence and hope lit up the darkest night. The fathers wept silently for their children. Hearts ached for wives and girlfriends, moms and dads who would spend another Christmas uncertain of their loved one's future.

The next morning was Christmas Day. The men woke before sunrise and lay on their mats staring at the tree which was lit up by an outside security light shining through the window. Many of the men discovered sudden memories of Christmas past and their hearts filled with joy and hope. From the darkness a single voice of hope rose softly:

Silent Night
Holy Night
All is Calm
All is Bright
Round yon Virgin
Mother and Child

At that moment, half way across the world a ten-year-old girl's voice carried the same message of hope:

Holy Infant
So Tender and Mild
Sleep in Heavenly Peace
Sleep in Heavenly Peace

"That was beautiful, Wanda Faye. Somehow, I believe your dad can hear your singing and his heart is encouraged and strengthened."

Wanda Faye sat on the sofa with her mom, little sister and Mrs. Katherine, admiring their Christmas tree. The fire in the fireplace brought the tree to life as the light of the flames fluttered about. It was Christmas Eve and presents were spread under the tree.

"Santa come tonight, Mrs. Katherine?"

"Yes, darling. He is on his way right now."

"I no want baby doll. Santa bring Daddy home."

"If he could, he would, darling. If he could, I believe he would."

✶   ✶   ✶   ✶

"You write!"

The American B-26 pilot sat in the chair staring, indifferent to the Chinaman's demands. His hollow eyes told the tale of months of isolation. Starvation had taken its toll, his body was down to a hundred and thirty-five pounds, compared to the two hundred-twelve he carried when he flew his first mission over North Korea. That was forty-two sorties ago. Nearly two years.

As he sat there, he thought of Joyce, his wife and their two-year-old son, who would probably never get to meet his father. He thought of the constant pain from the hunger and isolation. His only contact was with the beast that held him captive, caged like an animal. He had held on to hope, but hope had deserted him, as had death. There was no more hope, only the memories of Joyce and the faded memory of an infant boy.

"You write, Captain Matheson."

The Chinese officer put a pen in Matheson's hand. Looking down at the pen he gripped it, but felt detached. It wasn't really his hand anymore. It had belonged to the Chinese for quite some time.

"You write as I say, now," and the hand gripped the pen and wrote the words.

"As American flyer I been forced by the capitalists warmongers to drop germ bombs on the peace-loving people of Korea and the Chinese Volunteers. Ruthless greed of the Wall Street dogs have done this horrible crime against peace loving peoples."

The pen slowly moved across the page, writing down the bias words the Chinese officer spoke, in broken English, word for word.

"Despite my crimes, people of Korea have been kind to me. They give me good food and issue me warm clothes. I am much ashamed of things I do to hurt and kill innocent civilians and now realize my crimes. It is great burden that I carry and it good to confess and be forgiven by people of Korea."

Matheson looked down at the meaningless words on the paper and back up at the Chinaman.

"Now you sign," and he did.

"Very good, Captain. One must not carry such shame alone. Wall Street dogs share you burden now."

Reading the letter in length the officer smiled realizing the important propaganda treasure he held.

"You get better treatment now, Captain. Maybe you now survive to see son," and with that he turned and left the room.

Matheson sat looking straight ahead at the door that closed behind the Chinese officer. His stare was unfocused, not seeing the wooden door, or the walls beyond, or even the little brick, story-and-a-half home that sat quietly, half way around the world. He no longer saw his wife and son. He only saw darkness and despair, and burned in the depths of his soul were the words that would haunt him the rest of his long life with nightmares and constant self-doubt and humiliation, *"my crimes, my crimes, my crimes."*

CHAPTER 12

▼

Raymond Tracy's eyes studied the substitute teacher standing in front of the class. Marie Goldman was a graduate of Campbellsville Teacher's College. She was called to Tabor so Mrs. Lowe could have her baby. Marie accepted, seeing it as an opportunity to make steady money and gain experience that might impress a school superintendent on a job application.

Stephen Michael held up a small piece of paper with, "WE CAN DO IT" penciled on it. Raymond Tracy knew they could do it. The challenge was doing it in a dramatic fashion and not getting caught. He'd been sizing up Miss Goldman and saw her as a reasonable replacement for Mrs. Lowe. She wouldn't be a whiner like Mr. Tuckerfield. The class had managed to chase him off after two days. They hadn't tried to be difficult. Tuckerfield had actually started the whole thing by picking on the younger children in the class. He seemed to delight in tormenting the little ones who couldn't fight back. That in turn upset the older students and turned them against him.

The problem came to a head on his second day when he made fun of six year old Jimmy White by mocking his stuttering problem. Little Jimmy cried. Tuckerfield then put Little Jimmy in the corner where he sat sobbing until Beth Ann Browning went to see about him.

When Tuckerfield yelled at her to sit back down, she glared at him and said, "No, sir! I won't, and if you know what's good for you, you won't come back here tomorrow."

Tuckerfield jumped to his feet. "Is that a threat, young lady?" He demanded as he reached for Mrs. Lowe's paddle.

"Yes, sir! But, it's not me you've gotta watch out for, mister. It's Little Jimmy's daddy. He's gonna be waiting for you in the morning and likely whop some decency into you!"

The child's assessment of Tuckerfield's immediate future at Tabor worked on his subconscious throughout the day. He must have sensed the seriousness in her warning, as he didn't show back up the next morning. Standing in his place was Marie Goldman, waiting for the children as they arrived. She greeted them as they got off the bus, and walked over to meet Jim White as he helped Little Jimmy from their pickup truck. She listened sympathetically to his complaint and kneeled, giving Little Jimmy a hug. She advised Big Jim to bring his concerns to the attention of the school superintendent, so he could have a talk with Tuckerfield. He thanked her as Little Jimmy took her hand and they walked to the schoolhouse.

The general feeling of the class was that Miss Goldman was a good trade for Tuckerfield. Of course, that didn't stop some of them from being themselves. It just allowed them to be mischievous for the fun of it, instead of for spite.

Miss Goldman stood with her back to the class writing homework assignments on the board. It was a cool, crisp January day and the sky was a dark bluish gray, so she went ahead and wrote a week's worth of assignments in case school was closed on account of snow. With Adair County's narrow, hilly roads it didn't take much accumulation to make it unsafe for bus travel.

"Children, I have listed your homework assignments on the board for the next few days in case we are closed for snow. There will be a test on the Fifth and Sixth Reader on Friday. Those of you who have completed those readers study and be prepared on Friday."

"Miss Goldman, is the test on Friday an important test?"

"Why of course, Sherri."

"Yes, ma'am," responded Sherri as she sniffed her runny nose. The cold air from the windows across the back of the classroom and the burning wood tended to cause a lot of runny noses. Most of the children sat at their desk with a sweater or coat on, and when the stove got too hot, they would take clothing off and hang it on the pegs on the wall. There was constant movement in the one room schoolhouse.

"Sherri, it's important because passing the test allows you to pass on to the next reader, but why do you ask? I believe you are well beyond the Sixth Reader?"

"My brothers, Fred and Owen," *sniff, sniff* "are reading in those readers."

Marie picked up Martha's grade book, quickly scanned it for Fred and Owen Goode, and sure enough there they were. She had been at Tabor for three days now and had not seen, nor heard from the Goode boys. Looking at the grade book she saw that the boy's attendance at school was practically non-existent.

"Sherri, come to the front of the room please?"

Sherri walked up to the teacher's desk.

"Sherri, your brothers have been absent a lot this year, yet they seem to have fairly decent grades. Have they been sick a lot?"

"Oh, no ma'am. My mom says they are as healthy as a two-year-old coonhound. I take their school assignments home and I help them to study in the evenings. When they have an important test, I tell mom and they attend that day. They are really good students, but dad can't manage the milking and the chores by himself. He needs their help."

Miss Goldman and Sherri continued their conversation, their backs to the class while Raymond Tracy and Stephen Michael moved over to the window. Stephen Michael quietly lifted his leg up and out over the window sill, easing out and on to the ground. Raymond Tracy carefully followed.

The window had been opened because the student responsible for fueling the fire had done so, very generously. Children were coming out of their sweaters and Miss Goldman had asked that someone open a window. The window the two boys had just slipped out.

A potbellied, cast-iron stove stood in the center of the room. An older student was responsible for firing it up in the morning and keeping it going through the day. The student would usually get there before the teacher and start the fire with kerosene soaked corncobs. The wood was carried in from the outside and stacked against the wall, usually enough for the day. No one knew where the outside pile of wood came from. When the pile got low, it was mysteriously replenished.

"Okay, how do we get back in?"

The boys sat next to the schoolhouse, just below the window, whispering.

"Going through the door would be too easy. Where's the fun in that. I'm more inclined to try something different, something tougher, and something risky."

"What?" asked Raymond Tracy with a smile.

"Going back in the way we came out."

"Back through the window, are you nuts?"

Peeking up over the windowsill Stephen Michael said, "It's now or never," and up he went, through the window and quietly to his desk. The children watched out of the corners of their eyes in amazement, some holding their hands over their mouths, not to give them away.

Raymond Tracy was right behind him, nimbly through the window and as he stood up, Miss Goldman turned around. Grabbing a pencil off of Elizabeth Long's desk he turned to the pencil sharpener attached to the wall and began to grind away on an already sharpened number "2" pencil.

"Thank you, Sherri. Children these are the assignments. Write them down. By the looks of that sky out there, I think we will get some snow tonight. I also have a note here from Mrs. Lowe reminding you all that tonight will be the last night for the Methodist Revival at the Tabor Community Church."

She started for her desk and turned about. "I need a couple of you older boys to bring in some more firewood. Raymond Tracy and Stephen Michael, go out and get an arm load of wood, please."

"Yes, ma'am," the boys said together and stood.

"And this time, if you don't mind. Use the door and not the window."

Giggles rose across the classroom as the two boys headed out the door. Miss Goldman smiled and went over to the six and seven-year old children to make sure they had gotten their assignments written down correctly.

*　　　*　　　*　　　*

"Please stand for the reading of the scripture, *Philippians Four, Six through Seven.*"

"Do not be anxious about anything, but in everything, by prayers and petition, with thanksgiving, present your request to God.
And the peace of God, which transcends all understanding, will guard your hearts and your minds in Jesus Christ."

As the congregation stood, Brother Clarence Weber, hymnal in hand yelled out, *"Amazing Grace! How Sweet the Sound,* number three-thirty in your hymnal. First two verses."

"Amazing grace, how sweet the sound,
That saved a wretch like me!
I once was lost, but now am found,
Was blind, but now can see.

'Twas grace that taught my heart to fear,
and grace my fears relieved.
How precious did that grace appear,
The hour I first believed!"

Standing in the second row of the Tabor Community Church was Brother and Gracie Cook, and next to Gracie stood Martha Lowe, Mrs. Katherine, and the girls. Practically everyone in Gadberry, Fairplay and Hardscratch were at the Methodist Revival. It was a protracted revival meeting, lasting just as long as there was interest, and a need to save souls.

As in most protracted revivals, the last evening was lengthy. One soul remained unwavering, unmoved by the Holy Spirit. People prayed, scripture was read and hymns were sung. The church was so full of the Holy Spirit, surely some would leak over and move someone in need of being moved, up to the front of the sanctuary where the mourner's bench was located.

Brother George Mason Middleton stood at the front of the church, Bible in hand singing, his baritone voice ringing out above the rest. Most men of God would have settled for nine saved souls and considered the week a great victory, but not Brother Middleton. He had set his sights on one more soul, and wouldn't settle for anything less.

He had met Robert Lee Olsen the first night, and he and Clarence Weber had broke bread with Olsen and his wife on Wednesday night in their home. Mr. Robert Lee was seventy-three and still actively farmed his fifty acres. He was a good man, but had never given himself to the Lord. He was in his eleventh hour, and Brother Middleton was determined not to let him step out of the church without surrendering to Jesus with a public confession of faith.

"Our next hymn will be number two-seventy-five, *I Surrender All,* all four verses." Weber led them in singing the hymn as if he was conducting a full symphony orchestra.

"All to Jesus I surrender, All to Him I freely give
I will ever love and trust Him, In his presence daily live
I surrender all, I surrender all
All to Thee, my blessed Savior, I surrender all."

The young man held up two fingers and the people sung the second verse, then three fingers for the third and four for the fourth.

"Jesus Is Tenderly Calling," shouted out Brother Middleton as the last note was carried out.

"Number three-sixteen in your hymnal," responded Brother Weber, "all four verses!"

While the congregation sang, Brother Middleton fixed his stare on Mr. Robert Lee until he got eye contact, threw his arms out to his sides, Bible in hand, tilted his head back, looked to the heavens and prayed. He was unloading the heavy guns directly at Olsen now and tears welled up in the farmer's eyes. Olsen's wife, Minnie, a believer since childhood, held his hand giving him the only support she could give. It was his walk to make. No one else could walk it for him.

Brother Cook knew of the struggle that was taking place. Middleton had confided in him, asking for his prayers, which he was giving freely at that moment. The ministers and pastors around Adair differed somewhat in ideologies, but supported each other when it came to winning souls over for the Lord. Three local ministers sat about the small church that night, lending strength to the effort with prayer.

Mrs. Katherine leaned over and whispered into Martha's ear. "There's a suffering soul in this church tonight and my guess is it's Robert Lee. He's caught between Brother Middleton and the Devil, and I'm putting my money on the Lord."

Martha nodded her head and smiled. Mr. Robert Lee had been a close friend of her dad's and she had known him as long as she could remember. She had never known a kinder man in her life. Her dad had once said if he was ever in trouble, of any kind, he could depend on Robert Lee. She felt for Mrs. Minnie and prayed for Mr. Robert Lee to be touched by the spirit.

As the congregation finished the last verse and silence fell over the sanctuary, Brother Middleton stood at the front of the church on the small platform and stared in silence out at the faces of the people. Taking his Bible, he opened it to *John 3:16*, closed his eyes and loudly recited the scripture.

"For God so loved the world that he gave his one and only Son, that whoever believes in him may have eternal life."

Holding the open Bible in his left hand, Middleton took a step down on to the floor and reached his right hand out toward Olsen. The room remained silent as Olsen stepped out into the aisle. Middleton took another step, and closing the Bible in his left hand, held it out to Olsen. The Devil lost his grip, and Mr. Robert Lee, cane in hand, walked down the aisle and met Brother Middleton at the mourner's bench.

"*To God Be The Glory*, number four in your hymnal, first two verses," shouted Brother Weber and the people rejoiced and sang as Brother Middleton and Mr. Robert Lee kneeled at the bench and prayed.

That night before a mixed congregation, Mr. Robert Lee Olsen won a life long struggle. He professed his belief in Jesus, was baptized and went home a saved man.

At the front door of the church Brother Middleton and Mr. Robert Lee shook hands with the people as they filed out to their cars. Shaking Martha's hand Mr. Robert Lee smiled.

"Martha Ann, it was something your father said to me might near thirty years ago that finally allowed me to go up there tonight. I was standing there thinking about how disappointed Marshall would have been if he were here tonight and I didn't profess my faith, and then something came to me he used to say. He'd say, 'Bobby Lee, when nothing else makes sense, sometimes you just got to listen to your heart.' My heart was a telling me to go up there to Brother Middleton, so I listened and went. I don't know what I was afraid of. I should have done it long ago."

"Mr. Robert Lee, I know my daddy is rejoicing right now with the heavenly angels."

"Bless you child. Minnie and I have been praying that your Howard will get home soon."

"Thank you. It means a lot to know people are keeping Howard in their prayers."

As Martha walked to Brother Cook's car, large snowflakes drifted down from a dark blue sky. There was already an accumulation of six inches and it didn't appear it would stop anytime soon.

Once everyone was in the car, Gracie Cook said, "Thank the Lord, Henry had the good sense to put the snow tires on and some cinder blocks in the trunk. One could end up in a ditch on a night like this."

"Just take your time, padre," warned Mrs. Katherine. The Devil is unemployed tonight. Let's not give him any reason to land on us."

Everyone chuckled, but kept their eyes fixed on the road ahead. The adults looked out the windows with concern, as the girls stood in the back floorboard, peering over the adult's shoulders in the front seat, watching gleefully as the large flakes drifted down through the high beams of the headlamps.

Brother Cook carefully guided the car along the narrow two-lane road. Turning onto Long Cemetery Road he slowed even more, finding no tire tacks to center the car on. The snow cast an eerie white blanket over the landscape, giving shape and form to the roll of the fields and the buildings that sat on them.

The car reached the Lowe driveway, but didn't pull all the way up in the yard like usual. The headlamps lit up the front yard to the front of the house. Brother Cook jumped out and opened the back door, assisting Martha out onto the blanket of snow, her feet disappearing up over her ankles. Taking his arm, the two walked up to the house. Behind them came Mrs. Katherine with a girl on either hand, struggling to get into as much snow as they possibly could. She smiled, knowing the girls would have a full day of play tomorrow.

Mrs. Katherine was taking the coats and hats off the girls, while Martha watched Brother Cook attempt to back the car on to the gravel lane. With the back tires spinning, the rear of the car suddenly pitched and slid into the ditch, the headlamps shining up into the trees.

"Oh, my! Brother Cook just slid into the ditch."

"What I wouldn't give to be sitting in the back seat of that car right now."

"Mrs. Katherine, ministers are people too."

"Some more than others. You give Jordan Long a call and I'll go help them out of the car and up to the house."

In a few short minutes the Cook's and Mrs. Katherine were warming themselves by the fireplace. Brother Cook was silent, fuming over his miscalculation.

"Now Henry, it was just slicker than you thought, stop beating yourself up over it."

"Hum!"

"Besides, it gives us a chance to have some of Mrs. Katherine's peach cobbler and coffee while we wait for help to come."

"Brother Cook. Why you car parked in ditch?"

The minister stared at Amy Sue and a smile broke across his face.

"Why, darling. That old car of mine thinks for itself sometimes. It started telling me, 'Ditch, ditch, me go in ditch,' and I said, 'No, not ditch', and the car said, 'Yes, ditch!' and it jumped right in!"

"Bad car," said Amy Sue as she shook her finger toward the car.

From outside the chugging sound of a tractor slowly got louder, a signal that Jordan was coming down the lane. Brother Cook got to his feet, retrieved his coat and hat, put back on his rubber overshoes and slipped out the front door.

"Well, I had better get ready myself. It won't take Brother Long very long to get that car pulled out of the ditch," said Gracie as she stood and walked toward the front door.

"Thank you so much Martha for taking us in. I'm glad Henry decided to put it in a ditch right across from your house. We would have been in a pickle if we had been stranded half way between here and town."

Outside, Brother Cook stood next to the car as the tractor slowly chugged its way up the lane and stopped, the front end of the John Deere some ten feet from the front bumper of the car. Climbing off, Jordan took a logging chain from the back and handed one end to Brother Cook.

"Hook 'er up, preacher! It shouldn't take much pullin'!"

Nodding his head, Cook took the heavy chain and kneeled next to the front bumper, reaching underneath and hooking the large hook at the end of the chain to the car frame. Jordan ran the other end of the chain through a hitch loop twice at the front of the tractor and secured the hook over a link of chain.

Patting Brother Cook on the back, Jordan leaned over and yelled, *"Put 'er in neutral and let John do the rest!"*

Jordan pushed the hand clutch forward and as he predicted, the tractor eased the car out of the ditch with very little effort.

"What do I owe you, Brother Jordan?"

"Nothing," shouted Jordan as he hopped down, unhooked the chain and placed it back on the rear of the tractor. Gracie had made her way down the yard, waved at Jordan and got into the car with her husband, and they slowly drove off.

Back on the tractor Jordan locked the left brake and eased the front end around in a tight circle on the road. He gave a quick wave up toward the house and slowly followed the car tracks up the lane.

✷   ✷   ✷   ✷

The children were seated on the toboggan, up against one another, legs to the outside, bodies inside. They dug in their heels and scooted forward against each other in a caterpillar motion. There were five children in all on the four-man sled. Raymond Tracy piloted the toboggan, followed by Rebecca Long, Wanda Faye Lowe, Winnie Baumgartner and Otha Burton at the backend, each child tightly interwoven with the next.

"Everybody ready?" shouted Raymond Tracy over his right shoulder.

After a variation of *"Yes"* was repeated down the line, Stephen Michael put his shoulder to Otha's back and pushed the sled and its passengers on to the slope. As the toboggan gained its own momentum, Stephen Michael veered off to the side and grabbed his Flexible Flyer Airline Racer. Gripping the five-foot sled with both hands he ran and lunged out onto the slope. On impact the steel runners bit down into the snow and ice and quickly rose on top, casing and quickly catching the toboggan.

The hill on the back of Samuel Woods' farm was known as the best sledding hill in the Gadberry community. Depending on which side of the hill you went down you could have a ride equal to your skills and of course, your courage. The east side was the steepest. The southeast was longer, but not as fast. Halfway down there was a hump that would send sleds and riders airborne. Some said the hump was put there several years ago by some industrious young men, others said it was created by a large tree being blown over and pulling up its roots as it went down. No one rightly knew for sure.

With his load of passengers Raymond Tracy steered just wide of the hump, but Stephen Michael hit it dead center, and sailed through the air landing down in front of the toboggan. Toboggan and sled arrived at the bottom seconds apart. Ten heavily booted feet went down creating a cloud of snow bringing the toboggan to a stop.

Stephen Michael had steered a hard right and got another hundred feet of sledding around the base of the hill. Standing about were several children and adults with their sleighs, toboggans and inner tubes. They watched the riders come down the hill and waited patiently for a ride back up.

The day had long been referred to as "Sledding Day," in around the community. It celebrated the first substantial snow in the area. The hill on Woods' farm was simply referred to as the "Hill." There was always a good turnout. A large bonfire was maintained at the top of the hill, circled by bales of hay. When you felt chilled, you sat on a bale and had some hot chocolate, or coffee and warmed up a bit. Of course, for the men who were interested in a quick warm up, there was always a taste of shine available from someone's coat pocket.

This year transportation up the hill was compliments of Kate and Jack, Jordan Long's two mules. Hitched behind them was a wooden, flat-bed sleigh, some eight feet wide and twelve feet long. The runners were made of three-by-twelve oak planks. The sleigh had sideboards with an open backend.

As sleigh riders waited patiently for their ride back to the top, they kept their eyes on the slope above, hoping to be entertained by others. They were not disappointed. Down the hill came five teenage boys, stacked on top of each other, pyramid style, atop a large truck inner tube. Up and down the hill all eyes were focused on them as they approached the hump. Their speed was perfect and their aim was, well, one must face the fact that you simply can't guide a big black rubber donut full of air. You just go along for the ride. In this case their aim was lucky as the tube launched itself off the hump and sailed through the air.

Everyone held their breath. The ride was spectacular and if there had been a need for judges, the boys would have received a "9" for speed, and on this particular ride, a perfect "10" for artistic interpretation, for the fun of tubing is in the bounce, and the boys got their money's worth.

The tube hit the hump and went airborne for several seconds. The boys were elevated a foot or so above the tube, clinging as best they could to maintain contact with each other and their donut shaped aircraft. When the tube hit the ground the boys shot off it like they were coming off the back of a wild bronco at a county fair rodeo. Bodies were suspended in space for several seconds as they sailed down the hill. Gravity finally had its way, and each boy landed on the down slope, rolling, tumbling and skidding down to the flat. The crowd cheered as the boys got to their feet, pumping their fist in the air and bowing to appreciative fans.

Having watched the spectacle from the front end of his mule drawn sleigh, Jordan Long gave a knowing smile, remembering his younger days and exploits on the snow-covered hill. Behind him the children looped their sled ropes over hooks on the back of the flat-bed sled. Some sat or laid down on their smaller sleds, preferring to be pulled up the hill behind the larger sled, while others chose the warmth of the deep hay scattered about on the flatbed. The last to get on were the five boys and their giant inner tube, none the worse for their aerobatics.

With everyone on board and seated, Jordan whistled, gave the reins a flip and shouted, *"Get up!"* The mules obediently started the long pull back up, while others continued to race down the hill.

At the top of the hill sat two tractors, hitched to hay wagons, lined with hay. They had transported folks to the "Hill," and sat ready for the trip home at the end of the evening. A wooden table had been set up on the outside of the bonfire perimeter to serve hot chocolate and coffee. The table also had treats of brownies and cookies. All of the preparations, all of the doings, were for this one day. There would be other days of sleigh riding, but none with so much participation from adults. "Sledding Day" was a tradition, treasured by young and old alike.

As the timid and the reckless continued their fun, several adults sat around the bonfire warming up and swapping gossip. The conversation soon turned to war, as most conversations did in the small community.

"I'm telling you, it ain't right there being no ascapes from them camps. During the big war our boys ascaped from the Nazis and Jap camps all the time."

"What are you a trying to say, Hack?" said a man on the next bale of hay.

Everyone's eyes turned to him and then back to Hack Simmons.

"I'm just telling ya, it ain't natural for that many American boys to be held prisoner and none ascaping. There something strange a going on over there."

"It's that brainwashing them Chinamen are doing on our boys," piped in Dora Lynn Woods. "They're a doing something unholy to our boys and they can't think for themselves anymore. I read about it in a Life magazine at the beauty parlor. They called it men-ti-cide. Those Chinamen are messing with their mental side, and those boys are gonna come home with tainted brains."

"Ah, bologna! It's those boy's duty to ascape. There ain't nothing wrong with their brains. They just ain't as brave and dedicated as the boys who fought in W W II."

"*Hogwash!* What do you know about duty, or washing brains, Hack Simmons?" All eyes turned to Trilby Franklyn, who was now standing. "You never served and if I recall, you only read to the third reader. Those boys are doing the best they can just to stay alive over there. You go about with your idle talk, saying stupid things like that, it'll get back to Martha, and it'll hurt her feelings."

"Weren't talking about Howard, Trilby! He's as brave a man I ever met. Why, I saw him drag Ed Parker out from under a mad cow one afternoon. Ed got between that cow and her calf and she turned right quick on him. Howard didn't hesitate a second. He lowered his shoulder and rammed that cow, grabbed Ed and pulled him to safety. I weren't talking about Howard. I'm just saying the rest of them boys are . . ."

"Well, *Howard* is in one of those camps and when you speak badly of those boys, you speak bad of Howard." Trilby Franklyn stood with her hands on her hips, staring down at Hack Simmons, who wisely kept his mouth shut.

"I read where the Chinese are saying we dropped little germs on them. The paper called it germ-war-fare. Some of our boys even signed a confession of such. I thought everyone agreed after WWI to not use that awful stuff anymore."

Needing to add his two cents to Dora Woods' comment, Simmons jumped right back in the fire.

"There has been a lot of them boys signing confessions to everything those Chinese put in front of them. Weak o' character, I tell you. Weak o' . . .'"

That was as much as Simmons got out when a snowball disintegrated against the side of his head, knocking his cap off.

"Trilby, what the hell?"

There stood Trilby Franklyn, mother of three, a killing stare in her eyes, a second snow ball in her hand reared back and ready to wing it at Simmons.

"Say it Hack Simmons, you good for nothing know-it-all. Say another word against our boys over there and I won't aim high with this one. It's icy hard and sure to rattle that empty head of yours."

"You out of your mind, Trilby?" said Simmons jumping to his feet.

"*Sit!*" yelled the woman, and Simmons quickly sat back down.

"Can't a fellow express his o-pin-*yunnn,* about things around here?"

"Your opinion should stop where your friends and neighbors' feelings start. Why are you determined to hurt Martha Lowe's feeling?"

"*But . . .*" protested Simmons, as he started to stand.

"*Sit!*" shouted Trilby locking her throwing arm back once again, causing the man to flinch his arms up across his face and cower back on the bale.

"I'd like to see them Chinamen wash that brain of yours. Wouldn't they be in for a surprise," said Trilby as she sat back down.

"I'd like to see them disagree with you, Trilby Franklyn," mumbled Hack under his breath. "The war would be over in a week."

Off in the west the sun had settled in behind bluish, gray clouds, speeding up the onset of darkness. It was determined by responsible adults that the day on the Hill was at an end. Silas and Samuel loaded the bales of hay and cranked up their tractors, a signal to everyone that their ride home would soon depart. In fifteen minutes the wagons were full, including Jordan's sled. Silas and Samuel shoveled snow on to the smoldering fire, climbed on their tractors and headed out. Silas traveled west through the woods toward Gadberry, and Woods back down the hill, across the stream toward Yellowhammer and Fairplay.

Jordan brought up the rear, following Silas' tractor toward Gadberry. The children and adults on the sleigh were huddled together, covered with wool blankets and old quilts. An east wind had picked up giving a sharp bite to the air. The sun was completely down now and large snowflakes began to fall from the sky. The mules ambled along, seemingly indifferent to the falling snow and their passengers. Up ahead the sound of the tractor disappeared in the darkness as Jordan stood at the head of the sled, a tight grip on the reins, guiding the team through a fence gap and into the woods. On the right front of the sled, on a seven-foot pole, hung a double-mantled Coleman lantern, *hissing* out light and allowing Jordan to dodge the larger holes in the dirt lane.

Raymond Tracy rolled off the back end of the sled and fastened a barbed wire gate to close off the gap. Running, he caught up with the front of the sled and hopped on. Jordan stepped back a step and allowed the boy to step in front of him and take the reins.

"Hold firm boy. They'll follow the lane on through the woods. You just keep the slack out of the reins. Let them know you're back here."

"Yes, sir."

"See that big hole up on the right. Pull a little back on the left rein."

Raymond Tracy eased back a little on the left straps and the mules moved slowly to the left.

"At-a-boy. Now, ease up and let them straighten up."

Raymond Tracy gave slack to the left straps and the mules straightened up, passing the hole to the left, missing it completely.

"I recall that hole being particularly deep. We'd probably break the ice and splash water on the folks back there. A night like tonight is no night to get soaked. Keep your eyes on your animals and on the road ahead, boy."

"Yes, sir."

Behind them Sherri Goode broke into a snappy version of *"Jingle Bells"* followed by the rest of the group. Their voices rose in the silent surroundings of the woods, everyone joining in. The passing scenery was almost magical as the soft light of the lantern melted the darkness. Shadows leaped about from tree to tree with the moving light. All around them large snowflakes slowly drifted down, landing softly on the forest floor.

Sitting on the side of the sled, her chin resting on crossed arms supported by the sideboards, Wanda Faye Lowe stared out in the darkness, no longer singing. Tears welled in her eyes and rolled down her cheeks. She had joyfully sung the first verse and was *dashing through the snow, in a one-horse-open-sleigh,* when a memory of last year's Sledding Day and ride back through the woods flashed in her mind. She had sat where she now sat, her dad's arm around her. He was always close by, just a memory away from conscious thought, filling her heart and watching over her. Sometimes he would flood her thoughts, like he was doing at that moment. She had no control over when it would happen. The thoughts were from a year ago Christmas and the visions were distinct, the feelings as strong as if it had occurred yesterday. She was doing so good not to remember and then the holidays came. Knowing how emotional her mother was becoming due to her pregnancy, she worked really hard not to let her emotions get the best of her. She had made it through Christmas with only one or two good crying spells. The worst being Christmas Eve, after she and Amy Sue had been in bed for nearly an hour and decided that Mrs. Katherine and her mom were settled down. They agreed it was time to make their annual "sneak and peak" at the tree to see if Santa had come.

They had quietly moved down the stairs and when they looked around the corner they found their mother sitting there on the sofa, quietly sobbing, holding one of their dad's flannel shirts to her face. They ran to her and all three hugged and cried. The strong smell of their dad was still on the shirt. It was almost as if he was with them. They cried and sat there hugging and looking at the tree.

She didn't remember going to sleep, she just woke up in her bed the next morning, and it was Christmas day. Her mom said they would not cry on Christmas because it was a joyful day and their dad would be happy knowing they had a happy, wonderful day. Staring out into the darkness she could sense the smell of her dad. She could feel his arms around her, and she cried as the sled moved through the night.

"Land sakes, child! You're going to give birth to a ten-pound baby, if he weighs a pound. I don't think I've ever seen anyone so heavy with child, this far along."

Mrs. Katherine sat in the sofa chair and looked over at Martha lying stretched out on the couch. Martha was going into her seventh month and she had to agree with Mrs. Katherine, she was certainly much heavier and much more uncomfortable than with the other two.

From outside they heard the faint sounds of singing. Mrs. Katherine got up, went over and cracked one of the living room windows, and the singing became more distinct, growing louder as the sled grew closer to the house.

"to grandmother's *house we go*
the horse knows the way to carry the sleigh
through white and drifting snow, oh!"

"Would you listen to that Martha? Lookie, here they come."

Martha stood next to Mrs. Katherine at the window. Around the bend came the beginning of the light, followed by the movement of the mules and then the sled. The snow was heavy now and the children and adults on the sled were singing as loud as their voices would carry. Standing up and reining the mules was Raymond Tracy, Jordan at his side.

Reaching the Lowe drive, Raymond Tracy pulled back on the reins and shouted out, *"Whoa!"* and the team slowed.

"Gee!" he shouted and a flip of the reins turned the mules right into the drive and they came to a halt in the lower yard. Wanda Faye and Amy Sue climbed out and walked up the yard. Everyone on the sled yelled and waved at Mrs. Katherine and Martha, who were now standing at the front door.

Down in the yard Jordan waved as he took the reins from Raymond Tracy and said, "Now watch, boy."

"Jack, Kate, Gee!" and he whistled sharply between his teeth and repeated *"Gee!"* With a flip of the leather reins Jack and Kate worked together in making a slow, tight, right hand turn in the yard. The sled seemed to rotate on an axis until it and the mules were pointed and walking toward the lane. When they reached the edge of the yard Jordan yelled out *"Haw! Haw!"* and the mules made a left turn on to the road and headed back up the lane. Jordan handed the boy the reins once again and moved to the side. With years of handling a team around the farm he made it look easy. Most farmers had let their teams go, using tractors for farm work. Jordan used tractors, but he also used his mule team occasionally. He knew Kate and Jack would eventually go the way of his neighbor's teams, but for now he enjoyed working with the mules too much to give them up. He also enjoyed sharing that challenge and joy with a young man like Raymond Tracy. Before long he knew such treasures would be lost to the young people. The same was probably true for the "Sledding Day." It took years to create a tradition and only moments

for it to fade away. Tomorrow Jordan would be over yonder on the back of his place, cutting fence posts and wood to heat the house, but for the moment he enjoyed the singing, the snow in his face and the *clop, clop, clop* of Kate and Jack.

"What's wrong, darling?" Martha was tucking the girls into bed. She had noticed Wanda Faye was in a dreary mood the moment she walked in the front door from the sleigh ride. Amy Sue was completely worn out and was fast asleep before Mrs. Katherine could get her into her bed.

Wanda Faye looked up at her mom with big brown, sad eyes and said, "Nothing," very softly, half under her breath.

"Oh, come now darling. I can tell something is bothering you. Did something happen today at the Sledding Day?"

"You know that Allen Johnson and Stephen Michael Trace? They just won't leave me alone. I," and then she went blank, realizing she had made a crucial error in fabricating her story. Allen Johnson and Stephen Michael never did anything together.

"It seems like some boy or another is always pestering me, in school, on the bus, or out playing. Why can't I be like Winnie Baumgartner? None of the boys bother her."

Another mistake, since none of the boys liked Winnie because she was the biggest tomboy at Tabor. Boys didn't like girls they couldn't beat at arm wrestling. The more she made up, the more she opened herself to questioning.

"Darling, boys are never easy to understand, whether they are ten years old, or your dad's age." Martha could see the story was made up and understood her daughter's pain.

"I remember when your dad was ten and sat in the desk right behind me at Tabor. The only thing that interested him was farming, cowboys and playing baseball. There was this one time when he took some string and tied it to the end of my ponytail. On the end of the string he tied a big white turkey feather. I walked around for twenty minutes with that feather hanging off my ponytail, until Mrs. Crutcher noticed it and called me to the front of the room. She called your father up and tied the feather on top of his head. He looked so funny with the tip of that feather sticking out over his face. He had to wear it like that the rest of the day."

Wanda Faye giggled. "Was Dad a good student?"

"He was an excellent student, darling. He always made the highest arithmetic grades in the whole school. Even in high school. If he had wanted to do something besides farming, he could have been anything he wanted to be. He was just too busy being a boy most of the time to study like he should have."

"Like Raymond Tracy?"

Martha smiled. "Just like Raymond Tracy."

"Did Dad ever get in any bad trouble?"

"He was always lucky. Oh, he and Joey Houseman got their share of whoopin's, probably more than Raymond Tracy and Stephen Michael."

"More than Raymond Tracy?" asked Wanda Faye with wide-eyed disbelief.

"Your father was the luckiest boy I ever knew. I remember one spring day at recess. The yard was divided, the girls on one side, the boys on the other. On the dividing line, I was shooting marbles with May and Trilby Franklyn. I think Eddie Parker had marbles in the circle too. I'd won my share of his cat-eyes that day and Eddie was fit-to-be-tied. I just kept bumping his marbles out of the circle and he couldn't hit a thing. He'd lay his face on the ground to eyeball his shots, but it didn't do him any good. The boy had no depth perception and couldn't make his shooter go straight."

"Your father and Joey Houseman were playing behind the schoolhouse in the fence row when they came upon a large Black Racer snake. Your father trapped it with a stick, took out his pocketknife and whacked its head off. I like to think he killed it because he thought it would scare some of the small children, but I suspect it was just a boy thing."

Wanda Faye felt a warm loving feeling come over her.

"Well, just as Mrs. Crutcher rang the bell to end recess, your father came dashing out from behind the outhouse, the bloody, headless black snake pressed up against the side of his neck, screaming and running around the school yard in a frightful panic. Every time someone tried to help him, he would wiggle away from them. May Long chased him with a stick and swung at his head twice before Joey grabbed her and held her back."

"Mrs. Crutcher grew up on a farm herself and was unimpressed with his killer black snake trick. She stood on the schoolhouse steps, arms crossed, hiding a smile, watching as the drama played itself out."

"She was patient like you, Mom. Raymond Tracy says you got the patience of Job, and no matter what he and Stephen Michael do, you're always there at the end, waiting to whoop them."

Martha laughed. "Well, Raymond Tracy is about as easy to figure out as your father."

"What happened to Daddy and his big black snake?"

"The kids slowly circled your father, screaming and yelling, most of them held sticks and rocks. They figured that after it killed your father, they would have their best chance to beat it to death, before it slithered off and jumped someone else. As the circle tightened, the poison from the snake was taking a heavy toll on your father, as he dramatically staggered about, reaching out his hand, as if pleading for help. The kids would jump back, or swat at him with their sticks. He finally went to his knees and fell flat on his face in a cloud of dust. The children stood in stunned silence, their sticks and rocks at the ready. Mrs. Crutcher walked up and looked over the kid's shoulders at your father's lifeless body, the snake now wrapped around his wrist, its tail slowly twitching in the air."

"'Children,' she said, 'go to the classroom and take your seats. I'll send for Mr. Lewis at the funeral home to come and fetch Howard's body. It won't take long for him to get ripe in this hot sun and start stinking.'"

Wanda Faye giggled.

"As the kids tossed their weapons down and headed to the schoolhouse, I stood next to Mrs. Crutcher as she stood over your father and said, 'Coluber constrictor, Eastern Racer, commonly referred around here as Black Racer, a diurnal or day light hunter that feeds on rodents, birds, frogs, lizards and insects, prone to run from danger, and non-poisonous. Non-poisonous, Howard Delbert. Your passing should be the first recorded death by a Black Racer bite in these United States.'"

"Your daddy opened one eye, looked up at us and smiled. Mrs. Crutcher said, 'Get rid of that thing, so it won't scare any of the little ones, or stink up the school yard. Clean that blood off your neck and find your desk. You can remember where your desk is, or has the poison gone to your brain?'"

"Your daddy replied, 'No, ma'am, I mean, yes, ma'am.' He jumped up and tossed the dead snake over the fence row into the field. As we walked in Mrs. Crutcher added, 'I'll expect an oral report tomorrow afternoon on poisonous snakes in Kentucky. You can reference the subject in the encyclopedia under S, for snake-in-the-grass.' Your daddy's trick was the best I'd ever seen. We talked about it for weeks. There was even a rumor at Yellow Hammer's school in Hardscratch, that a Tabor student was bitten in the schoolyard by a rattlesnake and died."

"I miss Daddy," said Wanda Faye looking up at her mom. Martha laid her down and pulled the quilts up around her chin. Wanda Faye sank deep into the feather bed.

"I miss him too, honey. He loves you and your sister so much and I doubt that a day goes by that he doesn't think and pray about you. We will keep praying for him to return to us and if God's willing, we'll get him back soon.

"Goodnight, Mommy."

"Goodnight, darling."

★   ★   ★   ★

"Bzzzzzz, snip, snip, snip, bzzzzz, snip, snip, snip!"

"Well, I'll say this one thing about that and then I'll shut up! Harry Truman weren't no real president. He was a sitting in that White House for only one reason, and that was because President Roosevelt, God rest his soul, passed away in forty-five. The people didn't elect Harry Truman, he just happened to be in the right place, but I'm a thinking the wrong time for the American people."

"Snip, snip, snip!"

"Why, Jess Upton! You know darn well Truman got elected in '48 on his own. Beat Dewey good and proper."

Pulling the scissors back from Mayor Olsen's head, Jess Upton stared down at Mack Long seated in the row of chairs against the wall. With Mack sat Huey Trimble, Mr. Billy Hutcherson, and Johnny Ray Sarver with his five-year-old son, Derrick. In the barber chair next to the Mayor sat Theodore Graham, a student at Lindsey Wilson, down the hill between classes getting his flat top trimmed up. Graham was from Ohio, and a second-year student at the local Methodist junior college. Upton's brother, Josh, clipped away at his head, listening to his older brother trying to get the best of Mack Long, a rare Democrat in the predominately Republican county.

The Upton Barber Shop was situated just off the square in Columbia, on Campbellsville Street. On most mornings you could find Mack, Huey and Mr. Billy seated in the chairs against the wall, while the Upton brothers cut hair. Regular customers like Mayor Olsen, Sarver and his son and an occasional student from the hill, only tended to create a diversion from the normal discussions that went on every morning and afternoon. Jess Upton, a life long, straight-ticket Republican was riding high at the moment. After nearly twenty years of having a Democrat in the White House, the country had finally come to its senses and elected a Republican named Dwight Eisenhower to run the gaggle of politicians that waddled about Washington, D.C. A man the people could trust. After all, he had won the war in Europe, and Upton wasn't afraid to say it was so.

"That's another thing. Dewey won that election and the next morning the rich Democrats that run this country decided they wanted to keep someone in the White House they could control, so they fixed it so Truman could stay another four years."

Slapping his hand down on his knee, Mack Long said, "When you going to give up on that silly notion, boy?"

Pointing over his shoulder with the scissors Upton said, "Right there is all the proof a man's needs."

Taped to the mirror behind his chair was the front page of a newspaper clipping announcing in bold type, **"DEWEY DEFEATS TRUMAN."**

The men in the barbershop laughed.

"And, I'll tell you another thing."

"Whoa, now! You just stood there and said you were going to say just one more thing and you'd shut up," reprimanded Long, attempting to egg Upton on.

"You did say that," added eighty-four-year-old Mr. Billy with a smile, looking up at Upton. He had been a regular customer of the Upton Barber Shop for nearly sixty years, and had listened to the late Mr. Jonathon Upton's political bantering for most of that period. He had considered Johnny Upton a close friend and although he missed him dearly, it was sometimes hard to tell he was gone.

"Snip, snip bzzzzzz!"

"I recollect I did say just that, Mr. Billy. Thank you for reminding me and I'll stick to what I said, but that other thing I was about to say is exactly that, another thing. I was about speak of that young Senator from Wisconsin, who I think is doing some mighty fine work there in Washington, bringing all those communist to judgment."

Most of the men nodded their heads in agreement, but not all.

"While our boys are over there in Korea fighting the communist, he's back here leading the fight against Americans who done forgot where their freedoms come from."

"Snip, snip, snip, snip!"

"I hear tell he has a piece of paper with a list of eighty-one names on it, all card carrying communists, mostly government people, show business folks and college professors."

"I read it was might near two hundred," added Huey Trimble.

"Snip, snip, snip!"

Sounds of verbal agreement came from the seats against the wall, a couple of "yeps" and a "that's right." Young Derrick Sarver, the Lindsey student and Mr. Billy sat silently. Derrick's attention was focused on keeping his crayon between the lines. The student listened quietly, worrying more about how his flattop was shaping up with all the distractions. Mr. Billy listened intently, not responding one way or another.

"It's good to know someone is looking out for our freedoms and putting communist behind bars where they belong," stated Mayor Olsen.

"The government is full of Reds. Look at the fellow from the State Department who gave secrets to the Russians, what's his name?" Huey Trimble looked about the room for help with the name.

"Hiss!" replied Josh Upton.

"Now, there's no need to be ugly!" quickly responded Trimble.

"Alger Hiss is his name!" added Upton.

"That's it, and that commie couple who are on trial right now for selling information to the Russians about our bomb. Ah, what's their name?"

"Rosenberg. Julius and Ethel Rosenberg," came once again from behind the second barber chair.

"Yea! That be them, I tell ya. The government's full of 'em. Reds everywhere."

"I just don't know, Fellers." Everyone turned to Mr. Billy who sat next to the door. A seat reserved for the first to arrive, which was usually Mr. Billy.

"You just don't know what, Mr. Billy?" said Jess Upton, stepping out from behind his chair and speaking a little louder than normal, so the old man could hear him.

I've got a bad feeling about this Joe McCarthy. He's a Yankee and seems to have an awful lot of power for a first term Senator. Power he seems to toss around carelessly. Destroying people's lives for what they believe and don't believe just don't seem right. I, ah, I," Mr. Billy looked confused for a second, found his thoughts and continued. "I just think some of the things he's a doing just ain't American. It don't set right by me."

"Now, Mr. Billy. At your age you don't need to go and get yourself confused about what's been going on in Washington. It will take care of itself without you having to keep up with it."

Mayor Olsen said it out of concern. Everyone that heard it shared that concern. No sooner than the words were out of the Mayor's mouth, he regretted it.

"Bzzzzz, snip, bzzzzzz!" The mechanical sounds of Josh Upton's electric clippers refined the flat in Graham's flattop and filled the silence.

Mr. Billy sat for a moment in silence and with the support of his cane, scooted himself up on the edge of his chair.

"Let me tell you a thing or two, Tubby Olsen. I walked to town with my father when I was six years old, and stood next to him when he marked his ballet for Ulysses S. Grant's second term. Grant was a Republican, but Dad forgave him since he fought under him in the Wilderness Campaign in Tennessee. The first chance I had to vote in a Presidential Election was in Eighteen and 'eighty-eight. Benjamin Harrison got a hundred thousand fewer votes and beat Grover Cleveland in the Electoral College. I voted a straight Democratic ticket in 'Eighty-eight and in every Presidential Election since. So, you can guess I'm none too happy about having to breathe the hot air all the so-called Republicans in this county blow out every day."

The men in the shop chuckled, relieved that Mr. Billy was taking things light heartedly.

"But what's confusing me more than anything about this McCarthy feller, is that all those smart people in Washington are standing by and letting him trample on everybody's rights."

The old man hesitated, turned and looked at the young Lindsey student sitting quietly in Josh Upton's chair.

"What do you think young man? You're from one of those northern states. Do your folks up north have opinions on what this McCarthy fellow is doing in Washington?"

All eyes turned on the young man from Ohio. Looking down at Mr. Billy the boy sat in silence wondering why the old man had pulled him into their political bickering.

"Well, how 'bout it young feller?" asked Mack Long.

"I think, I think everyone has a right to their own opinion, and,"

"Well said," responded Mayor Olsen.

"Amen!" Jess Upton added. "Josh, that boy's haircut should be free today.

"And, that is all Senator McCarthy seems to be able to do."

The men suddenly sat quiet and stared at the young man.

"All Senator McCarthy has done is express opinions. With all his accusations, there has not been a single conviction resulting from his Senate hearings, nor has he produced a single piece of credible evidence that any of the people on his list are communist, or were disloyal to the United States."

Theodore looked around the room, unsure of himself until his eyes came to rest on the old man. The twinkle in Mr. Billy's eyes gave him the confidence to continue.

"Senator McCarthy has taken a good idea and has run out of control with it. I mean, it seems like all he has to do is mention he's got someone's name on a piece of paper and the person is ruined, and ruined for life. Everyone shuts them out. Friends stay away because they are afraid, afraid they will end up on McCarthy's list. Their career, their family, everything they have stood for their whole life, destroyed on the unsubstantiated gossip of a political opportunist, whose only goal is to improve his personal standing, politically and financially. The American people certainly aren't benefiting from the Senator's witch-hunts. When I said everyone has a right, Mr. Upton, I didn't mean the right to violate other people's rights. Senator McCarthy is violating those rights and abusing his power as a Senator. A lot can be written on a piece of paper, but his appears to be blank. Someone needs to stand up to him and expose him for what he is."

"Snip, snip, brush, brush, splash, splash!"

Josh Upton undid the cape from around Graham's neck and the boy, maintaining a hold on the chair arm with one hand, braced himself. Josh handed the boy two arm crutches, which he quickly slid his forearms into. He swaggered his crooked legs over to the cash register, took a dollar from his wallet, laid it on the cash register and started working his way toward the door. The men sat in silence as he struggled and opened the heavy wood and glass door. Blocking the base of the door with the tip of his crutch, he turned back to face the men.

"You all were talking about President Roosevelt. Well, he had polio just like me. I met him down in Warm Springs, Georgia when I was down there learning to walk. I was learning to live, the same time he died there. Maybe someday people will learn to respect the rights of people like him and me. Maybe we will learn to respect everyone for what they are."

Turning to go out the door, he hesitated, looked over at Mr. Billy and winked. Putting his shoulder against the door he went out and started down the sidewalk toward Lindsey Wilson Street. The long stretch of hill to get up to the campus was a tough walk, but he had done it many times before. Walking along, he physically rotated his hip in order to swing each leg out and to the front. The braces on his legs locked in place allowing a step to end, and the next step to begin.

He smiled to himself, remembering the paper he had turned in the day before in Mr. Edward's government class. The topic, "Communism in America" would have been a near death experience for most chemistry majors, but he had done his research on the subject and turned in an unusually good paper, so much so Mr. Edwards had him read it to the class. The direct quotes from his friend, the late President, were the highlight of the question and answer period that followed the reading.

When Graham reached the base of the hill and put his crutch tip forward, he looked up the steep incline and said to himself, smiling, "Thank you, Mr. Roosevelt."

CHAPTER 13

▼

It was March. It could have been any other day in North Korea. Colonel Pol sat at his desk reviewing paperwork. A career soldier, he was with Mao Zedong when the Communist Party lost control of their Jiangxi province base in October of '34. Chiang Kai Shek and his Kuomintang nationalist forced them to embark on a grueling six-thousand-mile march. The march started with a hundred thousand soldiers and party leaders, only twenty-eight thousand reached Shaanxi province. Pol fought under Mao and defeated the Japanese in World War II. He was there in '48 when the Red Army drove Chiang Kai Shek and his lackeys from mainland China to the island of Taiwan.

When ordered to take the commandant post at Camp Two he readily accepted, as he served without question. When a solution for the conflict in Korea was negotiated, he would retire from military service and actively pursue a career in public service through the Communist Party. A Central Committee seat was his future, if Mao stayed in power.

"One's duty was not always easy." Had not Mao himself said, *"Hard work is like a load placed before us. Some loads are light, some are heavy. Good commanders are the first to take the heavy loads themselves."*

The American people had no taste for a prolonged conflict, so the war would end soon. When the time was right, China would negotiate peace. Until that time he would run the camp and use prisoners to benefit the cause.

The door to his office swung open and Captain Lin burst in.

"Colonel Pol! I have . . ."

Colonel Pol threw up his hand. Holding his stare on the young captain for a moment, he finally asked, "What is so important that you show the camp commandant's office such disrespect?"

Captain Lin stood humbled, realizing that in his haste he had shown disrespect to his commander. Coming to attention, he bowed.

"A thousand pardons Colonel Pol. In my haste to bring you urgent news, I forgot myself."

Colonel Pol looked at his young officer and frowned, suspecting the news he was about to receive was going to be most serious.

"Sit and tell your news, Captain."

Lin bowed once again and with tears forming in his eyes, took a seat in one of the chairs. Looking up at Colonel Pol he could not find words.

"Come now, Captain. What has distressed you so? Has a great disaster befallen your family?"

Looking across the desk the young officer sat up straight, regained his composure and spoke. "It's Comrade Stalin, Commandant. Comrade Stalin has died!"

Pol's insides shook. His mind initially rejected the news, hoping the young officer was the bearer of an incorrect report, but he reassured himself that Lin was not an inexperienced officer. He would have most certainly verified the message.

"When?"

"March the fifth. Cause of death was not reported. Just simply that he is dead. The message came by courier, and I personally verified it with Peking."

Pol stood and with hands clinched behind his back, walked around his desk. Lin stood to meet him.

"Your haste is forgiven, Captain Lin. We have shared many insightful discussions about Comrade Stalin's thoughts and words. I know he is as special to you, as he is to me, and I apologize for not realizing immediately that you would not enter my office in such a manner, unless the circumstance was most urgent."

Col Pol bowed to the surprised young officer, who slowly returned the bow.

Pol walked to a cabinet, took two small glasses from the hutch and half filled them with rice wine. Handing one to Lin he held his glass up toward a picture of Joseph Vissarionovich Stalin behind his desk. Pictured in uniform, a full head of thick hair and his large mustache, Stalin stared down at the two Chinese officers.

"Comrade Stalin!"

"Comrade Stalin," repeated Lin and they both emptied their glasses.

"Go now, Captain. I must have some private thoughts on this most disturbing event."

"Yes, Commandant."

Lin bowed and left the room, closing the door behind him. Pol sat down at his desk, staring up at Stalin. Unlike some of the lackeys that kept easy jobs in Peking, he was not Russianized by long years of safe, decadent living in Moscow and Peking. He too was a Stalinist having studied and admired everything Stalin had written, but he harbored a tremendous dislike for those who chose the easy life to the top. It was now difficult to comprehend how China would deal with the loss of strong support they received from their Russian mentor.

Who's to know what direction Moscow would take once new leadership was established. He turned his gaze to the picture of Mao next to Stalin's.

"What are we to do now, my friend?"

The prisoners were lined up in formation in the camp yard. Captain Lin stood at the front of the formation as Colonel Pol came through the gate. Lin smartly stepped aside.

"I must now bring you very bad news. The world has lost great leader."

The death of President Roosevelt being fresh in memory of most of the men, they stiffened, their thoughts immediately turning to the present American President, Dwight Eisenhower. Others had visions of their country's leader.

"I must sadly inform you, that Comrade Joseph Stalin has died in Moscow on March five."

There were several seconds of silence as the men stood absorbing the news. Pol assumed that since prisoners had been obedient and studious in the indoctrination classes, they would take the news hard. He assumed wrong. His disappointment turned to anger as the men burst into spontaneous cheering. Pol stood in disbelief, his face turning red. He began to shout at the prisoners demanding they stop their disrespect and a silence fell over the crowd of men.

Lost for words to express his anger, he simply stood there in disgust, red faced and clinching his swagger strap. He finally turned and stormed out the compound gate, followed by Captain Lin.

*   *   *   *

"I miss my Mom and Dad. I want to go home."

"That homesickness will kill you boy! Get it out of your mind right now."

The young soldier looked up with intense sadness in his hollow eyes. He had been losing strength for months from bouts of dysentery and had only recently started talking about going home. It had started with sad eyed discussions about a disloyal girlfriend and had graduated to isolation and self-starvation. Mo Richards had noticed the mood change right away with the boy's decreased performance in the kitchen. He had been trying to intervene, without success. The outcome was predictable, if the boy didn't snap out of it.

"You've got to shelve those thoughts boy. The only way to survive this shit hole is to think about the here and now."

The boy looked up for a second and rolled over, facing the wall.

"Old Fu is treating us better. Word is the peace talks are moving along, and there are lots of bombers flying over going north. I tell you we are going to be out of here soon. You just got to hold on boy!"

The boy whispered, "Don't bother waking me in the morning. I won't be able to get up."

Richards looked down at Atkins. Shaking his head, he left the room and headed down to the kitchen to start the supper meal.

Outside, several men sat on the stoop watching the activities down in the village. The March air was crisp and fresh. The sky was blue and clear for miles. The cold was gone and the temperatures were livable, literally. The men around the camp busied themselves with odd jobs and chores. Several worked on the old schoolhouse replacing weatherboard, roofing and windowpanes. They were engineers and men who had experience in construction back home and some just provided assistance with a strong back.

The old schoolhouse was well built, but even it required maintenance. If the prisoners didn't see to it, it wouldn't get done. They had spent several weeks repairing buildings outside the compound fence where the Chinese worked and lived. When that work was completed, they were allowed to take the leftover materials for repairs in their own area. They had made sure there was plenty of leftover material.

Morrison Turner was on the roof of the schoolhouse repairing a stubborn water leak. He held a hammer in one hand and a small crowbar in the other. Looking up in the sky he caught the glimpse of a distant vapor trail left by an aircraft.

Turner carefully stood, balancing himself on the slant of the roof. He put his hand up to shield his eyes and stared, watching the vapor trail grow longer as it headed in their direction. It might be a bomber, but he really couldn't tell yet. Suddenly, behind it appeared another trail and then another. The closest aircraft made a sudden up turn and appeared to shoot straight up in the sky at tremendous speed, followed closely by the second, which was closing in on it. The third vapor trail swung to the west and behind it a fourth trail appeared right on its tail.

"*Boys, I think we got us a dog fight!*" shouted Turner.

Pointing, he shouted, "*South and west!*"

The men down in the yard stirred with excitement. Word traveled fast and men began to pour out of the schoolhouse and the kitchen sheds. All eyes were glued on the drama developing above them.

High in the sky the two aircraft that had broken away and gone vertical, curled to the east. The lead aircraft dove steeply, attempting to break away from the one on its tail. The two aircraft that had swung to the west were curling back north and closing on a line parallel with the camp, about a mile west.

"*Can you tell who's who, Morrie?*"

"*Not yet! Wait, I,*" Turner squinted in the sunlight and tried to see the fast moving aircraft as they sped past to the west. At that moment he made out a red star on the lead aircraft, threw a clinched fist in the air and shouted. "*It's one of our boys chasing a MIG!*"

The roar of the jets drowned out his report, but his reaction was clear. A cheer went up in the yard as the roar of the jets thundered and echoed through the hills and valleys surrounding the camp. The Chinese MIG 15 to the west turned sharply to the east and in a matter of seconds passed just north of the camp, an American F-86D "Dog Sabre" on his heels. The men were wild with excitement, jumping up and down, screaming and hitting each other on the back. The full noise of the jet aircraft came a second after they had flown by and it was deafening.

A small vapor trail suddenly shot out from under the Dog Sabre as the pilot let loose one of his "Mighty Mouse" rockets. The folding fin aircraft rocket shot forth from the underside of the American fighter with blazing speed, catching up with the MIG in seconds. The vapor trail of the rocket passed over the MIG's wing and disappeared on the horizon. There was a sudden silence in the yard as the men stood looking up at the sky, trying to comprehend what they had just witnessed.

"*Our boys are shooting rockets at 'em,*" screamed one of the men. "*We've got rockets on those firecans!*" The camp burst into hysterical cheering, the men running across the yard toward the east fence, to get a better look.

"Boom!" Heads quickly turned back to the south and there high in the sky was a big orange ball of fire and black smoke, falling toward the earth. The men held their collective breath as the remaining vapor trail swung to the east and streaked toward the MIG and the Dog Sabre behind it in hot pursuit.

The fireball continued to plummet to the earth and suddenly a loud shout came from the roof.

"It's the other Sabre!"

The quiet in the yard broke again with shouts as all the men closed in on each other on the east fence. There high over the river valley, two American "Dog Sabres" dogged the remaining Chinese MIG, whose pilot was trying desperately to escape their deadly bite.

A rocket erupted again from under the fuselage of the trailing Dog Sabre, the vapor trail zipping by the MIG and disappearing in the horizon.

A muffled, *"ba-boom,"* sounded off from behind the men. Heads turned to look back over their shoulders to the south. The downed MIG had crashed and a plume of black smoke began to rise. A loud cheer went up in the yard.

Back to their front the MIG turned sharply to the north to avoid the trailing jet and turned into the waiting sights of the second Dog Sabre.

A vapor trail shot out and raced toward the MIG. A sudden flash appeared at the MIG. It shuddered, flames and smoke coming out its back end. The men were dancing about, eyes to the sky as they watched the MIG make a wide circle back to the west where the Dog Sabre, on its tail, sent a second rocket toward it.

A burst of orange flame and black smoke erupted from the left side of the MIG, followed by a loud, *"boom!"* The jet began to spiral out of control toward the earth, its wing fluttering down slowly behind it. The men followed the falling MIG's path down and watched it crash in a ball of flames on the mountainside across the Yula River.

Several seconds later they heard a muffled, *"ba-boom!"*

There was considerable celebrating going on in the yard as the two American fighters regrouped north of the mountain. They appeared to be wingtip to wingtip as they swung south, dropping in altitude as they approached the camp. As they flew just left of the camp, they gently tipped their wings back and forth in unison. Flying at just over three hundred feet the Air Force symbol was clearly visible on the back of their fuselages. One of the pilots waved as the two aircraft roared past and the men went wild waving back and cheering.

After passing by the camp the engine exhaust flames burst bright with an orange glow, as two loud booms were heard, one right after the other. The F-86Ds quickly disappeared into the southern horizon, dragging the roar of the engines along with them.

The men's celebration continued until a loud burp of machine gun fire erupted at the front gate. The guard's show of authority silenced the men in the yard, but did little to hamper their smiles and excitement.

They had witnessed dogfights over the past month, but the aircraft were off in the distance, too far to tell who was who, and ended in apparent draws. They had witnessed nothing as close, or dramatic as what they just saw.

The American boys had shot two MIGs down. Right out of the sky, right before their eyes, and with rockets. That was very good news for the spirit of the prisoners. The war was coming to the north and their flyboys were knocking MIGs out of the sky. It was a major shot in the arm for the prisoners.

"I can't believe they got both of them," said Bob Green shaking his fist in the air. "Shot both of those dirty bastards down, and sent them to hell where they belong."

"Man! That was da . . . da . . . damn near the most exciting thing I . . . I ever seen," added Earl Davenport.

The men stood silently, looking at the plumes of smoke on the mountain to the north and to the south. The death of fighting men in Korea was commonplace in 1953, but as the men stood watching the plumes of smoke, hope rose in their hearts, a quiet hope that things were finally going their way. They watched quietly for twenty minutes or so. Occasionally a few words were said, but mostly quiet eyes watched the black smoke billowing upward.

Dan Welch wondered to himself if maybe the end of their hell was drawing near. There were the signs, the increase in bombers going north, the food was better and today, an honest to God dog fight right over their heads. Quiet hope was starting to spread.

*   *   *   *

Mo Richards kneeled down next to the Atkins boy and shook him. It was four-fifteen in the morning and Atkins was late for his shift at the kitchen shed. Richards shook him again, but got no response. He rolled the boy over and Atkins flipped over face up, eyes open and fixed. Richards looked down sadly and shook his head. He couldn't understand how people could just give up on living. He couldn't understand because he'd never been there, deep in the pit of despair, with no hope, overwhelmed in grief. Richards placed his fingers on the dead boy's eyelids and pulled them down. The eyes opened back up halfway, giving Atkins' face a very dead and haunting look. Richards took the boy's blanket and pulled it up over his head. Standing, he shook his head once again and left the room, headed for the kitchen.

"Masland!" A man moved forward through the crowd, reached up and took a letter from the mail clerk's hand.

"Lucas!" Another man moved forward and retrieved his letters.

"Monteux!" and so it went. The letters were coming in ones and twos now. The mail volume had increased. The letters were still three to five months old, but that didn't matter to the men as long as they came through.

Welch stood in the crowd. He had received an occasional letter from his Aunt Betsy, and had even received another letter from Amelia complaining that the Army wouldn't let her have all of his back pay. She wrote that he certainly didn't need it as bad as she did, since he was a captive and all, and he should call the Army and have them change her allowance. He had actually gotten a good laugh out of it and shared it with the guys.

"Bregoli!"

"Over here!" came a shout.

"Lowe!"

"Yo!" yelled Welch as his hand shot up and he made his way to the man standing on the wooden box.

"I've got that for Lowe!" and he took three letters and walked back through the crowd. Howard Lowe had been feeling poorly. For the past week he had been flat on his back. Welch walked quickly up the hill toward the building. He found Lowe where he had left him a couple of hours earlier on his mat.

"Hey, buddy, how about some news from home?"

Lowe's face lit up when he saw the three letters held up in front of him. He tried to speak, but only a whisper came out. Welch knelt down and lifted him up supporting his back against the wall.

"Let's see now, three letters. One, two from Martha and the third from," Welch held the letter close and studied the return address.

"It appears to be a Katherine Newhouse."

Lowe smiled and whispered, "Mrs. Katherine."

"Which will it be first, Mrs. Katherine or My Dearest Martha?" asked Welch.

Through the course of writing weekly letters for Lowe, Welch felt he knew Martha and the girls. The Chinese were now providing paper and pens for the prisoners, so writing was much easier, and safer. Welch tried not to embellish the letters and write the words as Lowe said them, but at times he would get carried away. When he read the letters back to Lowe, he would find several flowery words and lines he had added. He would apologize, but Lowe insisted the words be left in the letters.

"You got a way with words, Dan. You seem to write down just what I'm feeling," Lowe had said, so he left the words in.

"Let's hear what Mrs. Katherine has to say first," whispered Lowe.

"Mrs. Katherine it is. Saving the best for the last, eh? I'd do the same thing myself." Welch read Mrs. Katherine's letter, which was filled with news of the Gadberry community. He read slowly and deliberately. There were good stories about both the girls and several comments about this person or that, asking about him and praying for his safe return.

There was also some local gossip, written in the not so subtle way that only Mrs. Katherine could write, paraphrasing her favorite radio broadcaster and columnist, Walter Winchell.

"Good evening Mr. G.I.,

> *From Korean border to border and Pacific coast to coast and all the ships at sea. Let's go to press with Gadberry's latest gossip. I'm about to tell you nothing in a way that leaves practically nothing unsaid.*
>
> *It seems that one of Gadberrytown's favorite couples aren't talking these days. Everyone knows about the rift, but few know the real reason the man of the house is sleeping on the couch and eating out at the elegant Circle R diner nearly every night. This is the inside story from someone who promised somebody else that they would keep it a secret.*
>
> *It seems that the only ones who like Mr. C are his mother and his dairy cows. Mrs. C is ready to send him packing. An ultimatum was given and Mr. C is sleeping on it. It seems that he wants to keep milking his Holstein at home, while he is milking a Red Pole at someone else's barn. My source tells me that Mr. C was caught with teats in hand by Mr. S, the Red Pole's owner, who not only poked him in the nose, but immediately called Mrs. C to report that her bull had apparently followed its nose through the fence and wandered into his barnyard, breeding with his cow.*

Berrytown is where they Shoot-The-Moon in friendly games of Rook at the Gadberry General Store, but won't shoot a wandering bull. A real friend is one who walks in when the rest of the community only talks about it. Padre Henry is trying to save the union, but Mr. C can't make up his mind about which cow he wants to milk. Grazing on both sides of the fence is doomed to fail, and Mrs. C is ready to put her hoof down. Remember, today's gossip is tomorrow's headlines.

Take care Howard. God bless and hurry home.

Love Katherine"

Welch and Lowe chuckled through the reading of Mrs. Katherine's gossip column not once, but twice. It picked up Lowe's spirits.

"I really like this Mrs. Katherine."

"Maybe you two can meet someday. I want you to visit as soon as you can. You will always be welcome in our home."

Welch smiled and said, "Thanks, buddy. I may take you up on that." When Welch finished the letter he folded it neatly and put it back in its envelope. He looked down at Lowe and was amazed to see color had come back in his face. His eyes had a slight sparkle and a smile was holding across his face. Great medicine, these letters from home, he thought.

Looking at the other two he found the one with the oldest postmark, August 25, 1952, opened it and began to read. The news from Martha was generally about missing him and how the girls were doing with school starting back. Finishing the letter he folded it neatly and placed it back into its envelope.

Opening the second envelope and unfolding the letter, he said to Lowe.

"This one is dated October 10, 1952,"

"My Dearest Howard,

I am doing well. The girls are growing like weeds and miss their father very much."

Welch read on down the letter, repeating certain things at Lowe's request from time to time:

"I nearly finished cleaning out the garden today. Silas and Carl came by Saturday and finished harvesting the corn. The rains have made it impossible to use the corn picker, so they picked the whole barn field by hand. It's now safely in the corn crib, less for you to do when you get home, my dear."

Lowe whispered, "The crops, Dan. My neighbors are pitching in and helping." Welch smiled and continued reading until he read:

"I find it to be increasingly more difficult to see to everything, as I move further along with our unborn child."

Welch looked down at Lowe, a bit set back by the revelation in the letter. Lowe stared up, wide eyed, smiling ear to ear.

"More, more," he whispered.

"Let's see, ah, ah, here it is, *unborn child,*"

"I have been showing for about a month now, but have managed to hide it with clothing. Mrs. Katherine has been a tremendous help, coming down twice a week to wash clothes and prepare things in the kitchen. She turned to me last week and asked when the baby was due. I was dumbfounded for several seconds, but finally gained my senses.

She believes it to be a boy. I sense that you may finally have yourself a son to keep you company on the farm. At my checkup yesterday, Doc Slaton commented that it was acting more and more like a boy every time he sees me. He has set the date for the end of March."

Welch reached down and held Lowe's hand. It was trembling and tears where starting to run down his cheeks. Welch's eyes were also misty:

"Just think Howard, a son! Everyone will look at him and say, "There goes young Howard Lowe, my but doesn't he look just like his father," and someday they will say, "Why look at that Lowe boy hit that ball and run, just like his dad did on the '40 Indian team that beat Campbellsville so bad."

A boy, Howard! Oh, how I wish you were here to share the excitement the girls and I feel."

Lowe whispered, "I'm going to have a son, Dan, a son to work on the farm. My farm can continue to be worked by a Lowe."

Welch continued to hold Lowe's hand and finished the letter:

> *"I must go now darling. Know that I will hold you safely in my heart until you return.*
>
> *Sweet Dreams,*
>
> *Martha"*

Looking up at Welch, Lowe whispered, "Praise God, Dan. He works in wondrous ways."

＊   ＊   ＊   ＊

On March 26, a Chinese delegation representing Mao returned to Peking from Moscow where they attended Stalin's funeral. Two days later Chinese and North Korean officials sat down to discuss General Mark Clark's request to exchange sick and wounded prisoners. The communist group came to an agreement that they would meet Clark's request and carry out the provisions of the Geneva Convention in terms of the sick and wounded.

The message was delivered and they additionally proposed the resumption of serious peace negotiations. The break the free world had been looking for seemed to indirectly result from the death of one of the world's most ruthless and repressive tyrants.

"Praise God! He works in wondrous ways."

CHAPTER 14

▼

As Mrs. Katherine washed the dishes, Wanda Faye walked into the kitchen with her history book, the last of her homework that night. She sat at the table and turned up the coal oil lamp. Mrs. Katherine noticed the increase in light.

"Reading assignment, dear?"

"Yes, ma'am."

"What you reading?"

"The Civil War. Did you know my great-grandpa was in the Civil War?"

"Yes, I did honey, and you know what?"

"What, Mrs. Katherine?"

"My pa fought at your great grandpa's side in the 8th Kentucky Infantry. They were friends."

"Did you know my great grandpa?"

"Yes, I did. When I was a little girl we would come to visit. Mr. Lowe was a tall man with a long gray beard. He was always nice and gave us candies. When I was little, we lived in Barren County, outside Bowling Green. We traveled by horseback and wagon back then, so a visit lasted several weeks. My mama was in a wheelchair and traveling was hard on her. After a while she just stayed at home. Pa and Mr. Lowe would coon hunt three, sometimes four nights a week. Out all night and come in at sun up."

Wanda Faye listened intently as Mrs. Katherine recalled the memories from her childhood, but eventually she caught herself, "Child, weren't we talking about the Civil War?"

"Did your pa tell you about the war?" Wanda Faye grabbed her pen and paper, and waited.

"Darling, he had wondrous stories about the parades after the war. The truth is though, it was a horrible thing to live through. He would wake up in the middle of the night screaming out. Mom said he saw a lot of men die on both sides. They were American boys, killing American boys. It was a sad time in our history. After it was all said and done, he never could understand why the South wanted to fight in the first place."

Mrs. Katherine started rinsing the pots and pans, placing them on the counter to dry.

"Pa said everything was burnt to the ground. Dead horses lay along the roads, but they didn't smell nearly as bad as the dead men that covered the battlefields."

"I smelled a dead cow once," quickly responded Wanda Faye. "It stinked."

"It stunk, darling."

"You smelled it too, Mrs. Katherine?"

The old woman chuckled and hugged Wanda Faye.

"Pa said he was glad the North won the war, and glad they'd killed a bunch of them, but as he got older it bothered him a lot. On his deathbed, with kin and neighbors sitting with him, he talked about crawling up Lookout Mountain in Chattanooga a rock at a time, grabbing shrubs and pulling himself and his rifle along, an inch at a time, while sharpshooters below him killed the rebels above him." He hoped God would forgive him for all the men he'd killed. Brother Cox, our minister, told him that when he took to Jesus, all his sins were forgiven, including having to kill so many Rebs, who deserved to die anyway. Pa died a contented man.

Soon after that, Brother Cox's mule was shot out from under him one evening on the way back from his circuit ride. No one ever knew who'd done it, but the point was made. Brother Cox bought himself a new mule and toned down his words a bit."

Wanda Faye wrote feverishly the things Mrs. Katherine shared about her father and the Civil War. It was things she hadn't read in her books, things she would share with her class.

*   *   *   *

"Wanda Faye," said Miss Goldman. "You forgot to include the family radio in your floor plans. You can come and get your drawing to add it in, if you wish."

Miss Goldman had assigned fifth through eighth grades the project of drawing a floor plan of their home for home economics. She had provided a list of items on the blackboard that she expected in each floor plan. The Lowe home floor plan was the only one without a radio.

Wanda Faye stood. "Miss Goldman, we don't own a radio."

"You don't ever listen to the radio?"

"Oh, yes ma'am, we listen to the Lone Ranger and the Grand Old Opry most every Saturday night at Rebecca and Elizabeth Long's home. When the weather is bad, Dad borrows Mr. Silas' old radio. Mr. Silas charges the batteries all day, so they'd be good and charged up for Saturday night. Mr. Silas has electricity in his home to charge them with."

It hadn't occurred to Mrs. Goldman that some families might not have electricity in their homes. After all, it was 1953.

"That's all right Wanda Faye. Can you draw where Mr. Silas' radio would sit?"

"Yes, ma'am," replied Wanda Faye with a big smile.

She retrieved her drawing and sketched in a little square box on the table next to the fireplace. In small letters she wrote, "MR. SILAS' RADIO."

*   *   *   *

Grasping the handles of the posthole digger, Warren Clark raised his hands even with his nose and plunged the digger down into the hole. The five-foot mark on the handle was now even with the ground. He had dug and set in concrete five eighteen-foot poles. He would skip a day to let the concrete set up before he came back to run the wire to the meter on the side of the Lowe home. That would be Friday. On Saturday he would return on his own time and install the main electrical box inside the home.

Two weeks ago, his son was sharing his day at Tabor over supper. Ty described how Miss Goldman asked the older children to draw the floor plan of their home as a class assignment. Wanda Faye Lowe had stood up in front of the class and defiantly announced, by his words, "Her home didn't have electricity." The story got Warren to thinking about Martha being there alone with the children without the benefit of electricity. Yes, they had done without for years, but electricity was cheap and life was much easier with it. No one should go without it.

Martha and his sister, Shirley, were best friends growing up. He had known Martha practically her whole life and had met Howard on occasion. He wanted to help, so it had cost him a hot breakfast at Circle R to convince Bud Miller to let him run the line down to the Lowe home at no cost. Besides, as he had put it to his boss, "It's good public relations for the Rural Electric to take care of its neighbors when they were in need."

Warren stopped later that afternoon and spoke with Silas Long about the project. His Uncle Silas had patted him on the back and said, "Now, why didn't I think of that?"

They had talked it out. Silas knew a reliable electrician, Dale Conley from Cane Valley. Conley owed him a big favor and might be willing to do the wiring. Silas agreed to talk with Martha. Warren would get some wire scraps at the Rural Electric barn, as they had miles of it lying around. Silas would see to the outlets, switches and light fixtures. The old house would be easy to wire with the large crawl space underneath and no insulation in the walls.

Things would be easier for Martha and the kids with electricity in the home. The only thing Silas had to do was convince Martha, or maybe not.

"And that's it. Now, how can we convince Martha to let us do this for her and the kids?"

Mrs. Katherine sat for a moment, thinking.

"Tell me Silas, what had you and Dorothy planned to get Martha and Howard for their anniversary, this Saturday?"

"Well, Katherine. We don't usually get . . ." Silas looked at Mrs. Katherine and suddenly smiled. "Well now, come to think of it we talked about getting together with some of the neighbors and putting some electric in her home. But, we still got to get her to agree to it."

"Martha has said several times she and Howard talked about hooking up with the Rural Electric. She told me she wished they'd had it done before he left. I'll tell her about the anniversary gift this evening when I go back over. Go ahead and make the arrangements with Warren and Dale Conley. Trust me, she'll be delighted."

Martha was delighted. All the work was completed by the following Saturday evening. Mrs. Katherine cooked up a mess of fried chicken and neighbors brought side dishes. There was corn pudding, turnip greens, sweet potatoes, pole beans, potato salad and two or three different salads, and a variety of desserts that drove Brother Cook to distraction.

As the evening grew dark, two coal oil lamps lit the living room and kitchen, which were filled with neighbors, family and guests.

Silas got everybody's attention. "Now Martha, everyone knows if Howard were here he would have insisted on wiring the barn first." Laughter filled the room. "I'll answer for that when he comes home. But, for now, if you'll step this way, you may have the honor of flipping the switch to light up your new electric home."

Silas helped Martha up off the couch and they walked over to the light switches next to the front door.

"Brother Cook, shut off that lamp next to you. Someone get the lamp in the kitchen and Martha will flip the switch."

The living room and kitchen went dark one after the other. Everyone stood in total darkness for a few moments.

"There was a *click* and the living room lit up with a brightness that far exceeded the coal oil lamp. Everyone squinted, as their eyes adjusted to the light. Another *click* and the porch lit up, casting light down into the front yard. Martha walked over to the door going into the kitchen and *click,* the kitchen lit up like the bright noon sun and everyone applauded.

"There is just one more thing that we have to do," said Silas. May reached behind the couch, pulled out a gift-wrapped box and sat it on the ottoman. Martha walked over and sat down.

Teary eyed she read the tag on the box.

TO MARTHA AND HOWARD
HAPPY ANNIVERSARY
FROM NEIGHBORS AND FRIENDS

Martha unwrapped the paper, opened the box, and lifted out a modern electric RCA radio.

＊　　＊　　＊　　＊

"The girls really like Miss Goldman, and Wanda Faye says Raymond Tracy and Stephen Michael have even given her their stamp of approval. I hope the county school superintendent can find a place for her after I return to Tabor. We need to keep good teachers right here in Adair County."

"Well child, you know you've got his ear. A good word from you would go a long way," pointed out Mrs. Katherine.

Karen Spalding nodded her head in agreement. "You let her finish out the school year Martha. You don't need to go back to work with a tiny one to take care of."

"She's right, honey," agreed Mrs. Katherine. "By the time school starts in August your little man ought to be might near six months old, and you'll be recovered from birth'en. This war can't last forever and Howard will be a coming home soon. He'll start the farming back up good and proper, and he'll get a sizeable back-pay check from the Army that'll help you get caught up."

"Everything will be okay Martha. You'll see. Mrs. Katherine is never wrong, are you Mrs. Katherine?"

"Darling, you're sweet to think that, but I was wrong once. Unfortunately, everyone who was around then is dead and gone."

Martha and her sister laughed. Mrs. Katherine dressed a yellow pancake with brown sugar icing and as she spread the last bit, eight tiny feet were heard coming down the stairs of the Lowe home. Growing closer and louder, they rounded the corner and stampeded into the kitchen.

Mrs. Katherine let out a holler.

"Girls!"

Amy Sue came to a sudden stop and Nelly Ann, Wanda Faye and Coral bumped into her and one another.

"Ladies, and I say that with deep reservations, if you want to clean the icing pan and spoons, go back into the living room and come back in the kitchen like the nice young ladies I know you can be."

The girls shuffled out of the kitchen, giggling, and began entering the kitchen in single file, twisting and sashaying like New York models.

"Now that's a heap better. If you want to be treated like a proper lady, you need to start acting like one."

"Me no lady . . ." protested Amy Sue.

"Me Amy Sue!" added the other three girls loudly before she could finish.

"Well I plum forgot myself, Miss Amy," mocked Mrs. Katherine. "Miss Amy, ladies, there are spoons and a beater in that pan. When there is not a speck of brown sugar icing left on them holler and I'll come and clean you up. Your mothers and I are going into the living room so we won't get any icing flung on us."

In the living room Martha sat down on the couch and propped her legs on the ottoman. Karen sat next to her and Mrs. Katherine sat in her favorite rocker.

"I was shopping in the Louisville Store in Greensburg last Saturday and ran into Dotty Crisp."

"Who?" asked Martha.

"Little Dorothy Ham, surely you remember? She was in my class in high school."

"There was a two-year difference between us Karen."

"Little tiny thing. Lived on Burton Ridge. Dated Brad Fisher."

Martha looked at Karen with a blank look on her face.

"She dated Brad all through high school and married some Crisp boy from Green County, right after graduation. Surely you remember."

"Honest, Karen. I haven't a clue."

"Her dad worked at the Chevrolet garage in Columbia."

"You were saying you ran into her in Greensburg," interrupted Mrs. Katherine.

"Oh, yea. We were talking and when I told her about Howard, she said her younger brother was in Japan and wrote the war would soon be over."

"Oh, what a blessing that . . ." Martha cut herself off in mid-sentence, turned and looked at Mrs. Katherine. Her face tightened and she grabbed her belly.

"Are you okay, darling?" asked Mrs. Katherine as she sat forward in her rocker.

"I think my water broke."

Mrs. Katherine moved over to the couch and sat down next to Martha.

"Yes, I'm certain of it now. My water has broken."

Karen and Mrs. Katherine walked Martha to the bedroom where Karen helped her undress. Mrs. Katherine went to the kitchen to call Dr. Slaton. The girls sat at the table finishing off the icing. She picked up the phone and found May Long and Millie Parker on the party line, chatting.

"May, Millie, got to cut you off. Martha's water broke and I need to call Doc Slaton."

"You going to need any help Mrs. Katherine?" asked May.

"Karen's here. If her labor goes on too long, we'll need someone to run Nelly and Coral home to their dad. I'll let you know."

May and Millie hung up and Mrs. Katherine rung the doctor.

"Hello, Doctor Slaton speaking."

"Doc, Katherine Newhouse. I'm at Martha Lowe's. Her water has broken."

"Contractions?"

"One."

A loud moan came from the bedroom and the girls sat up straight in their chairs.

"There's number two. About fifteen minutes apart, I'd say."

"Make her comfortable Katherine. I'll be out there as quick as I can," and he hung up.

Mrs. Katherine turned to the girls. "Girls, it's time for the baby to come. Wanda Faye, you're in charge of cleaning up the kitchen and seeing that everyone cleans themselves up."

"Yes, ma'am."

Mrs. Katherine calmly walked back to the bedroom and found Martha propped up on the bed with several pillows. Karen was helping her get her nightgown on. Mrs. Katherine sat in a chair next to the bed.

"The Doc is on his way, darling. How are you doing?"

"I'm fine Mrs. Katherine. I hope this boy doesn't decide to be difficult."

Mrs. Katherine remembered the eight hours of labor that brought Amy Sue into the world and hoped for Martha's sake, the one on the way would birth easy.

"Where are the girls?"

"Don't you fret over them. I left Wanda Faye in charge."

"I feel so helpless."

"Of course, you do, honey. You remember how it goes. With a little luck, before long it will be all over. Now rest while you can, I'm going to put some water on and start gathering up some things we will need when that boy starts to get serious about coming into this world."

Martha smiled and leaned back against the pillows. The knowledge that Mrs. Katherine had assisted in most of the births in Gadberry over the past fifty years was comforting. The babies that wouldn't wait for Dr. Slaton to arrive, she had delivered herself.

"I see headlamps coming down the road!" shouted Wanda Faye.

"*Umph!* There it is again," grunted Martha as she caught her breath.

"This one isn't going to wait around like those other two. He's in a big hurry to see the world. How far apart, Karen?"

"Five minutes."

"It won't be long now."

"There was a rapid knock at the door. Mrs. Katherine went and let Dr. Slaton in.

"How far apart?"

"Five minutes."

"How's Martha?"

"Holding up just fine."

Slaton and Mrs. Katherine walked through the living room and the four young girls were sitting together on the couch.

"Hello, Doctor Slaton," said the girls in unison.

"Girls! I'm going to need you all to help me here in a bit. Can I count on you?"

"Yes!" said all the girls together again.

"That baby is going to be here before long, and when it gets here, I'm going to look it over, proper. Mrs. Katherine is going to clean it up and give it to Mrs. Karen. She's going to need help watching the baby until Mrs. Martha is ready to take it. Can I count on you all to do that for me?"

"Yes!" said the girls.

With that he went to the kitchen and scrubbed his hands and forearms in the hot water Mrs. Katherine had prepared. In a few minutes he entered the bedroom and closed the door behind him. The girls sat together on the couch holding hands.

"How you holding up, Martha?"

"Been better."

"Let's take a look," and he sat on the chair next to the bed.

Martha was lying across the bed, propped up with several pillows and Karen's support. Her knees were up in the air. Dr. Slaton reached under the sheet and examined her.

As the evening went on Martha's contractions grew closer together and when they reached thirty seconds, Dr. Slaton examined her once again.

"Well, Martha, it seems that boy of yours is ready to make his grand entrance. He's starting to crown."

In the middle of her smile Martha flinched and her muscles tightened.

"Ten seconds!" said Karen.

"On the next one, push!" said Dr. Slaton. "Push hard!"

The birth went well for both mother and baby and as Mrs. Katherine had predicted, it was a big healthy boy. He came out quickly, kicking and screaming.

The girls were still sitting on the couch holding hands, talking about birthing babies. Since none of them had actually witnessed the birth of a child they talked about what they did know, the birth of farm animals. As Wanda Faye was relating the story of their sow giving birth to a large litter, they heard the distinctive cry of a baby come from the bedroom. They jumped to their feet and ran to the bedroom door.

The baby continued to wail on the other side of the door and the girls squealed with excitement. Finally, the door opened and Mrs. Karen stuck her head out.

"It's a boy, girls. A baby brother."

"Good!" replied Amy Sue. "No need sister. Already got one!"

It was the fifth day of life for Howard Delbert Lowe II. He was fussy and demanding, as most newborns tend to be, and as Mrs. Katherine had told May Long, "Bless his heart, if he's not sleeping or pooping, he's got his face stuck to one of Martha's breasts."

He was a handsome baby with a full head of dark hair and a happy, little, round face. He was quite content to eat and sleep. The girls got to hold him some from time to time and they were amazed with his littleness. Amy Sue held his hand up against hers and announced that she was no longer the smallest one in the family. Both girls were right proud of him and studied everything about him with wonder.

Martha was overjoyed. Howard never showed any disappointment at the lack of a son. He loved his girls, but she knew it would please him to have someone to help him on the farm, someone to hunt and fish with, to toss a baseball with. She would call him Junior, as she was sure that was what Howard would call him.

The rocker had been moved into the bedroom and that was where Martha sat, rocking Junior during his evening feeding. She held him in the crook of her arm as he sucked away, his dark little eyes staring up at her. He was nearly done and as usual, his eyelids fluttered several times and eventually closed in sleep. Martha got up and laid him down in his crib, covering him with the little white blanket both his sisters had slept under the first several months of their life.

She had tried to sit down several times before and write a letter to Howard, telling him about his son. Each time she became very emotional, even before she had written the first word. She understood what was going on with her body. She had been through it before with the birth of the girls, but knowing still didn't make it any easier.

She sat down at her vanity and stared at the paper in front of her. She wanted to tell Howard about his son in a way that would encourage and give him hope.

Once again, she was overwhelmed with thoughts of what he was going through and tears welled up in her eyes, running down her cheeks.

Taking a handkerchief from her gown pocket she wiped the tears from her eyes, blew her nose and began to write:

March 30, 1953

My Dearest Howard,

We have a son. Howard Delbert Lowe II. Born the 25ᵗʰ of March.

Your loving wife,

Martha

CHAPTER 15

▼

"Young people fight wars, poor young people. Are you telling me that all the Chinese soldiers in Korea are poor?"

"That different matter."

Joe Albertson stood up. His beard and ebony skin hid most of the blush on his face, but not the fire in his eyes. "Why is it always different when it comes to your country?"

"You not understand!"

"Oh, I understand all right. I've understood my whole life. You people are no different than back home. It's always different for those of us who don't have anything."

"You think you have job when you get back home?" asked Captain Lin.

"Now you're telling me that everyone in China works. How about that Chairman Mao? How about your big boss man? Does he grow his own food, clean his house, and empty his own pot?"

"You reactionary! We punish you!"

"Punish me! You ask my opinion and when you don't hear what you want, you punish me. You're just like white folks back home in Birmingham. Coloreds are never right, even when we are, because, 'That different matter,'" Albertson said, mockingly.

"The day a colored man is born, he's nothing till the day he dies. He's called, Boy, whether he's eight or eighty. I don't need little yellow skinned shits like you to tell me what I have, or don't have back home!"

"You reactionary. Bad for other men. We shoot you!"

"Shoot me! Lord, you hear that?" Albertson threw his hands up in the air and lifted his eyes to the heavens, *"He's gonna shoot me!"*

Albertson turned his eyes to his captor and said through clinched teeth, "Why you wanna miss out on all the real fun, Captain, Sir?" He looked Lin straight in the eye. "What about a hangin'? I'll be damned if I'm going to deprive you and your boys of a good Sunday nigger hangin', and the pleasure of watching my dead black ass being dragged down a country road from behind a pickup truck. I got a family tradition to uphold."

"Shoot me! Lord God, Almighty!" Lin jumped back and Albertson gave him a cold stare. "You can shoot me right in the back, as I walk out on your yellow goon-ass!"

Captain Lin watched as Albertson walked out the door. The guard started to raise his rifle, but Lin threw up his hand.

Nate Smith sat on the wooden steps to his barracks smoking his pipe. Stomping down the road came Joe Albertson, kicking up the dust, and talking to himself as he came.

"Don't . . . don't tell me I can't find no job! And don't you even think you know what it's like for my kind back home, when you . . ." he stopped and shouted, *"you treat us the same over here! Don't you even think, you yellow . . ."*

"Joe! Whoa, *big fellow!* What's got you all riled up?"

Albertson stopped in front of the barracks and looked at his friend.

"Those . . . dat damn . . . one these days I'm a gonna . . ."

"One of these days they gonna shoot you!"

"Being dead ain't bad as it's made out to be these days!"

"What'd you know about being dead?"

"I've been close to dead since the day they captured me." Albertson stood there, his arms to his sides now, his shoulders slumping, a sad look on his face.

"Close to dead, ain't nowhere near dead, Joe. There's a lot of life between the two, and you got a lot of living to do yet. There's a rumor peace talks are going to work out this time. The Chinese apparently want to come to some sort of terms."

"We been hearing those same rumors since we got here. I've been living and slowly dying on rumors for might near two years now, Nate. I'm tired of rumors."

"The Chinese have been treating us better the last several months. I suspect something's gotta break soon. I got a feeling. A good feeling."

"You mean the chinks ain't been trying to kill us off the past couple of months."

"Damn right, and ain't the chow better? Ain't we a living better?"

Albertson didn't respond. He just walked over to the steps and sat next to his friend.

"You helped a lot of guys stay alive, Nate. Nobody cares how you do it, they just thankful for the medicine, or the extra rations. You got a way of getting along with people, especially those sneaky little chinks. I wish I had some of that, but I don't. You better be careful how you mess with them. People are gonna talk. You know a nigger don't stand a chance agin a white man's word in this Army. We may be free someday and you may have to answer for some things you didn't do."

Smith was touched by his friend's concern. Albertson was not easy to show emotion, other than anger.

"I'll be okay, Joe. I ain't done nothing, or told nothing that I'd be ashamed of. I learned to stroke white folks when I was young. Just doing the same here to makes life easier for us."

The two men sat talking, staring up the hill at the School House in the white man's compound.

*   *   *   *

"You. Tell about life in America."

A tall slender man with dark brown hair and a big round beard stood.

"Ralph Carson here. Not much to say about my life before I got drafted in the Marine Corps. I grew up in Gary, Indiana. My folks were average people for those parts. My mom was a doctor, a surgeon at the hospital. Dad was a lawyer. My grandparents were doctors and lawyers. We had a nice home on ten acres, in the middle of Gary. My sister, three brothers and I went to a private school. I wore a blazer and a tie to school every day. Never cared much for it all, but riding to school in our limousine sure beat the hell out of sitting on a bus."

The men sat quietly listening to Carson give the autobiography of his life, embellish somewhat. It was routine for the men to try and outdo each other. Two Chinese officers sat and listened intently.

"Mom loved to entertain, you see. That's why she worked part time. We had parties, two, sometimes three nights a week. Our house was built to entertain. Mom'd work with Bartholomew, our butler, and they'd tell the kitchen staff what to fix and the house staff where to put the flowers and things. We kids would just hang out by the pool while the grown-up folks were inside social-a-lizing, as mom liked to say. I really liked our pool because it was bigger and deeper than the one at the country club. Dad liked to say it was deeper than most rivers in Indiana. He was quite the talker. I tell you men, I always wished I had got some of Dad's gift for gab, instead of so much of Mom's intellect." The men shuffled their feet and moved around on their benches, doing their best not to laugh.

"When mom wasn't having parties, I'd hang out at the club, 'cause that was where the girls were. I had two or three girlfriends at a time, on most days. They always wanted to be with me. There were so many, it didn't seem right to break their hearts, so I'd give them all a chance at me. I never settled on one."

Restrained smiles were becoming difficult to cover and there were a few light chuckles, covered by coughs as Carson rambled on with his make-believe childhood.

"I can recall one sunny afternoon when I was sixteen. I was a lying out by the pool, a working on my tan. Tuesday was family day at the club, but I decided I needed the day off from my girlfriends, so I stayed home to rest up. I was sitting there reading that book *The Great Gatsby*, he was one of our neighbors, you know. All of a sudden Rosie, one of our maids, walked up and asked me if I could help get some sheets from the linen closet. The rest of the staff was off. I didn't mind since Rosie wasn't hard to look at. I got up and followed her into the house.

Well, I climbed up that ladder and grabbed an arm full of sheets and when I tuned around, there stood Rosie in her birthday suit, getting easier and easier to look at as I came down the ladder. It became obvious to me she had more on her mind than making a bed."

The men listened carefully now. Stories of home life were usually filled with fabrications, but this autobiography had taken an unusual but interesting turn.

"I tell you, comrades," Carson hesitated and looked longingly at the ceiling, "I went into that linen closet a boy, and I walked out a man."

Turning to the Chinese, Carson asked, "You ever been laid, Captain Lin?"

The two officers exchanged a few words in Chinese and Lin became angry. Flustered, he stood up and left the room, followed quickly by the junior officer.

"Well! I guess he never met Rosie," exclaimed Carson as he walked to his seat.

The men openly laughed now as they stood and made their way out of the classroom. A couple of men shot barbs at Carson, who sheepishly stuck to his rich-boy role. He was most certainly from Gary, Indiana, but his family was poor as dirt. Whether there was ever a Rosie in his life was debated for several days at the camp.

*　　*　　*　　*

"I'm really worried about Howard. He's not getting any better from this spell. It's been nearly a week now."

"Well, yelling won't work with a guy like Howard. He's got more than most of us to live for. He was too shot up and blown up when he got here, Dan. Anybody else would be dead by now. We just got to keep looking after him. Get him on his feet and keep him moving."

Green and Welch walked slowly across the yard, doing their daily exercise. Twenty trips total, back and forth. Several of the men had taken up exercise since the food and conditions had improved. Some of the more serious set up a workout center with large chunks of wood and rock to lift. It was good for everyone to see each other thinking about the future.

Finishing their last leg across the yard, they made their way to the School House and their squad room. There they found Lowe lying on his back, staring at the ceiling. When they entered the room his head slowly rotated to the side. A small smile formed on the corners of his mouth.

"Hey!" Lowe said in a whisper.

"Hay is for your horse, farmer," responded Green. "How you feeling today?"

"Like my horse slept on me. I gotta get up off my back."

"We'll roll you over on your side. We don't want any nasty bed sores developing on your pretty little behind," and the two men gently rolled Lowe over on his left side. Lowe slowly pulled himself up on his elbow.

The men glanced at each other, smiled and gently propped Lowe up against the wall.

"I was thinking more in terms of sitting up for a while today. Things seem brighter when I'm sitting up. On the farm when a hide gets down, you'd gotta get 'em up, if you don't, you'll lose 'em for sure. I've spent many a night in a barn, hoisting an animal to its feet and tying it off to a rafter or stall wall."

Since appearance generally reflects health, Lowe looked in trouble. His eyes were sunken and ghostly looking. His cheekbones were protruding from an emaciated face. His complexion was chalky white, with a yellowish tint. His hair was stringy and had a greasy, dirty look to it. On the back of his head the hair was flat from lying on the mat. His beard was thick and tangled. A lot of men looked rough, but Lowe had the look of someone who should have long since died. Green and Welch both knew how fragile life could be, and they were both worried about their friend.

"What's the word on the streets?"

"Rumor has it that something big is coming up in the next week or so. The chinks are acting strange, almost nice."

"And last night," added Welch, "In small group discussion class, Ralph Carson was being his usual self, telling a whopper of an autobiography and ended it by asking Lin if he had ever been laid?"

Lowe's chuckle turned into muted coughs. He raised his hand as Dan stepped toward him. "I'm fine, Dan. Go on."

"Lin blabbed something in Chinese and walked out of the room, followed by his toady, that skinny young Lieutenant. I thought for sure he'd be punished, but so far, nothing. The Chinese are definitely up to something and it can't be nothing but good for us. We're getting better treatment and they are trying to fatten us up. They're either going to eat us or they want us to look better. That's the way I figure it, anyway."

"We've been fooled before, Dan," whispered Lowe.

"But things seem different this time. Ever since they announced Joe Stalin's death, they have acted different. I gotta believe something good is coming."

"I agree with Dan, Howard. Something is definitely going on with the Chinese."

"Martha," whispered Lowe.

*   *   *   *

The men stood in the mess line, waiting for Mo Richards to signal that breakfast would be served. Down below on the other side of the fence several empty trucks began to stage, one behind the other, forming a convoy.

"New prisoners coming in," said a voice down the line of men.

They watched and waited for prisoners to be downloaded from the backs of the trucks, but nothing happened.

"Chows on!" bellowed Mo Richard's voice from inside and the men began to slowly move through the shed.

The prisoners formed up in the yard. It was mid-morning and all eyes were on the trucks below. There was considerable apprehension as rumors circulated that some of the men were to be transferred to another camp.

Up the road from the Chinese compound walked Colonel Pol and Captain Lin, trailed by the runty little Lieutenant. The guards at the gate snapped to attention as they passed. Pol came to a stop in his usual place before the men, his staff the appropriate number of steps behind him.

"Through generous mercy of peace-loving peoples of Republic of China and Korea, agreement met to release sick and injured prisoners. The following prisoners to be escorted to American lines for release." Pol turned and nodded.

Captain Lin stepped forward and began to read from a list of names. The men stood in silence as Lin read off the names of the injured and sick men in the camp. The tenth name shouted out was Howard Lowe. Bob Green and Dan Welch turned and looked at one another with huge smiles. If the Chinese were telling the truth there might be a chance now that Howard would survive.

In front of them Lin continued announcing names.

"Pat Doherty, Walter Fargo, Daniel Welch, Vince Brady, Jason Luckett."

Welch's body tensed. His knees became weak and his mind raced. His feeling of elation was suddenly overshadowed with suspicion, fear and confusion.

"It's not right," he said. "Something's wrong with this. I'm not sick, or injured. Those last three names are healthy guys." He looked at Green for reassurance. It wasn't beyond the Chinese to orchestrate a release, drive around the countryside, only to return to the camp in an attempt to break the will of a few men. Some men would give up. Some men would die.

"These men gather belonging and load on trucks," added Lin.

The men broke from the formation, going around shaking hands and hugging. Surely it was a sign that it wouldn't be long before they too would be going home.

"What's all the commotion, Dan?" Lowe was sitting, propped up against the wall.

"You're going home, Howard. The sick and injured are being sent to the American lines."

Lowe sat there staring, his mouth open to speak, but nothing came out.

"They called your name buddy. There are trucks at the gate waiting to take you. You're going home, Howard"

"What about the rest of the guys?"

Welch hesitated and said, "They called out my name along with the list of sick and injured. There were three of us that managed to get on the list. It might be a mistake, but we are going to get on those trucks like we belong there and see what happens."

Lowe's eyes lit up as a big smile came across his face, tears welled up in his eyes.

"Now don't go and start that. We're going to get on those trucks like we're going to a Saturday afternoon baseball game back home. You know the Chinese are capable of anything. We'll have to see what happens."

Welch gathered up the few belongings the two of them had, stuck it in the pockets of his coat and rolled up their mats. Bob Green came into the room as he was helping Lowe to his feet.

"Mr. Lowe. Mr. Welch. You have that look of freedom written all over your faces."

"We won't be free of anything unless we get on that truck, so help me here with Howard."

Howard placed his arms over their shoulders and they locked wrists, scooping him up in a seated position on their forearms. They made their way out of the squad room and down the hall. Outside men were carrying the sick and injured across the yard toward the gate and the line of trucks. Some were on stretchers. Some limped along slowly by themselves.

As they carried Lowe through the gate and to the back end of one of the canvas-covered trucks, Captain Lin spotted them and swiftly walked in their direction.

"*Welch!*" yelled Lin as he walked toward the back end of the truck.

Welch's stomach tightened and his heart sank.

"Welch, you not sick or injured, you . . ."

"We know," said Green cutting off Lin. "You called out his name Captain. We are just doing what we were told to do, by you."

Lin looked at the men for a moment and continued.

"Welch, you not sick, or injured. You and other healthy men freed as good will. The people of China and Korea are good, and generous people. Others soon, if armistice talks continue productive."

Welch turned toward him and said, "We are very much pleased with our release and freedom. We are pleased with generosity of the People of China and Korea." Welch slowly bowed his head toward Lin, who returned the bow.

"Lowe. You very brave man. Try not fall off back of truck when you arrive American lines. When you get to freedom, you tell American generals that you treated good at Camp Two. Tell that remaining men are treated good." With that said, Lin turned on his heels and headed toward the front of the convoy where a staff sedan awaited him.

Welch and Green gently lifted Lowe up onto the tailgate of the truck where two men pulled him up to a bench that folded down from the side. Welch turned to Green and stood for a moment in silence. Green finally extended his hand and Welch took it.

"You've been a good friend, Bob. I'm going to miss you."

They both pulled each other in close and hugged. Despite the happiness he felt for his friends, Green was feeling very alone.

"Take care, Bob. I'll be praying for you."

"Get on the truck and don't worry, Dan. I got too much living to do to have anything happen to me. You got my address. Write when you hear the rest of us have been released. We'll all get together for a few drinks and laugh about all of this."

Welch smiled and climbed on to the back of the truck. Green walked through the gate, turned and watched from the other side of the fence. The trucks started their engines, and one by one pulled away. The men of Camp Two stood behind the fence watching solemnly as the trucks drove off.

The ride lasted several days. The convoy traveled through the day and the drivers rested at night. The ride was particularly hard on the sick and injured. The roads were rough and the trucks were not designed with comfort in mind. Welch did his best to make the ride as easy as possible on Lowe, but there was little he could do about the bumping and bouncing around. Lowe was good-natured about it, but Welch could tell he was hurting.

The trucks stopped just north of the 38th Parallel at Pyongyang, where the men detrucked and were quartered in a North Korean compound. They were allowed to take hot baths every day and measured for new clothing. They were fed American food, one last attempt by the Chinese to appear they were treating the prisoners decently. The men ate up, but their digestive systems weren't able to retain the rich food. Most of them spent the evening out behind their tents throwing up what they had eaten.

On the day of their release, they were herded into a small room full of cameras and Soviet media. The prisoners stood quietly, feeling uncomfortable with the circus like atmosphere. A Korean general stepped forward and spoke. An interpreter translated.

"In accordance with very humane policy of government of Democratic People's Republic of Korea, you are being released to your homeland today."

When the interpreter finished, the cameras turned to the prisoners, who stood quietly, giving no response to the general's speech. The general spoke and the translator directed the cameras to stop. The general spoke again and the cameras once again turned from him to the prisoners, who stood as if frozen in time, giving no indication that they had heard anything the translator had said.

"You Americans. You go to homeland. You not understand? You go to families. Are you not happy you go home?" asked the general, which was repeated by the interpreter. The cameras were focused on the prisoners, who stood defiant. The general threw up his hands and stormed out of the room.

The press surrounded the Americans. "You don't seem happy about your release?" said one of the correspondents in broken English.

"We'll be happy when we're out of this God forsaken country," spoke out one of the men suddenly, and shut up just as quickly.

"Aren't you grateful to the Korean People's government for your," the correspondent looked down at his notes, "your very humane treatment?"

The Americans stood tight lipped and silent, knowing the truth would put the men they left behind in danger. As if scripted, several Korean civilians wearing Red Cross sleeve patches approached the prisoners.

"We are Korean People's Red Cross. Is anything we can do to help you?"

The men stared as a one legged American on crutches spoke up. "Well now, where have you guys been? We don't need you now. They need you back at the camps."

"We help."

"We don't need your help, now!"

One of the correspondents asked, "Come comrades. Tell us something. Surely there is something you wish to say to the Korean people about your captivity."

The men stood quietly, showing no emotion, giving no response. After several moments of silence the correspondents left the room.

The morning of their release the prisoners were loaded back on the trucks and rode the last couple of miles to the line. The trucks pulled up and stopped at a barricade, just outside of Munsan-ni. The men sat in the back nervously as minute after minute passed by. The barricade was rolled away and the trucks drove to a predestined exchange point in the neutral zone. Captain Lin got out of the staff car and walked to an American officer. They reviewed exchange rosters, and one by one called off the names, first by Lin and then by the American. Each man stepped forward as his name was called. Those men too ill to walk were assisted or carried on a stretcher to a tent. Each man in his own way was starting to feel the pressure of restrained excitement.

Inside the tent an American officer greeted them and gave them a packet with their name on it. As they exited the other side, they were escorted to ambulances. Welch insisted and was allowed to ride with Lowe.

The entrance to Freedom Village was a large arch with a sign at its crest that read, "REPATRIATION HERE." On the north side of the arch stood two North Korean soldiers, facing two American MPs on the south side. The MPs stood at parade rest and were dressed sharply. Their spit-shined boots gleamed in the sun. As vehicles drove through the arch, the MPs snapped to attention and saluted, not altering their stare at the North Korean soldiers. The ambulances proceeded to a large metal building where the men were unloaded. As each man exited the vehicle an American general greeted him.

Behind the general on the other side of the drive was an American flag, high on a pole, its blue field of white stars, and red and white stripes floating elegantly in the breeze. Next to it the United Nations flag flew. Lying on the stretcher, Lowe noticed the American flag and called to Welch.

"Look Dan, the Stars and Strips, we're finally free." He propped himself up on his left elbow and brought his right hand up to his forehead in a salute.

Welch turned and looked up at the American flag waving high on the pole and cold chills ran up and down his body. It was finally starting to sink in. Tears welled up in his eyes as he slowly came to attention and rendered a salute. Moved by the show of emotion and patriotism by the two soldiers, the general came to attention and joined in the salute of the Stars and Stripes.

"Welcome home boys," he said as he shook their hands."

Inside were several American officers, doctors and nurses. There were a few handshakes, but mostly immediate medical attention for the men. Welch stuck close to Lowe as a doctor began his examination.

"Soldier, *Soldier!* Move on. We have the sergeant now," said a nurse curtly.

Lying on the medical gurney Lowe looked up and quietly said, "Nurse, this man is Private Dan Welch and you will address him as such. He has treated my wounds for the past six months and without him I would be dead. I refuse to lie here and listen to him be talked down to," and Lowe started to raise himself up from the gurney.

The doctor turned and looked at Welch, who had begun to reluctantly move away from Lowe.

"Private Welch will assist me with Sergeant Lowe's examination, nurse."

Welch nodded his head and moved over to the gurney.

"Start by you telling me about the most serious injuries."

Welch stood next to the gurney and reviewed each injury with the doctor. They discussed injuries on Lowe's arms at length as the nurse and doctor unwrapped the bandages. The doctor then examined the entry and exit wound the bayonet left in his chest, and with Welch's help continued on down the list of injuries. As they talked, the nurse took notes.

Welch also relayed the details of the spells Lowe had that would put him near death.

The doctor examined Lowe's eyes, pulling down the lower lids, exposing his yellowish-tinted globes. Welch looked on in dismay. He had noticed the yellowish hue to Lowe's skin, but hadn't noticed how yellow his eyes were. The nurse scribbled down a half a page of notes related to the yellowish color. The only word Welch could make out was "liver."

"Here's what we'll do, Sergeant Lowe. I'm going to have Lieutenant Archer give you a shot of penicillin to work on those infections. We need to get you cleaned up good before we can start treating those wounds. After I examine Welch, I'm going to leave you in his competent hands. He'll stay with you throughout your cleanup process. I'll clear it with General Daniels. Lieutenant Archer will get a wheelchair that will make your movement from station to station a little more pleasant."

With that the young doctor gave Welch a thorough examination and when his examination was complete he found Lowe waiting in a wheelchair.

"Nice wheels, pal. Where can I get one?"

"We could race."

"It wouldn't be fair, I'd blow your doors off."

"Sure, you will, but give me a few weeks and I'll give you a fair race."

"I'll bet you will," Welch said as he wheeled Lowe through the door and into a small room where two men were getting their hair cut and beards shaved off. When their turn came Welch helped Lowe into a chair and took his seat in the chair next to him. Before they started, the barbers turned them around and the two men stared at their ghastly reflections in the mirror. They both sported shoulder length hair and beards. The barbers spun them back around and began cutting. The hair tumbled down onto the floor, which was covered with mounds of hair. Welch looked closely at the floor and was stunned to see the hair moving.

"The hair seems to have a life of its own," he commented to the barber.

"Lice. The hair is thick with it," he responded.

After the barber's work was complete, they turned the men once again around to the mirror. Both men stared at themselves, and then at each other in amazement. The transformation was stunning.

"Hello, my name is Dan Welch, and you are?"

"Howard, Howard Lowe from Kentucky. I feel we have met before, Mr. Welch. France, maybe?"

"I'm thinking a poker game in the back of Mitchell's Beer Depot in Valley Head, West Virginia. You were bluffing with a pair of eights and I took a week's pay from you with three little Queens. I never forget a pretty face."

The two men laughed and stared at the strangers in the mirror.

Leaving the barbershop, they entered another small room where they stripped and were sprayed with a delousing substance to rid them of the rest of the lice. The next station was a hot shower and the two men took their time. Waiting for them after they toweled off was a blue and white-striped bathrobe, pajamas and slippers. Welch quickly slipped into his pants, T-shirt and slippers, before turning to help Lowe get dressed.

"We are glad to have you back safe and sound my son. Is there anything I can do for you while you're here at Freedom Village?"

Lowe sat in the wheelchair in front of Chaplain Woodford's desk. Still dressed in the striped bathrobe, he sat for a moment contemplating the chaplain's offer.

"Yes, there is something. Ask your Boss to have mercy on the men who remain prisoners in North Korea. Ask him to keep them safe until they can be freed, and if they die before being released, see to it their remains are brought home to be with their families someday. The bodies of our dead American soldiers are spread all over North Korea. Their families will never rest until they're brought home. Do you think you can ask the Boss to consider those things?"

"I can, and I believe he'll listen. Now what about you? Is there anything I can do for you, son?"

Lowe looked at the chaplain.

"I would like to let my wife know I'm coming home. That I'm okay."

"We have a telegraph room set up so you can send a personal telegraph to your family. Washington will probably send her a telegram to let her know you're free, so it will probably reach her about the same time as your telegram."

"I'll push you over to the telegraph office myself and you can send one off." The chaplain grabbed the handles of the wheelchair and headed through the maze of rooms and halls in search of the telegraph center.

"Yes, sir! I knew Chaplain Burns. He was a good man who looked out for us. He got into trouble a bunch of times, standing up to the chinks. He spent a lot of time in the box because of it. As a matter of fact, he encouraged me to take care of Howard when he showed up at camp all shot up."

"Did you witness him spending long hours with the Chinese?"

"No more than Commander Fletcher. It was their job to raise hell with the chinks about how we were being treated. When Fletcher was in the box, Burns or Lieutenant Colonel Cruz was down at the commandant's office raising hell. Colonel Ling was a real mean one. The new guy, Colonel Pol wasn't as rough, but he wasn't against hurting someone. When they moved all the leaders away and we were on our own, everyone started understanding just how much they protected us."

Major Chester Paulson waited patiently for Welch to ramble on about things he had no interest in. There would be many more counter-interrogation sessions. He could afford to be patient. He had often referred to the first session as the "Be nice to the idiot session." At the first opportunity he skillfully redirected the questioning.

"Can you tell me why someone would write," and Paulson looked down at his notes, "the chaplain seemed to always be talking to the Chinese, spending time with them, carrying stuff from their side of the fence to ours. At times he seemed too polite. Almost friendly with the enemy."

Welch's jaw tightened as he glared at Paulson.

"Who wrote that?"

"That's doesn't matter, have you ever . . ."

"Wait a minute, Major, it does matter because someone is suggesting that Chaplain Burns cooperated with the Chinese and that's an out and out lie. He worked the chinks just like the other leaders did to get the things we needed to survive. He would never act dishonorably. Christ's sake, he was a chaplain!"

Major Paulson made some notes and continued his questioning. Welch went defensive, thinking the questions through before he responded. He didn't like Paulson, or the questions he was asking.

"Can you tell me anything about Nate Smith?"

"Can't say as I ever heard the name."

"Oh, come now. He was on the march from the Bean Camp, to Camp One. A colored fellow."

The image of the negro soldier standing by himself at Camp One after the march popped into Welch's mind, along with Jawaski's concern for the man being left alone as they walked off. Welch suddenly realized he had been so occupied with his freedom that he had not thought about Leo for several days. Thoughts of the little man flooded through his mind and he wished Leo were there with them at Freedom Village. The thoughts brought tears to his eyes.

"The King of Siam, I am." Welch whispered to himself.

"Pardon me, Private."

Regaining his thoughts, he looked at Paulson, "A lot of good men died on that march. I had my hands full taking care of a friend. I didn't notice much else, besides, we were always separated from the coloreds."

Major Paulson was trained in the art of counter-interrogation. An expert when it came to body language and Welch's show of emotion didn't go unnoticed.

"Thank you, Private. That's all for today."

Welch stood up and came to attention, wheeled about and left the room. Paulson quickly made notes. His last written remark was, "Knows something about Nate Smith."

"And then he asked me about some colored fellow. I never met the guy, but he may have been with us on the march from the Bean Camp."

Welch looked at Lowe with a serious look on his face. "Be careful what you say to this guy, Howard. He's fishing for something and he doesn't care if it's there, or not. If he gets a tiny bit of nothing, he'll turn it into a big something. He doesn't care if innocent people get hurt. I know his type."

"Knock! Knock!" came at the door and Nurse Archer came walking in.

"Private Welch . . ."

"You can call me Dan, darling."

Lowe snickered as Lieutenant Archer looked down her nose at Welch.

"Private Welch, Sergeant Lowe," dryly replied Archer, rolling her eyes. "This is the meal list of food that will be available for supper tonight. Tell me what you would like to have and I'll personally see that you get it." Realizing her words hadn't come out quite like she had intended, Archer blushed and looked away from the two soldiers sitting in their semi-private bedroom. The men looked over a meal list that rivaled any fine restaurant in the States.

"I'll have the roast beef, mashed potatoes and gravy, green beans and a small salad, with Italian on the side. And ice tea, lots of sweet ice tea. For dessert I want apple pie, a scoop of vanilla ice cream and coffee," ordered Lowe.

Welch looked up and smiled. "Make mine the same, darling, except I would like to have milk. Cold as you can get it."

Archer scribbled down the order, turned and left the room.

"Cute, isn't she?"

"Very cute," replied Lowe. "The only problem is that about forty-five other guys are flirting with her also. It's got to get old. I wouldn't hold my breath if I were you."

"Hold my breath! They talk to us about re-Americanization. This is just practice for when I get home to the land of the big round eyes. The pastures are green, and as Mrs. Katherine would put it, I'm a bull with a mission!"

The meal that night was wonderful going down, and rough coming up. The men had the appetite, but their stomachs were still affected by months of parasites, dysentery and other intestinal problems. Despite that, they forged ahead, partaking in the delights available to them through the mess. They were being treated like kings. Those with serious medical conditions received treatment. For the first time in what must have seemed like an eternity, the men felt good about themselves and their future.

At supper General Daniels stood and spoke briefly, announcing their itinerary for the next day.

"Men! Each one of you has been told individually, and I want to remind you that you must not talk about the things that happened to you while in captivity when you get back in the states. That's an order! Tomorrow morning at zero-nine-hundred hours you'll all be airlifted by helicopter to Inchon. The hop will take approximately thirty minutes. There you will be transported by skip to a medical ship, anchored in the Port of Inchon. The ship will be your home for three weeks as you sail across the Pacific to America, and home."

The mess hall exploded in cheers as the men who were able jumped up, shook each other's hands and hugged. After giving Lowe a gentle hug in his wheelchair, Welch turned and catching Lieutenant Archer off guard, gave her a big kiss. Welch was surprised to find she kissed back.

*   *   *   *

Johnny Roberts sat behind his desk, reviewing Western Union regulations pertaining to ordering office equipment. Mr. Alfred had directed him to review management material and operating procedures because he planned to turn a lot of the office management over to him. Roberts was a bit surprised since his boss had tightly controlled every aspect of the Columbia Western Union Office.

"You need to start taking over some of the management responsibilities, Johnny," Alfred had said. "When I step down, I want to be able to tell the Regional Office that you're trained and ready to take over." Roberts walked around the rest of the day on cloud nine and had been devouring everything he could about office administration ever since.

Now he sat behind his desk in a white, button down collar oxford shirt. His blue and white striped tie was neatly tied with a double Windsor knot that had taken him, with assistance from his Uncle Benny, a Sunday afternoon to master. He also sported a new hairstyle, a stylish flattop that was neatly brushed up in front. Since their talk that day, he had been promoted to Assistant Manager, and had gone from hourly wage, to salary. The move had nearly doubled his income, and provided him with health care benefits and retirement.

Alfred had, of course, lectured him on his newfound wealth. When Roberts received his first check, Alfred had escorted him over to the Columbia Bank where he opened a saving account. While they were there, they also talked to Mrs. Miles in the loan department about getting a new car.

"As soon as you save two hundred, take half out for the down payment on a nice Ford, four door sedan. As assistant manager you represent Western Union, and need to have a managerial look." Alfred had said.

Alfred had just stepped out for a haircut when the new teletype machine began to tick away. Roberts walked over to retrieve the message, and stood there reading a manual on office supplies, until the machine ticked its last tick. He reached down, tore off the message and scanned it.

"Yes!" he yelled and pumped his fist in the air. He stepped quickly to his desk and rang up the operator.

"Sally, Johnny Roberts, here. Can you ring up Upton's for me? It's important."

"Ring, ring!" rang the telephone behind Jess Upton's chair.

"Snip, snip, snip!" went his scissors.

Jess ignored the ringing as he trimmed Aaron Campbell's hair, and lectured Mr. Billy and Mack Long on the success of the Eisenhower White House.

"Ring, ring!"

"Snip, snip, snip, snip!"

"Gal-darn-it, Jess. Ike's only been in office for three months. How can a fellow fix anything in just three months?" rebuffed Mack Long.

"Ring, ring!"

"And besides," added Mr. Billy, "anything going on now is left over from the Truman years."

"Ring, ring!"

"Why, you can't even stop that god-awful ringing?"

"He can stop the ringing, he just doesn't know how to pick up the phone!" laughed Mack Long.

Jess looked at the two men and exchanged his scissors for the electric clippers, as Josh walked over and picked up the phone.

"Upton's!"

"Bzzzzzz!"

"Yep! Why, I'm a trimming his hair as we speak . . . well I reckon I'm not actually cutting right now since I'm a talking to you but . . . ah, yes, sure Johnny, I'll put him on." Looking at Alfred he said, "This fellow insists he's the new assistant manager at your office, Julius. But it sounds like Johnny to me." The men seated about the barbershop laughed.

"Yes, this is Julius Alfred."

"Bzzzzzz!"

"What's that you said?"

"Bzzzzzz!"

"Can you hold for just a minute?"

"Bzzzzzz!"

"Can you give me a second of quiet here, Jess?"

Jess Upton nodded his head and switched off the electric clippers. Everyone leaned forward and listened.

"Go ahead, Mr. Roberts."

"It's Mr. Roberts now, is it?" whispered Mr. Billy loud enough for all to hear.

"Mr. Alfred, we have a special delivery from the head office."

"I'll be right there." Julius recognized the code phrase for an extremely important message. It was a bit melodramatic, but the telephone line had big ears and her name was Sally Newman.

"Bzzzzzz!"

"What a going on, Julius?" asked Mack Long.

"Oh, nothing important. Just a message from the head office."

"Bzzzzzz!"

"Now, ain't that the secret code talk for important telegrams?" pointed out Mr. Billy.

Julius looked at the older man and remembered he worked as a key man for the company years ago. He made a mental note to have Johnny come up with a more creative code.

Turning to the Josh Upton he said, "Are we done, Josh?"

"You were done five minutes ago, Julius, I was just snipping around, 'cause it helps me to think. Here, let me brush the hair off you." Josh brushed off the loose hair, dabbed on a little bit of the skin burner stuff and walked over to the cash register with Julius' dollar bill.

Julius said his goodbyes in the barbershop and walked out the door. When he was out of sight around the corner his pace picked up, and in a short time he entered the Western Union office. Johnny had a grin on his face as he handed him a telegram.

"Praise the Lord, it's from Howard himself. It's a great day for a good Christian family. Good news like this can't wait, Johnny. I'm headed to Gadberry."

"Wait a minute, sir. Another came in while you were on your way back from Upton's," and Johnny handed him the second telegram:

WESTERN
UNION
W.P. MARSHALL, PRESIDENT

P. WAO 14 GOVERNMENT NL PD
WUX WASHINGTON, D.C. 4 30 53
MRS MARTHA LOWE
LONG CEMETARY RD. GADBERRY, KY

THE SECRETARY OF THE ARMY HAS ASKED ME TO
INFORM YOU THAT YOUR HUSBAND HOWARD LOWE IS
PASSENGER ABOARD MEDICAL SHIP DUE ARRIVE SAN
FRANCISCO PORT OF EMBARKMENT FORT MASON, SAN
FRANCISCO, CALIFORNIA 15 MAY 1953 HE WILL BE HELD
OVER AT THE NAVEL MEDICAL CENTER WHERE HE
WILL RECEIVE TREATMENT FOR WOUNDS RECEIVED
BEFORE AND DURING CAPTIVITY UPON RECOVERY HE
WILL BE PLACED ON LEAVE WITHOUT DELAY RELATIVES
MAY WISH TO GREET RETURNING SERVICEMEN IN SAN
FRANCISCO AND THE ARMY WILL DO EVERYTHING
POSSIBLE TO MAKE RELATIVES WELCOME HOWEVER
INDIVIDUAL ARRANGEMENTS WILL HAVE TO BE MADE
FOR MEALS, TRANSPORTATION AND LODGING IF YOU
PLAN TO MEET SHIP SUGGEST YOU WIRE OR WRITE
CG SAN FRANCISCO PORT OF EMBARKATION AND
GIVE NAME OF RETURNING SERVICEMAN UPON YOUR
ARRIVAL SAN FRANCISCO DETAILED INFORMATION
MAY BE OBTAINED FROM CG SAN FRANCISCO PORT
OF EMBARKATION TELEPHONE PROSPECT 62200
EXTENTION 251

WILLIAM E BERGEN MAJ. GEN. USA
THE ADJUTANT OF THE ARMY

Julius turned to go out the door.
"But, Mr. Alfred!" yelled Johnny, bringing him to a halt halfway out the door.
"What?"

"You drive up in Mrs. Lowe's driveway you'll scare the life out of her."

"You're right boy. Call the preacher and tell him to be out on the road." And as he turned, *"Mr. Alfred!"*

"What, boy?"

"Your hat, sir!"

Johnny walked up and handed him his tan fedora. The light brown summer grosgrain hat, with its open weave crown and brown pattern band was Julius' favorite summer hat.

Smiling, he took the fedora, squared it on his head and out the door he went. Walking to his car he felt as if he was walking on clouds. This was the part of his job he enjoyed, the part that kept things in balance. Good news was always a joy to deliver.

As his car slowed and approached the gravel road, he saw Brother Cook standing on the side of the road, waving his Bible in the air, smiling and darn near dancing, if that could be said of a preacher. He pulled up and came to a stop. Brother Cook opened the door and hopped in.

"Glory be to God!" said the preacher nearly shouting.

"I can hear you!" said Julius, "and I believe the Lord can hear you too."

"Make a joyful noise unto the Lord!" said the preacher.

"Amen!" shouted the Western Union man.

It was mid-afternoon and Martha sat in her rocking chair breast-feeding. While Junior focused on breast milk, she read progress notes on her students at Tabor. She had maintained an ongoing dialog with Marie Goldman, keeping up with the students and monitoring the young teacher's progress. Her work at Tabor was impressive, and Martha was determined to help find her a place in the Adair County school system.

Mrs. Katherine was in the living room tidying up and the girls were up the road at Jordan and May's playing with Rebecca and Elizabeth. Out the window Mrs. Katherine saw a black sedan pulling into the driveway.

"Got company driving up!" She walked over to the window.

"It's that padre friend of yours and . . ." She hesitated as she watched Julius Alfred step out of the driver's side of the car. "And it looks like he's awful excited about something. He must think there's a free meal waiting for him in here!" Mrs. Katherine walked to the door and stepped out on the porch.

"Martha's feeding the baby, gentleman, why don't you . . ."

"Howard's on his way home," whispered Brother Cook.

Mrs. Katherine stood speechless for a second and then surprised Brother Cook with a big hug.

"We need to . . ." and turning she found Martha standing in the door, the baby in her arms, a tear starting to run down her cheek. She stepped out on the porch, handing the baby to Mrs. Katherine.

"I hear joyous whispering on my porch concerning my beloved Howard. Brother Cook you act as if the Rapture has come, and Mr. Alfred you appear to be overcome with the Holy Spirit."

The two men just stood there smiling, speechless and overcome with the moment.

"Well! Must I turn Mrs. Katherine loose on the both of you to drag out the good news?"

"Telegrams! Two telegrams about Howard," blurted out Brother Cook, before Julius could speak. Julius stepped forward and eased between Brother Cook and his customer.

"Mrs. Lowe. Western Union Telegram has received two telegrams related to Sergeant Howard Lowe. Last October we brought you terrible news. Now I am pleased to bring you the most joyful of news," and he handed Martha the two telegrams.

Her hand was shaking as she reached out and took the telegrams, reading the one on top first, the one from the Department of the Army.

Martha read the telegram and slowly looked up at Mrs. Katherine and then to the men.

"It is true, then. My Howard is coming home to us. God is truly a merciful and wonderful God. He has rewarded our faith and prayers with Howard's safe return."

She took the second telegram and slowly read:

WESTERN
UNION
W.P. MARSHALL, PRESIDENT

OSFMO91 CABLE
TOKIO VIA RCA 4 31 53
MRS MARTHA LOWE
LOY CEMETARY RD. GADBERRY, KY

DEAR MARTHA:

AM FREE HEADED HOME AM FEELING FINE
TRAVELLING BY SHIP SEE YOU AND KIDS SOON

LOVE YOU DARLING

HOWARD

Martha slowly read the telegram and then read it a second time. She walked over to the swing, sat down and clutching the piece of paper to her chest wept with joy.

CHAPTER 16

▼

"Let's go over it again Private Welch. When you saw Chaplain Burns talking with the Chinese officer," Major Paulson checked his notes, "Captain Lin, did you hear their conversation?"

"No. I told you I was probably twenty yards away."

"Did Chaplain Burns seem to be smiling as he spoke to the Chinese?"

"No!" Welch caught himself and refocused on calmly answering the major's questions.

"Just how friendly did the chaplain seem to be with the Chinese?"

Welch looked across the desk at the Army major and his jaw tightened.

"As friendly as he needed to be to save men's lives. Look Major, sir! I don't understand why you continue to ask questions about Chaplain Burns. You don't have a case today. You won't have a case tomorrow. There's nothing there. You should devote your time to chasing some other shadow and leave the good chaplain alone. He saved a lot of lives."

Paulson looked at him and started scribbling down notes. Welch reminded himself there was nothing Paulson could do that could upset him. He had survived days of hellish interrogation by the Chinese. He had been beaten and threatened with death. Paulson simply didn't have what it took to get him upset, unless of course he allowed him to.

"Let's talk about your friend, Private Nate Smith, at the Bean Soup Camp."

"That's Bean Camp, sir!"

Lifting his eyes, he looked at Welch and said, "Bean Camp. Did Smith ever mention his conversations with the Chinese?"

"Sir, look at your notes and you'll see you asked me that same question back at Freedom Village. My answer hasn't changed, but I'll elaborate on it since you brought it up again."

Welch sat on the edge of his chair and leaned over.

"I never met Nate Smith. I haven't the slightest idea who he is. The coloreds were separated from the whites. Don't ask me why. The Chinese had their reasons. You can ask me about Nate Smith until you're blue in the face, Major, and my answer ain't going to change. I . . . don't . . . *know . . . the man!*"

"That's interesting, Welch. I've got a signed statement that says different." Paulson scanned the page in front of him and read, "I saw Nate Smith talking to the Chinese officer, Captain Lin. Dan Welch walked up and bummed a smoke off of Captain Lin."

Paulson lifted his eyes and studied Welch's reaction.

With restrained calmness, Welch said, "That's a bald-faced lie or you're just making it up. If someone actually said that, I suggest you get them in here and the two of us can discuss what is, and isn't the truth. You can sit and watch, since you don't seem to have a good grasp on it yourself. Maybe you can learn something. If you're just making it up, well, I suppose you wouldn't be doing your job if you didn't have something to give to the boss when we reach Ft. Mason, sir!"

Paulson stood up behind the desk. "Are you suggesting that I am lying?"

"Your words . . . sir!"

"I'm a Major in the US Army. I've sworn to uphold the US Constitution."

Welch tuned him out and sat there thinking about Leo. For some reason Paulson's little counter-interrogation session had sparked thoughts about Leo.

"Are you listening to me Private, *Private!*"

"Sir?"

"Are you paying attention?"

"Of course, Major!"

"What did I just say?"

"You were taking a break from interrogating me and just giving your autobiography, sir. You know, the Chinese made us do that too. And sometimes they would become upset, just like you."

"Are you saying that you know nothing about Nate Smith cooperating with the Chinese?"

"No, sir! That's not exactly so."

Paulson looked at him confused.

"I'm saying I never met the man, and therefore it would be impossible for me to know about him."

"So, you are saying that you didn't hear Smith's conversation with the Chinese officer," Paulson looked down at his notes, "Captain Lin, when you borrowed a cigarette off of him."

"That's bummed, sir. You're supposed to give back something you borrow, and no, I didn't overhear anything because you didn't bum smokes of the Chinese, nor did I ever meet Nate Smith. Now, for the record, what part of my answer do you not understand, sir?"

The major's questioning went on for two hours. Some questions were direct about certain events and others were open ended. Welch did his best to answer the ones that were answerable, and on the others, he did his best not to tell the major to blow it out his . . . and on a couple of occasions that's how close he came.

Paulson was an interesting diversion during the long boat ride across the Pacific. The major seemed to know whom he could push, and who wouldn't tolerate his cheap shot antics. On the weaker men, his counter-interrogations were almost sadistic. Dredging up their nightmarish past with the North Korean and Chinese interrogators. The sessions were intense, accusations were made and statements signed. He was doing his job and there would be considerable material to turn in when they reached port.

*   *   *   *

Seaman First Class Wes England had signed on with the Navy in 1942 to go kill Japs. After a battery of tests, he was trained as a ship's electrician and had served on various hospital class ships. He had developed an intimate knowledge of the special electrical equipment required aboard a floating medical center.

Between him and his friend, Stanley Whitman, a refrigeration specialist, there was very little on a ship that was mechanical or electrical, they didn't know about personally, excluding the ship's engines, of course.

England had decided he liked being the ship's electrician, shortly after serving on his first hospital ship. When the war against Japan heated up in the Pacific and the wounded marines, sailors and soldiers starting pouring on board, he realized that it took lots of different people to support the fighting men. He was proud to be there helping the guys who put the warriors back together after they got shot up, blown up, or both. He stayed on after the war because jobs were scarce in northern Wisconsin.

After fixing a light fixture in the patient ward, England was walking down the aisle and came upon a young man, not much younger than him, trying to go from his bed to a wheelchair. Both his legs were gone just above the knees. Thick bandages were wrapped around both stumps.

England looked around, but saw no one else on the ward.

"Need a little help there, eh?"

The patient looked up and smiled, "Maybe a little. They tell me I'll learn to do this on my own, but they don't tell me what to do in the meantime when I've got to take a leak."

England laughed, sat his toolbox down and helped the young man into the wheelchair.

"Leave something back there in Korea?"

"It was a mortar round. Mangled the legs so bad the medic had to clip them clean off just above the knees, after he pulled me to safety. God kept me alive for some reason. The mortar took three of my buddies next to me, but all I lost was about eighteen inches of height. What's in the tool box?"

"Tools, odds and ends." England extended his hand, "Wes England, Ship's Electrician."

"Kelly Pullman, Marine Corps," the young man said shaking hands with England.

"I wonder if I could learn to do that kind of stuff."

"They're probably going to discharge you, pal."

"I mean back home. I can't go back to what I was doing when I was drafted. Nobody's going to hire a four foot-three-inch hod carrier."

England pulled up a chair and sat down next to the boy.

"I'm guessing you could do electrical work. It would need to be a job where you sit in a chair, while the things you worked on sat on a table in front of you."

"The doctor told me I would be able to go to school on the G.I. Bill. My disability pension would support me until I got trained and a job."

"Sounds like a plan. You're going to be okay, Pullman."

"Hey! I'm going home! The rest should be a breeze."

England stayed and chatted with the Marine awhile, until he remembered the reason the man had caught his attention in the first place. When he reminded him, Pullman's body tightened and he rolled off toward the head.

He had seen a lot of damaged men over the years and figured attitude was half the battle in recovery. "Yea, he's going to make it just fine," England said to himself as he stepped through the bulkhead, and walked down the companion way to his shop.

*   *   *   *

Lowe sat up in bed as the nurse changed the bandage on his arm. The wounds, no longer infected, had scabbed over. The nurse applied a topical ointment and gauze, before wrapping the arm with a clean bandage.

When they had tried to send Dan back on a regular troop ship, Dr. Webb intervened, feeling strongly that Lowe's recovery needed Welch's support. A call to General Daniels made it happen. Welch's berth on the hospital ship was a vast improvement over what he would have faced on a troop ship.

"Private Welch, it looks like it's time for your patient's daily dose of fresh air. Have him back by 1600 hours."

Welch looked at his watch. They had a full hour to soak up some sunshine on deck. He started to help Lowe down into the wheelchair.

"Why don't you walk up today," said the nurse. "Have you been walking to the head like I asked you to do?"

"Yes, ma'am."

"And how's it going?"

"Tough, ma'am. I'm totally exhausted by the time I get back to my bunk. These crutches are killing my armpits."

"Wait here." As the nurse disappeared around the corner Welch gathered up two blankets and tossed them into the wheelchair.

"We won't be a needing that chair, Dan."

"You don't, but I do to carry our stuff in. This is as good as any wheelbarrow."

The nurse reappeared carrying three walking canes. Welch took one and gave it a good look over.

"A fine piece of hickory. The shaft has good mass and the handle is turned just right. It should support you easily. Let's see which length suits you."

Lowe took one of the canes and held it in his right hand.

"No," corrected Welch. "It goes on the opposite side of the weak leg, Howard."

Lowe switched the cane to his left hand, "Too short, but I could use it to scratch my back. Gees, it's been itching the life out of me."

Lowe balanced himself with the second cane. "This one feels good."

"Looks good. Try the third one to be sure."

As the nurse watched, Lowe took the longest cane and put his weight on it, as Welch sized up the man and the cane.

"No. The second one is the cane for you, Howard. Right, Captain Maxwell?"

"Not bad, Welch. Where did you learn about support canes?"

"When you're raised in the mountains, ma'am, you learn to do a lot of things. I used to help my granddad in his wood shop making canes, ax and grubbing hoe handles. He made canes for just about everyone in the valley that needed one. There's nothing like the feel of a good piece of hickory," Welch said as he slid his hand down the shaft of the shorter cane.

"Use the cane for support and balance. It will take some of the pressure off your weak leg. Walk down the aisle about twenty feet and back. I want to see how you ambulate." Maxwell walked out into the aisle where she could get a good look.

"Easy now," she cautioned.

Lowe smiled at the nurse and started walking down the aisle very slowly to the third bed, turned and came back. As he turned a sudden roll in the ship threw him off balance, but he quickly braced himself with the cane.

"Nice save, Howard," said Welch teasingly, but relieved he hadn't fallen on his maiden voyage with the stick.

"A piece of cake," laughed Lowe as he hobbled back to them.

"Okay, let's not get overconfident," Maxwell turned to Welch. "I'm giving you a semi-healthy soldier. Don't bring back any broken bones."

"Yes, ma'am!" said Welch as he snapped to attention and saluted the captain.

"Get out of here, the both of you. I've got people with serious health problems to tend to. I don't have time to mess with you two clowns and I don't want you coming back here for at least an hour . . . an hour and a half."

Welch and Lowe headed down the aisle and out of the ward. Welch pushing the wheelchair and Lowe hobbling along to Welch's slow cadence of *"Hup, Two, Three, Four!*

Out on the deck they were greeted with sunshine and a mild ocean breeze. Lowe had maneuvered carefully up the two companionways to reach topside. The cane was much easier to use than crutches, but he was still extremely tired when he reached the afterdeck and the helicopter-landing platform. There they found two empty wooden recliners next to the railing. Welch eased Lowe into a recliner and took one of the white hospital blankets and laid it over his legs, draping the other around his shoulders.

"Would you look at that!" said Welch in amazement. "We were in the belly of a troop ship on the way over. I didn't get to see a thing. Look at the size of those waves, Howard!"

"Looks like ten, maybe fifteen footers. We sailed through stormy seas my first trip across to North Africa. The Navy pukes said we sailed through thirty-foot waves. They felt like mountains down in the belly of the ship. This is a vacation cruise, Dan. First class all the way, compliments of General Daniels and the Navy."

The two men sat for a while taking in the fresh air, listening to the sound of the sea slapping up against the hull of the ship and watching the churning water in its wake.

"You've never said much about Leo, Dan. What was he like?"

"It's hard to talk about Leo. He was special."

"I would like to hear about him. He was somewhat of a legend at the camp. The men would always say, spit in his eye for old Jawaski!"

Welch sat reflecting on his friend Leo, and after several seconds of silence he began to speak.

"We met in the mountains after B Company was overrun. He was scared to death and was running like a bat out of hell when he came across me hiding in a bush. It was pitch dark, I was out of ammo and had my bayonet out ready to stick him. I thought he was a North Korean. We double-timed for hours, trying to put distance between us and the North Koreans. Sleeping through the day and moving at night. The second night we were running through a rice field and I ran right into a, well, it was sort of a pit thing." Welch hesitated and gulped, his breathing was heavy. "It was, full of, of . . ."

"A pit full of what?" patiently asked Lowe.

Welch sat there. Goose pimples rose on his skin and the hair stood on the back of his neck. In his mind he was back in the pit, under the surface of the thick liquid, drowning.

"It was dark. It was like the ground disappeared under my feet and swallowed me up. I thought I had fallen into a deep, pool of thick, muddy water. When I went down, I couldn't swim back up. I tried, but the stuff was too thick. It would suck me back down. I thought I was going to die. Exhausted, I broke the surface a final time and as I started to go back down something hit my shoulder and I grabbed it. Leo had cut his rifle sling at one end and tossed his Garand out to me. I grabbed it and he pulled me out."

"You fell into a croc pit?" replied Lowe as he reached up and scratched his neck vigorously.

"Yea." Welch looked at Lowe. "You can laugh."

"I don't want to laugh. That must have been horrible."

"I threw up for five minutes and smelled like the outhouse back home. Leo saved me and took care of me until I recovered from it. What we thought were the lights of division headquarters turned out to be a North Korean camp. I realized it, but it was too late to turn back. The Koreans would have killed me if a Chinese officer hadn't intervened. Leo was up ahead of me and got the worst of it. I thought he was dead, but he turned up when they moved us to the Bean Camp."

Welch sat for a second remembering the croc pit and shuddered.

"When the North Koreans interrogated Leo, they beat him so much his eye burst. He acted like he was going to sign a confession and stuck the pen in the North Korean officer's eye. We saw the man later. He wore a patch over his eye and was a mean son-of-a-bitch. He would kill men to make an example of them. He was looking for Leo the day we left camp, so we told him Leo had died on the march. We managed to get him safely to the permanent camp. Leo was somewhat of a legend with the Chinese, too. They admire courage and a Chinese colonel saw him stick the Korean in the eye despite the fact that he was beaten badly. They viewed him as a man of great strength and bravery. They gave him medical treatment when the rest of us got none. Some of the men resented it."

Welch was overcome with a sudden feeling of emotion. His eyes moistened and he looked over at Lowe.

"He was the bravest man I ever knew, Howard. He didn't look like he would be, but I can't think of a man I would rather be with when the chips were down than Leo. The night he died, he was still being brave for me. He'd lost his arm and was burning up with pneumonia and I . . . . I felt like I was losing the best friend I ever had. He was . . . he was the best friend I've ever had. He asked me to go see his parents when I got home. You know something? I don't even have a picture of him."

They were ten minutes late getting back to the ward. Captain Maxwell was busy tending to patients and didn't act like she noticed, although she did. On her ward very little escaped her attention.

Lowe walked down the corridor. His gait was slow and deliberate, as he utilized the cane to keep his balance. As he walked, he spoke to those he passed.

"How are you doing, seaman?"

"Fine, Howard. You?"

"Fine. Hey, Mark! Cards tonight?"

"Sure. How about Dan?"

"I'll say something to him."

"What time?"

"How's twenty hundred hours?"

"See you then."

"Sergeant Lowe."

"Ma'am." Lowe nodded his head to the ward nurse as he passed.

"Martin, how's the feet?"

Martin Lynch hobbled down the corridor. Both feet wrapped in bandages. He had lost all ten toes to frostbite and was relearning to walk.

"Feet are fine Howard. It's the toes I'm a missing. Feels like I'm walking on poles. Never figured them ten toes meant so much to walking. They say they can fit me with a pross . . . te . . . see, when I get to Fort Mason. Doc says I strap them on my feet just like a shoe and they'll act just like my toes, giving me balance and all."

"Where you headed, Howard?"

"Got an appointment with the good major. He wants to pick my brain a little. See if he can add someone to his little list of bad guys."

"He's a bastard!" said Lynch, with hatred in his eyes. "He's treated that young Gene Manning like he was a dog. He's been mistreating him ever since we got to that Freedom Village place. Gene's been swearing statements against all manner of people."

"I'll spit in his eye for you!"

Lynch laughed out loud and nearly lost his balance and said, "Do it for Leo, but watch your step, Howard. An unintended word can cause a lot of grief over nothing."

Lowe walked on down the alleyway and turned the corner, stopping to step over the coaming, the raised partition at the base of the doorway to keep the water out. It was a struggle each time he went through a bulkhead. Standing in front of Major Paulson's door he braced himself and knocked with his cane.

"Enter!"

"Preee, sent!" The Navy Ensign shouted the preparatory command and with a slight hesitation followed it with the command of execution, *"Arms!"*

The members of the ship's company and patients, who could attend, saluted. Six flag bearers surrounded the table where the flag draped body of Lance Corporal Thomas Jefferson Lincoln, US Marine Corps, lay wrapped and ready to be cast into the sea. An honor guard rendered a twenty-one-gun salute and the Navy chaplain read a short verse of scripture that referred to Jesus calming the sea.

A young bugler stood slightly off from the rest of the group and his bugle began to cry out the notes. Those who were ill or injured did the best they could to render some form of a salute. An old sergeant, who had lost his right arm to the shoulder and his left to the elbow, saluted with his bandaged stump. The flag bearers lifted the board at one end, the body slid out from under the Stars and Stripes and was committed to the sea. At the end of Taps, the Navy chaplain read a brief benediction. The Honor Guard encased the flag, folding it carefully, until it neatly formed the traditional triangular shape. The ship's Captain would see that the flag and a letter were forwarded to Lincoln's next of kin.

Thomas Lincoln was an honest, hard driven, young Marine. He had survived the hell of the camps in North Korea, only to succumb to kidney failure on the trip home. He had become another statistic.

"This group of men who cooperated with the Chinese. The ones who lived separate from the rest of the men," Paulson looked down at his notes. "The men who ate better. Did you have much of an opportunity to talk with them?"

Welch sat pondering the major's question.

"We lived separately from them. I'm not sure they told the Chinese information, as much as they just cooperated. The Chinese placed a lot on cooperation. Hell! They knew all the military information they needed, they just wanted stooges to show off in front of the cameras."

"Do you feel any of these men could have been brainwashed?"

Welch looked at Paulson with a puzzled look.

"What do you mean, brainwashed?"

"It's a word the press likes to throw around. Do you think any of the men could have been mentally reprogrammed? Involuntarily changed their loyalty toward America?"

Welch sat up on the edge of his chair, placing his hands on the front edge of the desk.

"Brainwashed! Now, that's an interesting word, and it fits what the Chinese tried to do with all their interrogations and reeducation. They tried real hard to get us to embrace communism. Nobody did, as far as I could tell. We'll see if any of them stay after everyone is set free. Captain Lin asked us before we left Camp Two if we wanted to stay, go live in China. We all looked at him like he was crazy. I think it embarrassed him."

"Did you ever hear anyone talk about going to live in Red China?"

"No, sir."

"Nobody ever said anything about being treated better under the communist?"

"No, sir."

"Did you ever hear anyone brag about the Chinese making a personal offer to them to come and live in China?"

"No!" Irritated, Welch said, "Listen, Major. When you live in a prisoner of war camp, you can't go around kissing the Chinese's ass and still be one of the guys. Those who made the decision to really collaborate had to be separated from the rest of us once it was obvious, they were traitors. There were men in that camp who would have killed a turncoat."

Paulson scribbled notes on his pad. He looked up and stared at Welch, and laid down his pen.

"Would you tell me the names of the men who collaborated with the Chinese?"

"First off, tell me exactly what you have to do to be a collaborator?"

"Cooperating with the enemy in any way, of course."

"Well, according to you we were all collaborators. We were trying to survive, Major. People were dying all around us, every day. What would you have us do? What would you have done, Major?"

Paulson sat quietly, giving no answer to Welch's questions. Welch looked Paulson in the eye and thought about his request. He wondered to himself how much his future depended on cooperating with the likes of Paulson. He had survived the Chinese, but could he survive the American interrogators?

"We're coming into San Francisco Bay. Let's go outside, the bridge is in sight."

Lowe was sitting up in bed. He didn't look too good. He had a darker, yellowish tint to his pale skin now. Nurse Maxwell noticed, as well as the doctor who had examined him and made notes. When they reached Fort Mason a specialist would give him a better examination.

"You know, Dan, I haven't been feeling too well, but maybe some fresh air and seeing America will lift my spirits."

Lowe slowly spun around and swung his legs out over the edge of the bed.

"Let's take the wheelchair. It will give you a place to sit and I can move you around quicker to get the best view."

"Sounds good to me," and he dropped down in the chair. Welch threw a blanket over his knees and started down the aisle of the ward. There stood Maxwell with her hands on her hips.

"We're going to see the Golden Gate Bridge. We're home, Captain Maxwell. We're home!"

"Okay. It's against my better judgment, but go ahead and take an extra blanket."

Welch grabbed two more blankets, tossed them into Lowe's lap and carefully maneuvered through the bulkhead. A split second later he came running back in and grabbed Lowe's cane, gave Maxwell a hug and left her blushing, as he ran back out of the ward.

Outside on the bow they stood with several men and women. Off in the distance were the twin towers of the Golden Gate Bridge. The people chatted, watching the towers grow in height as the ship steamed closer to San Francisco Bay.

"Fort Mason!" shouted someone from the upper deck. Everyone moved in closer to the railing and peered ahead.

"Where?" asked Lowe, looking up at Welch.

"Look under the bridge span, just beyond the point, boys." A Colonel standing next to Welch pointed to the bridge looming in the distance. "That's Fort Mason there. You see those buildings there on the point, under the bridge. That's the Presidio. The big two story, tan brick building, nestled just under the base of the bridge is Fort Point. A lot of those buildings have been there for over a hundred and fifty years taking care of our boys as they left or came back from overseas duty. Fort Mason, that's where we will be living for the next several days, and look there straight ahead, that's Alcatraz Island and to its port is Angel Island."

"Look, Dan, Alcatraz! Just think, Big Al Capone himself lived there."

"Pretty dreary looking place, isn't it?" said the Colonel.

"No, sir! It doesn't look so bad. I would rather have been there for the past year and a half, than where I was," replied Welch.

The Colonel looked at Welch and nodded his head.

As the hospital ship steamed under the bridge some of the passengers leaned out over the railing, straining to see the underside of the structure. The ship had already reversed its engines and was coming to a stop. Sitting quietly in the still waters of the bay, she waited as two tugs came along side and prepared to assist her to a berth.

Welch and Lowe looked across the waters at Fort Mason. Down on the water there were three long warehouse type buildings, located on piers that jutted out into the bay. Up behind them on the shore stood three, three story buildings and a single one-story complex. Scattered about behind them were several different types and sizes of buildings.

The powerful tugs were slow and deliberate as they went about the task of nudging the larger ship up against the pier. Sailors on the pier took the lines and slipped them over the large turnbuckles and flipped the fenders down to provide cushion for the vessel against the dock. Welch slowly pushed an exhausted Lowe back to his ward. They were finally home.

"Hello, Sally? This is Howard Lowe. I'm out in San Francisco. I need you to connect me to Martha Lowe, in Gadberry, if you don't mind."

"Oh, my goodness, Mr. Lowe. We have been so worried about you. Thank God, you're finally home. I'll put you through right away."

There were several seconds of silence and then, "Lowe's residence. May I ask who's calling, please?" The strong, authoritative voice of Mrs. Katherine sounded off at the other end.

"Hello Mrs. Katherine, it's Howard. Is Martha in?"

"Howard! My heavens, it's Howard. You hold on for just a second and I'll get her. She feeding that boy of yours."

More silence, and Lowe heard someone pick up the receiver at the other end.

"My darling is it, is it really you?"

The voice on the other end of the line brought tears to Howard's eyes. He was so choked up and filled with emotion he was unable to speak.

"Howard! Oh, Howard, are you there?"

Lowe struggled to speak but sound would not come forth. He fought to regain his composure and finally was able to get forth a few words.

"I'm here, darling." He was already tired. The excitement of the moment was draining his strength quickly.

Martha was talking and crying now, making it that much harder on him, but he didn't mind. Her voice was heavenly. In the background he could hear the snorting and babbling of his son, Howard Junior.

"Darling, I have missed you so. I can hardly stand to hear you and not be able to hold you in my arms. When are you coming home? Oh wait, there is someone here who has been wanting to talk to you." The jabbering of Howard Junior got louder as Martha put the receiver close to his face. Howard listened to his son.

"Hey, boy!"

Junior got quiet and his facial expression changed as he listened to his dad's voice. Martha brought the receiver back up to her face.

"He misses his dad and wants to know when he is coming home?"

"Soon, darling. I've got some medical problems that the doctors are treating me for. As soon as I get them taken care of, I will be home." His voice was becoming very tired.

"Howard, you sound so tired. What medical problems? Are you okay, darling?"

"I'll be fine, honey. Are the girls there?"

"They're at school right now. I'll tell them you called. Will you be able to call back?"

"Yes. Next week, I should be able to. I need to go, honey. I'm only allowed a few minutes on a call."

"Oh. It hasn't been that long, surely. Howard I . . ."

"I love you, Martha."

"Howard!"

"Click!"

＊　　　＊　　　＊　　　＊

"Look over there, pal. Look at the size of the ship."

"Looks like a tanker, must be six, seven hundred feet long."

"Mmmmmmmm!"

The ship sounded its foghorn as it prepared to enter a fog bank that had settled over the water. The sound echoed across the bay, fading into the fog.

"The Lord sure did a great job here. What a beautiful place this is," said Lowe. "I'm going to bring Martha and the kids here someday. We'll drive out here and see all the sights between here and Kentucky."

Lowe sat in his wheelchair. He hadn't walked since he had taken the step off the ship's gangway. His health had deteriorated considerably since their arrival. Welch took him for a walk in the wheelchair every day along the walkway that curved around the shoreline. They would go rolling along, talking about things, and seeing something new each day. They had been at Fort Mason three days now and the doctors were not encouraged with Lowe's lack of progress. Welch took long walks by himself every evening down along the bay on the walkways. One day he would walk north, up around to the Presidio, the next, in the other direction toward Fishermen's Wharf. The time alone helped him to think, to sort out things in his mind. There was a burden that weighed heavily on him. He was losing Howard. He could feel it, and he could do nothing about it. He'd lost Leo, and then Amelia, and now Howard.

Welch walked past the firehouse and over to a bench on the walkway. He sat down, staring out across the bay. This was the scheme of things he thought to himself. It was his destiny to only make someone's life a little easier, a little less painful for a short period and then they had to leave, depart from this life and move on. Why was his role always that of a caretaker? Would he ever be happy? He doubted it. Would there ever be a lasting friendship? Didn't seem to be in the cards. Would he be rewarded for his selfless stewardship? He looked up into the clouds for a moment and then back across the bay. His shoulders slumped and he sat there alone watching the sun set in the west.

"Open." The doctor laid the tongue suppressor on Lowe's tongue and shined a small flashlight in his mouth.

"Ahhhhhhhh."

He stood, reached down and lowered Lowe's lower eyelid, revealing his yellowish eyes. The doctor noticed his jaundiced condition the moment he saw him. He had read the medical file and it was clear there was some serious liver damage. He had also noticed in the medical file Lowe's continued weight loss, after repatriation. Not a good sign. His appetite was very poor, and while the other repatriated prisoners were gaining weight, he continued to lose at a disturbing rate. He had also noticed Lowe's tendency to scratch a lot. Lowe knew something wasn't right either and confronted the doctor that afternoon.

Colonel Oliver Sobkowiak looked over at Welch, pulled up a chair next to Lowe's bed and sat down.

"Sergeant Lowe. You have a very serious liver problem. My guess it's a form of amebiasis."

"Come on, Colonel. If there's bad news give it to me so I can understand it."

"Amebiasis is an infectious disease that is also known as amebic dysentery."

"Dysentery! I had it really bad the whole time I was a prisoner. Everybody had dysentery at one time or another."

"Yes, but in your case the parasite must have broken through the intestinal wall and was carried by your blood to your liver. A parasitic one-celled microorganism causes the disease. You, like most of the prisoners drank water contaminated by human feces."

"It was all we had, Colonel. We had no way to boil it. We had to drink it or die of thirst."

"I know. Damned if you do! Damned if you don't! A normal liver is soft and smooth. Nearly all the blood that leaves your stomach and intestines passes through your liver. The infection has scarred the tissue, so your liver isn't working so well. That's why you feel tired all the time. Your constant itching is also a result of your liver dysfunction. Bile products from the liver are not processed properly and they end up deposited in your skin. The jaundice and itching are both late stage symptoms. I'm not going to hold back anything from you on this. What you have is fatal and you're in the late stages." As Lowe lay there he smiled at the Colonel.

"You know, doc, I was in pretty bad shape several times in North Korea and I bounced back. I'm going to bounce back this time too. You wait and see."

The Colonel smiled, "Go get'em champ!"

Welch sat at Lowe's bedside. He had watched his friend deteriorate the past month since they left Korea. It was heartbreaking to suddenly be free from captivity, only to find out that he was still a prisoner of camp life after all. A Chinese death sentence had been carried home, unknowingly in his damaged liver. At least he had made it to America, Welch thought. At least he would die and be buried in American soil, a free man, and not in an unmarked grave back in Korea.

He had sat with his friend since the evening before. Lowe had been in and out of sleep. His liver had virtually stopped functioning. They would talk occasionally, mostly about Martha and the girls. It was as if he didn't know he had a son, the memory of the baby erased. His face was puffy and he was too weak to move. When he did speak it was brief and in short sentences.

It was morning. Welch sat looking out the window. The sun was rising in the east when Lowe suddenly spoke, so faint that Welch almost didn't hear him.

"Why have you done so much for me, Dan?"

Welch stared out the window contemplating Lowe's question. He finally turned and faced his dying friend.

"Because you needed me . . . and I needed to help. It was the least I could do, Howard."

"Thank you. Thank you for everything, Dan."

Welch smiled sadly, but couldn't find the words to express how he felt. Howard lifted his hand. Welch took it with tears in his eyes.

"Let's you and me walk across the road and get a cool drink of water from my spring, Dan. Martha, and the girls will be waiting . . ." As the sunlight filled the room and Martha and the girls passed from his lips, Howard was gone.

*   *   *   *

Welch sat at the airport awaiting his flight. The terminal was busy as people came and went. He was smartly dressed in his army dress uniform. There were other soldiers, sailors and marines around the terminal, but he preferred solitude and sat by himself. He was still haunted by Howard's death. The colonel had made arrangements for him to escort Howard's body home to Kentucky, and arrangements were being made with Fort Knox for an Honor Guard. He wasn't sure what he would say to Martha, but he would find the courage somehow to talk with her and share his memories of the last year of her husband's life. With each letter he had written for Lowe and each letter of Martha's he had read, he grew closer to the family. It was a strange feeling to feel so close to someone he had never met. He was filled with sadness, but even more so, he felt as if a great dread had cast its shadow over him with the task he had to carry out. The quad propped, DC-6 would speed across the country, but it would still be a long, lonely flight. By the time he reached Louisville he would surely have an idea about what he would say to Howard's widow.

As he sat, he heard children giggling, laughing on the other side of the bench. They had been there the whole time, but somehow his thoughts had shut them out. He slowly turned and came face to face with a young child kneeling on the bench. He had big brown eyes and his sandy brown hair was neatly parted on one side with a wave combed up in the front.

"My name is Clayton. I'm from Louisiana."

"My name is Daniel. I'm from West Virginia." He didn't know why he used his Christian name. His mom referred to him as Daniel till the day she died. It was her special name. No one but family used it. It had just popped out.

"Are you a soldier?"

"Yes."

"Where are your medals? My Uncle Ray killed Japs in his war and had lots of medals on his uniform."

Welch sat looking at the boy. It was a good question, for which he had no answer. Next to the boy sat his parents. His father held an infant, probably not more than three months old. The father played peak-a-boo with the baby and his efforts were rewarded with an occasional giggle and smile.

"Clayton! Don't bother the soldier. Turn around here, now. I'm sorry Private. He's always been a bit too curious for his own good."

"He crying, Mommy?"

Welch's eyes had misted up and he realized a tear had run down his cheek.

"I'm so sorry, Private. Clayton, turn around and leave him alone."

"That's quite all right, ma'am. How old are you, Clayton?"

"Seven. Why are you crying, mister?" the boy asked with childish innocence. *"Clayton!"*

Welch smiled. It was his first smile in two days.

*   *   *   *

Julius Alfred sat at his desk reading the Courier Journal. The big news was the governor's big battle with the legislators over coal issues in eastern Kentucky. As a Commonwealth, the Legislature only met every two years, but when they did meet, it was usually quite a show. As he read, the telegraph began to tick away. The office assistant manager was in Louisville attending a training meeting on some new equipment, so Julius manned the office by himself. Without taking his eyes off the paper, he stood, walked over to the machine and waited patiently for it to print out the telegram. When it stopped, he tore the sheet off and walked back to his desk. Taking a seat, he laid down the newspaper and scanned the message:

WESTERN
UNION
W.P. MARSHALL, PRESIDENT

P. WAO 14 GOVERNMENT NL PD
WUX WASHINGTON, D.C. 6 5 53
MRS MARTHA LOWE
LONG CEMETARY RD. GADBERRY, KY

THE SECRETARY OF THE ARMY HAS ASKED ME . . .

Julius was stunned. His shoulders slumped and his eyes filled with tears. Slowly picking up the phone he rang up Sally.

"Sally, ring up Brother Cook for me."

CHAPTER 17

▼

"Good morning Martha. I, Dutch and I, we were so sorry to hear about Howard's passing. If there is anything we can do, please call on us." The short, round woman hobbled over on her cane and gave Martha a hug.

"That is very kind of you Americus. My Howard was fond of you and Dutch. It's been touching to see how sad our friends have taken his passing."

Americus sighed a heavy sigh, her large, round chest heaving out and back in.

There was a long uncomfortable pause as the two women stood looking at each other.

"Howard was there for us when Dutch was down with his back in '48. We could have lost the store. We want to help. I'd be glad to watch the children. Why, they love to come and visit Mrs. Americus' store. You drop them off some morning and we'll have a grand old time trying on hats and dressing up."

Martha gave a faint smile as Americus took her hand.

"I promise I'll go light on the sweets."

"Thank you, Americus. What I do need now is a hat to wear to the funeral Thursday."

Americus put her arm around Martha's waist and they walked to a small room off the side of the Gadberry General Store. The building itself was narrow, but elongated. It sat across from the entrance to Long Cemetery Road. The store had been there longer than anyone could remember. Americus and Dutch Turner bought it from Nathan and Mini Peters, who had taken it over after Mini's father had passed away the winter of '05. Brice Spalding had built it in the late 1800's. The general store had served the Gadberry community well over the years. The wood slat siding of weathered oak was the original siding. The corrugated sheet metal roof was fairly new, installed since the last war. The structure itself sat on a quarried stone foundation. If you looked closely you could see the chisel marks left by the stonemason as he squared out the stone. An eight-foot deep porch extended out to the front, with a roof overhang.

In the front were two windows, with a door in the middle. The small amount of wood space available was covered with small tin signs advertising everything from Double-Cola to Whiting-Adams Vulcan horsehair shaving brushes. Hanging in the left window was a framed cigarette advertisement. Faded, but still impressionable to young ladies was the 1940 Miss America, Patricia Donnelly, of Detroit, pulling a pack of Chesterfield cigarettes from a heart shaped pocket on her dress. Over the porch roof was a weathered sign announcing, "GADBERRY GENERAL STORE, est. 1870"—something. The last digit worn down to where it was unreadable. Under the large letters U.S. POST OFFICE." On the left side of the building was a single Texaco gas pump that had sat idle since the gas-rationing period of WW II. Dutch decided not to install a more modern pump, so the tall glass top pump sat there, the glass bowl empty of fuel, a sign of days gone by.

"I've got several black hats, Martha and if you don't see one you like, I'll just have to make you one. Let's see now, this should be one right about here."

Americus reached up with her cane and nudged a round hatbox down from one of the shelves that lined the walls of the back room. Catching the box, she sat it on the glass top case located in the middle of the room. The case contained several hats, all very colorful and in the latest fashions. Lifting the lid of the hatbox, she saw a pretty light brown derby, decorated smartly with brown feathers.

"Well, dear me! That's not what we are looking for, now is it?"

Martha lifted it out and held it at arm's length. The felt hat was crested on one side with quail feathers. She admired the hat for a second and carefully placed it back in the box. Americus knocked down another box, opened it and removed a black felt hat with a delicate black lace veil. She removed the lid from several other boxes on the lower shelf, each containing a different style, all black, all unassuming. Martha picked out three, trying each on in front of a mirror, finally settling on a black beret with a black veil and a touch of black feathers.

"Have you picked out a dress yet, honey?"

"Mrs. Katherine is going to let out a dress I wore to Aunt Elizabeth's funeral. A slight alteration and it should fit fine. I've still got a little of Junior sticking to my middle," Martha said placing her hand on her stomach and pushing in.

"Babies do leave a wide girth, don't they child?" said Americus, patting her own stomach.

Martha held her stomach and thought of little Howard. For a moment she separated herself from the numbing pain she had felt since Brother Cook and Julius Alfred stood at her front door the day before, tears streaming down their cheeks. She knew instantly the news they had brought. There was really nothing else that could have wrought such emotions from the two men. When they finally found their courage and the words to inform her, she must have gone into some sort of walking shock, as she did her best to comfort them. Mrs. Katherine made some coffee, they talked for a brief time and after a moment of prayer the men left, with departing hugs. Only after she was alone with Mrs. Katherine did the numbing heartache begin.

"This will do, Americus." Martha reached in her purse for her wallet.

"That won't be necessary, Martha. You can settle up later, if you wish. After everything settles down."

"It's best for me to settle now, Americus. With so much on my mind I could forget, and I wouldn't want to put you in that kind of position." She took a ten-dollar bill from her wallet and paid. Americus took the cash box from under the counter and gave her back six dollars and forty-two cents change.

"I appreciate your kindness, Americus. Tell Dutch hello for me." Martha turned with the hatbox to go. As she stepped through the front door, she turned and faced Americus to smile, but failed miserably. Turning, she let the screen door slam behind her as she left the store.

✶   ✶   ✶   ✶

Welch peered out of the cabin window of the DC-6 as it approached the runway at Louisville's Standiford Field Airport. Down below were the twin spirals of Churchill Downs with its oval shaped dirt track and the long horse barns on the backside. The walled grounds were completely surrounded by small white, weatherboard homes. Which was there first, Welch wondered, the horse track, or the quaint little neighborhood?

The plane and passengers shook as the aircraft's landing gear touched down. A puff of smoke was left behind as the airplane raced down the runway. A second later the front landing gear touched down, the props reversed with a roar, slowing the airplane to taxi speed. The ground crew busied themselves as the props slowed and the plane came to a stop.

The American Airlines DC-6 was a handsome aircraft. Its four Pratt and Whitney piston engines turned out twenty-five hundred horsepower each. The passenger cabin and its hundred and two passenger seats allowed it to rule the skies. It had been chosen as Harry Truman's personal airplane when he was president.

A stairway was moved into place just behind the cockpit. The cabin door opened and passengers carefully walked down and moved across the tarmac toward the terminal building.

As Welch walked down the stairs, he noticed a black hearse parked off to the left, a man standing patiently beside it. He turned and walked over to the hearse. The man took two steps to meet him and extended his hand.

"Darren Lewis."

"Dan Welch. I've been assigned to accompany Sergeant Lowe's remains to Columbia." Remains sounded so indifferent, thought Dan.

"Howard was a good man. He will be badly missed. We'll wait here until the container is unloaded and they signal for us to drive over to the plane. If you want, you can go to the baggage claim while we wait and get your luggage."

"Everything I own in this world is in this bag." Not quite the truth, but at times he felt as much. The fact that he had lived the past year and a half with nothing but the tattered clothes he wore led him to believe little else. There was so much of his life to recover, so much to rebuild.

"You're welcome to sit in the hearse while we wait."

"I'll just stand, if you don't mind. It's been a long trip."

Welch's mind wandered. He studied the small hills that dominated the landscape on the southern edge of Louisville. It was a bright sunny day with unlimited visibility. Off in the distance another aircraft approached the airport. Staring at the shiny dot in the sky he watched intently as it grew. The noise of other aircraft and ground crews slowly faded until nothing else entered his consciousness except the approaching aircraft. Snapping into a trancelike state Welch's mind went into overdrive. Was the approaching aircraft North Korean or one of ours? He scanned his surroundings, sizing up everything, picking out potential hiding places, areas that offered protection against an air attack. Mentally noting three locations to avoid, he selected two escape routes as the aircraft came in low in a strafing posture. Instinctively, he went into action.

"Mr. Welch, Mr. Welch, *Private Welch!*" shouted Lewis.

Welch took a deep breath, opened his eyes and carefully looked up over the hood of the hearse. Staring down at him was the concerned mortician. Sweat broke out on his brow. Out on the runway a DC-3 cargo plane touched down.

"It's a habit that's hard to break, Welch. You've been through quite an ordeal, be patient with yourself."

Lewis walked around to Welch and stuck out his hand. "Captain Darren Lewis, 1st Infantry Division. I survived the drive across Europe, but it took a couple of years to find some peace of mind when I got back. I suspect you have been through a whole lot more, so be patient."

Welch walked with Lewis back around to the other side of the hearse. They stood silently as the ground crew unloaded the belly of the aircraft. The tarmac area was an organized clutter of aircraft, baggage vehicles with trailers, and a flurry of activity. The planes that had just arrived were unloading and those departing were loading. The aircraft he had traveled on had its belly open and a conveyer belt up inside it. Invisible men placed baggage on the belt. Visible men on the ground grabbed the baggage and loaded it on the trailers. Others were busy doing maintenance checks and refueling. Welch didn't know where the aircraft was headed, but he wished he were on it going anywhere but where he was headed.

"There it is," said Lewis, returning the wave of the ground crewman.

They got into the hearse and drove slowly over to the aircraft. With the help of the ground crew, Lewis backed the hearse up to the conveyer and the crew prepared to load the container in the back of the hearse. Welch had walked to the back of the vehicle and stared down at the shipping order taped to the large metal box:

LOWE, HOWARD D. #1725416
SERGEANT—US ARMY
DELIVER TO RICHARDS-LEWIS FUNERAL PARLOR
COLUMBIA, KENTUCKY

He reached out and touched the metallic box as it slid by and into the back of the hearse.

"Watch your fingers!" shouted one of the crew. The back door of the hearse was slammed shut and he walked back to the front and climbed in. In a few seconds Lewis climbed in and they slowly drove off the tarmac and out the airport gate. They rode without speaking.

After traveling on several city streets and roads, the hearse turned south on highway 31 West. Welch kept his eyes fixed, staring out the side window as they traveled.

"Where you from, Private?"

"West Virginia."

"What was it like being a prisoner?"

"Lonely, very lonely. If we hadn't had each other . . . we would have been lost souls, Captain."

The hopeless implication of Welch's answer unnerved Lewis so much he sat without speaking for several miles. Soon the hearse began to climb a steep hill leaving the Ohio River basin behind. At the top of the hill they entered the flat plain that cradled the knolls, rolling hills and meadows that dominated central Kentucky. The hearse carefully and patiently moved through the Fort Knox military post. Dan studied the movement of the young soldiers. Some walking along the sidewalks, others marching in columns in the streets.

"You've got to be careful driving through here," said Lewis. "Those boys are liable to march right out in front of you. That sergeant yells out, 'Column Right,' instead of "Column Left,' and that whole column will turn right in front of you before the road guards can post to stop traffic. Basic trainees. They train them to take orders without question and they do. They'd walk out in front of a car rather than get a tongue lashing from their Drill Sergeant."

As they left the post Dan struggled to control his thoughts of Howard.

Up ahead something on a billboard advertising a First Federal Savings and Loan Association caught Welch's eye. The "OF ELIZABETHTOWN" at the bottom of the sign triggered a memory about Howard and his friends stopping for lunch in a community Howard had referred to as E-town.

"Is there a small restaurant up ahead called the New Dairy Whip?"

"You must mean the Moo Dairy Whip," responded Lewis with surprise.

"Would it be too much trouble to get a bite to eat there?"

The rest of the trip was somber for Welch. Lewis pointed out Lincoln's Birthplace and they talked for a few minutes, but fatigue had taken hold and his thoughts were on Howard. The road snaked through several small communities eventually arriving in Columbia where the hearse pulled up to the back of the funeral home. The core of the white, two-story brick colonial was originally the county's jail built in the eighteen-hundreds, now one of Columbia's older homes.

The massive white columns that adorned the front had maintained their impressive stature for the century or so the house had sat just off the square. Although the room built off the back of the building was built to be more functional than for looks, the main entrance off Greensburg Street maintained its pristine, colonial appearance.

A man met Lewis and helped him unload the casket, while Welch walked around to the front and through the front doors. The exterior walls were almost a foot thick, as well as the interior. The ceilings were twelve foot high. The home was well built. Walking down the hall to meet Welch was Jordan Long.

"Private Welch, I'm Jordan Long. Martha asked me to meet you. You'll be staying with me and my family during your stay in Gadberry."

They shook hands and Welch followed him out the front door to a flatbed pickup truck. Stacked on the back were several bags of feed corn and a roll of barbed wire. The bags were contained on the bed of the truck with wooden sideboards.

"Visitation will be tomorrow, with the funeral Tuesday morning. If you're up to it, Martha would like to see you this evening."

"I would like that."

As they talked, down Greensburg Street toward the square, several people filed out the front doors of the Columbia Baptist Church. Some stood at the doors and talked, while others talked on the steps and down on the sidewalk. The grownups were laughing, shaking hands and hugs were plentiful, while small children ran about. It was a celebration and the smiles were for a young child who had moments before, given her life to Jesus Christ in baptism. Her family belonged to a small Baptist church east of Columbia. Their church wasn't equipped with a baptistery and regularly used the one at the larger Columbia Baptist Church. As the crowd milled about, a woman broke away and crossed the street, walking toward the two men talking in front of the funeral home.

"Good afternoon, gentlemen."

"Ma'am," said Jordan, tipping his hat.

Turning to Welch she took his hand and said, "I saw you standing here in your uniform Private and I was wondering if you were in for the Lowe funeral?"

"Yes, ma'am. I was with Sergeant Lowe in North Korea and was asked to escort him home."

"God bless you Private and welcome home." She reached up and grabbed Welch's shoulder, pulling him down and kissing his cheek. With tears in her eyes

Gladys Henry turned and crossed the street, walking back to the church where she joined her family to continue celebrating the baptism of their youngest daughter, Barbara.

Jordan pulled the truck up in his yard and the two men got out. From nowhere two little girls appeared, ran a loud circle around the truck before realizing their dad had company with him. Quietly they hid behind his legs, staring up at the stranger in uniform.

"Girls, where's your manners? Come around and introduce yourselves to Mr. Welch."

As the girls obeyed their father, May came out the kitchen door and walked to meet them.

"And this is May, my wife."

"Hello, May." Welch offered his hand and May shook it.

"It's an honor to have you stay with us, Mr. Welch."

"It's Dan. Please call me Dan."

"Well Dan, supper's cooking and will be on the table in another thirty minutes."

"Good, that will give me time to shave and freshen up. I've lived in filth the past year and a half and it's a treat to be able to clean up. I look for reasons to do it."

Jordan led Welch to the door of the mudroom, just off the kitchen. "There's the sink and there's a cot you can call home for as long as you're here. I stir pretty early with the milking, so I'll try not to disturb you as I slip on my overalls and gumboots."

May had prepared fried pork chops, fried potatoes, cream corn and green beans. It was delicious, but Welch tried to not over indulge, despite the fact that May kept insisting he eat more. His intestinal system was beginning to do a little better at handling the rich fried foods America cherished so dearly, but he still wasn't fully recovered. At some point soon he hoped to be and feel normal again, whatever normal might be. He wasn't sure anymore.

After the meal he straightened his tie and put his coat back on.

"Supper was wonderful, ma'am. I had forgotten what a home cooked meal tasted like. If I stayed here very long, I would put my weight back on in a jiffy."

"What's your favorite meal?" asked May.

"Whatever you're cooking, May!"

Jordan chuckled as he finished his coffee. "You opened the gate with that response, Dan. I hope you're prepared to live up to her notion of your appetite."

Martha paced the living room floor. Mrs. Katherine looked on concerned. Martha had not cried since receiving the news of Howard's death. She had been a real trouper, consoling Brother Cook and Julius as they stood in her living room, shedding large tears, barely able to talk as they delivered the telegram message. Mrs. Katherine knew what she was going through. When Monty had passed, she didn't have a good cry for a day or two. She just walked around taking care of others like she always did. The day after Monty's funeral, when everyone finally left and she sat alone in her home for the first time in her life, she finally cried. That was twenty years ago and there were times when she still felt lonely in her home. She still longed for Monty to come rolling through the back door, kicking his boots off and announcing his arrival with, "Where's my Kate?" Now it was Martha's turn and she would have to find her level of grief on her own choosing. Katherine would leave that to her, but she did pray for Martha's future. She was far too young to spend the rest of her days alone.

The sound of Jordan's truck in the front yard sent Martha out the screen door and onto the front porch. She had on a plain cotton dress that came down to just above her ankles. The tan color matched her hair, which was tied up in a bun on the back of her head. She looked, for all the world, like a proper one room schoolteacher. It was a look she never tried for, it was just her.

The two men walked across the yard and up the steps. Jordan removed his feed store cap and Dan his service cap, as they climbed the porch steps.

"Evening, Jordan. Private Welch." She extended her right hand toward Dan, who stepped forward and took it.

"I have heard so much about you, Mrs. Lowe."

"I insist that you call me Martha. Mrs. sounds so ancient."

"And what's wrong with that, child!"

"This must be the famous, or should I say infamous, Mrs. Katherine," said Welch, as Mrs. Katherine stepped through the door.

"The one and only, Private Welch! My friends called me Katherine. They're all dead so Mrs. Katherine will have to do. In time you may live long enough to find the courage to refer to me as Katherine."

"If that's the case, I'll call you Kate!"

Mrs. Katherine put her hands on her hips and threw back her shoulders. "If it's a first name basis you want, informality you will get. I need to see to the girls, so good evening, Private."

Jordan smiled. "Martha, I need to see to my milking. I'll be back as soon as I'm done."

"Thank you, Jordan. Come, Mr. Welch." Martha took his arm and walked to the swing, where they sat down together.

"First things first, since you must call me Martha, what must I call you?"

"Dan will do." He could sense the tension and grief in Martha's voice and it was understandable.

"Dan, the children and I are grateful for the things you did for Howard. His death was a tremendous shock to us all. We were so close to getting him back home." Martha paused for a moment and then continued.

"Colonel Bruce called me last night. He wanted to be sure I had received the official telegram. He explained what had killed Howard. He said you were with him the whole time, from when he arrived at the prison camp, to when he drew his last breath."

"I . . ." Dan hesitated, searching for the proper words, but found none.

"You have to understand Dan that no one's to blame, except the Chinese for allowing you men to live in such horrible conditions. You survived. Howard was hurt too badly and too weak to fight back. Colonel Bruce said he didn't stand a chance once the disease got into his liver. But now you must tell me about my husband."

*   *   *   *

Jordan awoke and sat up on the edge of the bed, reached over and turned off the alarm clock. In five minutes, it was scheduled to go off and, as on most mornings, he didn't require it to wake up. He quietly slipped out of the bedroom in the dark and made his way through the kitchen to the mudroom. Flipping on the light he remembered his guest and turned to find an empty cot. Slipping into his overalls and boots he went out the back door and found Dan sitting next to the woodhouse on a block of wood. He was dressed in brown combat boots, olive green fatigues and a matching soft field cap. There was a half-moon overhead and stars blanketed the sky. At four-thirty the sun had not yet decided to rise.

"Early riser, or trouble sleeping?"

"Got a lot on my mind, Jordan."

"Well, I know some good listeners. Let's go to the barn."

The Red Polls were lined up at the door, waiting to be relieved of their milk. Dan's scent unnerved them a bit and they began to stir about.

"Here cow, here now, here now!" Jordan said in a calming voice as he walked between them, passing his hands over their backs making contact as he went.

He repeated himself, "Here cow, here now, here now," as he opened the barn door slowly. The cows started walking in, taking their places in the stalls. Welch watched in amazement at the connection the farmer had with his livestock. When the eight stalls in the bottom of the barn were full, Jordan motioned for Dan to enter.

"They will be fine now. Just avoid loud or quick movements. Here, take this bucket and get some feed out of that drum. Give each hide about a half a bucket and start with the end stall, where I'll be a milking."

Dan did as he was instructed. When he was done, he grabbed a second homemade three-legged stool he saw sitting next to the milk cooler and sat down next to Jordan.

"How'd Martha take things last night?"

"She is a very brave lady. I think she has a lot of crying to do."

"Mrs. Katherine said the same. We're all concerned about her, but Mrs. Katherine says she'll grieve when she's ready and I believe she is right. How are you doing?"

"I think I'll be okay. I was worried about meeting with Martha, but now that it's over, I'm starting to feel a whole lot better. Howard got to be special with a lot of us, can't say as I ever heard a negative word from him. He encouraged others with words and actions. He never gave up, no matter how sick he got. He kept bouncing back, and because of him a lot of us kept fighting on."

"Sounds like Howard. He was a good man. Everyone was understanding he had recovered, that he was okay. His sudden passing came as quite a shock. I've seen that before, where everything is fine and something happens that takes the person all of a sudden like."

"Howard's liver was destroyed by an intestinal infection. All the prisoners in camp had it and it pretty much stayed in our stomachs, kind of like having the flux, with diarrhea, the cramps and all. It passed though Howard's stomach wall and attacked his liver. He was pretty sick when we arrived at Fort Mason. It wasn't long after that his liver failed."

"Did he know what was happening?"

"I was with him when the doctor gave him the news. He seemed more worried about Martha and the kids than himself. He passed in a couple of days. He didn't have the strength to fight."

Jordan stood and patted the cow on the backside. As she turned from the stall and left the barn, another one walked in and took her place. Jordan walked over to the milk cooler and poured the bucket of milk through a strainer that sat on top of a galvanized milk can. Dan got up, walked over and dumped a bucket of feed in the trough in front of the new cow.

"What do you know about livestock?"

"Some. Folks couldn't make much of a living from it back home. Most keep a cow around for the milk, butter and cheese, or kept one up to feed out for butchering. I reckon I could keep one alive long enough to get it to the stockyards."

Jordan moved his stool to the next stall and sat down just in front of the cow's right hind leg. Grabbing a teat in each hand he pulled down with his thumb and the first two fingers of each hand. Streams of milk shot out of the end of the teat, splashing off the bottom of the bucket. The sounds echoing off the bottom of the empty bucket, soon changed to a *"whoosh, whoosh"* as the bucket quickly filled with milk.

"Not all hides go to the market. I take the milk from these Red Polls. I've got a few Holsteins I breed for milking stock to sell to folks serious about milking, or I may take them to the market. Depends on where I can get the best price. The male calves are cut, raised as steers and sold at the market. Sometimes I'll buy a group of young steers elsewhere and raise them up to sell. Everything depends on the market."

Dan moved over to the barrel and refilled the feed bucket. "How do you know when to do what?"

"Right now, the market is slow, so I hold on to what I got. There is a good stand of spring pasture, so it won't hurt me. Come fall I'll have to sell and cut my losses. The market tells you if you know what to look for. Take hogs. I got a lot full of pigs down below the house right now that are all running about one-fifty, one-sixty. Another forty pounds and they will be at tops. If I sold today, I'd be lucky to recover my cost, but that could change next week. Market trends are as unpredictable as the woman up at the house. Cattle, milking stock, hogs, corn, soybeans, it doesn't matter. They are only worth what the market can bear."

Jordan worked away on the second cow. When he finished the first bucket Welch fetched it and strained it into the milk can. Cows moved in and out, the feed in the barrel went down and the large cooler chest filled with milk cans. On it went until the last cow was turned out.

"Get the truck while I drop the milk buckets off at the house to be cleaned. We should have enough time to go check on the steers before breakfast. I don't expect to get much work done today or tomorrow."

Jordan sat the milk buckets at the back door and walked back down to the gate, motioning for Dan to drive the truck down through the gate, into the barnyard. Closing the gate behind the truck, he hopped in the passenger side.

"Drive across the barnyard and over to that gap at the corner of the woods. The hides are grazing over yonder."

In the east the horizon was showing first light. Dan cut off the headlamps as they drove around the edge of a cornfield toward the back of the farm.

The two men were in the backroom washing up. Breakfast was on the table, hot and ready to eat. Outside the milk truck was letting itself into the barnyard to pick up the full milk cans and leave empty ones. Welch could hear the girls in the kitchen talking to their mother. Through the screened windows came the sound of a Robin singing and cows bawling. Somewhere down the hill a beagle bugled, hot on a rabbit. Jordan's eyes lit up as he listened intently.

"That's old Sam. Won't be long before Jess gets in on it too," and as he said it, a second beagle chimed in, yelping and howling. Jordan smiled.

"Let's get some breakfast." As the two men stepped up through the door into the kitchen, Jordan stepped up briskly with his five foot-eight-inch frame. Welch, forgetting the low door facing, stepped up and drove the top of his head into the top of the doorframe. The girls squealed as the kitchen shook. Lightheaded, Dan reached out and grabbed the sides of the door, bracing himself. Jordan gave him a hand and helped him to a kitchen chair. The girls giggled.

"Girls!" admonished their mother. "I declare Dan, as tall as you are, you're going to have watch your step around here. This old house has been around for a long time and the man who built it apparently didn't intend to waste any wood on tall doorways. Let's take a look."

Jordan held back a smile and the girls continued to giggle softly.

May walked over and parted the hair on Dan's head. A wide red whelp was visible on his scalp. Fortunately, he had driven his head straight up into the frame, catching it flat against his scalp. The skin was intact, and nothing was hurt badly except his pride.

"Are you okay, Mr. Welch?" asked Rebecca. Elizabeth had both hands over her mouth attempting to muffle her laughter.

Touching the top of his head Dan said, "I think I'll be fine, Rebecca. I just need to get used to these low door jambs."

"Papa and Nana fell off the wall," giggled Elizabeth, pointing at a picture frame on the floor next to the door. Jordan walked over and picked up the picture, placing it back on the nail it had hung on, undisturbed for several years.

"They're none the worse for their fall. Papa and Nana would have gotten a good giggle out of such a shake."

"Jordan! Don't encourage the girls."

"I'm fine May, and you have to admit it was a bit funny, the house shaking and all," said Dan, gently rubbing the top of his head.

On the table were scrambled eggs, sausage and bacon, biscuits and sausage gravy, and several jars of homemade preserves.

"Let's eat. I need to nail down the northeast corner of the tobacco barn roof. The thunderstorm last week bent back two sheets and the barn door to the milking parlor is loose. The rest of the hogs need to be rung and cut, but that will have to wait for another day."

"We shouldn't have trouble getting that done before lunch," said Dan with a grin. It felt good to talk about honest, hard work that didn't involve life and death. More importantly, work performed without a rifle pointed at the back of his head.

Jordan pulled himself up to the table and passed the plate of eggs over to Dan. Looking up at his wife he said, "May, did you find out about visitation?"

"Mrs. Katherine called and private visitation for the immediate family starts at one o'clock. They'll open the doors for public viewing of Howard at two o'clock. We'll have plenty of time to get ready after lunch."

The words were like a knife cutting through the pit of Dan's stomach.

$$\ast \qquad \ast \qquad \ast \qquad \ast$$

Martha stood in the arched, double doorway that separated the hall from the funeral parlor. She gazed across the chairs at Howard's body, lying in the casket in far end of the room. She had walked into the funeral home minutes earlier with Mrs. Katherine and Karen. Mathew had taken the girls and walked up to the square to Foster's Drug Store for an ice cream. Darren Lewis and his wife, Jennifer, met them at the door and once again expressed their deepest condolences, after having done so that morning as they met to make the arrangements. They quietly shared the expected pleasantries until Martha moved things along.

"My Howard waits for me, Mr. Lewis. I am anxious to go to him now."

"Of course, Martha. This way."

As they walked down the hall and approached the door, Martha reached out and took Mrs. Katherine's arm. When she stepped though the archway, she stopped and Karen moved to her left, taking the other arm. Martha hesitated for a moment, staring across the room. Mrs. Katherine could feel her grip tighten as she took one step and then another toward the casket. Not a word was said as they finally stopped even with the first row of chairs in front of the casket.

Howard was laid out in an army uniform. The thin, frail man looked nothing like the husband Martha had kissed goodbye in her front yard a year ago. Tears were running down Karen's cheeks as she sniffled and tried to contain her emotions.

Mrs. Katherine stood like a rock, firm and supportive on Martha's right. She could feel Martha's grip tightening on her arm. It became painful, but she remained quiet and calm. Martha finally broke the silence.

"Oh, Howard my love, what have they done to you?"

She released her hold on Mrs. Katherine's arm and loosened herself from Karen's hold, moving forward slowly by herself until she stood directly in front of the casket. Karen took Mrs. Katherine's arm, sobbing. Leaning against the coffin for support Martha placed both hands on the rim of the casket and gripped the white cotton cloth lining. Looking down at Howard her emotions began to betray her as big tears began running down her cheeks uncontrollably. Reaching out she bent over and laid her head down on his chest, hugging him and sobbing.

"Howard, Howard!"

Karen started to her, but Mrs. Katherine held her back.

Between sniffles Karen sobbed, "What can we do, Mrs. Katherine?"

Mrs. Katherine stiffened, tears forming in her eyes as Karen laid her head over on her shoulder. She half turned and whispered compassionately, "Nothing darling, nothing. Men die and we women are left to cry. That's a burden the Lord would have us carry." The older woman caught a half breath as she gazed through her tears at Martha sobbing and calling out to her dead husband.

*   *   *   *

Brother Cook sat motionless in a chair, in front of the room full of Lowe family and friends. He listened to John Stills play the organ and Bonnie Stills sing a mournful version of *Amazing Grace*. It was only at such sad occasions that he was able to hear the Stills make their heavenly music together, for they were Methodist. He made a mental note to ask them to play and sing at his next revival. Methodist song and Christian preaching would be a powerful force for the Lord. He closed his eyes and soaked up the blessed sounds.

To the preacher's right and just right of the casket sat six men: Jordan Long, Silas Long, Mathew Spalding, Samuel Woods, Ed Parker and Private Dan Welch, dressed in his olive drab, enlisted "Ike" jacket and pants. The room was full with several people standing at the back. Seated in front on a couch was Martha, Junior cradled in her arm, with Amy Sue and Wanda Faye on either side. With her on the couch was Karen. In a chair next to the couch was Mrs. Katherine. Martha was dressed in black, a black net veil covering her face. The girls were dressed in pastel Sunday dresses.

The song ended and after several seconds of silence Brother Cook stood and laid his worn Bible on the podium. He gripped the sides of the stand and stared out across the room of people.

"We have gathered here to pay our respects to a patriot and a warrior of two wars. He was a believer, a quiet Christian who witnessed for the Lord in his every action. Howard Lowe was a friend to everyone in this community. He was a good neighbor, who was always there when we needed him. He was a father, no, a daddy who worshiped his children and took every opportunity to be with them.

A husband who . . ."

No one in the room could see into Martha's eyes except Brother Cook as she stared at Howard lying in the casket.

"A husband who . . ." As he repeated those words, he looked down into Martha's face and felt her heartache and despair. Feelings he knew were so intense, it was impossible for him not to suddenly feel them himself. It set him back and tears swelled in his eyes.

"Martha. I . . ."

Martha slowly turned her eyes to his. Her face was sad, but her eyes showed a strength and grace he had never witnessed, or felt before in all his years of spreading the Word.

"Henry, the Lord is with you, and my Howard is with the Lord. Now you must preach his Word so that others may hear."

The preacher found strength in her words. His Bible was turned to *Galatians*, the letter the Apostle Paul had written to the churches in Galatia, but it wasn't necessary for him to read from it:

"Grace and peace to you from God our Father and the Lord Jesus Christ, who gave himself for our sins to rescue us from the present evil age, according to the will of our God and Father, to whom be glory for ever and ever. Amen

CHAPTER 18

▼

In the deepness of sleep some find peaceful rest, while others encounter deeply personal moments. It was the middle of the night and somewhere between deep sleep and consciousness, a loyal, loving husband came to visit his heartbroken wife. It was one of those deeply personal moments and the two souls involved were Martha and Howard Lowe. As she lay there asleep, Howard came to her and it was as real as anything she had ever experienced.

"Hello, darling."

"My dearest, Howard. I have missed you so much. The girls have missed their daddy."

"I've watched them. They're growing up fast."

"Are you hurting, Howard? Are you in pain?"

"No, darling. I'm fine. It is wonderful."

"Dan said it was peaceful in the end. That you didn't struggle."

"It was my time, Martha."

"Then it should be my time. Let it be my time too, Howard!"

"No, darling. You still have a lot to see and feel. It's okay to go on. I will be waiting here for you in the end."

"Come, lay with me, sweetheart," and Howard settled close to her. She took him in her arms and held his head to her breast. Stroking his hair she said, "I love you Howard," and fell into a deep, restful sleep.

"I dreamed about Howard again last night," said Martha as she handed a dish to Mrs. Katherine to dry and put up.

"It happens, child."

"It was real."

"I know, darling."

"He told me I should go on with my life. That I had a lot to feel and do yet."

"He was letting you go."

"I don't want to be let go. If I can't have him alive, I'll have his memory with me until I'm with him."

Mrs. Katherine stood there in deep thought, lightly drying a small black skillet.

"You see this little skillet?"

Martha looked up at the skillet.

"To season this skillet, you coat it with oil, throw it in the ashes of a hot fire and cook it good. Each time you use it after that it gets better at what a skillet does, frying food. Put it away and not use it for a hundred years and the day you take it out it will fry bacon just as good as it did this morning. That's what a skillet does."

Martha waited patiently, listening intently. She knew Mrs. Katherine was not one for idle ramblings.

"You, my darling, are not a skillet. You are a living, breathing woman. You have a lot of lonely years ahead, if you put yourself on a shelf and hide." Mrs. Katherine placed the skillet in the bottom of the cabinet and looked at Martha.

"Darling, don't deny yourself and the children a full life."

*   *   *   *

Fried onions and hamburger patties sizzled on the grill, the thick aroma drifted across the old wooden floor and the green felt topped billiard tables. The lunch crowd and loafers would soon roll in looking for relief in a quick game of Eight Ball. Others would come for lunch and some friendly conversation.

Dan closed his eyes and let the grill smells have their way with his senses. Vivid images of youth raced through his mind.

Rick's Cue Ball had been a billiard establishment just over four decades. It resided just off the square in Columbia on Jamestown Street. It was previously known as Rick's Pool Hall and long before that the original owner started the tradition by having his own name painted on the window, Rick's Billiards. Richard Waters, a short round man from Louisville with a loud raspy voice had a dream of owning his own pool hall for years. He worked at the Louisville Slugger Bat Company. On a Saturday afternoon in May he bet his life savings on a long shot in the second race at Churchill Downs, drove home with a small fortune, retired and moved back to his wife's hometown, Columbia. He bought the old building on Jamestown Street and opened his billiard hall. He ran the establishment until his untimely death in '36 from a stroke. During a friendly game of Nine Ball he slumped over in his chair, cue stick in one hand and a cold Budweiser beer in the other. His wife sold the building and its contents to a local automobile salesman, and so it went over the years.

The atmosphere today was no different than years earlier when the establishment opened. The sound of billiard balls cracking against one another and the smell of onions and greasy hamburgers. The low hanging lights hovered just above the tables and old beer signs hung on the walls, a sign of how things were before the county voted dry and outlawed alcohol after the war. Between the dusty signs, cue sticks lined the walls like rifle racks in an armory.

Dan studied the balls on the table in front of him, holding the weapon of his choice, a weighted cue stick with a well-worn tip. One other table was busy and three others sat idle, their balls racked neatly on the table. Jordan had asked him to pick up some things in town and suggested he take his time coming back. It was a Monday morning and the flatbed Ford sat outside with five tightly rolled bails of barbed wire and a roll of tie wire. That afternoon they would stretch and nail the barbed wire. Two fencerows had been cleaned and replaced so far that month. When this stretch was finished Jordan would find himself a full year ahead of his fence work.

Dan banked the blue 2 ball into the side pocket and the cue ball came to rest five inches from the red 3. Good position, but what would he do after that? He looked at the 4 ball at the other end of the table, resting on the side rail. The 5 sat nearly in the middle of the side pockets. Chalking the cue stick tip, he shot down on the cue ball with sufficient enough force to create backspin. The ball struck the 3, knocking it in the corner pocket and backed up to the middle of the table.

He chalked the tip again and sent the 4-ball sliding down the rail into the corner pocket. The cue ball stopped dead just off the rail, leaving a difficult shot on the 5. Dan frowned as he walked around the table.

"Good run, mister."

Dan looked at a young man standing at the next table. He was a country boy, hair greased back, jeans, cigarette pack rolled up in his T-shirt sleeve, common as the day was long.

"Would you like to shoot a game of Eight Ball?" asked the boy. "We'll just play for fun."

Dan smiled. "Sure, you break 'em."

"Rack!" shouted the boy. A skinny, toothless little man with a ball rack around his neck ran over and starting gathering up the balls, placing them in the triangular wooden rack. He lifted the rack and the fifteen balls lay at the other end of the table tightly grouped and undisturbed.

The man scooped up the silver dime Dan tossed on the table and scurried back over to the grill to finish his fried bologna sandwich.

The boy placed the white cue ball on the table and slid the cue stick back and forth on an open hand bridge. He eventually drew back and brought the stick swiftly forward. The cue ball shot off the end of the stick, barely catching the lead ball, rocketing off to the side into the corner pocket. The boy managed to muster a look of embarrassment. Dan dropped three striped balls before missing a difficult bank shot. The boy managed to sink one of the solid balls, but missed the next shot. The cue ball rolled to a stop leaving an easy shot on the 12 ball. Dan began to sense he was being hustled. Each time the boy missed, an easy one was left for Dan. He ended it by calling and dropping the 8 ball in the side pocket.

"Another one?" asked the boy.

"Sure," said Dan, motioning to the rack boy at the grill. As the man started to gather and rack the balls the boy said, "Why don't we . . ."

"Why don't we play Nine Ball, a dollar a ball with five on the nine," interrupted Dan.

The boy looked up and smiled, "You break."

The game went quick. Dan was more focused and held his own as they swapped shots and pocketed balls. In the end the boy ran the 7, 8 and 9 ball.

Dan laid seven dollars on the table.

"I would love to stay and win it back, but I've got a fence row to wire."

"Maybe next time," said the boy, folding the bills and sliding them into his jeans pocket. "Keep practicing."

✳   ✳   ✳   ✳

Jordan nailed the wire on the post while Dan worked the wire stretcher carefully at the other end. Barbed wire could get ugly and deserved respect. Overstretched wire could snap and whip back, wrapping around a man. The two men moved down the fence line stretching and nailing the wire. By suppertime they were done. They gathered the excess wire and tools, and placed them on the wagon.

Jordan climbed on the tractor and started it up. Looking back over his shoulder to make sure Dan was on board, he shouted, *"Going to drive over to the back real quick. Check on the hides."*

Dan nodded. At the bottom of the field, fence lines from three open fields intersected on a large beech tree. Dan hopped off the wagon as they approached and opened the gap.

"Leave it down," shouted Jordan. The tractor and wagon crossed the open pasture field and entered a lane that had long since been cut through the middle of the woods. Mature timber offered a shady canopy to a scattering of saplings below. Yellow poplar, red and white oak, cherry and beech trees towered up into the heavens. The floor of the forest was covered with a thick blanket of leaves cradling the rotting trunks of a few aged giants, diseased beyond their ability to stand. Up ahead a large fox squirrel scampered up a persimmon tree on the fence line, disappearing in the upper branches.

The tractor moved slowly through the lane and passed through a gap into an open, rolling pasture where the backfields from three different farms came together. It was isolated and beautifully tranquil. Scattered across the field were a variety of steers grazing on the early summer grass. Jordan stopped out beyond the gap and cut the engine.

"You count and I'll look them over."

Dan counted heads as Jordan walked among the stock giving them a good once over. He circled down and back around coming up the hill to Dan.

"Fifty-two," reported Dan.

"I had fifty," responded Jordan.

"How many are there supposed to be?"

"Fifty-one. Count again without me stirring them up so much." The two men started counting to themselves. Dan would point while Jordan simply scanned the herd.

"Fifty," said Jordan with a concerned look on his face. "How many did you get?"

"Fifty-three."

"Good enough. Let's look around a bit," and Jordan started up the hill toward the tractor. Dan walked slowly, looking over his shoulder, pointing and counting. As Jordan climbed up on the McCormick, he yelled down the hill, "How many?"

"With a dejected look Dan reported, "Forty-nine!" Jordan laughed a robust laugh as he switched the tractor on and pulled the starter. Dan climbed on the wagon as the engine turned over and started up. The tractor circled around, going to the left, up a small hill. Through another gap was a small field that ran along the northern fence line into the pond field. Jordan drove along the property line studying the fence. Halfway down the row there appeared a break in the middle strand of barbed wire. Across the fence in an open field stood the missing steer, contently grazing in knee high red clover.

Jordan cut off the tractor engine, hopped down and crossed the fence. Dan grabbed a pair of pliers and snipped off a two-foot strand of tie wire. Wrapping the wire around the end of the barbed wire he pulled it tight and wrapped the end of the wire around the post, nailing it in place. On the other side of the fence in Paul Walker's clover field Jordan moved up behind the steer and drove it back toward his field. The steer trotted to the fence, but couldn't decide where it wanted to cross. It dashed back and forth and as Jordan closed in, it stuck its head through the two middle wires and bulldozed through. Trotting up the hill it headed back to the herd.

"There's little damage to the clover. Those blasted hides will go anywhere their nose can get through, and you know what they say about the grass being greener." Jordan studied the repair job on the break in the wire and nodded approval. They climbed back on, the McCormick roared to life, and across the middle of the pond field they went. Halfway across Jordan diverted slightly to the west, passing close to a newly formed sinkhole. It was nearly ten feet deep, its dirt walls straight up and down.

That wasn't there two days ago, bellowed Jordan over his shoulder. The tractor and wagon chugged on across the field, passing below the pond, up the hill and out of sight in the direction of the house.

✴   ✴   ✴   ✴

"Move out, men!" The sergeant barked.

Welch looked down the hill below his foxhole into the smoke and dust the artillery barrage had kicked up. Nothing could be seen, but deep from inside the haze there came a familiar sound. Faint at first, it slowly grew louder. The muscles in Welch's body tensed, the North Koreans were coming.

"Fix bayonets and move out!"

Welch fumbled for his bayonet and attached it to the end of his Garand. The sound of thousands of North Korean soldiers, yelling and blowing whistles grew so loud it became deafening. The sound was no longer focused ahead of him. It was behind him and to his sides now, it was everywhere, they were everywhere.

The sound was so intense it echoed in his ears and his head began to throb. He gripped the Garand tightly as it lay on the sandbag at the front of the foxhole and waited. Beads of sweat were breaking out on his forehead. The screaming and shrill whistling rang in his ears and his head felt as if it were about to burst.

"I said move out, Welch! Move! Move! Move!"

Welch was up and out of the foxhole, screaming, charging down the hill and firing his Garand into the fog as he went. Fifty yards out ahead of him hundreds of North Koreans suddenly broke through the gray wall, the fog swirling about in their wake. He met them head on, kicking, screaming and slashing with his bayonet. The enemy dropped at his feet, twisting about like night crawlers dumped from a can. Behind him the butt of a rifle made contact with his hip and he swung about slashing down with his bayonet with as much force as he could muster.

As he did a voice screamed out, *"No, Dan!"*

Welch jumped back and there in front of him stood Leo. The bayonet stroke had severed his arm at the elbow and had continued on across his stomach. Jawaski looked down and as he touched his blood stained, fatigue shirt, his intestines spilled out. He tried desperately to hold them in, but to no avail. They rolled out over his hands and hung down to his knees.

Looking up at Welch, Jawaski said, "Dan, you've killed me! Why did you want to kill me, Dan? We were doing pretty good. I wasn't going to . . ." and in mid-sentence the little man's eyes rolled back and he fell forward.

Welch tried to step forward to catch Jawaski, but his movement was too slow. The little man fell to his knees and then on his face in the mud, just out of reach of his outstretched hands.

"Leo! Leo!" Screamed Welch as the fighting around him came to a halt. He stood there looking down at Jawaski, frozen in his tracks.

"Private Welch, you kill American buddy."

Welch looked up into the smiling face of Captain Jin, his left eye covered with a black patch.

"You kill. Take revenge from me. I have no path to honor now." The North Korean raised his boot and stomped Jawaski's face down in the mud.

"Bastard!" screamed Welch as he leaped across Jawaski at Jin, striking him on the patched eye. The North Korean squealed as pain shot through his face. He doubled over and Welch ran past him out across an open field. Behind him he could hear Jin screaming, *"Kill him, kill him!"*

Welch ran through the darkness blindly. His feet made contact with the invisible ground as his arms pumped up and down. They wouldn't catch him, this time. He had run full stride for nearly a hundred yards when he ran head long into a North Korean soldier. The force of their collision flipped Dan in the air and he came down on his face. As he tried to scramble to his feet the soldier bayoneted him around the waist and legs repeatedly. He kicked franticly as he low-crawled forward in the dark.

In the distance there was a shout. A flashlight came into view, searching. They were coming for him. With one final roll he was on his feet, up and running headlong into the darkness once again. He had only covered a short distance when someone brought a rifle butt down against his forehead. His head snapped back and he went down on his backside. Dazed, he sat up and attempted to rise to his feet, but couldn't. The blood was rushing from a gash on his forehead and the cuts from the bayonet stabs were causing excruciating pain in his legs. His heart felt as if it was going to pound right out of his chest as he gasped for breath.

The flashlight was only thirty or forty yards away now and sure to find him. The blood from his forehead was blocking his vision and as he reached up to wipe it out of his eyes he lost consciousness.

Several minutes earlier a loud crashing noise woke Jordan and May Long with a start. Jordan grabbed the double-barreled Stevens shotgun he kept under his bed and eased out the bedroom door, down the hall toward the kitchen. May was on his heels. In the kitchen they both peered out the window in time to see Dan darting across the yard in the moonlight, disappearing behind the smokehouse.

Handing May the shotgun Jordan said, "Put this up. I'll fetch him before he hurts himself." Down in the backroom Jordan quickly slipped into his overalls and boots, grabbed a flashlight and headed out the door. The wooden screen door had been ripped from its hinges and lay mangled on the sidewalk. He shook his head in dismay. He knew the door could be replaced. It was Dan he was worried about.

Jordan was no stranger to such behavior. His older brother had been a shell-shocked veteran of World War I. Hade Long would wake up in the middle of the night, in the middle of the war he carried home with him, frantically fighting imaginary soldiers of the Kaiser's army. As Jordan walked around to the back of the smokehouse he stood and listened. In a few seconds, off in the distance, he heard the unmistakable *ping* of barbed wire breaking. He knew the sound and guessed what it probably meant.

Shouting, *"Hey!"* He switched on the flashlight and headed quickly across the field in the direction of the noise. In a short time, he was approaching the fence and turned left up the row toward the woods. He hadn't traveled far when he came upon the break in the barbed wire. The top two strands were coiled up against the fencepost. Following the beam of light over the bottom two strands of wire he saw a considerable amount of blood in the grass. The trail was easy to follow and as he quickened his pace, he heard a thud up ahead and the sound of rustling leaves.

He found Dan lying on his side under a maple tree. As Jordan ducked under a heavy low hanging branch, the beam of light witnessed what had brought the big man down. A large gash on his forehead was oozing blood out on to the leaves. The rest of his body was covered with deep cuts and blood. Jordan whistled to himself. It looked like he had been in a catfight, especially where the barbed wire had wrapped around his waist and legs.

Jordan looked him over good and concluded the gash on the forehead to be the worst, with one other bad cut on his left thigh that was also a bleeder. He took a blue bandana out of his pocket and with his Old Henry pocketknife cut the edge of the cloth and ripped it in half. From his left pocket he took a white handkerchief and placed it over the open wound on Dan's forehead, tying it down with the bandana strip. With the other strip he tied off the wound on the leg.

Without wasting any time, he pulled Dan up by the arm, and pushing and twisting, got the larger man up and over his shoulder. Holding the back of his legs with his right arm, he reached back behind and grabbed a limp arm with the other hand, and slowly pushed up with his powerful legs until he stood. He wobbled a second, caught his balance and headed out across the dark field toward the distant porch light.

*   *   *   *

Dan lay there feeling the breeze through the window and the warmth of the afternoon sun on his face. As he brought himself up in the feather bed, his head throbbed painfully, forcing him back down. He reached up and felt a bandage on his head. Lying flat on his back he slowly opened his eyes and stared at the white tongue and groove ceiling. To his side he saw white curtains fluttering in the breeze. He recognized nothing, nor was he able to recollect how he came to be there. His head ached and his legs were burning. The confusion and pain he felt were real. He wasn't sure about anything else.

"Well, sir. You certainly gave everyone quite a scare last night." It was unmistakably Martha Lowe's voice.

Dan looked to the other side of the bed where Martha sat in a rocking chair, gently rocking. A quilt pattern she had been stitching together lay in her lap. He took in her angelic appearance.

"Jordan is out on the farm and May had to run to town. I'm watching the girls and sitting with you. I hear tell you had quite a night of it." Dan looked at her, but didn't respond.

"Come now, Dan. I can see you are a bit banged up, but I don't think the cat's got your tongue."

Dan spoke, very quietly and with much embarrassment, "I was back in the war."

"Your wounds certainly suggest you were in some sort of fight."

"My head is killing me and my legs feel like I've been stung by bees. What happened?" and then he remembered the North Korean soldiers charging out of the fog bank, Leo's death, Captain Jin and his attempt to escape. He looked away from Martha, out the window and across the field in front of the Long home.

"It always seems real. Sometimes it's Leo, sometimes Howard, and every now and then a soldier I don't know. They cry out and plead for help. I try to save them, but I always fail."

Martha looked on with knowing eyes, "I know."

Dan reached up and gingerly touched his forehead. "I'll always think I'm getting away and this time I thought I was going to make it. A North Korean caught up with me and bayoneted my legs and butt stroked me in the head."

With dazed eyes Dan looked around the room and then back at Martha again.

"I think . . . I mean I know it wasn't a North Korean, but something did cut me up and bust my head open."

"Jordan says you got tangled up in some barbed wire, ripped yourself loose and ran headlong into a low hanging tree limb. Doc Slaton stitched up your head and leg, gave you a tetanus shot and something to help you rest. There's no permanent damage, but for the time being you need to take it easy."

"I'm sorry. I didn't mean to upset the Longs."

"They're fine, just worried about you, and rightfully so." Martha could sense that he was drifting away. "You need your rest, so no more small talk."

Dan attempted to thank her, but as he tried to speak his eyelids fluttered. He focused on Martha, as everything around her got fuzzy. He sighed, looked deep in her brown eyes and smiled. As his eyes closed, he saw a sad smile come across her face.

Martha sat with her hands in her lap, a compassionate expression on her face. Dan was a living link to Howard, but he was also a man who was carrying an immense sense of pain and guilt. As she stared down at him a feeling within her stirred, she didn't embrace or repress it. It didn't frighten her. She just sighed heavily feeling the warmth of it and gazed upon the man lying in the bed.

The red and white bobber floated against the current of Russell Creek. Spring rains had come and gone, the creek stabilizing at its summer level. A night crawler impaled on a razor-sharp fishhook dangled about three feet below the surface, a cane pole's length from the bank. Stephen Michael sat in the shade of a large sycamore tree, his back against a log. Down the bank, against the same log, sat Raymond Tracy, a blue New York Yankee ball cap pulled down tight on his head. Peering out from under the bill of the cap, he studied the bobber attached to the end of his fishing line as it drifted back across the middle of the creek.

Both boys had been deeply saddened by Mr. Lowe's death. Raymond Tracy had moped about, weepy, depressed and worried about Mrs. Lowe. At the funeral he stood at the casket, turned and faced her. She was crying. No words were passed between them. She simply stared past him as his dad took his hand and led him out weeping. He had tried to comfort her and was ignored. He was miserable for over a week, feeling rejected until he ran into Brother Cook one afternoon on the town square. The minister shared with him how Mrs. Lowe had appreciated the support of her students at the funeral. She especially appreciated Raymond Tracy's attempt to comfort her. She hadn't responded because her grief was too overwhelming at the time.

The next morning, he had rung up Mrs. Lowe and rode his bicycle the three miles over to her home. They sat in the porch swing and talked about the war, and why God allowed such things to happen. He had cried and as she was comforting him she broke down and had herself a good cry. She talked and he listened for nearly two hours that Saturday afternoon. As he straddled his bike, she waved bye from the front porch. He felt the weight of the world lift from his shoulders as he pedaled up the road.

Now, out in the middle of the creek the bobber bobbed gently, sending out cascading rings. Raymond Tracy leaned forward and slowly reached down, gripping the handle of his dad's fishing rod. The bobber dipped again and he studied it carefully trying to decide if the action was the result of the minnow on the hook, or a hungry fish. The bobber dipped once again, ever so slightly, and he tensed his arm. The fourth bob was stronger, a quick jerking motion taking the float half way under, definitely more than minnow action. He looked over and winked at Stephen Michael, who was also watching the bobber intently. He looked back just in time to see the float disappear under the surface of the water with a bubbly *"whoosh."* Raymond Tracy snatched up the pole with a jerk and frantically worked the old Garcia bait caster reel.

"You got him, Ace! Keep the slack out, keep the slack out!" yelled Stephen Michael.

The seven-foot fiberglass pole bent down, its tip pointing toward the water.

The fishing line danced about cutting through the surface of the creek, being pulled and tugged by some unseen giant.

"Hold him high, Ray! Steady!"

"Get the net!" responded Raymond Tracy.

Stephen Michael rolled over, grabbing the fish net that lay between the boys and moved down the bank to take up a landing position. The excitement on the creek bank went up a notch as the fish made a swift run up stream toward the boys. Raymond worked the reel as fast as his hand would spin it. The bobber was visible just under the surface, but as it approached it rose out of the water until the fish was easily seen below the surface. The size of it made Raymond Tracy's knees go weak.

"Keep the slack out, Ray. Wear him out!"

As the fish passed them and ran up stream, the reel began to hum as the drag let out line.

"He's getting away," screamed Raymond Tracy as the fish continued its run up stream. Stephen Michael grabbed the limb of a small maple sapling, braced himself on the bank and prepared to net the fish.

"Get ready, get ready!" The running fish slowed. *"Now! Reel him back, now!"*

Raymond Tracy held the pole out, working the Garcia, reeling the line in with everything he had. On the other end of the line the fish broke the surface fighting with every ounce of its eight plus pounds. Its mouth, the size of a volleyball was opened wide, jerking back and forth, the minnow visible just inside.

"It's a largemouth, and it's a monster!" screamed Stephen Michael.

As the fish approached it turned and tried to head back toward the middle of the creek away from Stephen Michael and his net. The swift change in direction caused a backlash on the reel, creating a tangled mess of fishing line. Raymond Tracy raised the pole as high as his arms would extend and began back stepping up the bank. Stephen Michael readied the net and just as the fish was coming within reach, Raymond Tracy fell backwards over the log. The fishing line went slack and as he landed on his back with a thud, he saw the fish hesitate, its head and large mouth just out of the water. In a mocking gesture it jerked its head to the side spitting the hooked minnow out on to the bank and slowly turned to dive and search out the cool depths of the creek. The defiant jester cut deep into the boy's pride.

Down below at the water's edge, another warrior refused to accept the conditions of the draw. Stephen Michael lunged forward, out over the creek, jamming the net down into the water. The second battle on Russell Creek began at that moment, as the boy's momentum carried him in and under the water. The quiet waters boiled as he resurfaced, clutching the netted fish to his chest.

"Ray!" yelled out Stephen Michael.

Raymond Tracy scrambled down the bank to the water's edge. Grabbing the root of the large sycamore he hopped into the creek, reached out and grabbed Stephen Michael's outstretched hand. Slowly he pulled himself and his friend up out of the water as the fish pounded against the boy's chest. He continued to pull and climb the bank until both boys plopped down side by side in the tall June fescue above the creek. The fish flopped about in the net between them.

As they caught their breath they stared at the giant fish. Neither had seen a bass that big, even in Mr. Collins' *Field and Stream* magazines. The monster lay there on its side, its mouth and gills opening and closing, its tail slowly curling up. A black round eye the size of a nickel stared up at the boys in defeat.

Stephen Michael sat up, hooked his thumb inside the lower lip of the fish's mouth and struggled to lift it out of the net. Looking over at his smiling friend he winked and said, "Looks like a keeper, Ray."

*   *   *   *

A group of black and white pigs, fifteen in all, meandered up the barn lot past the lower barn. Among them was a large sow that easily weighed 350 pounds. Jordan walked behind, gently pushing them along, and just to the left of the upper barn, stood Dan. He was meant to be an obstacle of friendly persuasion. The swine eyed him and moved to their left toward the north barn door. Two temporary gates formed a gauntlet, which guided them into the barn hall. Inside another gate was tied to a hall pole with grass strings, further channeling the swine into an open stall. The old sow was stubborn, but finally conceded and stepped over the stall threshold with a nudge from Jordan, who closed the stall gate as Dan slid the south hall door open. The pigs milled about rooting and grunting.

At a hundred pounds they were half the size of the twenty or so hogs that resided in the lot next to theirs. At one hundred and twenty pounds a pig stopped being a pig and became a hog. At two hundred pounds the larger hogs reached tops and were ready for market, as soon as Jordan could make arrangements to borrow Silas' two-and-a-half-ton truck. But, even at a hundred pounds the pigs could still be a handful when it came to catching and holding them down long enough to be cut. Removing the testicles of a male feeder pig improved weight gain and the eating quality of the pork, come market time. While you had them up, or down on the ground, whichever way you wanted to look at it, rings would be crimped on their nose to keep them from rooting. Swine were clean animals, when you provided them a good reason not to root.

Jordan took out his Old Henry pocketknife, opened the blade and brought it across a whetstone several swipes. As he honed the blade, in through the south barn door came Rebecca pushing her doll carriage, trailed by her sister. Looking out over the rim of the carriage basket was a wide-eyed tomcat dressed in a doll's dress.

"Daddy, what ya doing?" asked Elizabeth clutching two dolls to her chest.

"We're going to cut and ring these pigs."

Elizabeth froze in her steps. Looking wide-eyed, she squealed, turned and ran out the barn door.

"Rebecca, make sure you get that dress off of Norman when you're finished playing with him."

"Yes, Daddy," and she turned the buggy around and strolled out. Elizabeth had already scaled the barnyard gate and Rebecca watched as she ran around the backside of their house, putting distance between her and the soon to be squealing pigs.

"Best mouser I've ever owned, despite the fact that he likes to dress up in doll clothes."

Dan laughed as Jordan spit on the back of his hand and ran the blade edge across the spit. The hair shaved off effortlessly. Near the front of the hall sat an old two-gallon oilcan, a box of rings, and a pair of ring pliers. Jordan walked over and laid the open knife on a board.

"All right, let's get a pig out here," he said as he opened and swung the gate back against the hall wall. As Dan made his way into the stall the pigs rightfully eyed him with suspicion, grunting and moving about nervously.

"If they knew our intentions, they'd sprout wings and fly."

"If I was in their spot, I wouldn't need wings to fly," chuckled Jordan as he closed the gate behind Dan. "Walk into the middle of them, reach down and grab a hind leg. Take both hind legs and drag him out in the hall, flip him over on the ground and put a knee in his side. I'll do the rest."

Dan stepped in slowly, reached down and grabbed one and the squealing began. Twisting and fighting the pig attempted to jerk away, but Dan kept a tight grip on its hind legs, pulling it into the hall. Jordan closed the gate to the stall as Dan flipped the pig over and put a knee to its side, penning it down. Jordan moved in with his pocketknife and skillfully castrated the pig. He tossed the testicles out the south hall door, where Sam and Jess, his two beagle hounds waited. Jess was a little quicker and gobbled the testicles down. Sam sat patiently, knowing there were more to come.

The pig continued to squeal as Jordan grabbed the pliers and quickly crimped four rings into the top of its nose, two in each nostril. Grabbing the oilcan, he poured a liberal amount over the open cuts between the animal's flanks. Stepping back he nodded and Dan released the pig. It jumped to its feet and wasted no time finding its way out the barn door and into the lot.

"You know in West Virginia we fry these up and have them with breakfast. Mountain oysters, we called 'em."

"Never developed a taste for them and the noise will bring tears to a grown man's eyes. You saw the girl's reaction. It's the one noise on the farm they don't care for. The oil works as a good disinfectant. It's just used oil from the crankcase of old John. I've never lost an animal from castration infection. I did lose a sow one time after ringing her nose. She walked about ten feet and fell over dead. She must have had a heart attack. Hated to lose that sow. Bring on another."

Dan went into the stall and grabbed another small pig by the hind leg, and so it went until the sow was the only animal left in the stall. Jordan walked over and handed him a wire with a slip noose on one end and a wooden handle on the other.

"I'll get her out in the hall and you slip the noose over her nose. Keep a firm amount of pressure on her snout and she'll pull against you. While you two play tug-of-war, I'll crimp four or five more rings in her nose. Her snout needs tenderizing. She's been rooting up a storm."

Jordan routed the large sow out of the stall where Dan quickly got the noose over her snout. Snorting and squealing vigorously she immediately pulled back against him, pulling him across the dirt floor of the barn hall.

"Dig in your heels, man!"

Dan dug in his heels and pulled against the grunting sow. As she stood her ground, Jordan moved in quickly and crimped five rings on her snout.

"Okay, I'm going to grab a hind leg and give her some pressure. When I do you slip the wire off her snout."

Jordan moved to the back of the sow. Grabbing one of her hind legs he pulled as Dan pushed the wire forward causing it to release from her snout. As he did Jordan released the hind leg. Free at both ends the sow turned and lunged for the daylight of the open hall door. Jordan started to sidestep and his boot landed square on top of a pile of pig manure he had failed to see. He sat down in the dirt just in time for 350 pounds of pork to stampede over top of him. He rolled backwards under her belly and came out the back end as the sow squealed and grunted her way out the barn door. In the commotion Sam and Jess had jumped up, giving her a wide berth.

Sitting up, Jordan yelled, *"Man, she's fast!"*

"You okay?" Dan stood over Jordan as he wiped the dirt and straw off his overalls. Jordan reached up and took a helping hand, pulling himself up to a standing position.

"I'm fine, just my pride that's hurting. Catching a sow in a pen is easy. Releasing her is where the problem lies. I know better, just didn't see that pile."

Jordan brushed off his backside with Dan's help and the two men headed out into the barnyard to drive the hogs back down to their lot.

✳   ✳   ✳   ✳

It was his last chore of the day and as Dan worked the handle of the jack, the corner of the small outbuilding slowly rose. A carpenter's level lay in the doorway. When the bubble centered, he worked the jack handle two more notches.

Kneeling down, he began rebuilding the corner column, one stone at a time. The day before he had replaced several planks on the Lowe's front porch and when he finished with the outbuilding he would spread a thick coat of paint on the repaired porch. It was things Jordan and Silas had a mind to do for Martha, but couldn't find the time away from their own farm to do so. As he studied the stones, down the path to the outbuilding came Wanda Faye.

"Mr. Welch, Mom says it is time for lunch and you should come wash up to eat."

Dan smiled, "Thank you, Wanda. Tell your mom I'll be there shortly."

Picking up another stone he placed it on the column and after several moments of thought, placed a thin sliver of stone under one corner to level it up. Reaching over for the final capstone he was surprised to see Wanda Faye was still standing there staring at him with tears in her eyes.

"What's wrong, Wanda Faye?"

"Did my dad talk much about me?"

Thoughtfully he sat the stone aside, sat on the ground and turned his attention to the young girl as she sat down on a large stone next to him.

"Your father talked about your mother, you and your sister all the time," replied Dan.

Wanda Faye smiled through her tears.

"He was very proud of you. He would tell me what a good student you were and how he expected you would be a teacher someday, just like your mother. His eyes would light up and he would tell me about the family trips to the drive-in or playing with you and your sister after he finished the chores. He said his favorite time of the day was helping with your homework. I'll bet I know what your most favorite book is."

Wanda's eyes widened with anticipation.

"Your dad would say, 'She'd read this book called *Little Women*, I don't know how many times.'"

Wanda Faye smiled and let out a sigh. "Mom says I should read some other books, so I'm reading *Tom Sawyer*. It's pretty good, but *Little Women* is my favorite."

"Your dad wanted to come home more than anything in the world. He was hurt really bad and he fought hard to get better. He loved you all deeply, and that kept him alive a lot longer. The morning he died, his last words were of his girls and your mom. He asked me to tell you that he loved you very much. He was a good man and I miss him."

"Mom says if you hadn't helped, he would have died and been buried in North Korea. She says because of you he will always be here with us over on the hill," and she pointed to the Long Cemetery just down the road.

Wanda Faye stood up and hugged Dan around the neck. "Thank you, Mr. Welch for taking care of my daddy and bringing him home," and she took him by the hand and led him down the path toward the house.

*   *   *   *

Martha sat in a chair in the superintendent's office of the Adair County Schools. She was dressed in a proper, light summer dress, with her hair professionally up in its traditional bun. The superintendent and his wife had attended Howard's funeral, but had not been able to speak to Martha personally, so he started the visit by expressing their deepest, heartfelt sympathy to Martha and the girls. Since it had been necessary for her to have the same conversation again and again, with everyone she met, her response could easily become routine, but it wasn't. She always managed to feel a deep sense of appreciation for the thoughts and feeling of those who showed concern for her and the girls. She thanked him, and with that out of the way, the conversation turned to business.

"Martha, I'm glad you were able to come in today. It's been some time since we've had a chance to discuss the upcoming school year."

"I'm looking forward to getting back to Tabor, Mr. Moreman. I was out quite a bit this spring with the baby, and I do miss the children."

"Well, there's something I would like to talk with you about, and I want you to think on it a day or two before you give me your answer." Clasping his hands together and placing his index fingers together under his lower lip, Moreman hesitated for a moment before he continued.

"Tom Wheeler's retirement has opened up the Director of Curriculum position here at the Board. He's given the children thirty years and deserves his retirement. He did a bang-up job, but the time is right for change. Time for new blood, a new way of looking at what the children should study, and the board and I think you are the best-qualified person for the job. We believe you can move our curriculum in the direction it needs to go for the future of Adair County's children."

Martha sat quietly listening to Mr. Moreman.

"I'm sure you're aware that the position is year-round. Here is the salary figure, and of course, it's negotiable. I don't need your answer today. You can call Friday with your decision." He leaned forward and handed her the slip of paper.

"Mr. Moreman I . . ." She looked down at the salary figure as she spoke. It was more than twice her present salary. After a long hesitation she calmly looked up at the smiling superintendent sitting across the desk from her.

"Mr. Moreman, I appreciate your kind offer but . . ."

"If the salary figure is inadequate, I have the board's permission to add an additional twenty percent to the figure. As our Director of Curriculum, we think it is a good investment."

"This is a most generous offer, Mr. Moreman, but I . . ."

"Thirty percent and that's our final offer. You surely drive a hard bargain, Martha." He stood and extended his hand. "Give me a call Friday with your decision"

Martha took his hand and shook it, but didn't turn loose, as he would expect.

"My students at Tabor, Mr. Moreman, I will not desert them without knowing they are in good hands."

Looking over his spectacles he asked, "Who do you recommend?"

Having his attention, Martha turned loose of his hand. "The substitute who filled in for me this spring, Marie Goldman, she would be an excellent choice. She's fresh out of Campbellsville Teacher's College. She has proven herself this spring at Tabor and I have confidence in her skills."

Moreman reached over and pushed the intercom button on his desk. "Mrs. Terry, what do we have on Marie Goldman, the substitute who filled in at Tabor?"

"She has an application on file for a full-time position, Mr. Moreman."

"Excellent. See if she can come in tomorrow to interview for the Tabor teaching position." Turning to Martha he said, "Miss Goldman will teach at Tabor, if she wants it."

Martha extended her hand and he took it. "Then I will be your Director of Curriculum, Mr. Moreman, at this salary, plus thirty percent." She held the slip of paper with the salary figures up in her other hand. "You have my word, Adair County will get their money's worth."

"Here's the key to your new office. Your first day will be August one. Make an appointment with Mrs. Hale in personnel to do the paper work one day next week. If you have any questions feel free to give me a call. Have a good day, Martha."

"I will Mr. Moreman, I will," and she left his office.

Moreman turned and stood looking out his window. In a few seconds Martha came into view and as she walked toward her car, she did a little hop-skip step.

Moreman smiled. It felt good to advance good people, especially when they were in fact, the best qualified.

*   *   *   *

"Director of Curriculum," Mrs. Katherine extended her arms, hands open as if picturing a title painted on the frosted window of an office door.

"Mrs. Martha Lowe, Director of Curriculum. You know it has a ring to it. How about, Mrs. Martha Lowe, Superintendent of Adair County Schools. I like the sound of that even better."

"Oh, flitter!" responded Martha to the suggestion she could achieve such a lofty goal. "You know how political the superintendent's job is. Besides, I'll retire before the position is ever available."

Mrs. Katherine proclaimed, "Mrs. Martha Lowe, first woman Superintendent of Schools in the Commonwealth of Kentucky."

Martha smiled, "Mrs. Katherine, I will sorely miss the classroom. There's a certain amount of excitement in watching children grow. There's satisfaction in meeting them when they're older, to hear them tell you about their jobs and families. Teaching is a wonderful way to spend your life, and I wonder if I'm doing the right thing."

"I know child, but you've got to think of all the children in Adair County. Since the big war ended, things have changed. The country is a lot smaller than it used to be and it won't be long until the world is just as small. Our kids need to be able to compete with the kids from Bowling Green, Lexington and Louisville for bigger and better jobs. They need to leave this county and build a future. Some will return with the knowledge and experience to lead Adair to a brighter future. We've got to catch up with the times and you're just the person to lead the way. That board wouldn't have asked you, if they didn't have confidence you'd get the job done."

"Thank you, Mrs. Katherine. I hope I can do a good job."

"Don't worry, honey. I have faith in you and that young Goldman girl. She reminds me of you when you first started. She'll do just fine." Mrs. Katherine picked up a hot dish of green beans and sat it down in a basket. Next to it sat a bowl of cucumber and onion salad. The serenity of the kitchen was broken as the girls came running in. Amy Sue bear hugged Mrs. Katherine's leg, as Wanda Faye got a cold drink of water from the bucket.

"We going to see Rebecca and Elizabeth, Mrs. Katherine," said Amy Sue unable to stand still. Turning to her mother she asked, "We take our bicycles, Mom?"

"We'll see about putting them in the trunk of the car, dear."

"*Yes! Yes! Yes! Wanda, we take our bikes. We can, we can, oh yes, oh yes we can! Rebecca and Elizabeth and we ride bikes!*" sang Amy Sue as she danced about the kitchen and out the back door to fetch her bike.

"Thank you, Mom", said Wanda Faye as she zipped out the back door.

"It was nice of Jordan and May to invite us up for a Saturday dinner. I just don't know how I would survive without friends and neighbors."

"Child, that's what friends and neighbors are for. Silas and Dorothy will be there and I believe that minister friend of yours and his lovely wife, Gracie. And of course, that nice man who brought back Howard. I hear he's heading back to West Virginia soon. Got unfinished business there with a wife that deserted him while he was a prisoner."

"Where on earth did you hear that?" asked Martha, not all that surprised Mrs. Katherine knew of such things.

"He and I talked a lot while he was recovering from those barbed wire cuts. He's a very naive young man and that girl did him wrong. He still thinks he might be able to salvage the marriage. It's sad to see that kind of loyalty wasted on such a tramp."

"Mrs. Katherine. 'Judge not, lest . . . '"

"Heavens to Betsy, child," interrupted Mrs. Katherine, "Ain't no Bible verse gonna make right what she did. The Good Book teaches plenty about forgiveness, but it also shows us treachery and betrayal in the likes of Jezebel and Delilah. You know as well as I do, Daniel Welch has had the bad luck of Job, and like Job he still has faith that things will turn out for the best. He deserves better than that trollop. I've known only a few men in my life with that kind of loyalty and you and I child, were married to two of them."

*   *   *   *

"Welcome. Welcome," said Jordan as he helped Mrs. Katherine out of the car. "Go out front and seat yourself in the shade and I'll see that the food gets into the kitchen."

"Good afternoon, Rebecca Lynn, Elizabeth Gail," greeted Martha. She carried Junior in an infant seat as she and Mrs. Katherine walked to the front of the house where two large sugar maples offered relief from the noon sun. The Long girls stood, straddling their bicycles behind their dad.

"Mr. Jordan, could you please get our bicycles out of the trunk?" asked Wanda Faye.

"Please?" repeated Amy Sue.

"Well, I don't know girls. I can get them bikes out, but then I'll have to find some girls to ride them." Jordan stepped around to the back of the automobile, "Why, yes! They're girl's bikes all right and my girls already have one. You girls have any idea who might want to ride them?"

"We can ride them, Mr. Long," said Wanda Faye trying not to giggle.

"Me ride blue one," added Amy Sue.

"Well, that's perfect because there are, let's see. Sure enough, there are two of them. I'll get them out girls just as soon as I carry this food into the kitchen." The girls dashed over to greet Rebecca and Elizabeth.

In the shade sat Silas, Brother Cook, May and Dan in folding lawn chairs. The group sat semi-circled around the front of a porch swing that hung from a metal a-frame where Gracie and Dorothy gently swung. Brother Cook held a fly swatter in his right hand, swatting at flies that were careless enough to land too close to him.

"Smack!"

"By golly would you look at that, two with one swat. Now, that's some serious fly swatting."

"Saints preserve us, if it isn't Samson himself with the jawbone of an ass. How many Philistine flies have you sent on their way this afternoon, preacher?"

"Look Silas, it's Goliath. Get my trusty sling and a nice smooth stone. There is much work to be done in the Valley of Elah before this day is done."

"She's left her bronze spatula at the Philistine camp kitchen, but be careful Brother, it may be a trap," cautioned Silas as he tossed a small stone over to Brother Cook.

"I doubt that the two of you are man enough to carry the stone needed to drop this giant."

"Run away! Run away!" cried out Brother Cook waving his arms in the air, as everybody laughed. "The giant is upon us."

Laughing, Dan stood, "I, for one, fear not this kind and gentle lady. Mrs. Katherine please, take my chair. I'll go and fetch one for Martha and myself."

"You sir, are a gentleman," said Mrs. Katherine, frowning at Silas and Brother Cook. "Ladies isn't it refreshing to have one around?"

"Is it true, Martha? Can you talk about it yet?" asked Brother Cook as Martha sat Junior down on a blanket in the middle of the gathering.

"In response to both your questions, yes. I will sign my contract this Tuesday."

"Mrs. Martha Lowe, Director of Curriculum! Impressive, isn't it?" chimed in Mrs. Katherine.

"Director of Curriculum, sounds important," said Jordan as he walked up with a chair. "We are pleased you'll be having say-so in what the children are to learn. I know Howard would be very proud."

"Thank you, Jordan. I'm looking forward to getting started. The girls really seem to be the only ones who are not sure about it."

"Little Amy wanted to know if she could still kick Bobby Joe Browning in the shins, if he pestered her," said Mrs. Katherine.

"That's my girl!" added Brother Cook, waving to the girls as they rode past them down the gravel driveway on their bikes.

"I recommended Marie Goldman to take over at Tabor. Mr. Moreman has already approved it. I worked closely with her through the spring and she's a fine teacher."

"Rebecca Lynn and Elizabeth Gail are crazy about her," said May.

"Jordan, how's your new hand working out these days?" asked Gracie smiling.

"He knows his way around a barn lot and he's a hard worker with a light appetite. Everything you want in hired help."

"My appetite is getting better, isn't it May," objected Dan patting his stomach as he walked up with a chair for Martha and himself. She's already put fifteen pounds on me since I arrived in Gadberry. I figure I'd better pack up and head for West Virginia, or none of my clothes will fit."

"You just got here, Daniel," protested Mrs. Katherine looking over at Martha.

"It's been three months, Mrs. Katherine and I've business to attend to back home."

"What could be more important than being around friends?" asked Dorothy innocently.

"Family, of course," quickly interjected Mrs. Katherine. "And a job. Didn't you have a good job in the coal mine before you left for the war?"

"I promised myself on the way home I wouldn't go back down in the mines. I hope to drive a coal truck or work at the coal wash, or maybe even one of those security jobs. I've learned that life is too valuable to cut short by filling your lungs with the coal dust."

"Ladies, it's time to warm things that need warming, and set out what's been cooling."

"Amen!"

"Amen, indeed Brother Cook. Dorothy, Gracie, let's get to the kitchen. Any more is a crowd. The rest can sit out here and help Dan plan his future. We'll holler when things are ready." May turned on her heels, followed by her appointed assistants.

Mrs. Katherine sat there listening to the men predict the fall crop yields. Dan and Martha sat quietly at opposite ends of the group, for the moment, each in their own little world.

Two lonely people, two broken hearts, Mrs. Katherine thought to herself and sighed. *Too many issues in one chair and too much heartache in the other, too soon for either to look up and find peace with one another.*

She watched as Dan sat down on the edge of the blanket next to Junior, showing him an inchworm he had found. The light green worm humped its back and pitched forward inching itself along on a twig. Junior babbled on wide-eyed reaching out with his finger, but not daring to touch the worm. Dan's eyes were bright with the happiness a young child can bring.

Too late, once Daniel leaves for home, she thought sadly.

*   *   *   *

The last Red Pole was let out of the milk barn. Dan straightened things up as Jordan poured the bucket of milk in a milk can and sat it in the cooler. As he walked out of the barn he met the girls.

"Daddy, can we ride Daisy down to the spring?" pleaded Elizabeth.

"Please?" added Rebecca.

"I'll see to these," said Dan with a smile, as he took the buckets from Jordan.

"I don't suppose down to the spring will hurt. Now you know it depends on Daisy. If she ain't up to it, she won't budge an inch. What do you think old girl?"

Chewing on her cud, a moan came from deep in Daisy's stomach. "Girls, she says down to the spring and then she's off to the pasture to be with her cow friends before it gets dark."

The girls giggled as their dad sat them up on the cow. The oldest milk cow in the herd, Daisy had been around the barnyard for years. She never refused the girls a short ride to the spring, but it was always polite to ask.

Dan started for the house and as he turned to latch the gate, he looked back at the girls riding atop the old cow, their dad walking beside them. A warm smile came over his face as he closed the gate and walked slowly to the house.

*   *   *   *

"Are you sure it's okay, Dan?"

"We'll be fine, Martha. Dorothy is going to sit with Junior. May is going to drop the girls off for the afternoon, and the five of us are going to town for lunch and catch a matinee at the *Columbian*. You and Mrs. Katherine go on to Bowling Green. Don't worry about a thing."

The babysitting arrangement appeared to be one of those spontaneous moments that afforded itself, but Mrs. Katherine's influence had been all over it from the very beginning.

The opportunity had presented itself a few days earlier at breakfast when Martha mentioned to Mrs. Katherine the need to get some outfits for her new job. Martha had commented that she hoped May would be able to watch the girls.

That afternoon at the Long home, Mrs. Katherine had asked May if she could take old Mr. Tyler into town for his doctor's appointment, if she would watch the girls. Martha's shopping trip and Mr. Tyler's doctor's appointment conflicted at the moment when Mrs. Katherine wanted them to, just as she, Martha, May and Dan were sitting alone together under the shade trees. Dan volunteered his services, as she knew he would. It was a spontaneous moment as far as the victims were concerned. Just the way great manipulators like Mrs. Katherine meant for them to seem.

Martha and Mrs. Katherine drove off in Martha's four-door Chevrolet just after breakfast, leaving Mrs. Katherine's '45 Plymouth for Dan and the girls.

"All right girls, what needs to be done here?"

"First we wash up the breakfast dishes and then our chores," replied a practical Wanda Faye.

"Chores," repeated Amy Sue, somewhat dismayed.

"Good," said Dan. "Wanda Faye, you take care of the kitchen and Amy Sue and I will see to the chores."

"Yes!" cried out the younger girl as she took Dan by the hand.

"Ah, but first what are the chores?" questioned Dan.

"I show you chores," said Amy Sue leading him down to the back porch. "Feed King his food and cow her corn, and water too."

Dan looked to Wanda Faye and she nodded her approval. After the kitchen and the chores were done, they retired to the front porch swing and waited for Dorothy, May and the girls.

"What cun-tree is Wes Ver-gin-nee in?" asked Amy Sue picking through the words very carefully.

"West Virginia is a state, just like Kentucky," responded Dan. "As a matter of fact we are neighbors, West Virginia and Kentucky."

"You could say we are cousins," lectured Wanda Faye. "West Virginia and Kentucky were both Virginia Territory before they became states. Kentucky was part of the frontier, until Daniel Boone opened it up to settlers. He was a great frontiersman."

"Me would like to be Daniel Boone," responded Amy Sue.

"I've read a lot about Boone and his adventures," said Dan. "Did you know he was captured and lived with an Indian tribe."

"Me like to live with Indians," said Amy Sue.

"Oh, flitter!" scolded Wanda Faye. "They would trade you for a horse."

"Me worth more than one horse!"

Out in the lane May pulled up in the yard. As Dan walked down to meet her, Rebecca and Elizabeth ran up and crowded onto the swing.

"Morning, Dan."

"Good morning, May. Thanks for letting the girls come with us. We have a big day planned."

"Have a good time," smiled May, "and if you need rescuing, just give me a call."

"Thanks, but we'll be fine. We are going to have lunch in town and stop by the Tasty Freeze on the way home after the movie. I promise to return two tired girls."

"Don't count on it," yelled May. As she backed out of the yard, Dorothy came walking up the lane.

*   *   *   *

"What do you think," asked Martha. She slowly turned in a circle to show off the calf length brown dress suit she had tried on.

"Very nice. I think that one, the two blues suits, blue is definitely your color, honey, and that forest green dress with the flowers."

Martha looked at her with surprise. "I thought we decided that the hem was too short on the dress."

"You decided the hem was too short. Just below the knee has a long way to go up before reaching too short."

"I've never worn anything that short," said Martha. "The white trilliums on the dark green background are beautiful, but what would people say?"

"They'd say you have the prettiest legs in Adair County."

"Oh, flitter!"

✳   ✳   ✳   ✳

Dan looked around the table at the four girls and then at their plates. There was enough uneaten food, hamburger and hot-dog parts to have kept two men alive for a week at Camp Two. An uneasy feeling had come over him as he watched the girls being so wasteful. They had starved and even used dead friends to get more food. They had eaten rotten fish with maggots on it. They ate the maggots! Now these children were wasting food while guys were still held captive in North Korea.

"Mr. Welch, Mr. Welch. Can I have some more ketchup, please?"

Looking down at Elizabeth and her big brown eyes, the bad memories melted away, "Of course you can, sweetheart," and he picked up the bottle and put a large helping of ketchup on her plate. She grabbed a fry, dipped it and stuck the whole thing in her mouth. Dan smiled.

On the ride home the girls sang fragmented songs, jumping from one tune to another, a melody of sorts, a combination of country, hymns and popular. When the girls were stumped Dan chimed in with a country western song he knew. The girls would pick up on the words quickly and sing along.

Judging by the mix of laughter and screams, they had enjoyed the matinee, *Abbott and Costello Meet Dr. Jekyll and Mr. Hyde*. He had bought them each a popcorn and soft drink. He saw most of the movie, except for the periodic bathroom trips the girls would need to take. Ice cream topped off the afternoon.

When he dropped Rebecca and Elizabeth off at their house, May waved from the kitchen. The girls stopped briefly to wave, before entering the back door.

As they pulled up in the yard, Martha and Mrs. Katherine sat on the swing talking, Junior sitting in Mrs. Katherine's lap. Of course, Dan was invited to stay for supper, and not wanting to overstay his welcome, he politely declined. But, as he sat at the table waiting for the fried potatoes to be passed around, he tried to remember how that sincere effort to decline ended with him at the supper table. He recalled how Mrs. Katherine was insistent and the girls had grabbed both hands and pulled him onto the porch. How could he refuse?

The girls picked at their food, until Martha excused them from the table to get ready for bed. Returning with lightweight cotton pajamas on, they gave Dan a good night hug around the neck and retired to their room to read. Exhaustion brought on sleep very quickly for little Amy Sue. Wanda Faye read for about thirty minutes, before turning over and going sound asleep. Martha checked on them just before the adults had dessert and placed *Little Women* back in Wanda's bookcase. She tucked in their sheets and turned out the light.

Dan sat at the table, covered with dishes containing various delights. There were pork chops, simmered in gravy, cream corn, garden tomatoes, and of course, the fried potatoes. It was just about as good as it could get. He had picked at his food at Circle R and resisted eating too much popcorn at the theater. But now, he ate until he was comfortably satisfied and then ate a little more, leaving room for a piece of butterscotch pie. Mrs. Katherine cut a healthy piece and placed it on his plate. The slice of pie held together perfectly, from its flaky crust, all the way up through the two inches of white meringue.

"Thank you," said Dan as she put the pie on his plate and poured hot coffee for him and Martha.

"Wonderful! If I were a few years older and you a few younger, I'd let you break my heart, Mrs. Katherine."

"Darling, I'd still be older than your mother and besides, I didn't make that pie. Direct all comments to the lady of the house."

He turned to Martha and smiled, "Perfectly delicious, Martha."

"Thank you, Dan."

"It shouldn't take but a couple of minutes to straighten up in here. Why don't you two go sit on the porch where it's cool."

"Yes, it would be nice to visit a while before you head up the road, Dan. You must come too Mrs. Katherine. The dishes will wait."

"It would be impossible for me to relax knowing this mess is here. You two go on and I'll be right out. Now go along." And she motioned toward the front door.

"It has been a blessing for the children to have so much of your time and attention, Dan. They seem to have taken to you, and I might add, you to them."

Martha sat in the swing while Dan sat in a chair, he had brought from the kitchen.

"Howard told me so much about them I feel like I've known them since their birth. I could have picked them out in a crowd. It's strange. I've got two families here in my heart that I brought back from Korea. Leo's parents," and he looked up at Martha, "and you and the girls. I feel close to both of you."

"It's God's gift that you brought memories of Howard back for us. I'm sure Leo's parents will feel the same when you visit them. In some ways your visit has helped ease the pain."

"It's something I felt I had to do."

"After your visit with Mr. and Mrs. Jawaski, what then? Surely you have family back home?"

"I plan to attend to my personal business before going to New York. It shouldn't take long. If there appears to be something to return to, I will go back to Valley Head and try to settle down." Dan looked downcast, staring down at the porch floor. "I'm not sure what my choices will be, but I'll have to see."

Martha looked at Dan with a deep feeling of compassion. Before her sat the man who had cared for and had been her husband's closest friend the last months of his life. She knew what she wanted to say, but wasn't sure how he would take it. Then she thought about how Dan had not hesitated to see to Howard when he himself was barely able to exist. She stopped swinging and sat forward on the swing. Dan looked up as she spoke.

"The one thing I feel compelled to point out is that you have the saddest eyes I have ever seen. Please allow me this slight indiscretion. I look into them, admiring their color and expressiveness. They smile when you're happy and seem full of pain when you're sad," Martha hesitated. "Your eyes should be full of life, but they are filled with sadness. I understand why they are like that now, but trust me Dan, things are going to get better. I believe our lives are an unwritten book that we can finish anyway we wish. We simply have to believe it to be so."

Dan sat in silence wanting to respond to what Martha had just said, but not knowing how to express his feelings. All he knew was that Martha was a very special lady, too fine of a lady for a country boy from the West Virginia Mountains.

If he actually had a choice, if his story was yet to be written, he didn't deserve a family like Martha and the girls. It couldn't be. He had the perfect wife and had lost her. He sat silent, watching as Martha sat back and began to swing back and forth again. The longer the silence continued, the more uncomfortable they both felt. Dan began to realize that maybe she was right. Maybe he could write some things about his future. He looked up to speak, to tell her what he really wanted, and the screen door opened and Mrs. Katherine stepped out on the porch. For the next hour small talk was made concerning the day's events, the shopping trip and the trip to town with the girls. They talked until dark and Dan finally stood, thanking them both for an enjoyable evening. It was a few minutes before ten o'clock and as he walked up the road to the Long home, he felt a sense of inner comfort. He had failed to tell Martha how he felt, but he had thought it and admitted it to himself. For once in a long while he felt good about his future and felt he was beginning to heal.

Back on the porch Martha and Mrs. Katherine sat on the swing and watched as Dan waved one last time and disappeared into the darkness.

"I like that boy," said Mrs. Katherine.

"He is a good man who took on a heavy burden and still carries a considerable amount of it deep in his soul. I just wonder what choices he will make, if he ever reaches a point where he can leave the burden behind."

Mrs. Katherine eyed Martha and wondered the same question.

*   *   *   *

The old suitcase sat next to Silas' automobile. In it were Dan's army fatigues and combat boots, along with a few other things he had when he arrived in Kentucky. There were also a few new things. A pair of partially worn bib overalls and brogans he had purchased. There was also a green John Deere cap. The bill was folded just right, the way he had folded and molded ball caps since he was a kid. The cap was sweat and grease stained, and would probably have been tossed by a less loyal owner, but to Dan it was only now reaching a point of acceptable wear.

It was late October and three days earlier the neighborhood had awakened to fall's first frost. The Long's, like most farming families, were ready for whatever the upcoming winter might bring. The feed corn was off the stalk and in the crib, the baled hay out of the fields and stacked in the barn lofts. The tobacco was hanging heavy on sticks in the barn, waiting patiently to come into case. Hams were hanging in the smokehouse curing and below them on the cellar floor, potatoes and walnuts were spread out on cardboard. Sitting on the shelves in the mudroom were Mason and Ball jars full of pork, vegetables and many other edible items. Practically everything that could grow in the garden was canned. The harvest was plentiful. The Long family was blessed with God's bountiful grace.

Dan came out of the mudroom door, dressed in his army dress uniform. It had hung loosely on him when he first arrived. Now it fit the way a uniform was supposed to fit. He carried his service cap in his hand.

May and the girls followed him out of the house. She carried a brown paper sack, something she had put together for his lunch while he waited for his flight. Jordan and Silas were chatting beside the automobile. Dan turned to May and she handed him the sack lunch.

"I don't know that I will ever be able to thank you for all your kindness," he said.

"It was our pleasure. You will always be welcome here, Dan. Remember that you have friends in Gadberry."

"I will, May," and they hugged. He stooped, motioning for the girls to come and give him a hug. As they did, May looked over her shoulder at the sound of a car turning into the driveway and smiled. It was Martha, Mrs. Katherine, and the children. Dan stood and a warm feeling came over him as the car pulled up.

"Lordy!" exclaimed Mrs. Katherine as she climbed out of the car. We thought for sure we were going to miss you. Little Miss Fancy Pants here just couldn't seem to get herself out to the car."

Amy Sue stood with her chin to her chest, looking at the ground, while Wanda Faye walked over to Dan.

"Mr. Welch, I am sorry that you must go."

Behind her Amy Sue quietly said, "Sorry."

Wanda Faye handed Dan a small gift wrapped in white tissue paper.

"Thank you, Wanda. You shouldn't have." He kneeled next to her and opened the gift, a small-framed picture of the girls with their father. Dan was overcome with emotion. The picture must have been taken just before Howard left for the war. There kneeling between the girls was a strong, handsome looking man. A broad smile on his face, registering the joy he felt when he was around his two girls. Tears burned Dan's eyes. He had only known Howard as a sick, emaciated man, weak from injury and disease.

"Darling, thank you, but I can't take your picture."

"My dad would have wanted you to have it. You can remember him and remember me."

"Remember me," came a soft echo from behind her.

Dan hugged Wanda Faye. He patted her on the back and said, "I will always keep it next to my bed and every night before I go to sleep, I will think of my favorite girls and their dad." Wanda Faye kissed him on the cheek and walked over to Mrs. Katherine. Taking a handkerchief from his pocket he wiped the tears from his eyes and reached out with his right-hand motioning for Amy Sue to come over to him. She hesitated for a moment and then ran to him, wrapping her arms around his neck.

"You no go." She whispered in his ear.

Standing up with the small child in his arms he said, "I have things I must see to, Amy. I have to go home."

"This your home."

Dan was speechless as he held the child in his arms.

He finally said. "Gadberry will always have a special place in my heart. You and Wanda Faye will always be special to me."

"You get home, I write," said the young girl.

"And I write you."

Dan kissed her on the cheek, handed her to Mrs. Katherine and said, "I don't know which I will miss the most, your cooking, your wit, or your friendship."

"I suspect it should be all of those things," said Mrs. Katherine dryly, but she gave herself away as a tear rolled out of the corner of her eye and down her cheek.

Dan took his handkerchief and wiped it away.

She hugged him and whispered in his ear, "Daniel look around you. There is a lot of love for you here. Always remember that you are cared for here."

"I will never forget, Mrs. Katherine." Dan turned and walked to Martha, her son in her arms. He noticed for the first time the stunning sundress she had on. The white Trillium flowers with the dark green background reminded him of mountain valleys back home. Taking her hand he said, "I'm sorry I couldn't bring Howard home to you."

"Oh, but you did Dan. More than you can ever realize. You brought us out of the darkness with memories of Howard's last days. That's very special to us. It's something that will help us get on with our lives, a gift we will always cherish."

With that she hugged Dan tightly for several moments, Junior grabbing at his ear. She finally turned and walked over to Mrs. Katherine and the girls. Dan walked to the auto and got in as Silas climbed behind the steering wheel and Jordan got in the backseat. As the automobile drove out the drive the mental picture of Martha holding Junior, and Wanda Faye, and Mrs. Katherine holding Amy Sue, was burned in his memory.

✴   ✴   ✴   ✴

Martha held a letter in her hand from Bob Green. He had arrived on the west coast full of hope for the future, only to learn that Howard had passed away at Ft. Mason. He walked around depressed and gloomy for a couple of days feeling sorry for himself. Howard was his inspiration, the camp inspiration. He was the guy who, despite his horrible condition, would never give up, always fighting, even when he couldn't do for himself and needed constant care and attention. He would always bounce back, defying the dark angel of death. There were times when despair and hopelessness were overwhelming and in the depths of self-pity he would look up and see Howard struggling down the hall, grimacing in pain on his way to the stoop to be with the guys. Instinctively he would move to assist him, taking a few moments to forget about his own plight. It was valuable medicine.

It didn't cure the feelings he was having, but it did snap him back to a level of emotional functioning that was survivable. He, like many other men at Camp Two, owed their lives to the Kentucky farmer. The realization that he hadn't survived long enough to see his family had shocked the men.

Sitting at the mess hall table sipping strong army coffee, he had stared blindly at a recruiting poster on the wall and finally came to the decision that he would write Martha and share his feelings concerning her husband. In doing that he might be able to pay back a little of the enormous debt he owed.

When Martha read the letter for the first time, she was moved by the emotion Green shared concerning Howard's impact on the men at the camp. The true significance of the letter didn't sink in until she read it aloud to Mrs. Katherine:

August 4, 1954

Dear Mrs. Lowe,

> *I have to beg your forgiveness for waiting so long to write. My thoughts and time have been with my family since my return to the states last November. It is difficult to find the words that I want to express. I, along with many other prisoners who served in captivity with your husband in North Korea, were shocked and saddened to learn of his passing when we reached the states. Howard was a true inspiration for many of us. I would*

not have made it back without the example he set in his daily fight to survive and get back home to his family.

Howard's thoughts were always with you and the children. Even in those times when he was so ill, he could barely speak a struggled word here and there, he confessed his immense love for you. In those periods of severe illness, Dan Welch, his friend and attendant, recorded his whispered devotions. Dan would lean down close to him to get every word for the letters he wrote for Howard. He was a very loyal friend to Howard and to my knowledge composed and wrote most of his letters. I pray that you might eventually receive all of Howard's letters. I would also hope that you might have the opportunity to meet Dan Welch.

I will soon be home with my Doris, but my thoughts will never be far from Howard. It is with great admiration and love that I can say I wish you and the children the very best in the future.

Respectfully, Bob Green

"I remember Dan talking about a Bob Green. He was one of the men that helped him take care of Howard. I suspect there's not a person in Gadberry that wouldn't be able to write a similar letter. At home or halfway around the world, your Howard shared himself with others."

Martha smiled, a bit misty eyed. "I shall write Mr. Green tomorrow, right after evening worship."

"Let me see that letter, child." Martha handed Green's letter to Mrs. Katherine. "Let's see now," she said as she scanned down the contents of the letter.

"Here it is: '*In those periods of severe illness his friend and attendant recorded his whispered devotions. Dan would lean down close to him to get every word for the letters he wrote for Howard. He was a very loyal friend to Howard and composed and wrote most of his letters.*'"

With a serious look on her face Mrs. Katherine looked down at Martha as she sat at the kitchen table. "I recall Howard's letters that got through. If I were you, I think I would want to read them again."

CHAPTER 19

▼

Dan sat up on the back seat of the Buick convertible waving to the people who lined Davis Avenue in Elkins, West Virginia. Next to him sat Joe Kirby, mayor of the small mountain town and a veteran of the First World War. He smiled and waved to the people taking advantage of an opportunity to be seen with the hometown war hero.

The Elkins High School sixteen-piece marching band marched ahead of the automobile. Just finishing Sousa's "Stars and Stripes Forever" they struck up "Yankee Doodle," to the cheers of the crowd lining the street.

Out into the street ahead of the car ran ten-year-old Denise Welch, Dan's second cousin. The Buick slowed to a stop and Dan leaned over, picked Denise up and sat her between him and the mayor. The child beamed with innocent pride. Mayor Kirby beamed with political savvy. Nothing increased voter appeal like a small child.

Dan gazed about as they drove along, taking in the crowd of familiar faces. Behind them an automobile horn blew, adding to the noise and commotion. As the Mayor and Denise continued to wave, he looked back over his shoulder, and the auto's headlamps flashed bright. Dan waved. Up ahead was the Randolph County Courthouse, its stone tower looming above them, visible in the moonlight.

From behind the horn blew again, much more annoying this time, much louder. The music of the marching band faded as the driver persisted in laying on his horn. Dan refused to look back at the driver, but did glance in his mirror as he gripped the steering wheel tightly with both hands.

In front of him the traffic light at the intersection of Davis and 3rd had turned red for a second time. To either side of the street, a few bystanders stared. There was no marching band, no mayor, and no white Buick convertible. He closed his eyes and squeezed the wheel with both hands.

From behind, once again the horn sounded causing him to open his eyes with a jerk. The traffic light was green. He reached over and turned the radio on, as the 1950 Pontiac Chieftain rolled through the intersection and down the street.

The music of Hank Williams filled the car.

Jambalaya, crawfish pie and filet gambo
'Cos tonight I'm gonna see my cher amio . . .

When Dan's flight arrived in Charleston that morning, he stood in front of the airport terminal and hailed a cab.

"What's the bus to Elkins going to run me?" He asked settling into the back seat of the cab.

"The train'll be a right smart faster. Bus'll stop fer every wide spot and coonhound in the road 'tween here and Kingdom Come. I'd be a takin' the train," the cabby looked back over his shoulder, "if I were you, but a course, I ain't."

"The train depot it is."

The cabbie flipped up the flag on the meter and drove down the terminal drive. "Jest gettin' back from the war, are ya?"

"You might say that. I'm looking to get my job back at the Tygart Coal Company."

"There's jobs a plenty, if you don't mind crawling underground. Coal's a riding high. You got a car waiting at home?"

"Nope, but I plan to get one."

"You'll want to be a visiting the bank, then?"

"Not necessary, I just got a couple years back pay."

The cabbie glanced in his rear-view mirror at Dan for a moment with a quizzical look, threw the cab in gear and gunned it into traffic.

Dan stepped on board and took a seat next to a window as the Western Maryland coach prepared to depart for Elkins. Moments after the conductor shouted, *"Alllll-aaa-board, Alllll-a-board,"* the engineer signaled with a double whistle, followed by the turn of the engine wheels. The engine moved, causing the line of coach cars to jolt, one after the other. The succession of motion slowly started the train of cars out of Charleston's busy rail yard. After the conductor called for tickets, Dan took off his coat, loosened his tie and took off his shoes. The engine gradually picked up speed and was soon making good time through the endless mountains and valleys. The autumn colored trees, the boulder filled streams, rock bluffs and meadows all painted a picture of home in Dan's mind.

The train climbed a steep grade, leveled out and picked up speed, only to slow as it went into a sharp curve. The clapping sound of steel faded behind him as the remaining cars shifted through the curve. He had grabbed a *Charleston Gazette* at the air terminal and read through it as the train crawled through the mountainous terrain. Articles on President Eisenhower and American POWs shared the headlines, equally. The subtitle on the POW article proclaimed, *"Some Choose Communism Over Home."* Dan's interest focused immediately on the POW article, which listed names of deserters and pending court marshals for collaborators.

As he read, he looked for the name Paulson had mentioned several times during his interrogations. When "Nate Smith" failed to appear, Dan grinned triumphantly.

Buried toward the back of the front section was an article about the continued repatriation of the American POWs. The article stated that Operation Big Switch was bringing the American boys home. Dan wondered about his friends, wondered if they made it home alive. They were all in pretty good shape when he and Howard had departed, but fortunes changed very quickly for POWs in a prison camp, and not always for the best. Several of the men promised to contact one another once they settled. Dan carried the list of addresses in his wallet. After he took care of his business he would write. That way he would have something to write about.

As they reached the east side of the mountain, the train slowed and began its decline into the Tygart River valley. The Charleston cabby's assumption that trains make fewer stops wasn't necessarily so. Dan's train had stopped in every little switch town between Charleston and Elkins. Switch towns or wide spots, they were all the same.

"Next stop, Tygart Junction!" yelled out the conductor as he walked from coach to coach.

*   *   *   *

The Pontiac dealer was a WWII vet. He and Dan talked about cars and about battles, won and lost until after dark. Dan told him about Leo, Howard and his stay in Gadberry. The dealer excused himself several times during the evening to close a deal, always returning with a big grin on his face. A middle-aged mechanic knocked at the door and waited patiently until the owner recognized him.

"Is she cleaned up, Paul?"

"We started in on her about an hour ago Mr. Clemons, and I got to tell you, she looks as good as new now. Mrs. Clemons sure took good care of her. You think she'll like the new Chieftain?"

Lester Clemons pointed his Dark Certified Bond cigar at a maroon two-door convertible sitting on the showroom floor. The chrome bumper, trim work and spoke hub caps glistened under the show room lights. The white top was down and the white interior matched the wide, white walled tires perfectly. A slightly larger body than last year's model, the automobile proudly featured a new design concept—a one-piece windshield.

"I might not be able to figure out where the wife wants to eat after Sunday service, but one thing I do know is, *automobiles!*" He said with a loud bellowing voice. "I've been trying to figure out what to get Harriett for our twentieth wedding anniversary and this young man helped me make up my mind. Oh, she'll be thrilled, Paul, or I'll have to give you a sweet deal for your Julie Ann."

"She'd think I was feeling guilty about something, Mr. Clemons," said the chief mechanic as he tossed the keys to the 1950 Chieftain across the desk. Clemons laughed as he caught the keys and quickly came around the desk.

"Let's go take a look at your new wheels, Private."

Dan obediently followed the retired Marine Gunny Sergeant. In the garage a few mechanics were punching out for the day, while a couple of salesmen bickered with the general manager about who got to drive a new Catalina home for the night. At the end of the garage was a small room where autos were detailed. A Pontiac Chieftain sat there shining under the bright overhead lights. Dan slowly walked a circle around the car, from the fender covers on the back-wheel wells to the trademark orange Indian head that adorned the hood. He thought the white wall tires were brand new, but after sitting behind the wheel he realized the three-year-old car had only two thousand miles on it.

"Beauty, isn't she? When I say she was only driven to church on Sunday, it's only a slight exaggeration."

Dan suddenly lost his smile and stepped out of the car. "I can't afford this, Mr. Clemons."

"Of course, you can, son. You've earned it. Let's go write up that contract."

Clemons wheeled around and headed back to his office. Dan caught up with him as he sat down and pulled a blank contract from a desk drawer.

"Seriously, Mr. Clemons, I don't think I should buy such an expensive automobile. I have lots of back pay, but I've got some business to see to at home and in New York. I don't think it wise to leave all of my money here with you."

Clemons looked up from his desk and nodded his approval. He scribbled a price on the contract and handed it to Dan. "Sit down son, and let's haggle over the price."

Dan looked at the price on the contact and looked up over the desk at the husky cigar smoking automobile dealer.

"I don't understand, sir?"

"Call me Gunny, and let me tell you something, son. I personally made five times that amount this evening while you and I traded war stories. I'm letting you have it at what I would pay someone on a trade in, less a dollar a day for everyday you were a prisoner in North Korea. I know it seems like a lot of people in this country don't appreciate what you boys did over there, but a lot of us do. I've been blessed and it helps me to look in the mirror every morning if I occasionally share that blessing. I can't force you to buy this automobile, but if you think you want to, you count out your money while I finish writing out this contract."

The men sat quietly on either side of the desk, counting and writing. Out in the parking lot, the 1950 Chieftain sat next to the newer '53 model.

"Clemons Pontiac, you'll always walk away with a smile," said Clemons proudly pointing up to a big sign with his cigar. He turned and shook Dan's hand. "Drive carefully and good luck, son. Bring that young lady of yours from Gadberry back up here for a visit, and maybe we can work out a nice deal for her on this little convertible."

Dan watched as Clemons climbed into the new Chieftain and drove off. Settling down behind the wheel of his new automobile he shook his head and mumbled to himself, "Is it that obvious?"

Pick guitar, fill fruit jar and be gay-o
Son of a gun, we'll have big fun on the bayou

"Good old Hank, man I've missed him," said Dan out loud to himself as he drove out of the Elkin city limits into the countryside.

As he pulled into Aunt Betsy's yard the radio was just finishing a song by the Texas Troubadour, Ernest Tubb:

I'm walking the floor over you,
I can't sleep a wink that is true.

Dan cut the engine and Tubb off in mid chorus, and sat there staring at his Aunt's home. Up on the veranda Aunt Betsy came out the front door and stared down at the parked car. Squinting, she peered out over her spectacles. Dan opened the door and as he stepped out in the moonlight, a smile of recognition flooded her face. She raised the hand that always held a handkerchief to her mouth and hurried down the steps, meeting him down in the yard.

"Oh, is it you, Danny? Are you finally home?" They collided in a big hug and stood together motionless under an age-old maple tree.

"Hi, Auntie. It is good to be home."

She took him by the shoulders and shoved him back an arm's length for a good look.

"Lord, have mercy! It looks like they starved you to death. I'll fix something to eat and you can tell me all about your big adventure. I've laid some of your things out in your old room."

The two walked up the hill together. Aunt Betsy went to the kitchen, reheating some leftovers, while Dan got out of his uniform and freshened up. He stood in front of the mirror and looked at his face. It was good that May's cooking had filled him out some.

On the bed lay a pair of pleated slacks and his favorite flannel shirt. His black loafers were parked on the floor. Walking down the wooden staircase he remembered how neat his aunt kept her place.

"My, my, you look so much better out of that stuffy uniform. That's the Danny I know."

In front of him she sat a plate covered with ample portions of corn, collard greens, lima beans, fried catfish, and a side dish of coleslaw. Dan sprinkled a touch of vinegar on the greens and a light dusting of pepper on everything. She poured a fresh glass of ice tea for both of them and waited anxiously.

"It's just leftovers. I hope it's okay."

"Everything's great, Auntie."

Betsy smiled. "I didn't think you were ever coming home. I got your last letter…I finally got all your letters a month ago. The mail must be awful slow. We'll sit down after you have rested and you can tell me all about your war. But first, I suppose you want to know about Amelia."

Dan didn't look up from his plate.

"I would like to see her. Maybe I can talk some sense into her."

Betsy sat across from him tightlipped, wanting to speak, but didn't. Dan looked up and said, "Straight up, the truth Auntie." Dan knew the circles his aunt associated with would have the latest on Amelia. He also knew he could trust her to tell him everything, straight up.

"She started stepping out just after you left," she sighed and paused for a moment, looking him in the eyes, "straight up?"

Dan nodded.

"She started running around on you long before you left for the war. All those nights you worked overtime trying to keep her in money, she was working some overtime herself."

"Anyone I know?"

"No, Danny. Your friends stayed away from her. Randy Singer confronted her at the Elks Lodge one night and she told him to get lost. The club manager showed her and her escort to the door. When she filed for divorce, Donna Lewis down at the County Clerk's office called me. It was quite a scandal around these parts, with you a prisoner and all. She couldn't find a local lawyer to represent her and I hear tell she had to go up to Barbour County to find one. When I got off the phone with Donna, I called her and she said she had your things boxed up and I should come and get them before she sat them on the corner. I asked her why, and she said she never bargained on being lonely all the time. I lost my temper and told her everyone in Elkins knew just how little she had been lonely, and she hung up on me. I shouldn't have lost control. I'm sorry I spoke like that to her."

Dan had listened very intently as Betsy recounted the events with some emotion in her voice. He looked up and smiled with an understanding look, and took her hand. "You have nothing to be sorry for, Auntie. It must have been very difficult for you."

"I drove over and when I got there all your stuff was sitting out in the hall. She wouldn't even answer the door. It took me five trips up and down those stairs to get it all out to the car. I haven't talked to her since."

"Do you think she will talk to me?"

"There's more, Danny."

The tone of his aunt's voice brought his eyes up from the plate.

"She's had a child," and she quickly added, "too young to be yours."

Dan stared out the window past his aunt's face.

"If you still want to see her, she moved out of your apartment and is with the father of the child. He has a little rundown house near the edge of town, in Elkins. I don't know if she will talk with you or not."

His aunt was having a harder time telling the news than he was taking it.

Amelia's behavior seemed insignificant compared to what he had been through over the past two years. The one thing he did know for sure was that he loved his aunt and she loved him. He got up and walked around the table and gave her a long hug.

"Thanks, Auntie. I knew I could depend on you."

＊   ＊   ＊   ＊

"Well, I'll be damn! Look at what the cat drug in." Mark Gregory pushed away from the corner desk he occupied in the mine shack. He'd been foreman at Tygart Coal Company's Number 2 shaft for the last fifteen years. His father held the position before him. He took Dan's hand and gave it a vigorous shake.

"It's good to see you, Mr. Gregory."

"We kept up with you best we could, Dan. We're awful glad you beat those bastards and made it back home safe. Have a seat, son. How long you been back?"

"Not long, sir. I spent some time in Kentucky taking care of some business for a friend. I've got something I have to see to in New York and I'll be ready to come back to work."

"Good! Production is running full steam right now and we need an experienced seam ripper, Simmons is down with the cough. We hit a wide seam over a year ago, and we're still working it. It's five-feet-high and we can't dig enough of it. It's always been boom or bust in the coal business. I'll hold your old job for two weeks so you can take care of your business. It will be good to have you back."

"I'm not sure I can go back down underground, sir. The prison camps changed a lot of things for me."

"Hogwash, boy, you belong down there. Coal is in your blood, just like your dad and his dad before him."

The phone on his desk started clicking and Gregory snapped it up. "Gregory here. Be right there." Gregory headed for the door. "Got a conveyer belt slipping and slate pickers standing around. Sit down boy, I'll be back in a few minutes."

Dan sat back in his chair as the door slammed behind the foreman. The metal shed rattled and small puffs of coal dust drifted down from the ceiling. The fresh smell of coal dust reminded him of his summers working at the mine as a slate picker. The Elkin's coalfield seams had impurities. The slate pickers would stand on a narrow platform beside the conveyor that carried the coal to the railroad hopper cars. They would pick the slate out and toss it over on a small platform.

When there was no more room on the platform it was shoveled down to the ground where a front-end loader picked it up and deposited it somewhere out of the way, usually between two hills. At a coal mine the landscape changed above the ground as well as below.

Those were tough times, but happy times when his dad was still strong and working. The three of them lived in a company house up in Barbour County, north of Elkins. The company store provided everything they needed. His mom was born a Hutton and became a Welch at fifteen, despite her family's objections. Aunt Betsy took him in when his mother died with the breast cancer, within a year of his dad's death. Betsy took good care of him, but Dan never got over the feeling of missing his parents.

The cabin door swung open and closed with a bang. "Why can't I find a damn machinist who can read a schematic? That's the third cog wheel Altman's made in the past month and he still can't get it right." Gregory stopped and looked down at Dan. "Now what's this foolishness about not wanting to go down in the mines?"

The words stung, but he didn't feel foolish. It was all about being trapped, the fear of confined places. It was the memory of listening to his dad gargling, fighting for every breath as the fibrosis finally turned his lungs to mush. He felt humiliated having to explain himself, so he didn't.

"I'd like to come back, Mr. Gregory," Dan said standing. "You know I can do any of the jobs above ground and I'm dependable, but I won't go underground. I would appreciate it if you would keep me in mind. It was good to see you and thanks for taking the time to talk to me. I need to go."

The phone clicked as Dan went out the door, "Gregory here, *Too much dust!* They don't get paid to whine. We needed to be through that sandstone yesterday . . . I don't care if he can't breathe, if he's not back on the miner in five minutes cutting through that damn sandstone wall, you'll be on it!"

He slammed down the phone and growled to himself, "These lazy asses are killing me!"

*   *   *   *

Dan parked his car just off the corner of Davis and 3rd, and walked down to a small diner. It was lunchtime and the place was beginning to fill up with customers. The waitress led him to a table out in the middle of the room.

"Could I have the table against the wall, please?"

"Why sure, darling, you can sit anywhere you want." She led him over to a table against the wall and placed flatware at the outside chair.

"Coffee, honey?"

"Yes, ma'am. Cream and sugar please."

"My name is Cynthia and I'll be back in a shake with some coffee."

When she returned Dan was sitting with his back to the wall looking out on the crowd and the front windows.

"So ya like to see whose coming and going, do ya?"

Dan smiled. He had tried to sit with his back to people in Kentucky, but it made him feel very uneasy. The waitress poured him a cup of coffee.

"What will it be, darling?"

"You still have the chicken salad sandwich plate."

"You got it."

"And a Coke-Cola soft drink."

"Done."

Amelia lived down at the end of the street. Dan had arrived in Elkins a little too early to call on her. He drove around town and decided a quiet lunch would settle his nerves a little. He had been feeling anxious all morning. It was a few minutes after eleven and the café was beginning to fill up.

"Hon, can I get you something else?" It was now a quarter after twelve and Dan had finished eating thirty minutes ago.

"No thanks, Cynthia." She eyed him, nodded and went on to check on her other tables. Dan left two quarters on the table. At the cash register he was standing in line with his wallet out and a five in his hand. Outside on the street a coal truck geared down to stop for a stoplight and backfired with a loud, *boom!* A lady sitting at the counter screamed. At the cash register another lady screamed and a man was knocked to the floor. Loud words were exchanged. The hostess who was ringing up the check for the man on the floor stared down at her feet and yelled, *"Bill!"*

The manager came out of the kitchen and quickly calmed the customers. The waitress continued to point down at the floor, until Bill leaned over and looked behind the counter.

"Hey! What's your problem, buddy?"

He leaned over a little further, "Hey! I'm talking to you!"

Dan looked up into the angry face of the manager. Sweat was already dripping from his pale face. His body trembled. He attempted to stand, but his legs couldn't hold his weight. Cynthia came around the counter and squatted next to him.

In a calm voice she said, "Are you okay, darling?"

Dan looked up with wide-eyed confusion.

"Come on, darling." She took him by the arm and gently helped him to his feet. Everyone stared at them as she walked him over to an empty table.

"Have him pay his tab and get him out of here, Cynthia. We don't need a nut case hanging around here scaring the customers."

"Can't you see he's a vet, Bill? What's wrong with you?"

"What's wrong with me? What the hell is wrong with him?" snapped back Bill with a restrained voice.

"You just leave him alone, you hear me. He'll be fine in a few minutes, once he catches his breath."

"He's got ten minutes. You go back to work."

"I'm on break," she said throwing back her shoulders. "Alice, can you take my tables?"

"Not a problem, Cynthia," said Alice as she stood defiantly with one hand on her hip and the other holding a tray with three orders of burgers and fries.

"Ten minutes," he repeated as he disappeared through the swinging door of the kitchen.

Cynthia poured Dan some coffee and added some cream and sugar.

"I Suwannee, all that screaming sounded like the ghost of Sharah Goodwest had dropped by for lunch." She looked down at Dan as he took the cup and saucer in both hands and brought both up to his mouth, the cup rattling against the saucer.

"I understand what happened, darling," she said as she pulled out a chair and sat down next to him.

"You could never understand," Dan said in a whisper.

"Oh, I understand more than you could ever imagine. Relax and have some coffee. I got your back. You'll leave when you're ready to leave. I'd like to tell you it's going to get better, but I won't lie. How long has it been since you were repatriated?"

Dan looked up from the coffee with sadness in his eyes and said, "About four months."

"You must be one of those boys I've been reading about who were just released in Korea."

Dan nodded his head and took another sip of coffee. The tension was beginning to fade in his body.

"Thanks for coming to my rescue. How'd you know?"

"Darling, that ain't nothing I haven't lived with since my Nathan got back from the Pacific in '45. I didn't pick up on it when you asked to sit facing the crowd and window. Lots of folks don't like people at their backs. When the truck backfired and I saw how quick you went over the counter, I knew. You see much action before you were captured?"

"Some. I spent my last eighteen months in the camps."

"Nathan spent thirty-three months in a Jap camp. He's tried to work, but can't stay focused. He won't tell me anything about what happened, but I know more than he realizes because I'm awake at night when he is having his nightmares. He goes to the grocery and keeps the pantry stocked with enough food to feed an army. I see him walking into the pantry three or four times a day checking to see if the food is still there. When we built our new home on the ridge, he wouldn't let the builder cut down any of the trees. He even planted pine trees to block the view from the road. I didn't understand at first, but now I do. It's the same deal as telling the builders to leave the windows off the side of the house the neighbor lives on. I thought it was the money, but now I know it makes him feel safe to have his own secure place. Sometimes it ain't easy to accept his anger, his loss of thought and mistrust."

"No one really understands," said Dan.

"You're right, darling, no one can ever understand who hasn't been through it. Nathan has a buddy over in Wheeling that was at the camp with him. He kept talking about him, about going to see him, but he never would go. I realized he could never talk to me, so I really pushed him hard to get in touch with him. Now they see each other nearly every month or two. His wife and I generally sit together while they go off someplace and talk about their secrets. We talk and compare notes. We know a lot more than they think we do. Nathan is kind hearted, but he has a tortured spirit. Despite all he goes through he's good to me, so I'll stick with him through thick and thin."

"He's lucky to have you."

"Yes he is, darling. Now, are you going to be okay?"

"Yes, I think so. Could you do this for me?" He held out the crumpled check and five-dollar bill.

"Sure thing."

"Thanks, Cynthia, you're terrific."

"You're welcome. You sit tight and I'll be right back with your change." She walked over and rang up the register. As she gathered his three dollars and something in change, a buffalo nickel appeared in her hand. Some good luck she thought, for someone who needs some. She looked up with a smile, but Dan had already left.

$$*\qquad*\qquad*\qquad*$$

It was mid-afternoon and the thunderstorm showed no signs of letting up. The dark clouds overhead hung low, barely visible through the heavy downpour. A black '46 Ford sat on the side of the street, its two passenger side tires on the curb. The hood was open and both tires were missing from the driver's side. A couple of cinder blocks held up each end. Unidentifiable parts were scattered about, suggesting the repairman might have been chased off by the storm. A closer look would have revealed the condition of the auto hadn't changed for several months. A steady stream of water ran down the street along the curb and into a distant sewer drain. The drain was partially clogged by a small moon shaped hubcap. A second hubcap inched along the curb, weighted down with rainwater and rusty lug nuts.

Parked down the street sat a Pontiac Chieftain, its headlamps off and windshield wipers fighting to keep the view through the windshield accessible. Inside the sound of Hank Williams filled the auto, keeping beat with the wipers:

I saw the light
I saw the light

Dan sat staring at the run-down home, next to the run-down automobile. The tops of scattered objects stuck up through the tall weeds in the yard. The weatherboard siding was void of paint and several boards were missing. He still felt tension and stress. The episode at the diner and the anticipation of seeing Amelia had combined to a point where he felt like an over inflated balloon that was ready to pop. He had sat for an hour waiting for the rain to let up. His patience was finally rewarded as the downpour shifted quickly to a light drizzle.

He jumped out and headed up the street to Amelia's home along the wide torrent of water streaming down the curb. He found a spot in front of the Ford that was narrow enough to leap across to the sidewalk. Walking slowly up the front walk, dodging the clutter he reached the door and knocked. Off in the distance a thunderclap rumbled. He waited a few minutes and knocked again, this time a little harder.

"Yes, yes, yes!" shouted a familiar voice from the other side. Dan's heart pounded. The doorknob turned, the door swung open and they stood face to face. Amelia stood there in a stained frock and house shoes. She appeared to be some fifty pounds or so heavier than when he saw her last. Her hair was bleached blond with about an inch of dark roots showing. A brush had been lightly run through it, sometime that morning. She wore no make-up and her face was puffy, especially around her eyes. Behind her on the floor sat a crying infant.

Dan smiled. Her demeanor remained flat.

"What do you want? I gave that nosey aunt of yours all your stuff."

Dan's heart raced. "I wanted to see how you were doing, Amelia. See if you needed anything."

"Does it look like I need anything?" Dan looked over her shoulder at the crying infant and the trash strewn about the small living room.

"I just thought I could . . ."

"Where's that beer? Damn it all! What do I have to do to get a beer around here?" came a loud, rough voice from somewhere in the house.

"In a minute!" Amelia screamed over her shoulder.

Dan suddenly felt chilled, damp and cold all over. The rain had picked up again. The gutter above him was stopped up and started spilling over, splattering on his shoes and pant legs.

"I wanted to . . ." A sudden lightening flash, accompanied instantly by a deafening *crack*, stood the hair up on the back of Dan's neck.

"Shit!" screamed Amelia as she slammed the door in his face.

Dan stood there frozen in fear. He could feel the cold steel of a pistol barrel against his temple.

"This time I not miss. What you unit?"

"Daniel Welch, Private, Serial Number 2165342"

"Then you die, American pig. Go through door. *Go now!*"

Dan stood for several moments staring at the door, fearing what was on the other side. He reached for the doorknob and gave it a shake. The door refused to budge.

"You go now!" and another shot was fired, causing the hair on his neck to stand up again and leaving his ears ringing.

He shook the door vigorously and it sprung open.

"Go! I said!" Somewhere in the distance Dan heard the faint sound of a baby crying.

"Gees, nobody's that stupid!" Amelia stood in the door, her face ugly, distorted with anger.

Dan looked down at her and was suddenly back in the moment. Behind Amelia stood an unshaven fellow in a tank undershirt and boxer shorts, with an empty beer bottle in his hand. He took Amelia by the arm and shoved her to one side.

"She's lazy and spends all my disability check. If you want her back the brat comes with her."

"What?" screamed Amelia, stepping up and slamming the door in Dan's face, once again.

Screaming and yelling started up on the other side of the door as Dan turned and walked away. He didn't feel at all like he thought he would. He did feel a deep sense of pity and sadness for the child, but profound relief as he slowly walked through the downpour, back to his automobile.

✱   ✱   ✱   ✱

"Danny!" Aunt Betsy stood in the middle of her kitchen with her favorite red and white checked apron on. Her hands were on her hips and she stared down at Dan sitting at the kitchen table. In front of him lay a day-old copy of the Washington Post. He stared out the window, tuning out the world.

"Daniel Owen Welch, you answer me this instant!" Betsy tried to sound loud and angry, but couldn't pull it off. Dan continued to stare out the window. She walked up behind him and calmly placed her hands on his shoulders.

He turned his head and looked up at her. "Hi, Auntie."

"Danny, are you okay?"

"Why yes, Auntie. I'm fine. Why do you ask?"

"I just, you seem so distant." She pulled the chair out next to his and sat down. Dan reached over and took her hands.

"I'm fine, honest, Auntie. I've got a lot of things on my mind, but Amelia is not one of them, if that's what's worrying you. She's out of my system. She seems to be in a very deserving relationship." Dan smiled and squeezed her hands.

"Danny, there are times when I speak to you and you don't answer. It's like you're not in the same room with me. I called to you twice just now and you never acknowledged you even heard me."

Dan looked surprised. He hadn't realized he was continuing to tune people out.

"I will do better, I promise. Sometimes I go into a trance."

As they talked a knock came at the front door. Aunt Betsy jumped up and hurried off. In a few moments she reappeared.

"It's a man from the government to see you. If he was any stiffer, he wouldn't be able to sit down."

Dan got up and as he walked past his aunt he stopped and gave her a hug and a kiss on the top of her head. In the parlor stood a man in a dark suit, holding a dark hat. The only color on him was a slight bit of blue in his tie and the thin red line in the band of his hat. His hair was short and neatly trimmed.

"What can I do for you, sir?"

"Private Daniel Welch?"

"Yes, sir."

"Field Agent Horn, Federal Bureau of Investigation. I have some questions concerning one of the men you were incarcerated with in North Korea."

"I'm not sure what I can add to what I discussed aboard the ship on the way home, but you're welcome to ask. Have a seat Mr. Horn," Dan motioned to the couch. "Would you like to have some ice tea or lemonade?"

"No thank you, but I will have a seat."

Dan sat on the veranda swing, motionless. He stared out across the treetops in the distant valley. The sixty minutes he had spent with Agent Horn had started off casual, but quickly turned negative. Once the initial "Hello, how are you" was out of the way the agent had started with the rapid-fire questions directed specifically toward what he knew about a Joe Albertson. Agent Horn's demeanor wasn't as cruel as Major Paulson, but it was just as unnerving. Albertson had apparently turned, voluntarily chose to stay in the North, when his time had come to be released. Dan couldn't recall his name, but why would he? He answered the questions with, "I don't know." As soon as he saw where the questioning was headed he informed Horn that he hadn't and couldn't have associated with coloreds, and therefore, knew nothing about Albertson or his activities at the camp. Horn was persistent, asking endless questions, trying to jog his memory, but in the end Dan's responses were accepted. Horn thanked him and left a card asking Dan to get in touch with him if he thought of anything.

Dan walked him out to his government car and bid him goodbye. As he walked up the yard toward the house he felt exhausted. He slowly walked up the porch steps and went over to the swing to sit and rest.

Staring out over the treetops he wondered why his own government felt it was necessary to continue harassing him. He had made it clear time after time that he knew nothing? Hadn't he done enough? Sacrificed enough? He sat in the swing, slump shouldered and pushed off the porch with one foot and gently swung for several hours.

✸   ✸   ✸   ✸

"Are you sure you have everything you will need for the trip?"

"Everything I own is in the trunk, Auntie."

Dan had tried the mines, even though he had promised himself he would not go back. He had worked up through the end of July in his old job as a seam ripper. The dampness seemed to affect him more than before, clinging to his skin and causing his joints to ache. The closed in feeling overwhelmed him from the very beginning, but he resisted the impulse to fight his way back up to the surface. It got the best of him eventually and two men had to help him make his way up to the surface. The men understood and he was glad he hadn't hurt anyone. He was sitting in the mine foreman's office, a thick layer of black coal dust covered him from head to toe, with the exception of his eyes and the top of his head where he had removed his helmet. He had been sweating profusely and the sweat had made streaks down his face. When Gregory finally showed up, they talked. Gregory's thoughts were elsewhere dealing with a loose belt or a tardy employee. They shook hands and Dan walked over to the pay office to draw his final check.

He had isolated himself at home for the rest of the summer and early fall. He had taken long walks in the woods like he had done as a kid. He spent most of August and September reweaving rush or splint wood strips in the seats of some of the old chairs that sat on Betsy's porch. Word got around and some neighbors starting bringing chairs in for repair. He fashioned several hickory canes and rode with his Aunt to deliver them to folks in need in the surrounding hills. It kept him busy and Aunt Betsy had enjoyed his company, but by the end of September, she knew he needed to get away for a while and had told him so.

Dan closed the trunk lid and turned to his aunt.

"Your smile tells me you find that to be convenient. I find it to be very sad that a man your age can get all his belongings into the trunk of an automobile."

Dan took both of her hands and stood for a moment looking into her tearful eyes.

"When will I see you again?"

"I'm driving up to Brooklyn to visit Leo's parents and then I'm not sure where I will go. I have a little money and I thought I would travel around a bit. See some of the country. You always told me that there was a lot to see out there."

"You should see it with someone you care about."

"That would be nice Auntie. Why don't you come with me?"

"I've already seen it, darling. I was referring to someone else. Do you think you'll be visiting your friends in Kentucky?"

"If I do, I'll let you know. The thing I want to do in Kentucky isn't as easy as you think. It needs time. I just can't show back . . ."

"Don't underestimate the strength of a young heart to heal, Danny. Think about what you've got, what you want and what you've got to give. Don't grow old being one of these sad people who walk around with something in their heart they were forever afraid to act on. If you hadn't gone over to see Amelia, you never would have got her out of your mind and your heart. Go see your friend's parents in New York and then go down there to Kentucky and see if she feels the same as you feel."

"Auntie, you make it sound so simple. You and Mrs. Katherine are one of a kind."

"I would like to meet your Mrs. Katherine."

"You two would hit it off."

"If I meet her, I would surely get to meet your Martha."

"She's not my Martha."

"She is, boy, you simply have to believe it to be so."

Dan stood silently staring at his aunt, still clinging to her hands. Her words, Martha's words ringing in his ears. His Aunt had no idea how much he wanted to make it so, or did she? He leaned over and kissed her on top of the head and gave her a hug.

"What would I do without you, Auntie?"

"Why, you would be very rich, Danny."

"As long as I have you, I am rich."

"You get along now. You've got a lot of miles ahead and don't try to drive them all in one day, and Danny."

"What, Auntie?"

"This came in the mail today. You may want to read it on your trip. She handed him a letter, the return address was, *"Martha Lowe, Gadberry, Kentucky."* He looked up at Aunt Betsy as tears ran down her cheeks.

"I love you, Auntie."

"I love you too, Danny. Listen to your heart, boy. Listen to what's in your heart."

Dan hugged her one last time and walked down the yard to his automobile.

As he backed out of the drive, he looked up toward his Aunt one more time and blew the horn. Handkerchief in hand she waved as he drove out of sight.

★　　★　　★　　★

The roadside café was tucked along the side of the highway that snaked its way through the Blue Ridge Mountains. Across the road was a spectacular view of the Shenandoah Valley. It was a clear September day and you could see for miles out across the valley. Dan had been driving the winding mountain roads nonstop for seven hours. He had stopped to top off his gas tank in Elkins, and had grabbed a Moon Pie and a grape soda pop for a snack. He wasn't in a particularly big hurry, as he intended to enjoy the trip, the freedom to go how and where he pleased was exhilarating. He stopped when he wanted and he drove when he wanted. The road map in the seat next to him served only as a guide to New York. The roads he took were his business. He felt like a child exploring a grand forest for the first time.

He had written Mr. and Mrs. Jawaski and advised them that he would be there sometime in early October. Mr. Jawaski had phoned, telling him they would be honored to have one of Leo's friends as a guest and were looking forward to meeting him.

Martha's letter was in his coat pocket, lying in the seat next to him. It had been constantly on his mind since Aunt Betsy handed it to him that morning. He was almost afraid to open it. He didn't want anything to spoil the joy and anticipation of having it.

He slipped on his coat as he stepped out of the automobile and stretched. The café was rustic, befitting the surrounding mountainous area. The valley below was covered with pastures and forest, Virginia farmland that had been farmed long before the Revolutionary and Civil Wars. The area was heavy with history.

Dan went in and was led to a booth next to the window. He could see out across the road and into the valley below.

"Beautiful view."

"That's why we call this little place Valley View, sugar. What can I get for you?"

"How's the meat loaf plate?" asked Dan looking at the menu.

"Terrific, vegetables?"

"Pinto beans and let's see, how's the collard greens?"

"Terrific, drink?"

"Coffee, cream and sugar, and bring a glass of cold milk with the meal."

"Terrific." She disappeared for a few moments and returned with a coffee cup and saucer, filling it to the brim. "If you need anything else, holler."

"Terrific," responded Dan as he spooned some sugar and poured cream in the coffee and sipped it. Perfect. He reached over and took the letter out of his coat and looked at it. Why would she write him? The thought suddenly occurred to him that maybe there was a problem and she needed help. Had something happened to one of the children? Maybe something had happened to Mrs. Katherine. He studied the letter, took the knife from the place setting and carefully slid it along the top of the envelope, being careful not to tear it anymore than he had too.

Inside were three separate one-page letters, from the girls and Martha. He slowly read Wanda Faye's and with a smile placed it back in the envelope.

He looked at Amy Sue's, carefully written in large letters, spaced generously across the page. At the bottom her full name was carefully and painstakingly printed out. Dan could visualize her sitting there, big pencil in hand struggling to make every letter as perfect as she possibly could. "I miss too," he said to himself as he folded the letter and placed it in the envelope along with Wanda Faye's.

He sat there for several moments looking at Martha's letter, still folded in his hand. Carefully he opened it and began to read:

September 16, 1953

Dear Dan,

I hope this letter finds you in good spirits. The girls, Junior and I are doing fine.

We have been blessed with an ample harvest, so far and I don't believe I have ever seen the fall colors so bright and vibrant, so early. Jordan and Silas have been generous with their time on the place and I'm most thankful for such good neighbors and friends, but I can't continue to allow them to forego work on their place to keep this farm afloat. The everyday routine of running the farm is overwhelming. I am always second guessing myself, but trust their judgment. I fear some difficult decisions are ahead.

Mrs. Katherine sends her best and hopes you have been successful with your business there in Elkins. She had grown quite fond of you and misses your company, as we all do. I want to thank you again for all the things you did around the farm and especially the time you spent with the children. Little Amy wanted to climb a tree the other day and wished you were there to lift her up to it. Wanda Faye talks of you over breakfast. I must also admit that I enjoyed the talks we had out on the porch. My new position is going well, but it does take me away from the children more. The days are passing far too quickly. My young ladies are growing prettier every day. Junior is growing faster than chickweed and is into everything.

I'm sure you are enjoying your reunion with Aunt Betsy. Considering what we have here your mountains must be breathtaking this time of the year. When the girls are a little older I plan to take them over to the Smokey Mountains for a long weekend, as they talk frequently about mountains now and want to see real ones.

A recent letter from Bob Green has helped me to better understand just how big a role you played in helping Howard at the camp. The Lord will surely bless you for the compassion you showed Leo, and my Howard.

You will always be welcome in my home and the children and I are looking forward to seeing you again. Do come when you can find the time to travel back down this way. Always keep in your heart that our prayers and thoughts are with you.

Sincerely,

Martha

CHAPTER 20

▼

Dan gazed down at the Silver Star in his hand. Below the red, white and blue-striped ribbon hung a five-pointed star with a tiny star in its apex. In his left hand he held the certificate that described the heroic action of Private Leonard A. Jawaski II. Irene and Leonard Jawaski stood beside him, tears of pride in their eyes.

He had arrived in the early evening with directions Mr. Jawaski had given him. The street was parked bumper to bumper on either side and although the Jawaski's had never owned an automobile, right there in front of their stoop was an empty parking place. The spot remained available the course of his stay, just as Lenny said it would be.

"The man from the Army came and presented us with Leo's Purple Heart and Silver Star," Leonard said very carefully, enunciating silver and star. "He was a colonel with lots of ribbons on his uniform. He even had a ribbon at the top, the same color as Leo's Silver Star."

"Got it in the big war, didn't he Leonard? Do you think very many soldiers get one of these, Daniel? Isn't a Silver Star better than a Bronze Star? Helen Civick's son got a Bronze Star in World War II. She brings it up every chance she gets and brags on him. Seems like silver would be more valuable than bronze? Did you get any medals, Daniel? I'll bet you got a bunch. That colonel had lots of pretty ribbons. Are you married, Daniel, Daniel?"

The voice and the mannerisms of Irene Jawaski warmed Dan's heart. She was sweet and energetic, just like her son.

"I have nothing as important and as beautiful as this. Leo would have been very proud. He was the bravest soldier I ever met."

"Come, Daniel. Irene will have supper on the table in just a few minutes. It's a feast you'll never forget and it's just for you. We'll eat, and then we'll talk of our son."

The evening passed too quickly. The meal was delicious with dishes from the old country. Irene had fixed a few American dishes just in case the ethnic dishes didn't suit their guest. Dan focused on the Polish dishes and neither he nor Irene felt disappointed. When they finally settled in the parlor, she disappeared and quickly returned with a tray of coffee and an array of tiny cakes. He was comfortably stuffed from supper. The dessert would top him off.

Leonard and Irene began by telling him everything they could think of about their son, from birth to when he left for the war. It was a tearful, but joyful journey for the couple and Dan sat back listening in wonder. Everything they shared confirmed what he already knew about his friend, there was nothing phony or pretentious about Leo Jawaski.

More coffee and one more delicate sweet cake and Dan began telling them about their son, the warrior. The couple listened intently as Dan talked them through the escape in the mountains and valleys, and to their eventual capture. There was laughter and smiles when he related things that only Leo would say or do, and they tried to be polite when he shared the horrifying story about falling into the croc pit. Irene squirmed about and finally jumped up, brushing off the front of her apron, letting out a loud *"Ugh!"*

"Sit down, Irene! Can't you see the boy almost died in that stinking pit?"

"Without Leo's fast thinking, I would still be laying on the bottom of it," said Dan his eyes moistening. Irene came over and kissed him on the forehead and sat back down. As Dan progressed through the camp stories the Jawaski's became very somber, their eyes and cheeks wet from the tears.

Occasionally one of them would say, "Listen to that Lenny" or "Irene, listen to how brave our Leo was."

At one-point Leonard stood and walked over to the window. Dan sat silently for several moments.

When he turned a steady flow of tears ran from his eyes. "Who is this animal that would do such things to my Leo? How can such evil exist?" He sniffed, blew his nose and stood there, putting his handkerchief back into his sweater pocket.

"I don't know, Mr. Jawaski. I have been trying to come up with some answers to those questions myself. I just don't know."

Lenny's shoulders slumped and an expression of regret came over his face. "Who am I to ask such questions? You lived through unspeakable evil. Forgive me Daniel and continue with your story. Please, we have put Leo's loss to rest in our hearts. Let us continue to celebrate his life."

When Dan started relating Leo's last night, he hesitated, went silent, broke down and wept. Irene rushed to his side and gave him a big hug. Lenny followed, a little slower, but feeling just as emotional about the young stranger who sat there sharing such deep emotion about their son. They sat there on either side of him as he shared with them the final moments of their son's life.

"That's my Leo. He was a fighter, a fighter to the end," said Lenny as he stood and walked over and got the Purple Heart. Sitting back down next to Dan he opened the box and they stared down at the purple and white ribbon.

"You see, Daniel, General Washington's picture there on that heart. That's for my Leo. General Washington himself, right there on Leo's medal. Someday we will find our son's body and bring him home, Irene. Before I die, we'll stand next to our son's grave." Lenny cradled the medal in his hand, resolute in his determination to bring his son's remains home from the North Korean hillside, to rest in the family plot.

Dan stayed a week in all, a guest in the Jawaski home. Lenny took off the whole week and everyday it was something different. The Jawaski's hosted a small family get together the second day at the Dock Workers Union lodge. It was just a small, extended family affair out to the second cousin, with about fifty people in attendance.

On Sunday Lenny had two tickets to Game Two of the World Series, a rematch of the '52 Series with the New York Yankees taking on the Brooklyn Dodgers. Lenny had made a habit of attending at least one Yankee game a month that summer, and never missed an opportunity to harass the Yankee players and management staff. Since he showered his beloved Giants with insults when they played poorly, he saw no reason to spare the boys in the pin-stripe uniforms. Mantle assured the Bronx Bombers' win at Yankee Stadium, with a two run homer in the bottom of the eighth inning, that night. Dan had a great time and although Lenny would have never admitted it, he was pleased Leo's team was taking a two-game lead to Ebbets Field the next day.

After the game the two men caught the subway home and walked to *Polanski's Deli and Grill* for some fresh pierogis, stuffed cabbage and a cool glass of ice tea.

Dan had the sauerkraut-kielbasa pierogis, while Lenny had his favorite, crab meat. There was lots of serious and lighthearted baseball talk, for both teams, in the deli. Before the men left to walk back home, they enjoyed a couple of kolaczkis.

The day Dan had planned to depart was a bright sunny day, so he dropped the top on the Chieftain and treated the Jawaskis to a ride. After tossing his bag in the trunk it took a considerable amount of coaxing to get Lenny to drive, but once behind the wheel he beamed from ear to ear. Dan climbed in the back and they waited patiently as Irene ran in to get a scarf to protect her hair in the open auto. She returned fifteen minutes later and sat next to her husband in the front seat.

"She'll be late for my funeral, Daniel," scoffed Lenny over his shoulder.

"Important things take time, you know. Drive carefully Lenny, you don't want to scratch Daniel's beautiful automobile." Irene sat back in the seat and smiled as Lenny eased out into the street. He carefully guided the automobile past an endless number of streets for about twenty minutes, circled a block and headed back home. At a stop light four blocks from the Jawaski home, Dan noticed the block ahead was congested with people.

"Sweet Mary! What's with this ahead," snorted Lenny. "It's a Saturday morning, for Christ's sake! Doesn't anybody work for a living anymore?"

"What's going on, Lenny? Can you see what's happened? I can't see! There are too many people in the way." She turned around to Dan and said, "Dan, can you see what's happing?

Dan stood in the back of the open auto and peered up ahead at the crowd of people in the street, lining the sidewalks and standing on their stoops.

"There's a big crowd of people, but I can't make out what's happening, Irene."

"Stand up on the seat, Daniel, you can see better that way," coaxed Irene. As Dan carefully stepped up on the seat, Irene learned over and whispered something to Lenny.

Once Dan was upright and peering over the windshield at the crowd ahead, Irene elbowed Lenny and he lifted his foot off the clutch. The Chieftain moved forward gently, throwing Dan off balance, forcing him to sit down on the top of the backseat and convertible top. He caught his balance and sat up straight just as the crowd on the street opened to let the automobile pass through. The Jawaski's neighbors and friends began shouting and waved as the auto carrying the war hero slowly made its way down the street.

Dan smiled and waved to the children and adults lining the streets and sitting on the parked autos. Here and there were old veterans sitting on their stoops, dressed out in their uniform jacket and service cap. They would stand and give a snappy salute as Dan passed by. He would respectfully return their salute and smile. The parade only covered four city blocks, but it seemed to go on forever as Lenny guided the automobile slowly down the street. When they came to a stop in front of their home the people gathered around.

"I don't know what to say," said Dan shaking hands with Lenny. "This should have been Leo's parade. He should have been sitting up there, not me."

Irene gave him a big hug. "It was yours and Leo's parade, Dan. He was sitting there with you. He will always be with you." She kissed him on the cheek.

"Let him go, already. He has driving to do today." Lenny grabbed Dan by the arm and sat him in the front seat.

"If the Giants make it to the Series next year, you come back for a week. We'll see some real baseball then." He leaned over and whispered into Dan's ear, "Even if those damn Yanks make it again, God forbid, you come up." Lenny straightened back up, "God bless you son. I hope you find what you are looking for."

Dan smiled as he closed the door. The crowd parted once more and he drove down the street, his hand in the air waving until he was out of sight.

*   *   *   *

He had driven nearly all day the day before, stopping at a small motel somewhere in the middle of Pennsylvania to rest for the night. About a hundred miles east of Indianapolis, Indiana, Dan climbed out of his automobile and said, "Fill 'er up," as a squad of Texaco attendants in dark blue uniforms and military style hats, converged on the Chieftain. One cleaned his windshield, while one pumped gasoline. Another checked the oil level under the hood, still another checked the air in his tires.

Standing at the next pump was an elderly gentleman next to his Buick Roadmaster. The attendants had just finished servicing the Buick as Dan pulled up.

"Where you heading, young fellow?"

"I'm not sure. I guess I'm kind of heading," Dan pointed down the highway, "that away."

"West, is it? There's a whole lot a road west of here. Going to see somebody?"

"No, sir. Got nobody to see. Just seeing the country."

"Lot of country to see. Nice automobile you got there. The Misses and I are traveling too. We're headed to Chicago, on to St. Louis and then Kansas City."

"Visiting family?"

"No, sir! The kids and grandkids live back down in Maryland. We're just traveling. I retired from the railroad five years ago and we're aiming to visit all forty-eight states while we can still get around. We have always wanted to see those places in the magazines. I drive and she's my co-pilot. We plot out the trip on a map and have quite a time. We stop when we want, eat when we're hungry. We see something interesting we stop and visit for a while. We haven't had this much fun since we were courting. Oh, there's the Misses now."

A petite, silver haired lady came walking up to the automobile, smiled at Dan and got into the passenger side of the Roadmaster.

"You be careful, young man. Traveling through life alone is no fun. You need to find yourself a co-pilot." The old gentleman smiled, opened his door and got in. Dan watched as they drove off down the road toward the setting sun, turned and gave the attendant three one-dollar bills.

"So, you're headed west too," said the young attendant, as he handed Dan his change.

"There is going to be a change of plans." Looking south, Dan said, "Things look sunnier down south."

"You'll like Louisville. It's a nice friendly little town that sits right on the Ohio River."

"My destination is just a little further south in central Kentucky."

"What do you think you'll find there, mister?"

Smiling, Dan said, "A co-pilot."

✴   ✴   ✴   ✴

"You haven't opened that letter, have you?"

"No."

"It's from Daniel, isn't it?"

"Of course, it is. You know that."

Standing at the washstand Mrs. Katherine finished drying the pan and lowered it down to her knees. A small hand shot out, grabbed the pan and pulled it back in between the curtains that covered the front of the stand. She took another pan from the rinse water and starting drying it as she continued to speak.

"You take your letter, go sit on the porch and read it. I've a hankering to hear what Daniel's been up to and it wouldn't be proper for me to sneak and read it until you have."

"I've a notion to keep it to myself, you old busy-body." Martha smiled and grabbed the letter off the table. As she walked across the kitchen she said, "Amy Sue."

"Yes, ma'am," came a small voice from behind the curtain at Mrs. Katherine's feet.

"Come out from under there and go ask your sister to help you fetch some fresh water from the spring."

"Yes, ma'am." The curtains parted and Amy Sue shot out on her hands and knees. She hesitated a moment and kissed Mrs. Katherine on the foot.

"Thank you for helping me stack the pans, darling."

"You welcome, Mrs. Katherine." She crawled on across the floor to the back screen door, jumped to her feet, grabbed the water bucket and dashed out.

As Martha walked past her bedroom she leaned in and listened. A soft cooing came from the baby bed. She went in, scooped up the baby boy and held him close as she walked out on the front porch and sat down in the swing.

Unbuttoning the top of her cotton dress, she gently cupped her milk heavy breast, bringing it up to meet the baby. He locked onto the nipple and began to suckle.

She closed her eyes, holding the baby in the crook of her left arm, with Daniel's letter resting in her lap. The morning sun warmed her face and a mild breeze blew in from the east, carrying the sweet smell of freshly plowed ground in the tobacco patch, just above the locust thicket. Across the road a chorus of laughter rose from the girls down in the shade of the woods. It was a beautiful October, Indian Summer morning.

"Mrs. Katherine is probably right. Now listen to me. What a silly notion", she said out loud as she stared down at the angelic face, "Mrs. Katherine is always right, isn't she Junior?"

"Ouch!" cried out Martha through clinched teeth.

Howard Junior looked up at his mother with big brown, smiling eyes.

"I think it's time I weaned Junior off the breast milk."

"He doesn't think so," responded Mrs. Katherine as she came out the door and walked to the swing.

"He's been eating solid food for quite some time now."

"A mother's breast milk is good for little ones."

"Yes, but little teeth are sharp. Have you forgotten?"

Mrs. Katherine responded after a moment of reflection, "Yes . . . maybe it's time." The three of them sat on the front porch swing, gently swinging.

"Did you read Dan's letter?"

"No," and Martha handed the letter to Mrs. Katherine. "Could you read it for me?"

"Be glad too."

September 27, 1954

Dear Martha,

> *I hope this finds you, Junior and the girls feeling well and enjoying a beautiful Kentucky fall. I am well, but sad as I miss you all, and all of my friends in Gadberry.*
> *I worked at the coal mine just long enough to remember why I promised myself I would not go back down under the ground. I'm not sure what I am good for, but I do know mining is not good for me. Another line of work will have to be found.*
> *I have closed out my business here in Elkins . . ."*

Mrs. Katherine looked up quickly from the letter, smiling at Martha and repeated the last sentence:

"I have closed out my business . . ."

Trying not to smile, Martha said, "Get on with it, please."

"Yes, Mum."

> *"I have closed out my business here in Elkins, and for the moment plan to visit Mr. and Mrs. Jawaski up in Brooklyn. After that I'm going to see some of the country. I have no definite plans, so it's hard to say where I will eventually land.*
> *If I sound a bit uncertain it is because I have learned that life is fragile and uncertain. The Lord put us here, but we are in charge of the rest. I have also learned that life is precious and the best part of it is the friends you find along the way. I think of you and the children often and wonder how you are doing. I would like to come down and visit again, but I worry about how the neighbors would look upon my being around you and the children so much. You are a respected member of the community, especially*

now with your new position at the Board of Education, and overdoing my presence might be viewed badly by some. I know there is much more to consider than just me. I hope you will understand and not think badly of me for sharing such feelings.

I must go now. Please give a big hug to the kids and Mrs. Katherine.

Fondly,

Dan

Mrs. Katherine folded the letter up and placed it back in the envelope. The two women sat in silence, as Junior cooed and hummed the contented noise he made when he ate.

"Mmm, mmmmm, mmm," he sounded off in muffled tones between his suckling.

"Martha Lowe, I dare you to sit and deny you don't feel the same way."

Martha had no response as she reached over and took the letter from Mrs. Katherine's hand. Looking at it she said, "Am I to lose again, without even a chance to know what might have been?"

"Love is not something you lose darling. Even when it's taken from you, like with Howard. You always have it deep in your heart. Sometimes though, you fail to recognize it for what it is and embrace it before it slips away."

"What do you think young man? Surely a little boy as smart as you would have a strong opinion on such matters as lost love?" As Martha brought Junior up to his feet he snatched the letter from her hand and stood wobbling on her legs.

After buttoning her blouse with her free hand, she reached out and took both of Junior's hands, steadying him as he hopped up and down without leaving his feet.

"Ba, ba, ba, mmm, ba!"

Down below an automobile came down the lane and came to a stop on the edge of the grass. The door opened and the driver stepped out. From the spring Wanda Faye's voice rang out loudly, followed instantly by Amy Sue.

"Dan!"

"Dan!"

The girls ran up the path and Dan knelt, embracing them both with a big hug. Martha caught her breath and turned to look at Mrs. Katherine.

"Go to him child. Take little Howard and go to him."

Martha leaned over and kissed Mrs. Katherine on the cheek. She stood and made her way down from the porch and yard, to meet Dan and the girls at the end of the drive.

"Good morning, Martha."

"It is a fine morning, Dan."

"I stopped by Jordan and May's and will be visiting them for a while. I've been told there is a spring down this way with cool, fresh water that bubbles right up out of the ground. I thought I would drive down and see if it's as good as everyone says it is."

Dan hesitated a moment and said, "If I could, I would like very much to see you and the kids as much as possible."

"We would like . . . I would like that, Dan," said Martha with a smile. "Why don't we all walk down to the spring and get a cool drink of water."

Dan took Junior from Martha, and the five of them walked slowly down the grass path to the springhouse.

"I'll dip the water with the ladle," said Amy Sue.

"Very good, Amy," said Wanda Faye with a big smile as she knelt and began rinsing out the Ball jars.

Up on the porch Mrs. Katherine sat in the swing watching Martha, Dan and the children down at the spring. She smiled knowingly, pushed off the porch with one foot and gently started to swing.

THE END

A U T H O R ' S   N O T E S

▼

Acknowledgments

I would like to thank the late Charlie Frost, US Army (Retired) for sharing his experiences as a prisoner of war in North Korea. Thank you for the courage to share your story and your encouraging remarks after reviewing the manuscript.

I would like to recognize the important contribution made by the book, *American POWs in Korea: Sixteen Personal Accounts,* edited by Harry Spiller, published by McFarland & Company, Inc. In my research I found no historical document more inspiring and insightful in terms of captivity and survival, than the personal accounts of these men.

A number of people have been very helpful with their thoughtful and objective reading of the manuscript. Your insight and generous comments were much needed. I am especially indebted to Libby Lunsford, David Lunsford, Denise Placido, Sue Dabney, Eddi Emerson, Larry Carter, Chris Kiger, Sue Simon, Janell Coyaso and Korean War veteran, Odist Riley. Your unique perspective of the manuscript was extremely helpful and greatly appreciated.

In addition, I am grateful to the wonderful people of Adair County, Kentucky for their inspiration and their friendship. I am eternally grateful to Arnon and Golda Loy for their love, and the memories they made and shared with me. The oral customs and rich traditions of Kentucky are fading away, but they are not lost; one has to simply ask, sit quietly and listen.

A special thanks and love to Janice for tolerating my need to write. Your patience was appreciated, your doubts were understandable and your astonished emotional reaction when you finished your initial reading of the manuscript meant more to me than you will ever know.

Most of all I am grateful to God for the abundance of blessings He has granted me in my writing. He inspires my thoughts, guides my words and occasionally tosses a great line my way.

Land of the Morning Calm

As in most cultures, history, art, and mythology come together to tell the story of the birth of a nation. In the small villages that have dominated the Korean peninsula for ages a story is told of a god named Hwanung who comes down from heaven. Lonely for companionship he transforms a bear into a woman. They marry and their union gives birth to a son, Tangun. Tangun is a great leader and builds the first capital of the Korean nation in 2333 B.C. He calls it Choson, Land of the Morning Calm.

Korea is a land of remarkably durable people, despite their country's difficult climate and turbulent history. Korea's geographical location places it at the crossroads to East Asia, resulting in a long history of invasion and domination by powerful neighbors. For centuries the people of Korea have spoken the same language, liked the same foods, shared the same traditional dress, and embraced the same age-old customs.

The Korean heart feels strong national pride about its homeland and longs for an independent Korea.

The Korean peninsula runs six hundred miles down from the eastern coast of Asia, pointing south toward Japan. The peninsula is surrounded on the east by the Sea of Japan and on the west by the Yellow Sea. It's a mountainous land in the north with rocky, mile high ridges along the Taebaek Range, rich with mineral deposits. In the north the winters are bitterly cold, with temperatures that dip as low as fifty degrees below zero, Fahrenheit. The southern part of Korea is primarily a farming area, with steaming hot, humid summers. For centuries the rice and cabbage fields of the south fed the entire country.

Japan's occupation of Korea during World War II led President Franklin Roosevelt, Winston Churchill and Chiang Kai-shek to agree in the Cairo Declaration that "Korea shall become free and independent." After the surrender of Japan in 1945 President Harry Truman suggested to Josef Stalin that Russia receive the surrender of Japanese forces north of the 38th parallel, an arbitrary line on a map, and America receive the surrender of Japanese in the south. The expedient agreement ultimately led to Stalin's choice of the 38th parallel as his line for dividing the country in half, once again destroying Korea's dream of independence. The Soviets controlled everything north of the line, relinquishing control of the south to America. The 38th parallel was nothing more than a line on a map. It was an unnatural boundary, with none of the common geographical features that usually determined national boundaries. The north had 58 percent of the land mass, but only one-third of the total population of 30 million. The north possessed Korea's industrial base, with the country's only hydroelectric power plant, petroleum, and cement processing plants. The south held the farmland to feed the masses.

Although America's goal was eventual disengagement, it encouraged a free democratic form of government in the south and attempted to train an army to sustain that government. In September 1946, President Truman tossed the hot-potato over to the United Nations. When the UN General Assembly voted for Korean elections, the Soviets refused to permit UN observers to enter north of the 38th parallel. The south subsequently elected Syngman Rhee the first President of the Republic of Korea. The communist in the north responded by forming the Democratic People's Republic of Korea and named Kim Il-sung to lead it. The two hostile forces began digging in on either side of the 38th parallel. In the south the US continued to train a poorly equipped ROK Army of sixty-five thousand. In the north the KPA Army was one hundred and fifty thousand strong, equipped with Soviet 122-mm howitzers, 76-mm guns, self-propelled guns, and T-34 tanks. Most of those troops, eighty-nine thousand, were Korean volunteers who had fought under Mao against Chiang Kai-shek's Nationalist Army.

Late in the spring of 1950 the North Korean Army prepared for a large military exercise along the 38th parallel. On the morning of June 25, the world realized the true intent of the military exercise as North Korea began a full-scale invasion of South Korea. For the Soviets, Korea was an ideological battleground for their relatively new form of government, Communism. For China, the Soviet's understudy and Korea's neighbor, the war was the continuing struggle in their search for respectability and power.

For America it was a limited war, a war the American people did not understand, want or feel a part of. The tragedy of any war is measured by destruction and human death, ground won and ground lost. In the end negotiations between countries establish the winners and losers. Heroes emerge from such conflicts and return home to an appreciative family and public recognition. The seldom talked about tragedy of captivity leaves deeper scars in both the men held in captivity and the families back home who await their return. Under the best of circumstances prisoners of war suffer immeasurable humiliation and pain in the hands of their enemies. Their families do their best to carry on back home, but they suffer deep heartache as they live with the daily terror of the unknown, not knowing if their loved one is dead or alive. Historically, the mortality rate for American POWs has averaged twelve percent. There is one exception, American POWs held in North Korea from 1950 to 1953 died at a rate of forty-two percent, nearly four times higher than any other war. Some refer to the Korean War as the "Forgotten War," a "Police Action" or simply a conflict. The fact remains, the human tragedy that occurred in the POW camps of North Korea and in the broken hearts of those waiting back home remains untold.

There is nothing more fragile than a captive heart and nothing more powerful than its story of survival. On the morning of June, 25 the Land of the Morning Calm woke up once again to find its dreams of independence shattered and its destiny controlled by others. On that same morning America found itself once again, at war. Although the characters of this story are fictional, the events are based on individual and historical fact. This is not a war story, as very little takes place on the field of combat. It is a story of honor, survival, and heartbreak in the POW camps of North Korea. It is the struggle and heartbreak of the American families waiting back home in Kentucky, the heartland of America. Korea and Kentucky share the same latitude and nearly the same land mass. Both have mountains rich with minerals, along with bountiful farmland. The people of Korea and Kentucky are durable and independently minded. In both settings, a world apart, this story took place.

Recommended Reading

If you would like to learn more about the Korean War and its POWs, the following books are recommended reading:

American POWs in Korea: Sixteen Personal Accounts

Edited by Harry Spiller, published by McFarland & Company, Inc.

The Korean War
Max Hastings, published by Simon & Schuster

In Mortal Combat: Korea, 1950–1953
John Toland, published by Quill, William Morrow, New York

The Korean War
Matthew B. Ridgway, published by Da Capo Press, Inc.

The Coldest Winter
David Halberstam, published by Hyperion, New York

Printed in the United States
by Baker & Taylor Publisher Services